Chapter One

Coarse haired or light wire? W
As problems went, it was of th
was still a matter that required some consideration.
had too many brushes to choose from. And alloy wheels scratch easily.

"It's only a bloody car," Amanda shouted.

It had become a mantra. She was right, it *was* only a bloody car. But his four wheel drive Volvo had been bloody expensive. Far more expensive than Amanda knew. It was the sort that was designed to go off road, although Will had no intention of doing that. It would take most of the weekend getting mud off the alloys.

"Have you found the wellingtons?" Amanda shouted.

A little part of his mind felt that his life should have greater purpose than cleaning the wheels of his car and locating rubber boots, but that was what life had become since the kids had left home. He thought the wellington boots were somewhere in the back of the garage. It was a garage that hadn't seen a car in a very long time, and was more the repository for things that eventually were destined for the dump. There were boxes of pictures which had come from his in-laws' house and which were, as far as he could see, decomposing. He moved them and found an old fridge. It had once been fully functional, but Amanda had decided that it was no longer large enough, and had promptly ordered a new American-style shiny coffin the size of a truck.

He wondered if the old one still worked. He felt a little sorry for the fridge, which had been retired before its time. That was ringing bells in his own life. The fridge prompted a further thought.

There was a door to the rear of the garage, which was easily accessed from the patio facing their garden. But he hadn't opened the door in ten years. He looked at the fridge. It didn't look too bad and could be, in modern phraseology, repurposed. It could become a beer fridge. He couldn't understand why he hadn't thought of it earlier. He opened the fridge and found two bottles of beer. Maybe he had thought about it. He examined one.

"Best before August 1998," he read.

He looked at it. It didn't look too bad. He certainly wasn't going to give up on it just because of its age. There was enough of that going on in the workplace.

"We were all best before 1998," he muttered.

Will set about moving the contents of the garage using the packing boxes to create a wall, so that he could make a small secret room. There was a long horizontal window that was set high in the wall and, as it was south facing and the sun was out, the little space was filled with light. There was also a small armchair which would have been in excellent condition had a cat – which had subsequently taken a one way trip to the vet – not torn pieces out of it. It was, he remembered, quite comfortable.

He shifted a few more boxes. It took a while, but eventually they fitted together quite neatly. It wasn't until he'd finished that he realised that the only exit was via the door which hadn't been opened in at least a decade. He unbolted it and gave it a shove. It was as rigid as the brick wall around it. He pushed it with his shoulder. Nothing. It was then that it occurred to him that he should probably first see if the fridge worked, otherwise the whole enterprise was flawed. He plugged it in. It whirred encouragingly. He put the two beers in the freezer section. Then he wondered whether he should continue to attempt to open the door, or wait. Will dropped himself into the armchair. It *was* comfortable. There was a pile of *The Cambridge Law Journal*. They were congealed with the damp, not that he cared. He'd been a lawyer too long to be interested in them. He looked at the boxes. There was one box left over. He put his feet up on it. Then he noticed that, unlike the others, it wasn't marked.

"Hah," Will said to himself.

There had been some debate about that box. Amanda had wanted to throw it out. Actually, now he thought about it, she'd instructed him to dispose of it. But somehow it had not made it to the last three trips to the dump. Will's father in law had been an upstanding individual who'd worked for a bank all his life. In retirement he'd been the secretary of the bowls club and had helped out in the local charity shop. There was some debate as to whether he'd known about his creeping illness. Amanda was convinced that he had, and that he had dealt with it with great grace. Will thought otherwise, and was convinced that his sudden death was as much a surprise to him as to everyone else. Otherwise he would have cleared out his extensive collection of magazines. He opened the box.

"Bloody wonderful," he said.

It was a treasure shrove of nineteen seventies and eighties pre-internet soft-core pornography. There were all the classic titles: *Mayfair, Playboy, Men Only,*

Penthouse and *Knave*. They were delightful period pieces, Will decided. Some of the pictures were quite demure, others not so. They'd survived in remarkably good condition and might even be valuable. But Will didn't want to sell them. He wanted to keep them for Jack, their twenty year old son. This was a family heirloom and far better than the other things he was likely to inherit, not least male pattern baldness. He picked up a magazine and began to read. For a few minutes – it might have been longer – Will lost himself in a piece about feminism and dildos. He guessed that those were two words which were unlikely to be paired today. The internet had, in his view, destroyed journalism and quality writing. He imagined that everything was written by spotty twenty-year-olds from universities which used to be polytechnics. It was a strange snobbery, as Will had been to just such a place when it had been a polytechnic.

He wondered how the beers were cooking and whether he could complement an eighties magazine with a nineties beer. He opened the little freezer at the top of the fridge and was reassured to see a vapour-like wisp escape. He took out a beer. It was pleasingly cool. It took a while to remove the cap from the beer, but when he did, he was rewarded with a satisfying hiss. He took a sip.

"Not bad," he said.

He took a further sip.

"Bloody good," he decided.

He delved into the bottom of the box and collapsed back into the armchair to discover that his late father in-law's taste had a rather harder edge to it. There were

Escorts, *Asian Babes* and *Big Ones Bimonthly*. There was no question what he'd find in that one. It wasn't long before a second beer was required and a further rummage in the box. A magazine, smaller in format, had been sandwiched inside a *Playboy*. It dropped on the floor. This was an altogether different proposition.

"You bad boy," Will muttered.

When he'd finished the second beer he decided it might be a good idea to open the back door.

It was then that he noticed the skis. They were next to the door and the poles were hanging off them invitingly. They were from the boys' ski trip. They'd gone for ten years until they'd been scuppered by children and a recession. The burden of responsibility. These were the boys from the Poly.

He looked at the skis with real nostalgia. Then a thought occurred to him. Their collective children were mostly at university, and they were reasonably solvent. Why not reinitiate the boys' trip? Will sat in the armchair, took another look at a *Colour Climax*, and then another magazine which was black and white and written in what he guessed to be Swedish. Then he got out his mobile phone and created a WhatsApp group. He searched through his list of contacts and ticked Judah, Al, Mac and Rick. When he'd managed that – he often asked Jack to help him with such things – he wrote, 'The Ski Team – who's in?'

It was simple, but they'd understand. He pressed Send and went back to another magazine in which the text was written in three languages – although he doubted, looking at the picture of a woman earnestly attending to three cocks of considerable size, that anyone had ever read it. It might as well be nursery rhymes.

"Will?"

It was Amanda. She was the other side of the wall he'd created.

"Yes," Will shouted.

He turned the page of the magazine taking him away from the woman and the three cocks and to a picture of a man dressed, he guessed, as Napoleon. Except his flies were open and his cock was hanging out. There was nothing diminutive about that.

"What the hell are you doing?" Amanda shouted back.

"Nothing," Will said.

"Have you found the wellingtons?" she shouted.

He slammed the magazine shut. He looked around. Was that a reference to Napoleon? Had she seen him? Wellingtons? What was she talking about? Then he remembered that he'd been sent into the garage to locate the boots.

Chapter Two

When the text arrived Judah was otherwise engaged. He'd heard it ping, but he ignored it. He should have been doing some marking, and in a way he was, but there had been a distraction.

"Harder," Julie panted.

He tapped her with a little horse whip. It might have been a little more than a tap, as it left what looked like a significant welt. There were marks all over her back and he was riding her like a jockey.

"Harder," Julie croaked.

Julie was an art student who was going through a phase. Her mother had told her that these were the years when she should do her sexual exploration, but she'd just meant that she should sleep with a few boys. Julie had embraced the suggestion and expanded upon it.

"Deeper," she commanded.

Judah was as deep as the physiognomy that god had given him would allow and, as he was now closer to his sixtieth birthday than his fiftieth, he was getting a little faint. He tried breathing a little harder, but it made him wheeze. He was grateful he was entering her from behind, as she couldn't see his face. It was florid with imminent heart failure. A hernia was the best he could hope for.

"Harder," Julie shouted.

She was racing to the final furlong and was now moving about to compensate for Judah's failure to achieve the required amount of 'deep'. She'd studied

Simone de Beauvoir and had written a paper on the pain/pleasure threshold, and this was fieldwork.

"Nearly there," Julie said.

She'd weirded out her fellow students when she'd made the suggestion, and they'd all had the foresight to realise the potential for disaster that lay in this kind of research. Judah might have too, were he not blinded by the opportunity of fucking Julie. He'd lived long enough to know that there were a few chances that just shouldn't be passed up, and fucking a hot twenty-two year old was top of that list. He'd have had sleepless nights regretting missing such an opportunity. He had no choice.

"Great," Judah muttered.

It wasn't quite as enjoyable as he'd hoped. It was a little too frantic, and although he'd taken an entire month's supply of viagra and feared he would be in priapic pain the following morning, he wasn't sure if he was going to get there.

"The whip," Julie hissed.

He tapped her back again in the areas he'd so far not marked. The problem was he was finding the whipping part rather distracting and he needed to concentrate on his own orgasm. But he also knew that if he concentrated on that it would suddenly become rather elusive. He'd race towards it and then it would disappear into the horizon. It wasn't like this when he was young.

"Harder," Julie shouted.

They were making quite a lot of noise and, as his wife had thrown him out and they were in student accommodation, most of the floor could hear. They were using it as an opportunity for a small party and a philosophy student had hit on the idea of a drinking game.

"More," Julie shouted.

Each time they heard the crack of the whip they took a drink. They'd mixed up Bacardi and vodka shorts and they were getting quite pissed. A music student had searched for whip-related songs to help the party atmosphere, and had found that while there was a lot which featured love and loss, very little had involved spanking or whipping. It was quite challenging. A business studies student had suggested he fill that musical gap.

"I'm coming," Julie yelled.

Judah was struggling with the multitasking nature of the activity. He cracked the whip a couple more times and felt Julie positively writhe with the agony and pleasure of it, and he could feel his body react to that. It was like a little stirring in his toes which, if he focused on it, it would disappear but, if he cleared his mind and attacked the task like Frankie Dettori three lengths from the finishing line, he'd race home. It might have been at this point that Judah became less than judicious about his use of the whip. Julie howled. It didn't take a medical student, although there were none on the floor, to deduce that they had reached a conclusion, and the party in the rooms around them finished with a long and hard drink.

"Beautiful," Judah said.

It was as his orgasm passed that other senses prevailed. The thinness of the walls in the little study room, and the complete lack of discretion he'd deployed when Julie had suggested the activity. Then there was the noise of the students cheering.

"Oh god," Judah muttered.

This could be his career in pieces. He withdrew himself from Julie. He hadn't used a condom. Who had a condom when they needed one? He certainly didn't. He could hear music. It was Sam Cooke. He knew which song immediately, as it opened with the sound of a whip cracking, although it took him a second to remember the name. He would eventually identify it as 'Chain Gang' and realise its significance, but there was a more distracting issue.

"Julie?" Judah said.

Julie was still howling. That wasn't good.

Chapter Three

Al's phone pinged and rumbled in his pocket, but he didn't notice it. He was driving at a bit over sixty miles an hour in a thirty zone and there was quite a lot to distract him. He was on a late shift and it was dark. He was in the rig and the lights and sirens were on.

"This is great," Darren said.

Darren was a trainee. He'd only been with Al a few hours, but Al already knew that if he was lying in a pool of his own blood or excrement, Darren was the very last person he'd want to come to his rescue. Al made a grimace in response and hoped that Darren would leave it at that. He didn't.

"It is so cool," Darren enthused.

Al had been a paramedic for nearly thirty years, and there had been moments. He'd saved lives and, once or twice, he'd ended a life. There was very little he hadn't seen and, in his last review, management had suggested he was getting too cynical. That was a managerial attempt at sugar coating. The other consistent aspect of his near thirty years was his loathing of the management.

"Okay," Al said holding his hand up.

Darren had started to wave at people. He'd lived in the area all his short nineteen year life, but he hadn't seen one person he knew. It was very disappointing. This *was* cool.

"We're here," Al said, bringing the rig to a halt and snapping off the siren.

Darren sat there as if his job was done. He really wanted to be an ambulance driver.

"Let's go," Al said.

Management, he knew, monitored the time between receiving the call and leaving, the duration of the journey, and the moments between arriving and treating the patient. The bizarre thing, he often said of management, was how minimal their own skills and talents were. They couldn't do half of what he did, yet they dictated what he should do. He knocked on the front door.

It was the last house in a terrace of two storey cottages which were on the cusp of being run down. There was one, further up the terrace, which was freshly painted with window boxes of brightly coloured flowers and a palm tree in the small front garden. Nothing said aspiration better than a palm tree, in Al's view. But this house was just sad-looking. There wasn't a light on. He knocked again. He pushed the door. It opened. Al looked into the gloom. A few years ago this would have induced a little tingle of nerves, but he mostly felt irritation. He leaned in and flicked a light switch. Nothing.

"Go and get the torches," he said to Darren.

He'd shown Darren round the rig, but he could sense he wasn't taking it all in. Actually, he didn't think he was taking anything in. He'd seen wallpaper rolls with a sharper end than Darren. Not that that made him unsuitable for the service. He'd be perfect in management.

"Under the dash," he reminded Darren.

Darren wandered off with barely a care in the world.

"Quickly," Al shouted and Darren hopped.

Al listened. He'd had people fly out at him in the past and he needed a heavy metal torch to smack them in the face should that happen again. He didn't mind inflicting injuries on them which would make the return trip to the hospital entirely necessary.

"Here," Darren said returning with two torches.

Al shone a light down the narrow corridor until he found a box above a door.

"Fuses," Al pointed.

Al realised he'd been there before. A depressed man of about his own age, which is to say mid fifties, or it might have been late fifties, who'd repeated the same mantra – 'I shouldn't be here, I went to Cambridge, you know'. Al relaxed a little. He didn't think he was in great danger.

"Put them on then," he said to Darren.

Darren's knowledge of Call of Duty was extensive, and he knew how to steal a car in Grand Theft Auto, but his grasp of domestic electricity was pretty minimal. He thought he was doing well when he found the trip switch and pushed it up. But it flicked off. The lights went on for less than a second. Then darkness.

"Bugger," Al said.

Al cautiously entered the kitchen. He'd referred to it as the armoury in the past, as it was full of knives. The lights flickered on again briefly and then he was plunged back into darkness. There was no one there. The lights came back on.

"Look, look," Darren said enthusiastically. "If I hold the switch up they stay on."

Al entered the sitting room. It took a very brief moment for him to take in the scene.

"You wanna let go of that switch," he said to Darren in a slow drawl, as if they had all the time in the world, adding, "if he wasn't dead before he probably is now."

Al looked at the convulsing form of the Cambridge graduate who had dressed himself in a rubber suit. Two metal studs were attached to his groin, from which two leads ran to the socket on the wall. Darren appeared next to him and followed the beam of the torch.

"Have I? Did I?" Darren said.

Darren's easygoing outlook was destroyed in a moment as he saw the rubber-clad body. Al unplugged the Cambridge graduate and flicked the fuses back on.

"I guess he didn't study physics," Al muttered.

He sat down. They were going to have to wait for a while, and he took his phone out, and checked his texts.

"The ski team," he muttered.

That really brightened his day. There was no question, he was up for it. Al looked around for Darren, but Darren was no longer by his side. He was leaning against a wall outside emptying his guts and feeling fairly certain he was going to have nightmares for the rest of his life.

Chapter Four

Mac was contemplating a third pint when his phone would have received the text, had he not been in the basement of a pub. It had been modelled on an older building and, coincidentally, he'd been involved in its design as a young architect. It hadn't looked much like it then, but now it was old and a little dilapidated and more closely resembled the original. There had been a lot of concrete and, although it wasn't pretty, it might have withstood a nuclear explosion. Mac had trained for seven years and he'd worked for a further thirty. He'd even won awards. But he'd spent most of the week designing a toilet block and arguing with the client. Treve had unconventional views as to the positioning of the toilets, and not the remotest understanding of the services that were required. On closer examination, Mac had decided, Treve's views weren't unconventional. They were fucking moronic.

"A pint of IPA, please Frank," he asked the barman.

He wouldn't normally drink on Fridays, but there was a great jazz band playing and his head was still ringing with the cretinous remonstrations of Treve. He needed a beer or two. He was fairly convinced that Treve's real name was Trevor, but he was far too pretentious to be a mere Trevor. Mac was surprised he hadn't chosen to rearrange the letters further and arrive at Revtor or something equally ridiculous. Treve had insisted he locate a toilet next to a vast window. The man was a fucking idiot.

"Thanks, Frank," he said, and settled in for the next set.

But Treve was the fucking idiot who held the purse strings, and Mac's practice was going through a rough time. An outsider might observe that his practice had never known any other kind of time. It was why he was designing toilet blocks.

"Thank you!" the sax player said to no one.

Mac wished he'd been a saxophonist. He remembered a ski trip ten or so years ago when they'd visited a bar overlooking the Alps. There were huge speakers and a vast crowd of beautiful young people, and the sax player was up high on a balcony. And he was god. It was Mac's feeling that if that man did not get laid every day of the week the whole of mankind was in trouble. Not that Mac didn't get laid. That was why he was hesitant about the third pint.

Friday nights the kids were always out – not that they were technically children any more – and the house was empty. It had become a sex night for him and his wife, Anita. That was one area of his life that did work well. Mac had made many mistakes, and taking Treve on as a client was certainly one, but marrying Anita had been the best thing he'd ever done. The only perfect part of his day was going home. But she'd gone to see her mother and would be a little late. Normally he'd steam into a couple more pints. But he couldn't be certain he'd be able to get it up, and that would be a waste of a Friday night.

The third pint was disappearing quicker than he'd have liked, and he decided to take a break and go up for air. Or in his case, a cigarette. He remembered the same venue when it was wrapped in a thick cloud of smoke. It was beautiful. The climb to the surface was further than he remembered coming down, although he'd had gravity on his side then. If he could he'd have taken a break half way, but there was quite a lot of movement in both directions, and it was too embarrassing to stop. He pulled harder on the handrail. It helped, but when he got to the top he was out of breath. A cigarette sorted that, and he decided to go straight home and leave the remains of his pint. It was then that his phone found a network and pinged. He looked at it.

"The ski team," he said.

It was strange, as he'd just been thinking about that. That sounded like a bloody great idea, he thought.

Chapter Five

Rick didn't notice his mobile vibrate. He was distracted. He was standing on a bridge which sat above a deep ravine in South Africa, which meant that if the drop didn't get him, the crocodiles would. As soon as he stepped up onto the handrail the wind seemed to triple in force. It was howling round his ears and made his eyes stream. It had been a terrible couple of years.

He'd met Annie at the polytechnic and he'd known immediately. They were a perfect fit and were rarely parted. As his career soared he'd been forced to spend the occasional week abroad and had hated it. When he'd been alone in a New York bed, he'd thought of Annie. It wasn't because he didn't want to be unfaithful, although he had no interest in that, but because he could think of no one else he desired.

When the cancer came and took her it was quick. They'd never been able to have children and it left him alone. His work kept him going until a year later a buyout made him rich, but took away his remaining lifeline.

"Are you alright, man?" a voice shouted.

Rick wasn't sure whether this was a phase. If it was a phase it was one that involved hazardous activities. He liked to think of it as an exercise in facing his fears. This was a life long terror of heights. Right at the moment he couldn't see what the fuss was about. He was a bloody long way up and there wasn't much to hold on to. His phone rumbled in his pocket a second time.

"Hey man," the voice shouted a little louder.

Rick wondered who it might be. He was swaying in the wind, but his curiosity got the better of him. He decided, despite his fear, that it would be worth checking before he jumped. He put his hand in his pocket and took out the mobile. It refused to accept his thumbprint, so he looped his arm through a steel stay, steadied himself, and tapped it in. It was a text from Will.

"The ski team," he muttered.

They were good memories. Rick had always been the most skilled skier, but tended to be cautious. He wasn't like that anymore. There was something freeing about that feeling. It made him feel immortal, which was slightly counterintuitive. He put the phone back in his pocket and jumped.

"Annie," he shouted.

He really did fall in slow motion. Time slowed right down and gave him an opportunity to deliberate over everything. He'd lived comfortably. Rick's house was large and faced an open park. He'd been told that pilots used it as a navigational landmark. His wine cellar dwarfed that of a Park Lane hotel and he'd invested in vineyards all over the world. He had an encyclopaedic knowledge of grape varieties and an exquisitely honed sense of taste to identify them. He'd amassed an art collection which reflected that fine taste, and he'd bought on beauty, but been rewarded with astronomical value. His vast garage housed a classic Jaguar and a Bentley, although he hadn't found a reason to drive any of them for some while, and preferred to take the modern Mercedes. He'd holidayed in the Caribbean, toured Europe and Asia, and eaten in the finest restaurants. Rick had lived very well. But without Annie they were just useless trinkets.

He looked down. He could see a crocodile thrashing around like a pet dog waiting to be fed. The crocodile salivated at the prospect. Was this a Pavlovian crocodile? Rick closed his eyes. It was then that he could feel something yanking at him. It was partly the ski team. Old friends. Life was about recognising what you do have and not what you don't have, the therapist had told him. But it was mostly the bungee rope attached to his left leg.

He'd seen a flyer for the bungee jump. It was a makeshift operation, and the majority of those who'd reviewed them on Tripadvisor had suggested you'd have to be 'fucking crazy' to use them. They did look a little dissolute, although they had been very generous with their cannabis, which was probably why they spoke in staccato sentences punctuated with lots of 'mans'. It hadn't worried Rick.

Now the deceleration was becoming eye ball stretching, even though one reviewer had said that he doubted they'd remember to tie the other end of the rope. Rick hadn't checked. It was so severe that his mobile shot out of his pocket and rocketed toward the ravine. It buried itself in the centre of the crocodile's head. The crocodile had not had the benefit of a therapist and had less than a second of life remaining but, he too, was rewarded with a slowing down of time giving him the opportunity to reflect on the life he'd led. He'd always wanted to try sex with another male crocodile, but that sort of thing was frowned on in his community. He started wishing he'd killed more things, but he didn't get that far. That was his lot. Death by the latest iPhone. The other crocodiles looked on a little bemused, unaware how fortunate they were that it wasn't an Samsung Galaxy, which might have killed them all.

But Rick was getting alarmingly close to the water, which was also riddled with large protruding rocks. He was reminded of another reviewer who suggested that the rope would be longer than the fall. It turned out the reviewer was wrong and Rick bounced back into the air. The worst thing, Rick knew, was that he wouldn't have minded if he hadn't.

Chapter Six

"Aren't you too old for that kind of thing?" Amanda said.

Will could see that there were hurdles in the way of getting the ski team together and Amanda was the first one. If he couldn't convince his own wife, what chance did he have?

"I don't think so," Will said defensively.

He was going to have to do better than that. He knew he had an ace card, but he didn't want to play it too early.

"It will be good exercise and a good opportunity to get together," he said.

Amanda frowned. This meant that she didn't believe a word he was saying and would not support the project. That wouldn't stop him doing it, but it would make it a bloody sight harder.

"And, as we're all a bit older, we'll be a little less crazy," he continued.

But Amanda was still frowning. He needed to change tack.

"I've organised a drink in town to talk about it," he said.

It was met with a silence. Silence was worse than a frown. That was a step in the wrong direction. He got the sense she didn't believe him. And she'd have been right to, as Will had yet to organise anything. He was bluffing, but he'd learned to phrase things as if they were a fait accompli. There was nothing wrong with organising a drink, and she often encouraged him to go out when she was at her book club.

"Okay," she said finally.

Will wasn't sure where that stood in the hierarchy of bad responses.

"When?" she added.

Will floundered. He should have organised it first before mentioning it.

"We haven't set a date yet," he said.

"Haven't you," Amanda said rather cynically.

This was one of the drawbacks with living with someone for a long time and there was no question what this meant. She didn't believe him. It didn't matter, as it was the next thing on his list. As this wasn't going well he was going to tell her he was going to do some work in the garage, which really meant he was going to have a beer – the fridge was now fully stocked – and commune with nineteen seventy-four Miss February and the further possibility, outside Scandi-noir, of brushing up on his Swedish. He thought it best they agree a date first.

"Maybe Friday," he said.

Amanda frowned. This wasn't so bad, as she'd accepted the drink and, having got that far, he decided to press ahead with his knockout ace card.

"And it will be good for Rick," he added.

Rick hadn't answered the text, but Will was fairly certain he'd be back in time, and absolutely certain he'd he up for a ski trip. He was currently specialising in falling off things.

"He's taken it hard," Amanda said.

The collective wives had their own WhatsApp group and they'd missed Annie too, and had encouraged the others to be as supportive as they could, particularly as Rick had begun to seem a little suicidal.

"True," Will said and his mobile rang.

It was Judah. He'd yet to hear from Judah and could guess what he was going to say. Will wandered out into the garden and then into the shed.

"How're you doing?" he asked Judah.

There was a pause. This was also a pause that Will recognised, and it normally preceded an admission that Judah had got himself in trouble.

"Fine," Judah said.

"Good, are you up for the ski trip?" Will asked.

Will could tell that Judah wasn't telling him something, but he knew he'd find out eventually. He could guess the nature of the trouble, as it had always been thus in the thirty years they'd known each other.

"Well, about that," Judah began.

Will also knew what was coming next.

"I'm not sure I can afford it," Judah admitted.

Fifteen years ago there had been tour rules and they revolved around supporting each other. The year Mac lost his biggest client the others had covered his costs, and when Rick had a financial blip they filled in for him, and the same when Will had been made redundant. They'd subsidised Judah more than most. But he was part of the ski team.

"You're in the ski team," Will said. "We'll sort it."

He spoke as he'd attempted to with Amanda and made it an unarguable fait accompli.

"Are you sure?" Judah said.

"Of course," Will said, adding, "Are you up for a pint this Friday?"

"Sure," Judah said.

Will also knew that Judah always said yes to a pint. Whether he actually made it was another thing. He texted the others.

Chapter Seven

"I reckon," Al said, "that there is a reason."

Al looked down at the woman. She was enormous, not just fat or obese, but vast and they were going to need another crew to shift her. She was lying on her back and her stomach was exposed.

"Look at this," Al said to Darren.

Darren hesitated. His school reports had never been glowing, and they'd mentioned a variety of traits, but not once had they called him sensitive. He'd only been on the job a day and he'd electrocuted a Cambridge graduate. He'd slept with the lights on that night, and when he'd put on some rubber gloves that morning he'd felt a bit queasy. His relationship with rubber would never be the same. He looked down at the great mass of quivering flesh. Al wobbled the woman's flesh and they watched as the ripples ran across her stomach until they got to the other side. Then they started rippling back. Darren looked a little shocked. The woman groaned. She was coming to.

"We'll wait in the rig," Al said to the woman.

The woman might have responded, but Al didn't wait. He'd done this before and it had resulted in six weeks at a chiropractor. They got back in the ambulance and Al opened a part eaten sandwich.

"What do you think she weighs?" Darren asked.

Al played with the sandwich as he thought about it.

"Forty stone," he said finally.

But this wasn't very helpful to Darren, who was fully metricated.

"In kilos?" he asked.

Al was munching the remains of the sandwich. He'd bought it the previous day and, by the look of it, it had been assembled the day before that using ingredients which were sourced a few days before that.

"Two fifty maybe. A quarter of a tonne," Al said.

"Fucking hell," Darren said.

His tour with Al had been a steep learning curve. He thought of it as a tour in the sense of Afghanistan or Iraq. The world wasn't what he thought it was. But he was there to learn.

"What was it you said about a reason?" Darren asked.

Al looked at him a little confused. He'd forgotten about their earlier conversation. Then he remembered.

"The husband feeds her for a reason," Al said adding, "she's too big to feed herself. She can't reach the kitchen counter. Her stomach gets in the way."

"Yeah," Darren said slowly, "but why does he feed her?"

Al was waiting for him to ask. Over the years he'd come up with a few theories and then one day he'd asked. And the woman's husband had told him.

"The husband – the feeder – goes down the pub and he says to his mates, 'you'll never guess where I fucked the wife last night'."

Al left a big dramatic game show host. He could see that Darren was confused.

"Last night it was her armpit," Al said.

Darren wasn't sure whether to look confused or horrified. This wasn't the sort of thing he'd hoped to learn.

"The night before it was her belly button," Al said.

Al used his hands to illustrate how this could be achieved. Darren did not have the most extensive of sex lives, it was primarily a solo pursuit, and he was a long way from exploring the outer reaches of sexual activity. He felt a bit sick. Al could see it in his face and couldn't stop adding a few more prurient details.

"Tomorrow it's going to be between the folds of her thighs," Al said.

Darren put his hand up. He'd had enough. He really had.

"I get it," Darren said.

They sat in silence for a while. Al rummaged through the various cubby holes to see if there was anything else he could eat. He couldn't be certain he hadn't forgotten something.

"If Micky doesn't turn up soon, you're on your own. I've got a drink planned," Al said.

This alarmed Darren even more. He did not want to face hauling the huge woman out of the house without an old hand like Al directing him. But Al wasn't going to miss the ski team drink.

Chapter Eight

The escalators were broken. Mac looked up. They disappeared beyond a bulkhead and he couldn't see the end of them. It was like Jacob's ladder stretching into heaven. Although this job was in New Cross, which made it closer to hell. If he'd known they weren't working he'd have had a cigarette first. It looked a bloody long way without a fag. He stood on the escalator with a spirit of optimism.

"It's broke," someone said.

Mac sighed and started climbing. He looked down at his shoes, so as not to be intimidated by the journey. People were overtaking him. Old people were overtaking him. Then he looked up. It was a mistake. He'd barely managed a dozen steps. He was growing faint. He took a rest.

"Are you all right, mate?" someone said without stopping.

Actually, he was fine. He was just pacing himself. He'd get to the top eventually and there was no hurry. He was going to take an Uber to the pub afterwards. He'd promised some clients he'd look at the building and that was what he was going to do. He hoped it resembled his drawings. His heart rate and blood pressure had subsided enough for him to continue the climb. It might have been the light headedness that such extreme exercise prompted in him, but it was making him philosophical.

"It's a bloody disgrace," an old lady said, and overtook him.

And his conclusion was that he was actually quite a happy man. His clients were pests but, now he was older, he saw them like recalcitrant mosquitos, or charity muggers, or traffic wardens. They irritated him, but no more than being in a crowded bar, and being unable to get a drink. Actually, that irritated him more. He had them in perspective. He looked up. There was still quite a long way to go. He stopped for a moment.

"Are you okay?" someone asked.

He really was okay. His architectural practice careered between prosperity and ruin, but he'd got used to it. He'd accepted that riches were never going to come his way, but he didn't mind. Every now and again he got a job which he actually enjoyed, and in which he could take some pride. There weren't many people who could say that.

"Nearly there," he said to himself, and carried on climbing.

He knew he should lose weight, give up smoking, and possibly even cut down on his drinking, but these were elements of his life which were only contributing to his happiness. Things weren't drastic enough for him to do something as serious as giving up drinking. There was plenty of time. He was close to the top and really didn't want to take another rest. But he didn't have to. There was a rumble and the escalator began to chug. Mac was a happy man because he liked his wife and kids and that he'd concluded, after more than half a century's existence, is as good as it gets. He was at the top, through the barrier, and into the air. He saw the building immediately.

"You're a long time dead," he muttered and patted his pockets until he found a battered packet of cigarettes.

There were moments when he was convinced that there was someone moving the cigarettes from one pocket to another. They were never quite where he'd left them. He lit one and looked at the small block of flats. There had been budgetary constraints and the planners had been bastards, which meant that his original drawings had morphed into something else. It was like taking a supermodel's face and rearranging her features. Not everyone understood that proportion was everything.

"Not bad," he said to himself.

He'd managed to convince the developer to lose a floor and keep the ceilings high which, with the premium the apartments could yield, would make it more profitable. It didn't look bad at all. It would have looked better still if they'd gone with the brick cladding he'd suggested, but the developer put his foot down on that. Mac walked round the building.

"Oh dear god," he said.

The developer had made a further economy, and the rear of the building looked like it had been designed by someone who'd never seen the front. The windows and bricks had all the elegance of a public convenience. Although he'd designed prettier toilets than that. He walked round to the front.

"Much better," he said.

He hoped that prospective owners wouldn't study the rear of the building, but the front really wasn't bad at all. He took a quick picture, and headed back for the tube now that the escalators were working. Just before he entered the underground he took one more rearward look. Actually, it was better than not bad. Something that had started as a scribble on a piece of paper in front of him had become a big permanent edifice, and a damn good looking one at that. That made all the toilet blocks and Treves worthwhile. He got on the escalator going down into the underground. It stopped again.

"Bugger," Mac muttered.

He had gravity on his side now, and he was motivated by the drink he was very much ready for. It was the ski team drink. He'd be a little early, but he was happy to get a few in first.

Chapter Nine

Rick should have been been ready, but his mind had a tendency to drift. As soon as he'd landed in London he hadn't wasted any time. He'd dumped his things in his flat in the West End and felt the silence. His replacement phone had arrived and he'd restored it. It had pinged and he saw the same text he'd seen before he'd jumped off the bridge in South Africa. He'd replied. He was definitely up for the ski trip and the ski team drink. And then he'd left the flat. Rick really should have been ready. He had his gum shield in, and his boxing glove-clad hands were up but, for the briefest of seconds, his mind wandered again.

He was twenty and he'd bought a Citroën Deux Chevaux and they were driving to the south of Spain. They were somewhere between Madrid and Malaga when the car began to make mysterious knocking noises. And then it had stopped. The engine was still running, but there was no forward motion, instead just a thump, thump noise. They came to a gentle halt. Rick had tried to remain calm. He'd wanted to impress Annie and a screaming fit of anger, which was what he might have done fifteen years later, wouldn't have achieved that. A collection of carefully strung together swear words would not have helped.

Rick had got out of the car. The road was empty and the landscape parched and desert-like. There was a gentle wind which whistled in a desolate way. He tried not to panic. He opened the bonnet. Rick's knowledge of car mechanics was less than extensive, but he could see something wasn't right. It looked as if the engine had broken free and the drive shafts had dropped out. It was probably them that were doing the thumping. Annie had got out of the car. She'd stretched. It seemed to last an eternity. It was very feline.

"Can you fix it?" she'd asked.

Rick's initial thought was 'I have no fucking idea', but instead he'd said, "Sure." Annie pulled out a small rolled up mattress and lay it down by a tree, which was too skeletal to provide much shade, but it didn't matter as she always took the sun well. She had a book in her other hand. Rick tried to remember what it was. Was it *Catcher in the Rye*? He wasn't sure. He'd looked under the bonnet. What the fuck was he going to do? A second later he heard a car. He didn't expect it to stop, but it did. The car parked fifty yards away and a tall man got out. As he approached Rick realised he wasn't tall. He was enormous.

"Can I help you?" the man said in a French accent.

Rick was surprised until he realised that the Frenchman had recognised the English registration plate.

"I've got a problem," Rick said pointing to the engine.

"I've been everywhere in these. This happened to me once."

He waved to his girlfriend, or wife, and she too, took something out of their car and lay in the sun. There was music coming from the car. It was classical, and it seemed to dance in the wind, and with it Rick's worries disappeared.

"Stand here," the tall man said.

Rick did as he was instructed and the tall Frenchman leaned over him and gripped the engine and gearbox and lifted it up.

"Feed in the driveshafts," he said.

It always seemed a mystery to Rick as to how, or why, a Frenchman would know the English word 'driveshaft'. It was said as if it was a rude or lascivious word. It almost made Rick chuckle. Two minutes later everything was in its place and the French couple were back on their way. Then he remembered Annie lying in the sun reading that book. Now he thought about it, he reckoned it was *To Kill a Mockingbird*. It concerned him that he couldn't remember, giving that detail more significance than it needed. He often thought about the tall Frenchman who'd come from nowhere, as if he was a guardian angel sent to help him. Unfortunately he wasn't there when Rick had really needed him. And then the punch came.

"Are you alright?" Sensei Walter asked.

Rick was on the mat. He wasn't out cold, but his mind was muddled as if he was his twenty year old self for a moment. He'd taken up kickboxing to help channel his aggression. It had helped and most of the time it kept his mind off things.

"Yeah, I'm fine," Rick said, getting up.

Now his mind had rearranged itself, and he was his fifty-seven year old self, he felt a little fleeting sadness. The sense of loss returned to him.

"You need to keep your guard up," Sensei Walter told him.

Rick knew the truth of that. Letting it down was too painful.

Chapter Ten

Terry had discovered which way she was orientated a long time ago. She hadn't had to have the awkward conversation with her parents, as they'd sussed rather sooner than she had. And Terry was fully invested in the business of same sex love, and had adopted a style which left no question as to which way she leant.

"You should try it," she told Julie.

Julie had not been long out of hospital. The third year student who'd dressed her wounds had not slept for around a hundred hours and had dressed them skilfully. But he couldn't remember whether he'd opened the packet which contained the dressing or not. He just assumed he had. It was certainly already open and he applied it neatly, and then he crashed out in on-call room, and dreamed about all the women he hadn't had sex with which, given his work hours, was most of the female population.

"Yeah," Julie said, "I'll give it a go when I'm a bit better."

Terry couldn't believe it. Gay men, she reckoned, had it easier. As a lesbian she was still required to seduce, and merely suggesting that the evidently heterosexual Julie 'give it a go', didn't sound much like seduction. Internally she was shouting 'wey-hay-hay'. She was very political about her sexuality, and held firm views about women's right to say no, although she occasionally waived those rights when she was confronted with the prospect of getting laid. Particularly when the girl was as hot as Julie.

"It will be tender and gentle," Terry said softly.

That was much more like it. She'd have told her she loved her if it would get her out of her clothes. That girl had a killer body. Terry was grateful that the Mind Police didn't exist as, in her head, she frequently sounded like a nineteen seventies male comedian at a working men's club.

"That would be great," Julie said quietly.

Lesbianism was part of the portfolio of sexual adventures she wished to undertake, but her normally reliable libido was at a low ebb. The dressing the young doctor – a doctor who in different circumstances she would have taken for a ride – had been previously applied to someone whose day had not gone to plan. Donald had lost his job and his girlfriend, and had stamped his full weight on a pressed steel manhole cover, which had the word 'ductile' embossed on it. Neither his girlfriend, or his boss, had been very flexible and nor, he discovered, was the manhole cover.

"But this hurts like fuck," Julie added.

Terry knew that now was her opportunity to display sympathy and support, but she wasn't very good at that. Although, if Julie took her clothes off and actually showed her her wounds, she might find it easier. She had to say something appropriate.

"That's terrible," Terry eventually settled for.

And for Donald it had been terrible. He fell a very long way, although things might have been much worse if the drain had not been blocked. His fall was cushioned by a deep pool of what the paramedics, who dragged him out of it, referred to as shit. It was positively oozing and suppurating, as if it had a life of its own. It was certainly sustaining a quite considerable pack of rats led by a large buck, whose name in rat language translated most closely to Louis. The rats were impervious to disease although Louis, who was quite narcissistic by nature, was easily wounded by sarcasm.

"Can I do anything?" Terry ventured.

What she wanted to say was 'Can I whip your knickers off and bury my face in your minge?' But she feared it was too soon for that and she was more than happy to settle for rubbing something into her skin. There was a pause.

"Have you got anything to drink?" Julie asked finally.

Julie had decided to self medicate in the hope it might lessen the pain. She was, as the young doctor's consultant had observed, 'a gnat's bollock' away from Weil's disease. If only Donald had been so lucky. It was a section of drainage in which a half pipe was elevated some three feet off the bottom of the drain to maintain levels and, although the effluent had lessened the impact, Donald's crotch took a fair bit of it too.

"Vodka," Terry said brightly.

She didn't normally share her vodka, but this was very definitely different. She opened a cupboard and extracted a cardboard box of cereals and, like a magician, she extracted the bottle.

"Ta-dar!" Terry said.

Terry was getting quite excited. She'd have Julie's knickers in her teeth in no time. But Julie was frowning.

"There's fuck all in that bottle," Julie observed.

Terry looked at it with panic. The bottle was tall and cylindrical and she'd repurposed it on a number of occasions. Mostly on herself.

"I'll tell you what," Julie said, taking control, "If I give you my card can you get a bottle of gin – Gordon's – and some slimline tonic – Schweppes. Only Schweppes. And a lemon. Don't forget the lemon."

Julie had standards and, while she didn't want to become her mother, this was what she really wanted and she was a nice girl at heart.

"Sure," Terry said, and Julie handed her the card.

Terry, who was normally a little averse to exercise, didn't hang around and Julie rearranged herself on the sofa. She lay face down. She was unaware that Donald was also laying face down, and a little part of him was wishing he was in the morgue. His fall had been further cushioned by the large rat, Louis. Louis didn't respond well, and took a considerable bite out of human testicle. It was delicious and he would refer to it as the ultimate delicacy until the end of his life which, due to a storm and a flash flood, was less than nine hours later.

"Hey," Terry said when she returned.

She'd been working on that and was pretty pleased with 'hey'. She began making the gin and tonics.

"Where's the lemon?" Julie asked. "You didn't forget the fucking lemon?"

Terry looked at her. Evidently she had. She'd blown it.

"I can go out again," Terry volunteered.

"Forget it," Julie said.

She had standards, but now she really just needed a gin and tonic, with or without lemon. Terry handed back her card.

"It says Julie Panter," Terry said, "I thought your name was Brown."

"Oh, Brown is my mother's name," Julie said.

"Isn't there a politician called Panter?" Terry asked.

"Is there?" Julie said innocently, but fearing she might have been rumbled.

Chapter Eleven

"What happened?" Judah asked, pointing to Rick's face.

Rick shrugged. It was nothing. He'd even taken a little pleasure in it, as if he felt he deserved it.

"Got punched," he said.

"You're still doing your mad martial arts thing?" Judah asked.

As Rick's life had been an oasis of calm and Judah's had been a little crazy, careering from one crisis to another in both his relationships and work life, this seemed a bit strange.

"I guess so," he said eventually, adding, "blue stripe belt now."

This didn't mean much to Judah who had, as ever, problems of his own. They were in Rick's central London flat. Judah had gone into hiding. He was hiding from his students and hiding from the vice chancellor. News of his little distraction with Julie had spread rather quicker than wildfire.

"More importantly," Rick said, "what happened to you?"

Judah gave a blow by blow account and, in this particular instance, it was precisely that. He took a prurient pleasure in describing everything including a very specific and detailed analysis of Julie's young and apparently very nubile, yet surprisingly curvaceous, body. In Rick's view Judah hadn't changed much in thirty years. Nor had his issues. He hadn't done a lot of maturing.

"With a riding whip?" Rick asked.

Judah nodded.

"And it got out of control?" Rick asked.

Judah nodded.

"How did it get out of control?" Rick asked.

Judah was reluctant to give too detailed an account as to how it had fallen apart because, while he hadn't matured, he had grown pretty old, which was something he wasn't keen to admit to anyone including himself. But Judah had asked if he could stay in the flat, which meant he owed him. He needed to explain.

"It's like this," Judah began and then after a pause he said, "do you mind?"

He produced a small tin in which there was some cannabis resin of great quality, which he'd confiscated from a student. Rick pointed to the balcony and they moved out. Judah assembled a joint at record speed. It was something for which he'd always had a great talent. He lit it and took a few tokes.

"You know when you're trying to come and you're distracted by things and the more you concentrate the more, sort of elusive it becomes?" Judah explained.

Rick didn't know.

"And I sort of closed her out and went for it, and I guess it must have happened then," Judah continued.

"What exactly happened? Rick asked.

"I think I must have hit her a little harder than I'd intended," Judah admitted.

"Oh dear," Rick observed.

"But she asked me to. She kept shouting 'harder'," Judah said.

Rick raised his eyebrows. He didn't understand Judah's predicament.

"Anyway I can't go back to the student accommodation," Judah said.

"Hold on," Rick said, "what were you doing there? Did Kath chuck you out again?" Rick asked.

Judah nodded. He was homeless again. He'd first met Kath at the poly, but he'd left her for Celia, and then returned. But a dalliance with Claire had intervened and then he met Bea, which ruined things with Claire. He was on his way back to Kath when he came across Lexy in a train station and stayed with her for nearly three years, until she caught him with Grace. Grace lasted a week and he returned to Kath, but Kath wouldn't have him back, and he met Glynis, which lasted a year until he got trapped in a lift with Melissa. Melissa was gorgeous. More than gorgeous, she was spectacular. He'd begun to salivate just looking at her. It was, they both said, fate, and two weeks later fate intervened and she left him for Tom, who she subsequently married, and with whom she now has two children. Judah returned to Kath, but Kath wouldn't have him again and he met Siobhan at a wedding. By now a pattern was emerging. Siobhan was striking and sexy and much younger than Judah. He tried very hard with Siobhan, but one drunken night he woke up with Sally. He couldn't quite remember how it happened, and he was surprised to discover he was sixty miles away from where he'd started the evening, but he made the most of it. Sally was older, and what might reasonably be termed as age appropriate. She was so age appropriate she turned out to be Siobhan's mother. That was a shit storm. The year that followed was so chaotic he couldn't remember the names but, at Will's youngest daughter's christening, he bumped into Kath. She might have been feeling vulnerable as they ended up together and, at the time, it was good. It was easily the best sex he'd had in years and their conversation flowed with shared cultural references. And then disaster struck. The mobile phone arrived and someone had invented dating apps. He didn't have to wait to get trapped in a lift, the supply was endless. Kath threw him out. He would have stayed out, but they bumped into each other again at Will's oldest daughter's wedding. That was three months ago. Judah needed to change the subject.

"I've brought a couple of bottles of wine," he said, removing them from a plastic bag.

Rick looked at the wine. He could do with a glass or two, but this barely qualified as wine.

"I'll sort the wine," Rick said.

He went back into the flat and ran his hand through the wine rack. The really good stuff was in the house in Blackheath, but there were a few French highlights hidden away. He chose a light burgundy, opened it carefully, sniffed the cork, poured it, swirled it, and observing the tears of the wine, he passed his nose over the wine and finally tasted it.

"Jesus Christ," Judah said, "you take more time faffing around with the stuff than drinking it."

Judah took a glass and drank it rapidly.

"Excellent," he said and put his glass out.

It wasn't long before Rick opened the second bottle.

"How are you?" Judah asked.

"Oh, I'm fine," Rick said.

"No you're not. You're still pining. You've got to move on," Judah said, his sensibilities clearly blunted by the wine and the joint.

Rick felt a flash of anger. He didn't want to take advice from someone who was such a royal fuck up while, at the same time, seeing there was some truth in what he had to say. He couldn't stop himself pining.

"I'm trying to adapt," Rick finally said.

Judah finished his wine and rolled another joint. He wondered where his students managed to source such high quality stuff. He tried to change the subject.

"What did you think of the skiing trip?" Judah asked.

"I'm all for it," Rick said.

It was a distraction he was looking forward to. His life was one distraction after another and this seemed like a better idea than most.

"It might be pricey," Judah pointed out.

"You'll be fine," Rick said.

Rick didn't know it yet, but there was a collective mentality with the ski team. Everyone was going. No excuses would be accepted. They'd have to be incapacitated or incarcerated. There was a knock on the door.

"Is that your door?" Judah asked.

"What do you mean?" Rick said.

His mind had drifted, which it appeared to do often, but he didn't worry about it. It gave him comfort.

"There's someone knocking at the door," Judah said.

It surprised Rick as he didn't spend much time in the flat. He preferred the large garden in the house in Blackheath. Annie had been passionate about it and he felt a duty to keep it in good order. Nobody ever knocked on the door in the flat. He got up and went back into the flat. He'd bought it when Annie had got into theatre and it was part of a redevelopment of Covent Garden. It was on the top floor and was high enough up to be light. He'd been thinking about living there. He opened the door.

"Hello," Rick said.

There was a policeman and a policewoman. They looked a little out of breath.

"Is Judah Wheeler here?" the policewoman asked.

It was then that it occurred to Rick that the flat smelled of the two joints that Judah had rapidly consumed. He sensed that might be the least of Judah's problems, and he nodded and pointed through to the balcony.

The policewoman gave an angry snort and talked into her lapel, which evidently contained a radio.

"We've got him, sarge," she said.

Chapter Twelve

Will had taken Friday afternoon off. There were a couple of property exchanges and, as the younger partners were biting at his heels, he thought he could leave it to them. He'd not done this before, particularly as he had nothing specific to do. When he got home he found that Amanda had gone out. She had mentioned it, but he'd forgotten. Occasionally on a Friday he'd go to the gym, and then grab a drink with Mac. Mac was a very reliable drinking partner. But he'd come home and gravitated to the garage. He wanted to check his skis and was thinking about looking at a YouTube video, and doing a bit of home waxing. But he'd forgotten his iPad. Instead he dipped his hand into his father in law's packing case and became distracted by a very intense article about erogenous zones. He was discovering that there were rather more than he was aware of. Will hadn't bought a pornographic magazine in over twenty years, and he was beginning to think he'd missed out. This was really quite interesting. He'd mention it to Amanda – and she'd probably agree – until she realised that his reference source was one of her father's magazines. That idea would make her choke. If the same thing appeared in one of her magazines, like *Marie Claire*, it would be different. Except modern women's magazines were more explicit than nineteen seventies pornography.

He looked up at his skis. They were a little battered, and very probably dated in design, but he'd only had them a couple of years before they'd abandoned the boys' ski trip. He feared it was going to morph into the old man's ski trip. He was looking forward to the drink.

It was likely to be a biggy, as that was one of the reasons they'd stopped going. Or was it? He couldn't remember precisely why they'd stopped, although he knew that money had been involved. Amanda had pointed out that their drinking and hence their expenditure got very much worse when they got together. As a collective they were inclined to excess. But, he thought, they were older now. They were more sensible. He went to grab his phone, but found he'd left it in the house. He wondered whether he could live without it and then decided to try and read a further piece about the practice of S & M and bondage. Thankfully it had a glossary, as he wasn't entirely aware as to what the 'S' or the 'M' stood for. He read it with interest, despite not having the slightest interest in being tied up, or in tying anyone else up, and certainly not inflicting pain or receiving it. Apparently, in order to set boundaries, it was important to have a safe word. He wondered what his would be.

Will grabbed another beer and decided that, although he wasn't addicted to his mobile phone, and could certainly live without it, he'd better get it anyway. It took a while to find, as he'd left it in his jacket pocket. He took it out and found a series of missed calls from Judah. One would suggest he wanted to talk about the drink, two that he had something to say prior to the drink, three that he had yet another relationship issue. Seven suggested he was in trouble. Will phoned him.

"Will! Thank god," Judah said.

This sent a little shiver of panic up Will. He feared Judah was going to ask him to do something he didn't want to do.

"I need you to come down and explain to them what happened," Judah said.

"What?" Will said, adding, "where are you?"

"I'm in Bow Street police station. I need a lawyer," Judah explained.

Will realised he was right to panic. This was something he really didn't want to do.

"I'm a conveyancing solicitor," Will said.

But he knew that that wouldn't bother Judah.

Chapter Thirteen

"Here's the cavalry," Al said.

He could see the ambulance at the other end of the street, which was a shame as he was rather hoping he could leave Darren to it. They got out of the rig and waved. Micky, a pretty fat man himself, got out. His colleague looked like he was asleep and stayed in the van.

"What have we got, Al?" Micky asked.

"She's a biggy, isn't she Darren?" Al said.

Darren nodded. He'd never seen a human quite so large before and hadn't the slightest idea how they were going to get her out.

"Where is she?" Micky asked.

Al pointed upstairs. Micky nodded.

"Why are they always upstairs?" Micky said with a sigh.

Micky went into the house and up the stairs to take a look. Al waited for Micky's evaluation. A few minutes later he got it.

"Fucking hell, how the fuck are we going to fucking get that out?" Micky said.

It was not correct protocol to refer to the patient as 'it', but Micky had the honour of being a little more cynical and jaded than even Al. Micky pulled his trousers up. He was sweating already.

"Is the feeder around?" Micky asked.

"I think he's down the pub," Al said.

"Well, if I'm going to risk putting my back out, he might as well give us a hand," Micky grunted.

"Feeder?" Darren asked.

But then, at the last moment, Darren realised Al had already explained. It didn't stop Micky.

"She doesn't get that big on her own. She can't even reach over the kitchen cabinets with that stomach in the way," Micky said, giving his trousers another tug.

"We need to get a move on," Al said.

It wasn't a job that anyone relished and they stood around doing nothing for a moment.

"Fuck it," Micky said, "Where is the pub?"

Al pointed to the other end of the road.

"What's her name?" Micky asked.

Al told him.

"I'll be a minute," Micky said and got back in his rig.

Darren watched as the ambulance shot up the road.

"What if he doesn't want to come?" Darren asked.

"Micky will drag him down the road if necessary," Al said.

Two minutes later Al watched as Micky returned. They'd worked together a number of times and they generally took turns when it came to taking the lead. This one, Al had decided, was on Micky.

"Right," Micky said.

There was a further pause as Al looked for the husband. He hadn't noticed him standing the other side of the bonnet of the van. Micky rolled his eyes as they focused on the diminutive form of the husband, as if to say 'he's not going to be much use.' They went upstairs.

"Right we have to roll her onto this," Micky said, pointing to a sturdy piece of canvas, "and then slide her down the stairs. I reckon she's about two fifty kilos and there's five of us. That's fifty each. That should be doable."

The cottage was small, and although the bedroom was the largest room in the house, there was wasn't much room once they'd all assembled around the sweating form of the woman. Al had the defibrillator with him. You never know, he thought.

"First we roll her that way," Micky said.

Al pointed to the patient to remind Micky that there was a protocol for this sort of thing.

"Oh yeah," Micky said carelessly, "we're going to roll you over first, love."

Having performed that duty they arranged themselves in a row and placed their collective hands on her.

"Go," Micky said.

They pushed and Darren watched as his hands became buried in flesh.

"Fucking hell," Micky said, sweated a bit more, and muttered, "I think she's bolted to the fucking floor."

And then suddenly, as if she was held by suction, she suddenly shifted.

"Hold her!" Micky shouted.

For a second it looked as if she was going to roll off the bed. She tottered and quivered as they spread the canvas sheet and a second later, completely out of their control, she slapped back onto the sheet. They looked at each other. There was a sense of success, but at the same time a feeling that they weren't going to manage it. Micky knew they couldn't take a pause. They had to get on with it. He motioned for them to arrange themselves around the patient and grab the canvas sheet.

"Lift," Micky said.

There was a lot of heaving, but very little movement. Micky had to revise his plan.

"Maybe not lift. Slide," Micky said.

This was more effective, but Micky had not devised a plan for when they arrive at the end of the bed. She very nearly crashed to the floor. It was more of a plop, which they took as quite encouraging. Getting her into the hall was easier than they'd hoped. Al looked down the staircase. It was steep and narrow, which meant they would have to attempt to hold her from the top and the bottom. Micky and his colleague, who Al had not met or been introduced to, went first and continued pulling her with the momentum they'd acquired in the hall until she made it over the edge and down the stairs. There was no question she was accelerating.

"Fuck," Micky said.

There was no stopping her and a second later she was at the bottom of the stairs with Micky lying on top of her.

"Do you mind," the husband, who had been quiet up to now, said.

Al attempted to pick his way down the stairs and then gave up and slid down the bannister. It was an unspoken rule that while Micky was in charge of the removal, Al should be in charge of the patient.

"Heart attack," Micky said, who was closer to the woman.

Al shifted gear. It was what he was trained for and he was calm. He'd done this many times and saved a number of lives. He'd also seen people break ribs, pressing them into the heart and guaranteeing the patient's exit from the living.

"Defibrillator," he shouted to Darren, who ran into the bedroom, and passed it down.

Al checked the patient. It wasn't immediately obvious she'd had a heart attack, but it wouldn't have been a surprise either and, if Micky said it was so, it was likely. She was breathing erratically and sweating like she'd done the lifting, but Al thought there was no obvious evidence that she was having a heart attack.

"No, she's fine," Al said.

"Not her, you fucking idiot," Micky said. "Me."

Chapter Fourteen

"Didn't you have a safe word?" Will asked.

Judah looked at him open mouthed. He looked at Rick. Rick shrugged.

"What the hell is a safe word?" Judah asked.

It was a strange thing to ask in a small grey, windowless room with a chipped Formica table and four plastic-backed chairs. They'd made little drag marks in the Lino floor. It was a strange thing to ask in a police cell.

"You know," Will said, wishing he hadn't mentioned it, "to set boundaries."

Judah had done most things, but he found the possibility that Will and Amanda indulged in such practices a little disturbing. It was like altering the natural order of things.

"How do you know about that?" Judah asked.

"That's not important now," Will said, wishing he was in the garage with a beer and copy of something which might involve readers' wives.

"But no, I guess we didn't," Judah said.

"What happened next?" Will asked.

"Judah couldn't come," Rick said.

"No," Judah interrupted, "it wasn't that."

"What was it?" Will asked.

"He couldn't come," Rick said again.

"Well, not exactly that," Judah said.

"What was it then?" Will asked.

"I became a little distracted," Judah explained.

"Because you couldn't come," Rick said.

"And then?" Will prompted.

"I might have smacked her with the whip a little more than I should have," Judah said finally.

"Whip?" Will said, "you didn't mention a whip."

They fell into a silence. Will broke it.

"Was she shouting stop, stop, stop?" he asked.

Judah tried to remember. There were some things that were really clear, particular the image of the way her breasts bounced, he could see them in the mirror, other details were hazy at best.

"He was too distracted trying to come," Rick said.

Judah looked at Rick. He wasn't sure if he was on his side.

"This is pretty bad," Will said.

"Are you saying that as my friend or my lawyer?" Judah asked.

"I'm not your lawyer!" Will said, but he knew he'd lost that argument.

"It wasn't my fault she was studying the boundaries between pain and pleasure," Judah said, as if he was hard done by.

It prompted a further realisation in Will.

"Was she a student?" he said.

Judah nodded.

"You didn't mention she was a student!" Will said.

"Yes," Judah said casually, "didn't I mention that?"

There was a tap on the door. It was the young policewoman.

"Mr Kingwill?" she said to Will.

He wanted to protest that he wasn't Judah's lawyer, but he didn't seem to have a choice. He left the room.

"We have decided," the policewomen said, "not to press charges at this time."

She said it as if she was passing a particularly painful kidney stone. It clearly pained her that this misogynistic, manipulative, predatory bastard should walk free. She'd not had a good time at the police academy.

"But," she cautioned, "we will be continuing our enquiries."

"Thanks very much," Will said adding, "he's free to go?"

The policewoman nodded reluctantly. Will went back into the cramped little room.

"You're free to go," he said.

"I knew I could rely on my lawyer," Judah said, and jumped up as if he didn't have a care in the world.

Will and Rick looked at him a little bemused.

"Come on," Judah said, "those beers won't drink themselves."

"We're late," Will said checking his watch.

Half an hour later they found Mac and Al propping up the bar. There were a few empties in front of them.

"Where have you guys been?" Mac asked.

"Don't ask," Will said pointing to Judah.

"Five of Alf's finest lagers?" Mac asked.

Mac had a talent for establishing the name of the barman or landlord, as he'd discovered this was the fastest method of delivering lagers to his right hand. This was the same pub they'd met at for twenty years and there had been a number of barman, landlords and managers. Most knew Mac.

"Here already," Mac said, "cheers Alf, and one for yourself."

A second later, after a couple of mouthfuls of lager, Rick launched into his interpretation of Judah's predicament. There was no question that the piss was going to be taken.

"So he couldn't get it up?" Al said.

"It sounds like that to me," Will said.

"No question of it," Mac said.

It was a banter which they all knew had legs and was good for at least another two pints until a further question was asked.

"Why did they let you off?" Mac asked.

Will didn't know the answer to that and suspected that this was an issue which wasn't going to disappear in a hurry. But he didn't let that upset his stride. He'd managed to get everyone together for the Friday drink and he'd doubted he'd manage that.

"More beer?" Mac said, but it wasn't really a question.

Chapter Fifteen

"Are you okay, darling?"

Julie was in a hammock which was strung between two three hundred year old yew trees. She'd gone home or, as her brother had said, 'reverted to the mothership'. The house had been in the family for generations, and it had a slightly jaded grandeur which only the truly wealthy could achieve. Money was spent, but only with the utmost discretion.

"Yeah, I think so," Julie said.

Julie was reading a book. It was punctuated by the occasional 'plunk' as tennis balls hit the ground in the court behind her. Her mother had just finished a lesson. If Julie had thought about it, and she was feeling too languid for that, she might question why her mother's progress on the tennis court was so minimal, while Jesus – it was pronounced with an 'h' – her coach, was making huge linguistic strides.

"Are you sure?" her mother insisted.

Julie was, by nature, pretty robust, and she'd almost forgotten about her ordeal. She just felt like a little luxury 'me' time accompanied by a few of her mother's hefty gin and tonics. There was a lecture she had to attend although, as she was studying art, there was no harm in being a little rebellious.

"I'm fine," Julie said.

Her wounds had healed as had her desire to explore and break through new sexual boundaries. As she was recovering, so was her heterosexuality. She was going to have to tell Terry, who wouldn't be pleased, but she'd understand. It was Julie's body and her choice with whom she chose to share it. Terry had been on demonstrations declaring the same.

"When are you going back?" her mother asked.

Her mother tried to make it sound as if her prime concern was Julie's welfare, which it was, but she'd established that Julie was fine and now she was feeling pretty horny. She'd run round the court, mostly just a little bit too late, and worked up quite a sweat and, as it was a warm day, so had Jesus.

"Soon," Julie said vaguely.

It hadn't occurred to Julie that this was the time when Jesus would learn her mother tongue, or it could have been her mother's tongue and then very much more. He was, as her mother had confided at a charity lunch recently, a gift from god, as his name suggested.

"Soon?" her mother asked, hoping for more specific details.

Julie put down her book and picked up her phone. There were twenty-two texts, although twelve of them were from Terry, but she was a very popular girl despite treating most people with indifference. Julie was a master of wilting indifference. Her astonishing good looks gave her a power she was only half aware of.

"I guess later today. I haven't checked the train times," Julie said.

The country house would have been empty as Julie's brother was in Ibiza, and her father was in the House making impassioned arguments about immigrants, and the creative ways in which funding could be cut from the NHS. He was going to stay the night in the London flat, although it was actually a house, and quite a large one at that.

"Would you like Jesus to take you to the station, love?" her mother asked.

It was a strange family dynamic that meant that when her mother wanted to have sex with Jesus, or her brother with Stephen, or even Julie with anyone she chose, that they were all able not to notice what might be obvious to everyone else.

"Hold on, I'll just check," Julie said scrolling through her phone.

She knew she ought to go back, but she was feeling seriously chilled. She checked the train timetables. Then she checked a few more texts. Another two had arrived from Terry.

"In half an hour?"

Her mother smiled. There was enough time to get a shower, but she didn't need to as Jesus liked her with a sweat on. He'd told her she tasted better and she had no reason to question him. Jesus's devotion to her mound, as she liked to think of it, was quite astonishing. She was fairly sure he'd spent more time down there than her husband, and they'd been married thirty years. The strange thing was that when he came up for air his language seemed to improve, as if her mound was the font of something quite profound.

"Are you okay, mummy?" Julie asked.

Her mother's mind had been elsewhere and a small smile, which she was unaware of, had appeared on her face. She had to make the most of it as Jesus was talking about attending a tournament in Barcelona. He'd mentioned something about sponsorship, and it was something they had to discuss once Jesus had performed his other duties.

"I'm fine," Julie's mother said.

Chapter Sixteen

It was Monday and Will was back at the office. He wasn't entirely certain he'd didn't still feel hungover. Saturday had been hell with a heavy breaker in his head, and Sunday had only been marginally better until he'd repaired to the shed and grabbed a couple of beers, after which he felt much better. Then he felt much worse. Amanda had barely spoken to him, particularly after he'd declined her kind offer of sex. He wasn't sure if he could manage it, which reminded him of Judah. He wondered if he could introduce not getting it up as 'doing a Judah' to the ski team banter. They'd certainly welcome it. Thankfully, most of the urgent business had been concluded on Friday and the day inched forward at a glacial pace until he gave up and started to google ski chalets in the Alps. There was a bewildering number of alternatives, which distracted him enough not to notice Jim Beresford standing in front of him. Jim was the senior partner.

"Planning a skiing holiday?" Jim asked.

Will was sufficiently senior, and knew Jim well enough, not to be embarrassed about searching for a holiday at work.

"I thought I'd get the old ski team together," Will said.

Jim was five years older than Will and had such a firm grasp of the business that no one could unseat him, and he had no intention of going anywhere.

"Let's have a look," Jim said.

Will turned the screen. Will scrolled through the alternatives until Jim said, "You could always take my apartment."

"Have you got a place in the Alps?" Will asked.

"Yes, I've told you about it," Jim said.

Will couldn't remember, but then his skiing antenna had been turned off. It was very much on now. Now he thought about it he did remember. Jim had paid nigh on a million euros for it, which would make it a good deal nicer than the places he'd been looking at.

"I'd forgotten," Will admitted.

He kept scrolling, but wondered if Jim was waiting for him to ask more, although he feared it would be beyond their budget. Not that they'd set a budget.

"How much is it?" Will asked.

Jim frowned. They'd had this conversation too, but clearly Will had no recollection of it.

"Nothing. I mean it's free to you," Jim said.

Jim was not generous by nature, but his accountant had told him he could offset some expenses if he used it for business. This wasn't exactly business, but it was near enough.

"Just pay for the cleaning," Jim said.

"That would be great," Will said.

"I just need to check when my wife is not there," Jim said.

Jim disappeared back into his office. There were rumours about Jim and his wife, some of which were quite fanciful and were to do with his slightly camp flamboyant nature, and others to do with the secretaries he grew so close to, who subsequently disappeared. That's wasn't to say he was a mass murderer but Jim, who'd once been a lay preacher, had thoroughly embraced the 'lay' aspect and was a serial philanderer who swung both ways. At least that was the latest theory and, now that Will thought about it, male interns had disappeared too. Will was quite resistant to connecting the dots, but when he did, it did suggest there was some truth in it. The idea of it, the complication, the deceit and the energy required horrified Will. Why were some people constructed that way and others preferred to lead a comfortable life? Perhaps that was why Jim had the drive to build the company, while Will was happy just to have a coattail of it. Was that why Jim would be marching on into his seventies sailing yachts, skiing down mountains and pulling women, long after Will had retired? Or been retired. Will might have been having a crisis of self worth.

"Right," Jim said.

Will hadn't noticed him reappear, as his mind had been elsewhere.

"The wife's there quite a lot this season," Jim said.

There was no question in Will's mind that Jim's tone of voice suggested that this was a situation that Jim was very happy with. It would give him the opportunity, Will guessed, to seduce women and men. The idea of sex with a man was pretty abhorrent to Will, who did not know any gay men, although he had his suspicions about a few. Not that he cared what they chose to do, and he wouldn't have had an issue if any of the kids had turned out to be gay.

"Except next week," Jim said.

"Next week?" Will said.

"From next Saturday," Jim added.

That made Will panic. It gave him five days to corral everyone together. And he'd have to tell Amanda. He thought about it, while Jim looked at him and tried not to get irritated by his lack of decisiveness, although Will was insightful enough to know that that was what Jim was thinking. He also knew that a free million euro apartment was not to be passed up and, if he did pass it up, it wouldn't be available again. Jim could be a bit like that.

"Brilliant, that would be great," Will said.

When Jim left Will thought about it. It was rent free and, from the look of the pictures, far nicer than the others he'd seen. He opened the WhatsApp group and typed, 'apartment in Val Thorens sorted for next Saturday. Who's in?' It was short notice, but he knew he could rely on Rick and Al, and he suspected Mac would find a way, and they would just just have to rope in Judah. Literally. A second later his phone rang. It was Al.

"Are you in?" Will asked.

"Yes, sure," Al said, although he'd not seen the text, adding, "Any chance you could come round and give me a hand?"

"No problem," Will said without asking what kind of a hand was required.

Al lived one stop before him and he often dropped in on his way home. He wasn't going to stay for long, as he didn't feel he had the stamina, and Amanda would probably complain. He'd yet to tell her that the vague dates he'd suggested had moved forward and become a certainty.

"The usual?" Will asked.

There was a pub opposite the train station.

"Great," Al said.

"Half an hour?" Will said and left the office.

When Will stepped out of the station he was surprised to see Al waiting in his car.

"We're going somewhere?" Will asked.

"We are," Al said and started the engine. He gave it a little burst of acceleration.

"Has something happened?" Will asked.

"A couple of things," Al said.

Al was driving quickly, but had yet to inform Will as to the destination, although some part of it was that Al was still turning things over in his head.

"You remember me telling you about my colleague, Micky?" Al said.

"Yeah, I've met him at yours. The fat guy," Will said.

"That's him. Well, we were doing a job together – it involved a bit of heavy lifting – and he had a heart attack," Al said.

"Shit, was he okay? Did you do your defib thing?" Will said.

Al had done his defib thing and he'd done so in a slight panic. While he'd pressed the paddles onto the chests and applied the electricity to hundreds of people, maybe more, he'd never done it on someone he knew. And they both knew the odds of survival. Suddenly he was leading the job.

"Not at first," Al said, remembering the slumped form of Micky.

The problem was that Micky's slumped form lay on the obese patient's slumped form. He'd had to do some clambering. It was a bit of a mountain to climb. He'd had to drag Micky off her so that he didn't electrocute the both of them.

"It took quite a few goes," Al said.

"But he's okay?" Will asked.

"Not exactly," Al said.

They drove a little further in silence and Will wondered if Al would get to the point.

"But he survived," Will said finally.

"Kind of," Al said. "He had a stroke after I got him back."

"Shit," Will said, "Are we going to the hospital?"

Will assumed the help that was required of him was of the emotional variety. He was okay with that.

"But they think he'll be alright. They reckon he'll make a full recovery. His paralysis was only mild and he was recovering movement on the way to the hospital." Al said.

"That's good then," Will said.

"Yes, it's a wake up call. He needs to lose a bit of weight," Al said.

That was certainly Will's impression of Micky, but it didn't explain where they were going.

"So what's the problem then?" Will asked.

"The problem was the woman lying under him," Al said.

"He was having sex?" Will said a little surprised.

"You've spent too much time with Judah," Al said. "No, she was the woman, about quarter of a ton of her, who we were trying to move."

"What happened to her?" Will asked hoping to tie up a few lose ends.

"We left her there," Al said.

The protocol was to see to the patient in need, as he'd explained to senior management. He'd been in a bit of panic too and forgotten about his responsibilities to the woman. He was coming off his shift as well. As far as he aware she was still lying at the bottom of the stairs.

"Did she make a complaint?" Will asked.

"She certainly did," Al said.

The small and largely insignificant husband, the feeder, had turned out to be not as insignificant as they'd assumed. He'd kicked up quite a fuss. One thing was certain. The husband wasn't able to get his wife back up the stairs, or in a car. The woman was rooted to the spot by gravity.

"I kind of had to scramble over her to get to Micky and I may have done so in a less than conscientious way," Al confirmed.

"But Micky's health was the more critical factor," Will said.

Al relaxed a little. That kind of reasoning would be useful. He knew he could rely on Will.

"So, where are we going?" Will finally asked.

"The police station," Al said.

"The police station?" Will said, a little concerned by the direction this was going.

"Yes, there was talk of assault. I thought I might need a lawyer," Al said.

"But I'm a conveyancing solicitor," Will said, quietly.

"It's near enough. I think they're going to charge me with assault," Al said.

"Charge you? But I'm only a..." Will said, but he didn't have the energy to finish the sentence.

Chapter Seventeen

Terry was furious. She'd spent the last half hour giving herself one with the long cylindrical vodka bottle, but it hadn't helped.

"Shit," Terry spat.

She needed something a little softer and more human. She put the vodka bottle back in the cereal packet, although as it was empty there was little need, and she pulled her knickers up. There was a fruit and veg store around the corner and she was going to invest in a few suitably shaped fruit, or veg, to get through her mourning period. She was mourning the fact that Julie wouldn't sleep with her. Julie had been very clear on the matter and that was that. No sex. Terry could only deal with this by locking the door and undergoing one of her monster masturbation sessions. She'd tried therapy, and she'd attended a few self help classes, but she generally found that this was the most effective way of beating away her frustration. Twenty minutes later she came back with what looked like a bag of groceries. She was a student so she was going to have to further repurpose them for food, although she didn't much care for cucumbers.

"Let me see," she said, once she'd locked the door and removed her clothes.

The last time she'd been so angry was when Valentine, who was French, had left her for Steve. She couldn't believe it. Valentine was a full-on jackboot-wearing dyke who'd joined her at rallies and demonstrations. And then she'd acquired a sudden yearning for happiness. Except she hadn't meant that.

She had, rather shockingly, meant 'a penis'. Who'd have thought? It had taken Terry a few days to thrash that one out of her system. She looked at the array of suitably shaped fruit and vegetables. It was quite a collection and she'd had a good squeeze checking everything for ripeness.

"Okay," she said.

Terry wouldn't have minded so much, but Julie had definitely led her on. She was on a promise. It was practically a done deal and then that bloody dirty lecturer had stepped in and practically flogged her to death. It wasn't fair. Terry squeezed an aubergine. Its girth was a little intimidating and she picked up a cucumber.

"Better," she said.

It was, but she decided to start with a banana. It was a pretty green one, really quite firm, and it posed the skin on, or off, question. She went for off, peeled it, closed her eyes and thought of Julie. It was a mistake. Despite her love of the vagina there was no way she was going to eat that. She grabbed the cucumber and tried that. She rubbed herself a bit. Then a lot. She was determined to banish this ghost and she stepped it up. She was gyrating and rubbing and thrusting. It was quite noisy. But she could feel something coming. It was a little distant and very much on the horizon, but she was racing for it. The cucumber, however, had had enough and started to disintegrate. It didn't matter as she was now ready for the larger girth of the aubergine. She hurled down the cucumber, which collided with a part filled ashtray, and grabbed the aubergine. She applied it without mercy. If the cucumber could have talked it would have looked up at the aubergine knowing it didn't have a chance. A minute later it wasn't providing the kind of stimulation she was hoping for and a few seconds after that it looked like a traffic accident. DNA analysis would be required to identify it as an aubergine.

"Shit and fucking bollocks," Terry swore.

This wasn't working. Vegetables were not what was needed. She heard a tapping at her door.

"Terry?" a voice said.

Terry looked around her small room in the halls of residence. It looked like a terrorist had attacked the place.

"Yes," Terry said.

"Are you alright?" the voice said.

Terry was fairly sure it was Pam. She was in the neighbouring room and she didn't know her very well. She was another posh girl like Julie.

"Yes, I'm fine," Terry said through the door.

Terry wasn't sure if she wanted to continue with this exercise, take a long walk, or drink vodka. She knew medication of some sort was required. She'd just not decided what.

"Terry, it's Pam," the voice said again.

Terry knew she should have grabbed the vodka bottle. That was where she went wrong. But the moment had sort of passed, although her frustrations hadn't. It wasn't simple, but she felt certain she could get through it without therapy.

"Do you want to share a joint?" Pam said.

Terry wasn't one to pass up a free drink, but a free joint was even better, and probably just what she required.

"Yeah, that would be great. Give me a minute," Terry said.

Terry was studying biochemistry and had a special interest in infectious diseases. Despite that, she grabbed a tea towel with which she'd dried dishes for the last three months, and she used it on her crotch and legs. She chucked her dungarees on, slipped her underwear under the sheets of her little single bed, and looked around. It was a bit of a mess. She used the tea towel on every surface which had been infected, but it was making things worse as bits of fruit and vegetable were falling out of it.

"Fuck it," she said.

She didn't want to miss out on the joint. She took a quick look at herself in the mirror and while she had also campaigned for the right to not be subordinated by man's vision of what a woman should look like, she did look like shit. But Pam was a resolutely heterosexual woman. She didn't need to worry. She opened the door.

"Hi," Pam said.

Pam looked in. There was a strange smell, she couldn't place it. Terry looked like she'd been in a hurricane. But Pam was waiting for her parents and it was a little tense at home. She needed something to relax.

"This joint won't smoke itself," Pam said.

"Come in, come in," Terry said. "I'll get a light."

Pam looked for somewhere to sit which didn't have a stain or the remnants of something she couldn't identify. She wouldn't have knocked on Terry's door, but everyone was out, and she had been making a strange racket which suggested she might need help, or company, or a joint. Terry passed her a plastic lighter and then, as an afterthought, she lit it and held it for her. But her hands were a bit shaky and Pam had to hold them. It made Terry feel better much more effectively than an aubergine had managed.

"Thanks," Pam said and drew in some smoke.

She would have left it until she came back, but her boyfriend had keys to her room and he would probably have smoked it for her, as if he was delivering a useful service. She was growing a little tired of him. Pam knew Terry was in distress and wondered it she could help her, although if she'd suggested this to Terry she would have been very clear as to how she wished to be helped.

"Are you okay?" Pam asked.

Terry sighed. She wasn't sure whether she wanted to confide, but the joint wasn't doing very much. Masturbation hadn't worked either. Hey-ho, Terry thought.

"I was a little upset about Julie," Terry admitted.

"Yeah, Judah gave her a right beating," Pam said, inhaling a little more smoke.

Pam wasn't great at smoking and she'd wished she'd practised it on her own. She was always one puff away from a cascade of coughs.

"That's true, but I meant..." Terry started and then stopped.

It took a few moments for Pam to connect the dots although she'd learned, as this was their first year and they were still in the halls of residence, that most conversations was about who was doing who.

"Were you guys an item?" Pam said passing the joint.

It was a good question and one that Terry wasn't immediately able to answer. They hadn't actually got it on which is where the agony lay.

"I thought so," Terry said, finally feeling the effects of the joint.

"Ohh," said Pam.

She very nearly said 'there's nought so queer as folk' as her dad might have, but she managed to keep it in. She'd heard Terry could be quite political and she didn't think she'd laugh at herself. She tried changing the subject.

"Did you hear that Valentine and Steve split up?" Pam said.

As she said it she realised that there had been some gossip which had connected Valentine to Terry. This was awkward, but she didn't know where to steer the conversation.

"I didn't," Terry said.

Terry wasn't sure if that meant that Valentine was back on the vagina, as she liked to privately think about it, but she'd changed her style to ostentatiously hetero so she doubted it.

"Oh," Pam gasped, remembered some more gossip, "and Steve was caught with Dave!'

Terry had to laugh at the irony of that. Her world was a little upside down. But she did feel a bit better about Julie.

"Funny thing is," Terry said, her mind reverting to Julie, "Julie's real name isn't Brown."

"Isn't it?" Pam said, taking the joint before Terry had entirely consumed at it.

"It's Panter," Terry said.

Pam was studying politics, and even had an interest in how power is brokered, but her mind had wandered now that the marijuana was properly infiltrating her system.

"Like that politician," Terry added.

Chapter Eighteen

"We need to turn the house round," Mac said.

He'd read the text from Will and replied immediately. It was Monday. He was definitely on, and then something unusual happened. He wasn't sure how, as he loathed Treve as a man and a client. Treve was difficult, lacked judgement, insight and taste and was a complete bastard to work for. More surprisingly he'd expressed this thought to Treve, as Mac's diplomatic powers were limited. It was therefore something of a further surprise to discover he'd been recommended by him, and rather warmly at that, and he'd acquired a new client.

"I'm sorry?" Beth said.

Beth was American and that rarest of things, a client with money. And she had every intention of using it, which meant he had to get her sorted in a week. Her house was in the Californian hills and she'd flown him there business class, and the only issue was getting back in time for the ski trip. His return flight was early Saturday morning.

"Reorientate," Mac said quickly.

The house was subject to a five year remodelling whether it needed it or not, like a London pub, and Beth's face.

"If we put the front door there and turn the hall round," Mac said.

Beth liked the exotic. Previous remodellers had been Mexican, Phillipino, German and French. Scottish seemed particularly exotic as she found his accent charming – it was the series *Outlander* set in Scotland that had convinced her that a Scottish architect should be her next choice – rather than Treve's recommendation.

"I'm sorry?" Beth said.

And, to Beth's eyes, he had a robustness which mirrored the highlands in the late seventeen hundreds. His ruddy, incredibly lived-in appearance represented a kind of lost masculinity. Californian men were too aware of their grooming and more interested in themselves.

"And then if we take this bedroom out at first floor level, we can give the room a triple height grandeur from which we can suspend a magnificent chandelier," Mac said.

He could tell by Beth's confused face that they were having wavelength issues and he began to use his hands to illustrate. As far as he could tell he'd already won the job. She'd even invited him to a drinks party.

"I'm sorry?" Beth said.

Beth also liked his mischievous smile and the clatter of British teeth behind it – just like teeth might have been in the seventeen hundreds – before dentistry had been invented. It was so charming.

"And then," Mac said, building to the grand finale, "that opens out this aspect which liberates some space but, more importantly, provides morning sunshine for your breakfast balcony."

While Mac had never encountered a house which required less remodelling, it was a joy to do so without any apparent budgetary constraints. The practice had suffered a setback that morning when a cheque had bounced and his secretary was forced to pay for toilet paper herself. Treve was not the most rapid of payers and Mac was waiting on payment from three other clients. Beth was temporarily taking him away from that world unless, she too, was a terrible payer. He'd negotiated a storming fee.

"I'm sorry?" Beth said.

Beth loved that wild accent. She just wished she didn't find it so impenetrable. She was picking out more of it, but only the odd word. She'd found the Filipino and the Mexican easier to understand. But that was part of the challenge. She listened carefully. It was like learning a new language, Beth thought, not that she spoke another language.

"And also," Mac said, nearly forgetting, "it creates a new room for the dogs which gives them a freer run."

Beth smiled. There was only so long she could go on saying 'I'm sorry' and she'd distinctly heard the word 'dogs' which was good news as Poly, Jasmine, Peachy and Blossom were the love of her life. At least they were while other lovers were absent. Beth had been looking for a man for over ten years and it was proving to be a little troublesome. It wasn't, she thought, as if she'd set her standards too high although, looking at Mac, she was certainly addressing that issue.

"Lovely," Beth said.

It was the most positive thing that anyone had said of Mac's work for a while and she followed it with the nicest possible thing anyone could say.

"Oh, and I transferred your fee," Beth said absentmindedly.

Mac's employees could wipe their arses now. He wondered whether she'd sent some or all of the fee. All would help with the ski trip.

"And will you fly over and check progress with the builders?" Beth asked.

She was going to stay in her London house for the duration of the work in the period that passes for summer in London, and then she'll probably have that house remodelled, while she gets back to Californian life. She'd dropped that hint already and Mac had taken a bus to Highgate to check it out. Cash registers were ringing in his ears.

"Er...," Mac said.

He didn't mind overseeing work, but travelling to the US would take a considerable bite out of his fees.

"Obviously I'll pay more and cover your expenses," Beth said, studying the plans Mac had drawn up.

"I'd love to," Mac said, with a jagged smile.

Beth cast a quick glance at Mac's slightly dishevelled appearance, and his many pocketed cargo pants, and slightly droopy tweed jacket. She could almost imagine him on horseback. She wondered what he'd wear for the drinks party that evening and whether she should attempt to suggest he go for something a little smarter.

"Excellent," Beth said, adding, "you haven't forgotten the black tie drinks party this evening?"

She'd cunningly inserted the words 'black tie' in the sentence as a hint, although she was unaware, having only met Mac a few times, that he was immune to hints. She'd certainly agonised over her own wardrobe and was inclined, particularly as she'd put on a bit of weight, to the outrageous and the hope that her swelling breasts would distract the eye from her generous stomach.

"Yes, or course," Mac said, adding, "I hope a kilt is okay?"

Beth smiled broadly. A kilt, in her view, was very much okay.

Chapter Nineteen

When Pam's father came to collect her she had sobered up a bit and changed her clothes in case the smoke had clung a little too needily to her. That could easily prompt an argument. She wasn't sure if he was attempting to set a divorce record. He didn't say much after they'd exchanged greetings and pleasantries. Eventually the silence began to get to them.

"How's it going, then?" her father asked.

"It's fine," Pam said trying to think of something more to say.

But the silence was too painful, and she spoke a bit about the course, and the halls of residence, and that helped pass the time for a while. He seemed to relax, but she could tell he was under pressure.

"How are things with you?" Pam asked.

Her father sighed. When Bill Tuft had started work he was William or Will, but there had been a collective unconscious decision to call him Bill, although he'd thought of himself as someone a little softer than a Bill. It hadn't taken long for him to become a Bill and he'd grown a little impatient and monosyllabic with it. But Bill was going through a period of middle aged depression – the kind of thing the newspaper he worked for often spoke of – and he was struggling to find a starting point. He decided not to mention her mother.

"Work's tough," he said.

Her father had left university with radical ideals and a determination to change the world but the world, particularly with a couple of kids, was an expensive place to live. Consequently he'd abandoned social comment and now worked for the kind of salacious newspaper which carries very little news.

"All that social media," he muttered.

Although he'd been neither Woodward or Bernstein, he had investigated and unearthed enough stories to send him up the ladder. He hadn't exposed government corruption, but the world now knew that a Hollywood actress had secret plastic surgery, a leading actor had waved more than a truncheon in a thirties drama about the police, and they were now aware of an MP with a predilection for dressing in women's clothing. Bill Tuft was the go-to man for juicy, borderline slanderous gossip.

"But we're still knocking it out," Bill said.

The problem lay in the economics of the printed word, and he was required to administer an online version of the paper which confused him. He struggled to operate his old Nokia mobile phone and, when he did manage to access the online paper, he found it riddled with errors. Young people seemed barely capable of reading and writing, let alone spelling or grammar. He tried not to think about it.

"Have you met anyone interesting?" he asked.

"Terry is in the room next to me. She's a committed lesbian," Pam said, adding, "But she's angry because Valentine left her for Steve, although Steve left Valentine for Dave."

Bill laughed. There seemed to be a diminishing number of heterosexuals these days. The list of what was wrong with young people was getting longer.

"But Terry," Pam continued, "was upset because Julie wouldn't sleep with her – apparently she'd promised to

– after she had a sort of sado kind of sex session with a lecturer."

That was pretty heady stuff even for Bill, who'd seen it all.

"The strange thing," Pam said remembering something else Terry had said through the marijuana haze, "was that her real name – she uses her mother's surname – is Panter."

Bill registered this. If he'd had three eyes they would be rolling like the tumblers on a one armed bandit. They were searching for the jackpot.

"Have you got your phone on you?" he asked.

He knew the answer to that question. There were people who were less connected to their colostomy bags, and in his view there was more shit on the phone.

"Yeah, sure," Pam said, getting her phone out.

"Google images of Harry Panter and family," Bill said.

Pam expertly tapped it in and a page of pictures appeared.

"Nice house," she said scrolling through.

"Here they are," Pam said.

Bill took his eyes off the road for a second and looked at the picture. Like all politicians it looked like a staged photo of familial perfection. He doubted that very much.

"Well?" Bill said.

"Well what?" Pam asked.

"Is it her? Is it, what was her name? Was it Julie?"

There was no getting away from the excited tone which had entered her father's voice. Those tumblers were rolling.

"Yes," Pam said. "That's Julie."

Bill started tapping the steering wheel as if he were typing out a story on his old Olivetti typewriter. This would raise circulation and up the hits, or whatever they called it, on the online paper. They'd missed the deadline for tomorrow's paper, but that didn't matter. He might even have to do some footwork of his own on this, like the old days.

"What did you say happened between her and a lecturer?" he asked.

Pam explained the horse whip and the noise on her floor of the halls of residence. Then she remembered something else.

"I think someone recorded it," she said.

"Recorded what?" Bill said excitedly.

"Julie was shouting something like hit me harder and then there was the noise of the whip," Pam said.

Bill knew he needed that recording. He could transcribe it for the paper. Better, he suddenly thought, he could – if legal allowed him – put it up on the online version. It might, if he was lucky, even crash the fucking thing. He needed to track down that lecturer.

"Do you know the name of the lecturer?" Bill asked.

Pam had the feeling that she'd given something private away but, as it was making her miserable father a good deal less miserable, it was worth it. She had to think of the lecturer's name, as she'd only seen him in passing in the halls. She found it eventually.

"Judah. Judah Wheeler," she said finally.

Chapter Twenty

Most of the time Rick had been listening. His mind had only wandered a couple of times and he was fairly sure nothing significant had been said. He'd texted Will immediately. Of course he was on for the ski trip.

"Okay," the instructor said, "to recap, you steer like this and pull these up to slow you down."

The instructor looked at his audience. They seemed attentive enough.

"Now," the instructor continued, "the wind and the thermals are strong today, so there will be no problem taking off."

His audience nodded excitedly and the instructor led them out to their hang gliders. Now that the talk had finished, and they were nearing the point at which they had to strap themselves to a small kite and hurl themselves off the cliffs at Dunstable Downs, there was apprehension in the air.

"Is this your first time?" a nervous looking man asked.

Rick often thought about first times. It was why, if it was possible, he'd like to rewind his life – and probably keep rewinding it – to experience certain things again for the first time. At the time it might be different as nerves, or uncertainty, might taint the joy of the moment, but often there is nothing greater than a first time.

"Yes," Rick said with a smile.

"You seem very calm," the nervous man observed.

He remembered the first time he met Annie. She was out of his class and he commented later that he knew immediately that she was the one, but it took a little longer to convince her that he was the one. She had what she referred to as a sort-of boyfriend at the time. He was Hispanic.

"Right," the instructor said, "get yourself strapped in."

The class stepped into the flimsy looking devices and fastened the strap around themselves. The instructor checked everyone.

"Are you okay?" he asked a girl of around thirty who seemed to be shaking.

"I can't do it," she said.

The instructor frowned. When people show an interest, he tries to put them off, when they sign up, he tries to put them off, and when he talks them through it he tries to put them off. He'd found that when one person unbuckles it takes the others with them.

"No problem," he said casually, "you can go up later."

"Are you okay?" he asked Rick.

But Rick's mind was elsewhere. He was thinking about how much he'd loathed Annie's Hispanic sort-of boyfriend. They were about the same age, but the boyfriend was hideously hairy when Rick was only beginning to sprout hairs. He looked like a child next to him.

"Me?" Rick said, "I'm fine."

The instructor nodded and led them towards the launch site, as he liked to refer to it, as it was less intimidating that calling it the edge of the cliff, which was what it was. As they approached the wind whipped up suddenly and the sails of the glider filled and tugged Rick back. There were a few muted screams. Other members of the class were reconsidering. It was a very long drop.

"Ready?" the instructor asked.

Rick thought about the Hispanic sort-of boyfriend's confidence. It was more than confidence, it was a kind of conceit. He took Annie for granted, as if he was doing her a favour sleeping with her. Just thinking about it made his mind reel, and he wish he hadn't. It gave him a jealous stabbing pain, which made no sense, but he couldn't stop himself.

"Just a few feet," the instructor reminded them.

The instructor stepped a little quicker into the wind and the glider rose into the air and, with a deft tug, he brought it back down again. He was still a long way from the cliff.

"Go," the instructor said turning and waving for them to do the same.

One person started to get out of the glider, but the wind was giving it a life of its own like an animal reluctant to be trapped, another stood rigid and unable to move, Rick ran towards the edge. But he never made to the edge, he wasn't even close, as the glider rose into the air and spiralled upwards until the cliffs seemed to be a distant mark on the landscape. He'd climbed so high he couldn't hear the instructor's screams, and had no idea that he was supposed to only travel a few feet and land. He was flying like a bird for the first time, but it wasn't giving him the first time thrill he'd hoped for. He felt like he was an observer insulated from it and, if it should crash, it wouldn't be him crashing. He remembered something the instructor had said about what he needed to do before he flew. What was it? Was it learn to land? It wasn't something that could ever be applied to life.

"Bugger," Rick muttered.

He was crying, but he didn't know why, or maybe he did, but he didn't want to think about it even though he could rarely stop himself. He cleared his eyes and looked around. It was a clear day and, as he turned, the sun hit his face. He was Icarus flying too close to the sun. He looked down. He could see the faces of his class mates, and the instructor who was talking on his mobile phone summoning the emergency services. But Rick continued to circle. He vaguely recalled the operation of the device, but he'd flown light aeroplanes, and had a bit of a feel for it. He could have come down, but there was a peaceful solitary silence which was relaxing him. As he passed over the cliff he felt a thermal buoying him up. He could stay here all day. But every now and again the panic stricken screams of the instructor carried their way up to him and he wondered what landing was like. He'd not really been listening. He started to come down.

"Rick!" someone was screaming.

Rick waved at them as if he didn't have a care in the world but, as he got closer, he realised he might have been travelling too fast. He banked and turned again. He could hear the instructor shouting commands. It was as he turned he vaguely remembered seeing the instructor pulling two cords simultaneously and Rick gave them a yank, which braked the device, and the ground came up suddenly to meet him. For a second he was bewildered and then the comfort of blackness took him away.

"Are you okay?" the instructor said.

If Rick had heard he would have said he wasn't really okay. He was barely coping. But he had to carry on.

Chapter Twenty-One

The police station Al eventually took Will to was brand new and state of the art. It wasn't just ready for the digital age, it was saying bring it on. DI Wilkins had retirement in his sights and was bewildered by this brand new form of coppering.

"What did you say your name was again?" Wilkins asked.

Al looked at Will. Will shrugged and told Wilkins. They watched as Wilkins' finger roamed around a keyboard in the hope of finding the appropriate letter and entering into the new system. Despite the bluff, Al was nervous. This sort of thing could jeopardise his career and he didn't want that. But the gentle way that the police officer blundered along was taking the edge off the tension Al felt about a possible assault charge and where that would lead.

"Right," Wilkins said. "Address?"

Twenty minutes later Al's basic details were residing in the police database, although it would require opening a subsection of a subsection of a drop down of a drop down and Wilkins prayed that there was no merit in the case, as he doubted he'd ever find that information. There were lost burial grounds which would be easier to find.

"What is the relationship between you and Mrs Parry, who claims you assaulted her?" Wilkins asked.

"She was my patient. I'm a paramedic. I was called to her because she was having difficulty breathing. The patient was, is, severely obese," Al said.

In the old days Wilkins would have duly noted this down in his notebook and now he had to find the right electronic column to put it against, and that was akin to a hunt for truffles, or a white peacock. The alternative required asking one of his younger colleagues, and that would feel like defeat. He grabbed the mouse and, as he moved it across the page, alternatives kept scrolling up and down. His feeling that operating the system was like a personal assault was not shared by his colleagues who seemed to take pleasure in never leaving their desks. Policing wasn't what it used to be.

"Getting there," Wilkins said.

He wasn't. He might as well have been navigating the Darien gap in a storm, but Wilkins didn't want to give up. He had made complaints about the system, suggesting that the software was villainous and deliberately obstructive, but he'd been ignored and it had just pushed him further in the direction of retirement.

"Got it," he said, a little too triumphantly.

He hadn't, but a menu had appeared temptingly and then evaporated as if it was taunting him. He was unaware, as were most of the staff, that the software was indeed devised by a criminal and its sole function was to obfuscate the case and, if that didn't work, it could easily be hacked by those who paid a subscription. The criminal in question lived on a very large boat, on which he employed celebrity chefs, and toured the Caribbean. Type two diabetes was a bigger risk than prison for him.

"Fuck it," Wilkins said suddenly, realising he'd been in his own world. "Sorry about that," he added.

As if by magic, or if someone was actually listening to him, the correct screen appeared and Wilkins tapped in the information. He was a little inclined to give in and go back to the old fashioned way, but he persevered. An hour later Al and Will left the police station and stepped into the fresh air.

"Pub," Al said.

Will was surprised he'd said it as it was, quite plainly, a statement of the fucking obvious. They chose the nearest. Will waited while Al bought the beers. It was only right.

"That was strange," Will said.

"All hail technology," Al said downing a generous gulp of beer.

"Does he know what he's doing?" Will asked.

"We'll find out," Al said, "you know, when the shit hits the fan and the patient crashes, and everyone is running about panicking, it's not about the technology. It's useful, but it ends up being about the ABC. About the basics, about airway, breathing, circulation and an instinct and an experience about knowing what to do."

"We're going to need a few beers, aren't we?" Will said.

"We may," Al said, adding, "I thought he was going to arrest me."

"That would have scuppered the ski trip. We've only got four days," Will said.

"Oh yes," Al said a little absentmindedly.

Will worried that he wasn't entirely committed to the trip, but then he had problems of his own.

"Have they suspended you?" Will asked.

Al nodded. He'd become a paramedic after a career as a civil engineer and had done so with passion. It was more than just a job, and he'd let it absorb his life to the point where there was very little left for him. Or perhaps that's why he'd chosen it. He didn't know.

"Let's have another," Al said, and got up and went to the bar.

Chapter Twenty-Two

When Beth had admired herself in the full length mirror she'd worried that her chosen clothing might be just a little too much. Lawrence had designed it, and fitted it especially for her, and she wasn't sure about it, as Lawrence clearly preferred men, and probably had no idea what a real man, like a Scotsman, might find attractive.

"What do you think, Peachy?" she asked Peachy.

Peachy had no views on haut couture, although she was quite specific about fresh meat versus dried biscuits. She didn't care how nutritious they were, or how glossy they might make her coat.

"Too much, do you think?"

There was no question that what was on show was more than just décolletage. Even the word cleavage didn't quite cover it.

"And you, Blossom?" Beth asked.

Blossom also had views on fresh meat, although she liked it to be lightly fried. The rest of the time she spent sleeping and none of it extended to views on the ridiculous concoction that Lawrence had thrown together for an outrageous fee.

"It is quite daring," Beth said.

It was also, Polly thought, a vast amount of exposed flesh and, were she familiar with sheep-based metaphors, it might have prompted a less than flattering comparison. But Polly preferred Winalot, which the others frowned on.

"You like it, don't you, Polly?"

Beth prodded herself in an attempt to reorganise and minimise the substantial sea of flesh that Lawrence had seen fit to expose. But it was held too tightly in place, and whatever she did it reverted to a kind of default setting. It sort of wobbled back to where it had been.

"Do you think I should go for the elegant?" she asked her dogs.

But Peachy and Blossom had left the room. She looked at Polly and then she looked at the mirror. She did, as Lawrence had pointed out, have very fine breasts. They were her assets and she had to 'work them, darling'. Men were very basic creatures. She patted her stomach and then regretted it. Her stomach couldn't take much patting. It was being held in as if a sumo wrestler was sitting on her.

"What do you think?" she asked Polly again.

The dress, although it was more of a bustier, did do a very good job of disguising her stomach. She'd given up on her personal trainer, and juicing gave her appalling diarrhoea, and she did like her gin and tonics. Keeping that stomach flat was akin to seeking a resolution to the crisis in the Middle East. She'd tried, god knows she'd tried, but she couldn't stop it looking like a freshly plumped up pillow. There was no question that the mechanics of the dress held her in, and the vast exposure of upper body flesh did a good job of drawing the eye away, like sleight of hand. She just hoped her stomach could take it.

"Damn it," Beth said.

Life could be so difficult. She didn't ask for much. Beth had decided she wasn't going to eat anything that day and now her stomach, the thing she was trying to hide, was drawing attention to itself with gurgling noises.

"Are you ready B, darling?" a voice the other side of the door said.

It was Davy, although most people called him Daphne, and she was fairly certain there was something going on between him and Lawrence. Davy was organising the drinks and the waiters. It was an all male team of quite the buffest creatures she'd ever seen.

"Nearly," Beth shouted.

This meant that people had started arriving. She had to make a decision. She could get out her default dress. It was long and elegant and hid the fact she wasn't much more than five feet tall, but everyone, simply everyone, had seen it before. They expected something new from her. What did Lawrence say? Wasn't it der rigger or something? She breathed in, but it was like her stomach was permanently in. There was no breathing out. She finished the last drops of her gin and tonic. A girl, she thought, needed some calories, and gin and tonic supplied them in the most pleasant way she knew. It was now or never. She left the room and descended the curved staircase which had been Jean-Pierre's, a previous architect who'd remodelled the house, signature feature. She was surprised to see the large double height, soon to be triple height, entrance hall was full of people. Time had run away with her.

She walked slowly, partly for the dramatic effect, a little bit because her shoes were high and required some negotiating, but mostly because she wasn't certain her breasts wouldn't fall out regardless of the careful structure that Lawrence had put in place. There was another issue. The issue which concerned her most. It was her stomach. The dress kind of clamped it in place, and she feared she wouldn't have room for a gin and tonic or two, let alone a cocktail. Or three. She stood as tall as her diminutive height, her heels, her clamped stomach and her overhanging and weighty breasts would allow. She might have thought that it was outrageous that a woman should have to subject herself to this kind of medieval torture to hook a man, but Beth didn't think that way. She looked around the room.

The previous evening when she lay in her bed with her dogs she'd rewatched a couple of episodes of *Outlander* to reacquaint herself with the accent. Mostly she had no idea what they were saying, but she loved the way they said it. And then she saw him. He was wearing a velvet dinner jacket over a tartan kilt. It gave her a frisson of excitement. Mac the Scotsman had arrived. Her Scotsman.

Chapter Twenty-Three

The Right Honourable Sir Harry Panter was playing with himself in the bath. It irritated him that he had to, that things had come to this, but he was pretty well known and the world was full of camera phones and social media. He admired his cock. It leant very definitely to the left and his wife had been very clear on the matter. She'd said she 'didn't give a fuck where he put it as long as it didn't mess up his career'. And that was why he was playing with himself. He didn't want his left leaning cock getting in the way of his right leaning politics.

In the old days he always had one on the go – usually, as his mother might have referred to them, from the lower orders. If Harry knobbed a Deb, she was more likely to be a Debbie from Romford than a debutante from the Home Counties. He liked them a little rough and tacky, and plump and bosomy, and playful and mischievous, unlike the debutantes, who were invariably stick thin and stuck up. At least that had been his experience, as he'd married one. Harry was missing that old life, although he was quite enjoying the new one in which his influence had grown, and he'd become something of a power broker. He'd always been fascinated by the dynamics of how it could be achieved. Two men of equal background, education and intellect could hold very different positions in the party. It was a balance between ingratiation and intimidation, and he'd got very good at it. But the latter, the intimidation, brought with it some risks. He was a big man from a monied family who'd made money of his own but, if he stood up and made a speech about the importance of family, and he got caught with his left leaning cock in Debbie's cooky jar, then the media circus would kill him. He didn't want that.

The Right Honourable Harry Panter continued to masturbate. It was more out of necessity than desire, as he'd reached an age when he was never certain he could do it twice in one day. This was an insurance against temptation. Knocking the need out in the morning was the best way, he'd decided. But it was becoming a shade too clinical and he needed a little more stimulation, which meant he'd have to get out of the bath, as he'd discovered that iPads don't recover from a dunking. He'd lost two that way. He stopped masturbating.

The political world was more fragile than ever. It was like spinning plates. But if he could keep some up and knock others down he could pick his way to the top job. Harry's wife had decided that that was where he should be and, if he played his cards right, it was entirely possible. She liked the idea of mixing with world leaders and their wives. Name dropping didn't get any better and, if he could get his finger out of his arse, or off his cock – his wife could be quite blunt – it could be in time for whoever succeeds Trump. She had no intention of meeting that ghastly man. And Harry wanted it too. He'd given favours and steered people around him and established a hierarchy which placed him at the top. It wasn't rock solid, but he was the bookies' favourite. His cock wasn't rock solid either, and he resumed the masturbation with renewed vigour, as he pictured himself, and his elegant wife, at the top table of life. A master of the universe.

"Damn," Harry muttered.

His phone was ringing. He'd placed it by the side of the bath in case the PM required his urgent advice, or needed him to converse with high level diplomats or, even better, world leaders. He looked at it. It was even more elevated than the PM. It was his wife. He stopped masturbating and answered it.

"What are you doing?" she asked urgently.

"I'm masturbating," Harry said with a languid tone.

He knew the languid tone irritated her and there were times when he'd rather she was attending to him rather than playing tennis or doing whatever it was she did.

"Well stop it and have a look at the Slime-Online and call me back," she said and hung up.

"Damn," Harry muttered again.

It was most awkward as he'd nearly finished but she, as was often her way, had taken him off the boil. On the other hand there was an urgency to her voice that suggested something serious might have happened. Perhaps there had been another Twin Towers? If so, why hadn't the PM called him? But then his wife would have suggested the BBC news website and not the Slime-Online. This was a scandal of some sort and, as he was now too clean living for such things, it might be something from which he could profit. He gave his penis a few more tugs, but it had lost interest, and he got out of the bath. He wrapped himself in a bathrobe, picked up his iPad, and sat in the elegant sitting room.

The Slime-Online had become their shorthand for the most salacious of the newspapers and the nickname had spread after he'd mentioned it in a speech. He loathed and despised everything about it and consequently accessed it every day hopeful that someone from the opposite benches had done something which could induce schadenfreude pleasure in him. But it wasn't a politician, and he didn't have to scroll down to find it. It was the lead story and his name was slapped all over it.

"Oh shit," Harry said.

It was about Julie and a university lecturer and, as the paper had shrieked, their perverted sex.

Chapter Twenty-Four

"What the fuck were you doing?" Will asked.

Rick had woken up to a harsh brightness and, if he had a religious bone in his body, he might have thought he'd arrived in heaven. It made him pause to think about whether he'd be allowed entry there, or whether he'd be destined for a darker, warmer place. He'd worked in the business of money, in a hated institution, yet he'd only ever shown charity in his life. Then he thought what kind of shitty god would put him in hell, and was reminded why he wasn't religious.

"Hang gliding," Rick said simply.

"Hang gliding?" Will spluttered.

"Well, it wasn't the hang gliding, more the crashing," Rick said.

"What have you broken?" Will asked.

The doctor arrived at this point, although Will's primary concern was Rick's fitness to ski, and the possibility it might mess up the trip. It was Wednesday. There was less than three days left and Rick looked a little crumpled.

"He's fine," the doctor said, "just some mild concussion."

"Very mild," Rick said, looking at his watch and making a drink sign to Will.

Thirty minutes later they were in the pub.

"Have you heard from Judah?" Rick asked.

"Not yet," Will said.

"But you've seen the piece in the Slime-Online," Rick said.

"No," Will said slowly.

Rick chuckled.

"It turns out that the student," Rick said just as slowly.

"Which student?" Will asked.

He knew the answer to the question before he'd asked it, but he thought he'd ask it anyway.

"The one Rick couldn't get it up with," Rick explained.

"I think you'll find, in Judah's defence, or the defence of his masculinity, he did get it up. It just distracted him," Will said.

"Well, her name is Julie Panter," Rick said.

It took a while for Will to connect the dots.

"She's not related to Harry Panter, is she?" Will asked.

He knew the answer to this question too, but he was hoping it wasn't true.

"She is his daughter," Rick said, "and the shit is hitting the fan."

"I'm going to get a call soon, then," Will said.

Will checked the time. He really needed to get back to work.

"Panter's lawyers are making a noise," Rick said.

"Oh shit," Will said.

"There is some outrage and talk of a moral decay at the heart of our education institutions," Rick said.

"They've met Judah," Will muttered.

Will decided to change the subject and bring it back to the skiing trip. He had his iPad with him and took it out.

"This is Jim's place," Will said.

They scrolled through the pictures showing a large sitting room overlooking the main concourse in Val Thorens.

"Very nice," Rick said, "is it ski-in, ski-out?"

"It is, with a heated boot locker, and a jacuzzi, and steam room," Will said.

"And I imagine it's close to shops, restaurants and, more crucially, bars," Rick said.

"So I'm told. We're on the seven o'clock crossing, although I bought a flexible ticket in case we have any problems."

"Like Judah?" Rick asked.

"Or you killing yourself, or Al getting arrested for assault, or in case Mac's plane from LA is delayed."

"There's a lot to go wrong," Rick said.

It called for another beer. Will looked at his watch. He was getting close to the time when there was little point in returning to work, although going back with too many beers in him might be counterproductive.

"Cheers," Rick said raising a beer.

Will looked at the beer in front of him and found it surprisingly alluring.

"Fuck it," Will muttered and picked up the beer.

Will had another question.

"How come the hospital called me?" Will asked.

"That's because," Rick said, toying with his drink, "You, my old son, are my next of kin."

"Well, as your next of kin, can I suggest you stop trying to kill yourself?" Will asked.

Rick stopped toying with his beer glass and downed the rest of it.

"Another?" Rick asked.

"I've got to get back to work," Will said and got up. Duty was calling, but not very loudly.

Chapter Twenty-Five

Mac sat on a small balcony drawing furiously on a cigarette. He calculated that the opportunities to smoke were going to be severely limited, and it made sense to cram as much nicotine into his body as he was able. He lay back and looked at the Californian landscape. There was a fair bit of evening sun, but Mac's complexion didn't favour sun, so he was sitting in the shade. He was finishing the last of the little scotches he'd found in the room and was looking forward to the vast quantity of free booze which would be on offer at Beth's drinks party. His flight was late that evening and he had no intention of falling into his business class seat anything less than completely pissed. Then he had a few hours to get home, after which he intended to collapse into the back of Will's car for the ski trip. He finished his scotch, although it wasn't really what he'd call a scotch, as he favoured an aged single malt, but it contained alcohol and that was enough. Mac packed his small bag, adjusted his sporran, and went downstairs to find his car was already waiting for him.

The car cut through the urban sprawl and then up into the hills towards Beth's villa which, from the outside, appeared to be suffering an identity crisis. Too many cooks, or in this case architects, had been involved. But he was happy to be one more. He hoped to sharpen it up ready for Mario or Paquito or whoever would be tasked with remodelling it again in five years time. The car took him to the front door which had once sat on the east face of the building, and before that the west, and before that the north. Mac favoured the south face of the building. He got out of the car and took the glass of champagne that was offered to him.

"Thank you," Mac said.

He was in an unusually good mood. All his stars had aligned and he had money in the bank. He had Beth to thank for that and he knew he had to be on his best form. This was a golden goose and a gravy train he didn't want to hop off. He looked round the room. There were a lot of plastic faces and he searched for Beth. He couldn't immediately see her until someone looked up, stretching taut skin unused to such movement and as if they were about to declare, 'Is it a bird? Is it a plane?' When Mac's eyes finally landed on Beth he wasn't sure what it was. She looked like a mammary gland.

"Bring it on," Mac declared.

Not that he wished to bring it on, but he knew that special attention could only help the perilous state of his bank account. Beth walked slowly down the staircase, and for a moment Mac's eyes were distracted by the staircase, which was probably the nicest thing about the house. It had a beautiful curve to it. His attention switched back to Beth's even more considerable curves as she slowly descended one step at a time with just a small wobble on each impact. There was no question that Mac's gaze had moved to that wobble, like the ripples on a pond, and almost as big. Then his eyes met hers.

"Beth," Mac roared.

It was probably the first word he'd uttered that she'd understood and with it his face broke into a huge smile, which was made possible by the loose skin which hung round his face, and was often disguised by a slightly disorganised beard. As they approached each other it was clear that he should have given the nature of his greeting more thought, but as she was moving a little faster now that she'd reached the end of the staircase, he didn't have time to consider. When she collided with him it was as if he'd hit the dashboard of a fast moving car in which both airbags had been deployed.

"Mac," she said with real joy, planting poorly aimed kisses on his face.

Mac's normally exuberant spirit was a little dampened, as he was beginning to get the impression that he might be out of his depth. He was used to his flirting being met with some resistance, as he did not have a history of women hurling themselves at him. Although, if he hurled himself at Beth he was certain of a comfortable landing.

"I love the kilt," Beth said admiring more than just the kilt.

By a strange genetic collision Mac was gifted with quite the largest calves found on a human being. Athletes and body builders had nothing on the monumental muscles sandwiched between his knees and ankles. His skiing boots had to be specially made and it had been necessary to remeasure his calves three times, as the manufacturers were certain a mistake had been made.

"Oh my," Beth said.

Beth had never thought of calves as something to admire in a man, but she couldn't help noticing that these hairy muscles could prop up a small building. She made a note to herself to check out a few more

'Outlanders' with reference to seventeenth century calves.

"Beth, love," it was Davy.

"Yes, Daphne," Beth said.

"I need you to look at something," Davy said.

Davy looked between Mac and Beth. There was chemistry flying about like shrapnel and if he wasn't careful he might get caught by flying debris.

"Okay," Beth said slowly, and moved away.

Mac grabbed a passing drink and downed it one. His hands were shaking a little. What, he thought, was that about. He needed to make a concerted effort to downgrade his charm, which was bizarre as no one had ever accused him of having any. But then he was wearing a kilt. What did he expect? This thinking was an indication of the subtle inebriation of several whiskies and two glasses of champagne. He grabbed another and then went to the bar, which Davy had helpfully created for those who wished to drink something other than champagne.

"What's your name?" he asked the occasional model.

"Arthur," the barman said.

His name wasn't Arthur but, as his parents had named him Merlin, he was experimenting with different names.

"Can I have a whisky, Arthur?" Mac asked.

He'd noticed that few Americans tended to say please, but this was more of a medicinal requirement. He needed fortification and nothing fortified a Scotsman more than a whisky.

"Which would you like?" Arthur asked.

"What?" Mac said, still a little distracted by recent events.

Arthur, who mostly worked with his shirt off, stood back and ran his hands along the bottles behind him.

"Nice," Mac said and chose a Muckle Flugga to begin with.

He had to admire Beth. She was a stand out client. He could see her in the distance. She was unquestionably stand out. Mac had always rather liked large breasted women, but Beth was something else. She looked a little fetishistic.

"Thanks Arthur," Mac said, as a very generous measure filled his glass.

He decided he'd done his bit, and he needed to keep an eye out for Beth, and move around the room keeping a reasonable distance from her. He'd swoop in just before he had to leave for his flight which should, he hoped, provide the right kind of equilibrium. Mac moved around the room, but couldn't resist the magnetic powers of the free bar, and returned there every now and then or, more accurately, every fifteen minutes. After a couple of hours of avoiding Beth he decided, although his judgement may have been impaired, to make eye contact across the room. That seemed safe. It helped that Mac's vision was a little blurry, but it seemed to keep her content, as she worked the room. An hour later he found himself back at the bar. He didn't have long before the driver turned up to take him to the airport. But there was always enough time for another.

"A Muckle Flugga, my old mate," he asked Arthur warmly.

Arthur picked up the empty bottle.

"Oh," Mac said, "what an excellent opportunity to try Aultmore."

"I thought I'd find you here," Beth said pressing herself against him.

Mac was barely aware of it and gave her his fullest smile, put his arm round her, and gave her a gentle squeeze. When he did so her breasts jumped up like little dogs waiting to be taken for a walk.

"I need to show you something upstairs," Beth said.

Chapter Twenty-Six

"What the fuck are we going to do?" Harry Panter asked.

Rumball looked down. He was the chief whip, and the party's strategist, and the colleague Harry most feared. Harry couldn't figure out whether he was a man who wanted to be in the shadows, or whether he was just hiding there and waiting to jump out at the last minute. He *did* know he needed Barry Rumball on his side.

"I know what I'd do," Rumball said.

He was a big man who carried his weight daintily. But there was nothing dainty about his voice which rumbled like distant thunder. His father had worked in the mines in Grimethorpe and if he'd been on the political left he would have brandished those credentials like a weapon. But most of the time he hid them, unless he was annoyed. Then he couldn't stop himself, as if he was baring his teeth.

"What would that be?" Harry asked very reasonably.

Harry was there for advice, so it was a little irritating that he should have to extract it from the man. Rumball grunted in response. It was the start of the distant thunder and he used those grunts like punctuation. When his underlings heard a grunt they braced themselves, mentally clearing their desks.

"I would," Rumball said slowly.

He had two daughters who he adored. It filled him with anger whenever they were violated or, as they thought of it, introduced a boyfriend. He had to suppress an urge to rip the nervous young men apart. The girls were still single.

"Flay the fucker alive," Rumball finally managed to say.

Harry was a little bit taken back by this. He knew his daughter's shenanigans were something of an embarrassment, but flaying her alive seemed a little extreme. A beat later Harry realised Rumball was referring to the university lecturer. The working class, he thought wryly, were so prudish when it came to sex. It didn't even occur to him to judge his daughter's indiscretion, and he was sure she was completely complicit.

"I dare say," Harry said, "but how do I get this to go away?"

Rumball frowned and then he grunted again. He was equally confused by the machinations of the upper classes. They seemed to revel in the cruelty they inflict on their children. The whole absurd public school boarding ethos operated that way and was why, in Rumball's view, most of the country was as fucked up as it was.

"Optugg," Rumball grunted.

It took a moment for Harry to recognise that there was a word bound up in that grunt and, once he'd discerned it was the word 'options', he waited to hear what they might be.

"Do nothing," Rumball said.

Harry thought about this. It was tempting, as this sort of thing was a tightrope, and it was easy to make things worse. He hoped it might just go away.

"And the story will escalate," Rumball said filling in the blanks.

"Oh," Harry said.

"And you're fucked," Rumball concluded.

That didn't sound good to Harry and he waited for further advice.

"Issue a soft liberal sounding statement," Rumball said.

That was more like it, Harry thought, he hated all this below stairs talk and this was how he felt.

"And it sounds like you don't love your daughter," Rumball said.

"Does it?" Harry asked.

"And you're fucked," Rumball added.

"Oh dear, do you think so?" Harry said.

"Issue a hard hitting, no shit taking statement," Rumball said.

"Excellent idea," Harry said hopefully.

"And it sounds like you're trying to hide from it," Rumball said.

"Does it?" Harry said weakly.

"And you're fucked," Rumball said.

"Oh dear," Harry said.

The situation was making him feel a little feeble. Harry could feel more rumbling, as if a tube train was approaching. He was about to ask what he should do when he sensed that Rumball was about to tell him.

"You use every resource the law and the police have to nail the fucker to the wall," Rumball said.

This time Harry was certain he was referring to the university lecturer, and not his daughter although, if it would further his career, he would give it some thought.

"Judah Wheeler," Rumball spat.

If one of his daughters had been whipped to within an inch of her life by a university lecturer he would grab the old gun his grandfather had bought back from the Great War, and he would blow the man's genitals off. He would splatter them across the family hearth, decorate the woodchip, purée the little sperm and testosterone factories.

"Yes," Harry confirmed, but Rumball had drifted into a trance in which he considered every form of appropriate retribution.

Harry took this as the conclusion of the meeting and it was giving him the distinct feeling that the power was shifting away from him. It felt as if he'd been dismissed.

"I'll get on to my lawyers," Harry said and got up.

Chapter Twenty-Seven

Rick had arrived at the corner quicker than he'd expected. It was like the ground when he'd bungee jumped and the unscheduled landing of the hang glider. It wasn't there and then suddenly it was. Rick had promised Will that he wouldn't indulge in any high risk sports after the hang gliding incident, and he hadn't intended to. For years he'd been a Mercedes man, tripping from one to another every few years, and keen on the comfort and reliability. He'd never actually been tempted to change gear himself in about thirty years and it would have stayed that way, but after he'd had that beer with Will he'd pottered home, and it had taken him past a car showroom. He saw a low slung thing shining jewel-like, and he returned to take another look. He wasn't particularly interested in cars, but there was something about the way light reflected off the undulated surfaces that caught his eye. It was more the shape of it, than the promise that it could do two hundred miles an hour.

Actually he believed it could do two hundred and ten miles an hour which seemed a little crazy. Three times the legal limit. He wasn't travelling at that speed at the moment, but then the scenery was flashing by at a velocity which didn't provide enough time to look down at the speedometer and check. Not that he really understood the graphics which flashed and popped, or the flappy paddle gear change, which seemed to be an equal mystery. It didn't seem to matter as the thing leaped like a squirrel on speed. He was hanging on for dear life.

Not that Rick felt his life was that dear. He'd been detached from it for a while, although he was stamping on the brakes now, but that wasn't a metaphor for his life. The corner was approaching him as if it had movement of its own. The engine made a whole cacophony of noises from, he understood, its twelve cylinders and now it still seemed to be making noises even though he was decelerating and not asking very much from it. It was the Italian spirit, he assumed. He'd been a salesman's dream. He'd walked into the showroom, looked at the light glinting as if some of it emanated from within, and he hadn't noticed the price tag. His sudden desire to own it had got the better of him.

He was on his way back from hang gliding. He didn't tell Will, but thought it would be a good idea to learn to land. There was no metaphor here either, but he'd enjoyed the quiet and serene freedom of his time in the sky. The instructor had taken some persuading, not least because Rick had a black eye from the sparring class that morning, but he'd kept a close eye on him and concentrated on landing, which Rick had now mastered. It had been quite pleasant and distracting. He liked to be distracted. Those moments when he really had to concentrate on something else successfully took his mind away from the thing he didn't want to think about. The car had arrived at the corner. Although he was driving the car he was beginning to feel like a passenger. A passenger who'd fallen asleep.

Despite the car's Italian heritage it was loaded with electronics which were designed by sweaty, pore-blocked geeks who still had posters of exotic cars on their bedroom walls. If these people were the last remaining males on the planet, then the human race would die out. The car might have been Italian, but the geeks were British, which was why those electronics were now thinking 'what the fuck'. The steering input and the speed suggested that death was a whisper away, a snort of the cocaine that the programmer now found himself able to afford. The tyres were wide enough to make shoes for an entire African village, and they had been engineered with something more challenging in mind than a Hertfordshire country road. But they too were panicking.

It didn't help that there had been a dispute between the council and the subcontractor who was tasked with repairing the roads, and keener on taking the money than carrying out the work. The backhanders had dried up and the Masonic lodge had closed, and this particular sharp right hand bend hadn't seen much attention since Margaret Thatcher was in power. There were quite a few patches scattered on the road and this was confusing the electronics, which were recalculating every millisecond, and still concluding that someone was in very deep shit.

The steering wheel was moving about in Rick's hands as if he were holding a live rat and he supposed that this wasn't a good thing. But he held on as he also assumed it was better than letting go. But that *was* a metaphor for his life at the moment. He was choosing to hold on because it was expected of him and he'd always been good at coping. There was a time, many years ago, when he'd found himself holding a position which indebted the bank nearly half a billion when the prevailing wind was in the opposite direction. He'd held firm, he'd not panicked and, when the loses came, they were slight enough for the bank to merely raise an eye. He had 'bollocks of steel' someone had said.

Rick hadn't studied physics and wasn't aware what constituted a 'G' force, but he and the car were experiencing a few now. There was a slight skip and a mild squeal and then he was out of the corner and travelling on the road in the right direction. If he'd been overseen by the geeks and the engineers like an Apollo landing, they would be celebrating with champagne and patting each other on the back, while at the same time saying they knew it would be fine all along. What wasn't fine was the quartet of policemen armed with radar and a determination to take him down who were waiting the other side of the corner.

"Shit," Rick muttered.

Chapter Twenty-Eight

"I need to show you something upstairs," Beth said.

Mac was at her beck and call for any of her architecture related questions but, despite that, he was a little surprised to make it to the bedroom, although it wasn't without potential for some remodelling.

"How do you think this could be changed?" Beth asked.

She'd emphasised the word 'changed' by thrusting her chest out, but Mac hadn't noticed. His plans hadn't included much alteration on the bedroom front because, he seemed to remember, she said she was happy with it.

"Well," Mac said.

It was than that Mac turned and looked at Beth. He was not a man sensitive to subtlety of tone, and he'd consumed enough whisky to anaesthetise a bull, but even Mac could sense there was something in the air. Although it wasn't in the air, it was spread out in front of him. He was being asked how to change her bust.

"Er, it's perfect, just as it is," Mac stammered.

Mac looked at her chest, as if he were studying an architectural detail such as a mantelpiece, although this mantelpiece looked a little out of proportion to the rest of the room. Someone had planted a Louis XV in a council house. But it wasn't without merit.

"Generous, of course," Mac continued.

Mac looked into her eyes. Bloody hell, he thought, this was more than just a mantelpiece. It was a fire blazing. There were several issues. Principle among them was that Beth was his temporary route to solvency and he didn't want to mess that up.

"And so womanly," Mac observed.

And a rejection might be messing it up, he thought. She might not take well to it and then the gravy train, which had only run a brief service, would come to a halt. By this logic he would be a fool not to see to her every need.

"Really nice," Mac said still stuttering, and turning to face the windows.

He needed to change the subject. There was a further issue. If eternal happiness and prosperity depended on it, if a life of uninterrupted joy was guaranteed, if it would ensure world peace, if it would make the green and pleasant land that is Scotland a continual Provençal summer, if a cure could be found for every major malady, if all of that could happen, Mac could still not get an erection. Too many whiskies had made it down his throat. A failure to erect might also be interpreted as reject.

"And perhaps we can move this wall and alter those windows to get the morning sun," Mac jabbered.

Beth had moved closer to him. So close he could feel a part of her brush lightly on his arm. There was no question which part. It was prompting panic in him. But not the kind, he feared, that would induce sobriety. He'd left too many empty glasses at the bar for that.

"And maybe introduce another small balcony here," Mac said moving away.

He daren't turn and make eye contact. But they were moving around the room. He was being chased. It was fox and chickens and there was no question which one he was. He needed to think.

"A roof light," he said, inspired.

He'd forgotten there was another floor above, and Beth hadn't noticed as she had other things on her mind, and was moving in for the kill, or it might have been kilt. She knew she was getting on and not in the finest shape. She knew that her best days were behind her and that there were flaws. But that was why they were so perfect together. Mac was riddled with flaws, almost entirely composed of them. She looked down at his legs.

"Just here," Mac said moving away and a little desperately.

Beth moved with him. Mac was waving his arms around maniacally in an attempt to illustrate the potential remodelling and Beth caught sight of those hands, which could do with a bit of manicuring, but she overlooked that. They were the hands of a creative person. Mac hadn't noticed that he'd arrived at the bed. Beth joined him and then sat down.

"Oh," Mac said.

He looked down. He had no idea why she'd sat down and all he could see was a sea of mammary. Then she grabbed his calf.

"So much muscle," Beth said.

She had quite a firm grip and it felt as if he'd stepped in a bear trap. She began to caress his calf without releasing her grip. It was a talent she had no idea she possessed.

"Is it true what they say?" Beth asked.

Mac had a suspicion he knew where she was going. But he couldn't be certain.

"I don't know," he said with faux confidence, "What do they say?"

He tried to move away. But as he moved her hands moved higher. He stopped and her hands stopped. It was an armistice. It was then that he saw the clock that sat on the bedside table.

"Jesus, is that the time?" Mac said.

He was going to miss his flight if he didn't get a move on. It was late Friday night and he needed to get that flight. He tried tugging, but her hands went higher. They were only a handspan away from discovering the truth about what a Scotsman didn't wear under his kilt.

"I've got a flight to catch," Mac squeaked.

There was a further issue. Anita would kill him. But worse than that, the guilt would kill him. Mac didn't want to have sex with anyone else. That thought brought him back to his current predicament and a second later Beth had her hands around that predicament. Mac jumped up like a baby deer. It was enough to release him from her grip. Beth got up.

"You're playing hard to get," she observed.

Mac opened his mouth, but nothing coherent exited it, although that was how it always sounded to her. And he hadn't noticed that Beth had manoeuvred herself between him and the door. He had to reason with her.

"I'm going to miss my flight," he said.

Beth smiled. That was fine with her. She felt loose and free. She probably shouldn't have had that fourth cocktail. She moved with her back to the door and dropped her hand to the lock. She turned the key. It made a click.

"Oh, I say," Mac said, losing his Scottish accent.

Beth continued to smile. She took the key out of the lock and waved it in front of him.

"You can leave once you get the key," she said.

Mac watched her drop the key into her cleavage. She wobbled and her cleavage swallowed it like a snake consuming a rabbit.

Chapter Twenty-Nine

Harry Panter decided to have lunch at the club. The world was going a little crazy and there was nothing more comforting than the leather wingback chairs and chesterfields of the ancient organisation of which he'd been a lifelong member. There could be a nuclear war outside, the sky could be filled with fighter planes and bombers, and the streets lined with tanks, and yet it would be near silence in the club. The only noise would be the clink of cut glass and ice refreshed by a suitably alcoholic liquid.

"I don't mind if I do," Harry said.

A large scotch was placed in his hand. The press were everywhere. At his flat, at his office, at the House and, according to his wife, at the fucking country house. Apparently it was upsetting her tennis. It was upsetting the PM. Harry's supporters, the ones that could take him to the top job, were hiding in corridors. He was going to need a scotch or two to get through this.

"Harvey, old boy," Harry said.

Harvey was an old school friend on whom he could rely on to talk of nothing of significance for the duration of the meal, which would calm him for the storm ahead. Harvey had made a career of falling from grace. He'd been expelled from school when the headmaster's daughter found herself pregnant. He'd lost his safe seat when it was discovered that he was something of a lead player in a rather substantial orgy. He was caught taking backhanders during his time at the Home Office, and his subsequent role in the planning committee had been no different. His career even included a short stay at Ford

Open over a dispute as to whether he should, or should not, pay tax. Harry could rely on Harvey to make him feel good about his life.

"It's a bit rum, this," Harvey said.

Harvey rarely referred to matters directly, although the general consensus was that he'd found discretion rather late in life.

"Indeed it is," Harry said. "What do you think I should do?"

Harry took the view that he should do the opposite of whatever Harvey recommended as Harvey's history of bad judgements was a very consistent one.

"Release a statement saying how much you love your daughter and how people should be free to express themselves as they wish. Bang on about freedom for a while to take their minds of flagellation," Harvey said.

Harvey nodded for another scotch. Unfortunately Harvey's advice made perfect sense. This was what he had wanted to do, but Rumball had been quite clear. For a second Harry wondered if he should talk to his daughter, but the starter had arrived, and that needed to be attended to first.

"A new chef," Harvey said.

The new chef had been trained by the old chef, who'd been trained by the chef before him and so on since the club's inception in 1676. Harry looked at the rather substantial helping of belly pork wrapped, as it was, in a good deal of fat. Neither the chefs, or the club members who dined regularly, enjoyed a long lifespan. He tried some.

"Very nice," Harry said.

The subject of Julie's unfortunate escapade with the lecturer wasn't mentioned again and when lunch was concluded, with a further portion of something also swimming in fat, he made his way to the lawyers. The offices of Ringham, Rougham and Shankly lay discreetly above a gentleman's outfitters in Mayfair, and a very small brass plaque announced their name on an anonymous Georgian door. He pressed the bell and realised he hadn't drunk a scotch or two. He'd drunk five or six and a bottle of wine with the meal, not that plebeian concepts such as intoxication concerned him. He was let in and led up to a small meeting room which was a masterpiece of discretion. Harry sat down and thought about Harvey's advice.

"Good afternoon," a man who'd introduced himself as Shankly said.

They sat down and, after the briefest of pleasantries, Shankly got to the point.

"How do you want to proceed?" he asked.

Normally Shankly would talk pleasantries for at least fifteen minutes. It wasn't to put his clients at ease, but because he charged four hundred quid an hour, and it was an easy hundred quid. But he'd been primed by Rumball and no one in their right mind takes the piss out of Rumball.

"Hang him by the balls," Harry said.

This seemed like a much safer bet than taking Harvey's advice, and Rumball had convinced him that this Judah character was responsible for the fall of civilisation and should be hung, drawn, quartered and urinated on from some height.

"Precisely my thoughts," Shankly said.

When it came to generally dumping on people, a kind of legal excretion, they were the go-to company, and Harry knew it. He was about to resume his natural urbane charm when he reminded himself he had to access his inner Rumball.

"And get the police doing their bloody jobs," Harry added.

But Shankly was ahead of him. He'd done some research.

"About which," Shankly said slowly, "I took the liberty of making some enquiries. We have a very reliable contact there."

Shankly paused. A 'reliable contact' was Shankly speak for 'on the payroll' and was part of the service they offered. It was clearly lost on Harry, so he continued.

"It appears there is a recording," Shankly said.

"A recording? A recording of what?" Harry demanded.

It coincided with a vibration in his pocket. He ignored it, but whoever was calling him was quite insistent. Shankly appeared to be having difficulty finding his words. Harry looked at his phone. It was his wife. He doubted she was calling about her progress with her backhand.

"Have you seen the Slime-Online?" his wife shouted.

Harry was certain his wife had never enquired after his health. Her calls tended to involve the imperative.

"No," Harry said slowly.

A moment later Harry and Shankly listened to Julie demanding further whipping and the possibility that Harry would become the laughing stock of the House.

"Don't worry," Shankly said dryly as if they'd been listening to cricket scores, "we'll bury the bastard."

Chapter Thirty

"I'm a conveyancing lawyer, not a litigator," Will complained.

It was Friday and Will's day had been interrupted yet again. Rick shrugged. He could have hired a specialist, but he'd asked around and the collective advice was that his licence was doomed. They were waiting in a draughty corridor, in a building patinated with brown stains, and surrounded by people having urgent whispered conversations with their lawyers.

"Why don't you get someone who knows what he's doing? Will asked.

"I don't want to have lunch with them afterwards," Rick said.

The car's collective electronics had reduced his speed, but he was still travelling fast enough to ensure an immediate court appearance was obligatory.

"And what made you buy a bloody Ferrari?" Will asked.

Rick had forgotten the thought process that had resulted in a shiny red car, or whether there had been one, and just grinned.

"Because you could?" Will said.

"Maybe," Rick said.

"Ninety-six miles an hour," Will said.

"At least it was under a hundred," Rick pointed out.

"But you were in a forty. They might send you to prison," Will said.

The general consensus of the advice Rick had taken was that this wouldn't involve a custodial sentence, although he wondered what prison would be like, and whether it would be all that bad. It would certainly be distracting. Rick shrugged. The shrug concerned Will. It wasn't a good sign. There was a reason why the prosecution had been expedited, and that also wasn't a good sign. A bored voice with a nasal Estuarial accent called Rick's name.

"We're on," Will said.

They moved into an airless court in which there had been an ongoing battle to install air conditioning. It was a battle which the presiding judge had won, but it had gone wrong, and he was losing the fight to have it repaired.

"Rick Ford," the judge called.

Rick and Will stood up.

"Ninety-six miles an hour," the judge said, reading the sheet in front of him.

"In a Ferrari," the judge added and most condemningly, "In a forty."

"What do you plead?" the judge asked.

"Guilty," Rick said, a little too cheerfully for Will.

"You understand I'm at liberty to hand down a custodial sentence?" the judge said.

"I do," Rick said equally cheerfully.

Will did not like the sound of this. A sentence, however short, would jeopardise the ski trip. Will was becoming a little obsessed about his determination to get everyone on the trip, but it was getting like spinning plates. He had to intervene before this went wrong.

"My lord," Will said, standing up.

"I'm a recorder. A straight 'sir' is sufficient," the judge said.

Will hadn't been in court for years and he knew this wasn't a good start, but someone needed to protect Rick from himself.

"There were extenuating circumstances," Will said.

"How can there be extenuating circumstances when your client – I assume he is your client?" the judge asked.

"Yes, he is," Will said nervously.

"When your client is using the public road as a race track?" the judge continued.

Will paused. This was the point when he needed to deliver a speech which would sway the judge in his favour. An emphatic address in which travelling fifty-six miles an hour over the speed limit could be considered perfectly reasonable. Bugger, Will thought.

"He has not been himself recently," Will began.

The judge gave an expression which suggested that he was even less impressed with the notion of someone with mental health issues driving at high speed.

"Since Annie, his wife, died he's been searching for something and I think he now realises that it isn't speed, or a Ferrari. Prior to today he's had an unblemished licence for over thirty years, and has always been a pillar of the community. And, although the speed which was registered was high, it was on the edge of the village in an area which was not built up. He was only a danger to himself."

The judge sighed. He looked through some papers. He sighed a bit more.

"And he will be selling the Ferrari," Will got up and added.

"He might as well," the judge said, "he certainly won't be driving it any time soon."

The judge paused and shuffled a few more papers. He knew what he was going to do. He'd known before they'd walked into the court but the pause, of gameshow dimensions, was part of the punishment. It was as if air was being pumped out of the airless court, and there would have been mounting tension, but Rick wasn't sure he cared.

"A driving ban of twenty-four months," the judge said finally, adding, "and you're lucky not to receive a custodial sentence."

"Thank you, my sir," Will said clumsily.

"There will be a substantial fine," the judge said.

Another name was called and they were out into the corridor and into the clear air of the street.

"What are you going to do?" Will asked.

"Do?" Rick asked. "Lunch," adding, "And, as I have nowhere to drive, at least one bottle of wine. This way."

Will followed as Rick walked confidently in the direction of a restaurant and Rick said over his shoulder, "how did you know it wasn't a built up area?"

Will shrugged. He might have got a little carried away.

Chapter Thirty-One

"Don't be a wee clipe," Mac said.

For a moment his language had morphed into an Englishman at a vicar's tea party but now, as panic began to rise in him, it was reverting to something more guttural. It was returning to his childhood just outside Glasgow.

"Whit's fur ye'll no go past ye," he blathered.

He was losing the plot. This didn't seem fair. Beth was his first decent client in years and he was about to blow it. Beth began to fumble with his kilt, suggesting that she was likely to do the blowing.

"You're a wee scunner," he said.

This wasn't helping. If anything his return to a childhood dialect was stoking her fires and, as far as he could tell, they didn't require any further stoking. He tried to compose himself and address her in an English she might understand. He needed to come up with something, or he'd miss his flight, and the ski trip. But the key to the room had disappeared, as if it had fallen in quick sand. He had to start talking.

"The thing is," Mac explained, "I would absolutely love to..." he paused as he thought of the right word, "ravish you."

Beth smiled. She hadn't caught much of the sentence, or anything that had preceded it, but she'd caught the word 'ravish' and that was much more like it. He needed to get a move on, as she was feeling a bit lightheaded. The structure of the dress was pressing on her stomach and she hadn't really noticed it until she'd filled it with a couple more cocktails. Or it might have been four.

"But, you know, I've drunk a lot of scotch. It was great scotch, really top notch malt and, well, I've had quite a bit of alcohol and with that, I'm pretty certain I couldn't get it up if the Swedish volley ball team tickled my bollocks and waved their fannies in my face." Mac rambled.

It wasn't quite expressed with the clarity that Mac was hoping for, but to Beth's ears it sounded joyous. The stabbing noises of his archaic, in her view, and deeply charming accent. She hadn't understood a word.

"And any other time, I'd be up there," Mac said illustrating his up there-ness with a clenched fist and a cocked arm, "and I'd be banging away like a record breaking steam train like," Mac hunted for an appropriate metaphor to illustrate the lustiness with which he'd ravish her, "what's it called, you know, the Jacobite."

Beth was delighted to hear the word 'Jacobite', which completely suggested that they were on the same wavelength and this long, arid period of her sex life was about to come to a riotous end. Although there was no question that if Mac had been part of the Jacobite rebellion, and he'd been captured by English, he would have blathered away and told them anything they wanted to hear and a bit more. Beth was still smiling, but she was having issues of her own. There was a rebellion going on and it involved her stomach and the confined space Lawrence had decided it could fit into. If she didn't get out of the dress pretty soon the contents of her stomach were going to make a hasty exit and she wasn't sure which route it would chose.

"Take off my clothes," Beth rasped.

"I'm sorry?" Mac said.

Mac wasn't sure if he'd made himself clear. He thought he had, although he could see now that the train reference might have been a bit confusing.

"I'd happily make, er…" he struggled for the right word again, "passionate love. Love with real passion." Mac said.

He looked at her and found she was still smiling, which suggested that she hadn't quite grasped the other issue to do with the physical limitations that he was bound to as a consequence of consuming most of her whisky.

"But," he said, "I find myself temporarily, indisposed. The service is currently suspended. That train and that tunnel…" he paused again.

Her facial expression had changed, and he could see he wasn't making himself clear. He hoped she hadn't found the tunnel reference offensive. He couldn't tell. But he needed to make his point. Mac flopped his hand down to express limpness, but then wondered if she might interpret that as homosexual. If she thought he was gay would she still want to employ him? Was it his overwhelming masculinity she was drawn to? This thought was an insight into the vast quantity of scotch Mac had consumed.

"Damn," Mac said.

This wasn't working. He realised he was going to have to bite the bullet. Anita would understand that he had no other choice. He moved forward and lay his hands on her breasts. Then he thought that he might have made too presumptuous a move and lowered his hands to her waist. He gave her a little squeeze and moved in for the snog.

"Mac," Beth whispered.

Her stomach felt like there was a poltergeist in it and Mac had added further pressure. She'd been silently grappling with it, clenching the muscles in her stomach, attempting to force everything into place, and hold back that rebellion. But she was losing the battle. When Mac lowered his puckered lips to hers she knew which exit route the contents of her stomach would chose to take, and Mac was too busy biting the bullet to notice. But the retch came with a suddenness that took her by surprise and with it her chest expanded and the carefully constructed bustier-type dress came apart like a hot air balloon wrenching itself from its guy ropes. Beth threw up on him. Mac staggered back, a little insulted by her reaction to his kiss. And the key pinged into the air and, with uncharacteristic dexterity, he caught it.

"Are you okay?" he asked Beth.

Beth nodded and waved him away. Mac took the hint, inserted the key and made his escape, grateful that the car was still waiting to take him to the airport.

Chapter Thirty-Two

When Will had bought his four wheel drive Volvo it was suggested that the only off roading it would ever do would be a trip over a kerb in a supermarket car park. It was a big, tall sturdy thing and it was going to earn its keep on this journey. No one had arrived yet and he worried he'd be going on his own. It had been a hectic week, although less so at work. He rang Judah again. Nothing. That was typical Judah.

"You've packed the chains?" Amanda asked.

Will jumped. He'd not noticed her beside the car. He'd read that the forecast was for heavy snow and the conditions going up the mountain were treacherous. He wasn't going to let that stand in the way.

"Ready?" Rick asked.

He hadn't noticed Rick either, and Al was paying the cab. He relaxed a little. At the very least the ski team would be the three of them. He got out of the car and opened the boot and packed their bags into the back. Despite the size of the car the bags were packed almost to the ceiling, leaving just enough room for Judah's bag, as Mac had dropped his off before flying to California. Although he doubted Judah would have anything as organised as a bag.

"Yes, we just need to pick up Mac and Judah," Will said.

"Where are they?" Rick asked.

"Good question," Will said and pulled out his phone.

Neither Mac nor Judah were responding, although in Mac's case it was probably because he was still on the plane. Judah was a different matter.

"No reply," Will said, checking his watch.

It was early and he'd allowed plenty of time to get to the channel tunnel. He'd even bought a flexible ticket, as he'd guessed it wouldn't be straightforward.

"Do you know what time Mac lands, or who he's flying with?" Rick asked.

"Yeah, we talked about it. He's flying from LA with British Airways," Will said.

"Okay, I'll look into that," Rick said.

Will ran though his last conversation with Mac, which was laced with a half dozen beers. It made his recollection a little blurry.

"Scrub that," Will said, "he's flying Virgin."

"Do you know where he's landing?" Rick asked.

"Good question," Will said and gave it some more thought.

Mac had told him about his new client, Beth. A client with money and a willingness to spend it which was the Shangri La of clients and, in Will's view, was more a function of statistics. Mac had worked for thirty years and this kind of client was a once in thirty years kind of client. It was probably his turn.

"Gatwick," Will said.

"Are you sure?" Rick asked.

"He has a new client with money," Will said.

"About time," Rick said.

Will wondered how they were going to locate Judah. He always had his doubts that he'd make the trip. He was many things, Judah, but reliable wasn't one of them.

"I've found it. It was delayed, but it should land in about an hour," Rick said.

"We might as well head there," Will said.

"Hi," Al said.

He'd drunk a little more than the others the previous evening, which was a mixture of drowning his sorrows, and starting the week in a holiday spirit.

"I feel like shit," Al said, getting into the back of the car.

It had been an unspoken rule that those who sat in the back were allowed to doze throughout the journey, while the front seat passenger must navigate and entertain the driver. Will looked at Rick.

"Let's go," he said.

Unlike the previous trips which they'd taken over fifteen years ago, Will's Volvo was equipped with Sat Nav, and the screen lit up and Will tapped in their destination.

"You want to keep trying Judah?" Will asked.

They set off and forty minutes later they were at the airport. Al was fast asleep and they would have left him in the car, but he grunted and woke up as they got out of the car.

"Hold on," Rick said.

They went into the terminal building and headed for the bar and checked the screen for arrivals.

"Another twenty minutes," Rick said.

"I'm going to grab a coffee," Al said.

They watched as people arrived in little crowds. There were drivers waiting for some, and others were greeted by family, friends and lovers.

"I like the movement of airports. I like the emotion," Rick said.

Will and Al looked at each other. There we certain things that set Rick off, and this was likely to be one of them.

"Don't get too emotional when Mac turns up," Al said.

"No chance of that," Rick said.

Rick looked out for the plane. Ten minutes later it landed.

"There it is," Rick said.

Fifteen minutes later the LA crowd flooded into the terminal building. They seemed to be smiling more than those who'd arrived from Stuttgart, but it wasn't long before the crowd began to thin.

"No bloody Scotsmen," Rick said.

"What about that one in the kilt," Al said.

Mac was strolling as if he had all the time in the world, although he didn't have a faster setting. He waved and smiled.

Chapter Thirty-Three

When Judah took exercise it generally involved thrusting his hips, but today he was running. He was running faster than he'd ever run before and his lungs were having difficulty supplying his blood with sufficient oxygen. He'd jumped on a bus and they'd followed him, then a tube and they'd followed him, now he was just running. He had no idea where he was. He turned quickly. It felt like he was safe and he saw some toilets. They were old and lay by the side of a park and were scheduled for renovation, but the part of London he found himself in was not awash with money. He ran in and locked himself in a cubicle.

He sat down. He got up. Whoever had used the toilet before him had been less than fastidious with his aim. It was all over the place. Judah grabbed some toilet paper and tidied up. He sat down again and put his head in his hands.

"Oh fuck," Judah muttered.

His life was a shit storm. Someone had tried to serve a writ last night and then again that morning, which was when the police had turned up. He was grateful he was on the ground floor. He'd escaped through the toilet window. And they were waiting. It was as if they knew he was the kind of person who would escape through toilet windows. The press. If he'd known he'd have faced the police. They were positively benign compared to the British gutter press. And he was very much in the gutter. That was when he started running. He was thankful that the members of the tabloid press were no fitter than him.

"Fuck," Judah said.

One of the more politically active students had launched a campaign against him. They'd protested all night outside his flat. Women against exploitation. He tried to point out that as far as his liaison with Julie was concerned he was the more exploited party. It wasn't an argument they responded well to.

"Fuck," Judah said.

He'd called Kath. He needed somewhere to hide but Kath, he discovered, was now shacked up with Cyril. Who the hell is called Cyril? He probably shouldn't have said that as it gave her the opportunity to list, in near exhaustive detail, why Cyril was a far better partner than he'd been. He came close to pleading, but she'd already hung up, and he was talking to thin air.

"Fuck," Judah said again.

He took out his mobile. He'd turned it off earlier, as it was loaded with calls he didn't wish to take. He turned it on. As it whirred slowly into life he looked around him. There was graffiti everywhere and it appeared that someone called Boris was only a phone call away should he wish to receive a blowjob. Although it might be Doris, he couldn't tell. There were a lot of basic spelling errors.

He checked his missed calls. The vice chancellor had attempted to call him. Seventeen times.

"Shit," he said.

Judah was qualified enough to be a university lecturer but not, he feared, to do very much else. He couldn't see himself working in an office, or on the telephone, or interfacing with the public. If the vice chancellor had called him seventeen times it was unlikely it would be to express his support. What the fuck was he going to do?

"Bugger," he said.

There were five missed calls from Will. Judah had lost track of the day. It was Saturday, Saturday morning. It took a moment for him to process this – there had been a number of other things on his mind – but he remembered something Will had been hacking on about. The ski team. Judah hadn't thought it likely he'd join them. The phone vibrated in his hands. It was Will.

"Where the fuck are you?" Will asked.

"I'm not sure," Judah said. "Somewhere in south east London."

"You'll have to be more specific than that. I'll come and pick you up."

"Okay," Judah said.

This was good. He was going to be saved. Things were looking up.

"I'll find out and text you. It's Lewisham, somewhere."

"Okay, I should be there in about half an hour," Will said and hung up.

Judah put his head back in his hands. He didn't think it likely that the press would follow him to the Alps, and nor whoever was trying to serve him a writ. He couldn't be so sure about the police. He relaxed. It was then that he became aware of the presence of someone nearby. He turned his head slowly to discover that someone had taken the time and trouble to drill a hole between the cubicles and whoever was in the neighbouring cubicle had decided to avail himself of the opportunities this presented.

"Oh Christ," Judah said, and ran from the cubicle into the street.

Chapter Thirty-Four

"Why are you wearing a kilt?" Will asked.

Mac wasn't sure whether he should tell them about Beth. He suspected they wouldn't believe him.

"I went to a party," Mac explained.

"Jesus," Rick said, "you smell like shit."

Mac had just flown for eight hours and he'd smelled pretty bad, but he had nothing to change into, and even less under his kilt. A stewardess had quarantined him in a corner away from complaining customers.

"Someone threw up on me," Mac said.

"Why didn't you change?" Will asked.

Mac paused as he thought how to explain the events that led up to his hurried escape.

"I had an altercation," Mac said.

"Not again," Rick said.

"It wasn't my fault," Mac said.

Rick looked at Will. Mac's capacity for putting his foot in it was legendary, and there had been times at university when there had been nobody he hadn't offended. And that was before the era of political correctness.

"Had you been drinking?" Will asked.

Mac grunted.

"Hold on," Will said with concern, "it wasn't your new client?"

"Not the gravy train?" Rick said.

"The meal ticket?" Will said.

"The golden goose?" Rick added.

Mac grunted.

"Back to a life of penury," Rick said.

"A world of bouncing cheques," Will said.

"Will you guys give me a break," Mac said.

Mac didn't know what was going to happen, but he wasn't hopeful.

"What happened?" Will asked reasonably.

"She came on to me," Mac said.

"That explains why she threw up," Rick said.

Will and Rick laughed so heartily that it woke Al.

"What's happening?" Al asked.

There were a few seconds while Al attempted to take in what was happening.

"Jesus, what the fuck's that smell?" Al asked. "I'm not spending twelve hours in the car with that smell."

"He's right, we've got to sort that out," Will said stopping the car.

Will got out and went into a small corner shop returning a few moments later with bottles of water and a roll of black plastic bags.

"Did you pack jeans in your bag?" Will asked.

"I did. Good idea," Mac said.

Will drove a little further, out of the built up area, until they arrived at a quiet country road.

"This will do," Will said.

Will got out of the car and opened the boot and rummaged through the pile of bags. Mac followed him and dug through his bag.

"You're going to need underpants," Will suggested.

They had been at too many events when Mac had demonstrated what wasn't worn under his kilt. He grabbed a pair of underpants and debated whether he should remove his shoes. It seemed easier to keep them on. It might have been the scotch the previous evening, or the disturbed sleep during the flight, but raising his feet and inserting them into the holes of his underpants was proving a challenge. He loosened his kilt and tried again. It was then that a series of coaches came tearing down the road the first of which seemed to be pushing a bow wave of air, which challenged his tenuous balance.

"Shit," Mac yelled.

Despite the heavy tartan, the wind whipped up the kilt like Marilyn Monroe on a subway grate. The coach that followed was carrying a hen party from Essex on its way to Dublin. Alcohol and strippers were promised and, although Mac's pale, hairy arse was not what they would want to pay for, it prompted a roar of cheers. Mac waved. He changed quickly and put the kilt in a plastic bag and then covered that with a second bag. Five minutes later they were back on the road.

"What about Judah?" Al asked.

"He's somewhere in Lewisham. He's not sure where," Rick said.

"You need Find-a-Friend on his phone," Mac said.

"I'll try him again," Will said.

Rick had synced the telephone to the car's handsfree, which Will had never bothered to do, and he pressed dial. This time it started to ring.

"That's encouraging," Rick said.

A second later it stopped ringing. There was a pause. And then they heard Judah's voice. It sounded a little desperate.

"Will! I need you to get me!" Judah said.

Chapter Thirty-Five

"Can you see him?" Will asked.

They were next to a park with a long ragged grass verge, somewhere in South East London. There were a few cars lined up along side them.

"No," Rick said, "we better give him another call."

Will tapped Judah's number in. It rang once.

"Where are you?" Judah asked.

'Where are you? Will asked.

"I'm just after the park, down an alleyway," Judah said.

They looked for him. Judah inched out slowly.

"There he is!" Rick said.

Will threw the car into Drive and pulled out into the road, but it seemed as if everyone else had the same idea. A line of cars moved at the same time. Two cars collided, bringing them to a halt.

"Go!" Rick said.

But they were jammed in. People were running towards Judah armed with cameras and microphones.

"I can't," Will protested.

"Drive over the kerb. This thing's four wheel drive," Rick yelled.

Will wasn't keen to admit that he didn't want to damage the wheels. He edged slowly towards the kerb.

"It's quite a high kerb," Will said timidly.

There was a growl from the back of the car. It had a Scottish accent.

"Floor the fucking thing," Mac shouted.

It made Will jump and prompted an involuntary flick of his right foot. The car leaped over the kerb and into the muddy grass verge. Will would have slowed down, but he was weighing up the reckless illegality of his driving against the scorn he would receive. They overtook the cars and the people running towards Judah. Mac opened the rear door. A light came on the dashboard accompanied by a persistent buzzing noise in a reassuringly Volvo kind of way to remind the driver of the open door and the perils that might present. Then the grass verge ended and they were on tarmac. There was a drop between one and the other, and the car took a little jump and landed with a bounce. Will winced and a second later he screeched to a halt. Judah threw himself across the back seats.

"Go! Go! Go!" Mac screamed.

The two cars behind had disentangled themselves and were heading in their direction. Will hesitated.

"Get a fucking move on, you poof," Mac shouted.

And Will floored the throttle. He'd owned the car for two years and, as he took the train to work, it was mostly used by Amanda to do the shopping. She favoured the more expensive supermarket. He occasionally used it to go to the garden centre, and they'd had a few long journeys to the various in-laws, and a couple of holidays in France. In the course of these trips he may have overtaken the odd car, he'd certainly exceeded the speed limit on the motorway, but no more than anyone else. He'd squeezed the throttle early on to see what it would do. But he'd never floored it before. He lifted off and they were flown forward.

"Fucking hell," Al said.

Al had been asleep until the moment Judah had landed on him.

"Rick, you might have to take over," Mac yelled.

There was no way Will was going to allow Rick to drive. He didn't even have a licence. Will floored the throttle even though his every instinct was to release it. Rick leaned forward and tapped in the Eurotunnel into the Sat Nav, although he had a good idea which way to go.

"This way," Rick said.

"But that's a bus lane," Will whined.

There was another growl from behind.

"For fuck's sake," Mac roared.

Against his better judgement, Will turned into the bus lane hoping that there weren't any cameras, as this sort of driving tended to lead to fines and points on his licence. It didn't stop the cars that were following them.

"Through the lights!" Rick shouted.

There was no question in Will's mind. The traffic lights weren't green, they weren't amber, or on the change. They were very definitely red. He was a fifty-seven year old man bowing to peer pressure. He shot through the lights.

"Fuck!" Rick shouted.

There was a lorry. A lorry, Will knew, which had legitimately crossed the junction when the lights were green. The Volvo was a solidly built thing, but this was a skip lorry and, as it was empty, it was driving at some speed. The driver was on his mobile talking to his wife, although it was less a conversation, and more a shouting match.

That morning, while the driver had been in the shower, his wife had looked through his texts. When he got out of the shower there had been some discussion about interpretation, which was a subject about which they clearly took opposing views, with his wife explaining that she wasn't a 'fucking idiot'. The driver led a fairly sedentary life, which was mostly spent sitting on his arse and consequently, when his wife ran off with the phone, he had difficulty following her. She did Pilates. They ran around the house until they got to the back door. It was at this point that she whipped off his towel and ran out in the garden feeling fairly confident he wouldn't follow her.

And he very nearly didn't, but there were messages on that phone he did not want her to see. They'd bought their house off the council and, at the time of its construction, there had been a discussion about garden size. Theirs was big and she was running down it at a far greater speed than the driver was capable of but, in a subsequent change of council policy, a block of flats had been built at the end of the garden. He could see people having breakfast. He'd looked around the kitchen for, at the very least, a tea towel, but he'd never dried up anything in his life and had no idea where his wife kept them. But he had no choice. The skip driver had sprinted naked down the garden. That moment of indecision would prove costly.

A lesbian couple lived in one of the flats that overlooked his garden. They had two young children and they were sat at the kitchen table quietly eating breakfast. The children had seen plenty of naked women, but they'd never seen a naked man. They'd seen Action Men dolls, but they had slim muscled stomachs and not the quivering paunch the lorry driver was carrying. They also didn't have genitals. It was a warm period and the window was open. The children looked on with their mouths open. Their two mummys were very specific about the kind of language they were allowed to use and none of it contained the words that the lorry driver's wife was about to read out.

"I want to suck your hard throbbing cock," she shouted.

The lorry driver had skidded to a halt. There was a little slap as he did so, and which would become a topic of discussion between the two children when their mothers were not in the room. But the lorry driver knew he was banged to rights.

"Have I misinterpreted that?" his wife yelled.

The lorry driver had walked up to his wife and grabbed his phone, gone back into the house, got dressed and driven to work. It was the subsequent phone call from his wife, while on the way to collect a skip, which had distracted him.

"Fuck!" Mac screamed.

In the fraction of a second that was presented to Will there was no time for calculation. It was instinct. Could he stop in time or get past? He went for the latter applying even more pressure on his right foot. There wasn't any more throttle travel, but Will was committed to it, and they watched as fifteen tonnes of lorry slowly hove into view, like an eclipse. It wasn't travelling slowly, but their collective perceptions had altered time, aside from Rick who was more accustomed to such things.

"Sh…" Will said.

And then they were through and the shadow went back to moving at real time. It took a second for them to notice that the rear of the car had been clipped. The skip driver noticed it too, but it was more as if he'd encountered a deeper than usual pothole. He'd spent the last hour attempting to create an interpretation in which 'I want to suck your hard throbbing cock' could mean something other than an intent to perform fellatio. It was proving to be quite an absorbing exercise not least because he knew, as his wife had pointed out, that she wasn't a 'fucking idiot'.

He'd given up. He'd held his hands up and then had a further thought. The key was in the grammar, which was ironic as he was a skip lorry driver and rarely got his 'was' or his 'were' right. But the text clearly said that she – Lorna who works in the office – *wanted* to suck his cock and not *had* sucked his cock. As far as his wife knew he could be entirely blameless. Lorna might be a mad, psychotic bitch, a proper nymphomaniac, he'd told his wife. And that had prompted a further thought and a plan. But the lorry driver paused for a second as something seemed to flash in his rearview mirror.

"Sh..." Will said, still not quite having the time to complete the word.

The Volvo was a pretty substantial vehicle and, with five paunchy men on board, it weighed nigh on three tonnes, but they were no longer moving in a forward direction. They were spinning. Will had washed the car every weekend for the last year regardless of whether it had needed it. It had once acquired a small nick on the passenger door, and Amanda had professed innocence, claiming it was a supermarket trolley or a neighbouring car door. But it had irritated him. When the light caught it, it was all he could see and he'd taken it to a body shop, after which they'd had difficulty matching the metallic paint, and he'd sent it to another body shop until it was perfect. It wasn't perfect anymore.

"...it," Will said.

It was at that moment the skip lorry driver hit on an inspired plan. The solution to his immediate problem. After he'd collected the skip, and returned to the office, he was going to grab Lorna's mobile – she always left it lying around – and he was going to send the text 'I want to suck your hard throbbing cock' to all the drivers. His wife and Ed's wife were thick as thieves and they'd be talking in no time. It would be even better if his wife spoke to Ed's wife first and encouraged her to investigate his phone. The lorry driver was feeling much more comfortable now, but he was certain he'd hit something, and planted his foot on the brakes and the lorry screamed to a halt.

The Volvo was still describing circles in a South London high street. And then it stopped and instead it rose up onto two wheels. It went higher and higher until slow motion time was restored to the occupants, apart from Rick who was wondering what it would be like should it roll over, and then it came down. It took a moment for everyone to take this in. Mac got it first. They'd turned seven hundred and twenty degrees. They were pointing the right way. The reporters were approaching.

"Go! Go! Go!" Mac shouted and, despite his better judgement, Will floored it again.

Chapter Thirty-Six

Nine hours later they arrived at a service station somewhere near Dijon. The car was gently ticking.

"Are we nearly there yet?" Al asked.

Al had slept the entire time and for him it had passed in a few seconds. He looked up, saw where they were, and closed his eyes and went back to sleep.

"Not yet," Will muttered.

Will hadn't got out the car yet. He'd refused when they'd sat in the Channel Tunnel and no one had said anything. But his back was beginning to play up and they needed fuel. He wondered if he could achieve that without looking at the rear of the car, but once he was out he knew he had to take a look.

"Look at my poor car," Will simpered.

The others joined him wondering if they should say anything. They were standing as if they were attending a wake.

"Where's the bumper?" Will muttered.

"Lewisham," Mac said and went into the building to take a piss.

Will looked at it. It wasn't just the bumper. It was the rear door and the rear wing. It looked a mess. He grunted and filled it with fuel. He grabbed a coffee and a sandwich, took a piss and they were off again. Up until now the temperature had been mild, but a few hours later they passed through a tunnel the other side of which lay the Alpine views they were waiting for.

"Finally a bit of snow," Mac said.

A few flecks of snow hit the windscreen and the snowcapped mountains appeared. The temperature was dropping. Will relaxed a little, feeling genuinely excited. They'd nearly made it. An hour later they were stuck in a traffic jam, as the roads had converged and they were now in the valley queuing to take the various turnings which led to the skiing resorts. It was slow moving, because it was changeover day, and the weather had turned.

"It's chucking it down now," Rick observed.

Will had the wipers shifting as fast as they were able and they were struggling to clear the dense snow. He was grateful he'd bought the big four wheel drive Volvo. Twenty minutes later they turned off and began their assent to Val Thorens, one of the highest resorts.

"No shortage of snow," Rick said.

The road snaked up the mountain with a series of hairpin turns, and every few minutes Will could see the temperature shown on the dashboard drop a further degree.

"Minus six," Will said.

It began to look a little chaotic as cars were stuck by the side of the road unable to proceed, and others had stopped to put on snow chains. Will could feel the occasional jiggle through the steering wheel as the car lost and found traction, but it felt reassuringly solid. Rick looked at the stationary cars.

"Do you think we should put the snow chains on?" Rick asked.

Will was beginning to wonder the same thing, but the car was still pulling them up the mountain.

"Nah, not in this," Mac said.

They turned a further corner and it no longer felt like snowfall. It was a blizzard.

"Fuck," Will said, trying to pick his way up the mountain.

Rick was studying the Sat Nav. He didn't always agree with it, as he'd always had a facility for finding short cuts.

"If we take a left here," Rick said.

Will had stopped following the Sat Nav and hadn't looked at the signs. He was just trying to manoeuvre the car so that they'd didn't collide with anyone, or fall off the mountain. Without thinking he followed Rick's instruction.

"There's no one up here," Rick said.

Will was beginning to have a bad feeling.

"There might be a reason for that," Will said.

"Do you think?" Mac said.

Will couldn't tell whether he was being sarcastic or not.

"Do you think we should put the chains on?" Will asked.

"No," Mac said, "chains are for pussies."

It didn't matter as the road had narrowed, and there were no flat sections on which he could park the car and fit the chains. He just had to keep going. At the next hairpin he slowed to almost a halt.

"Fucking hell," Will said.

It was steep. Behind them was a sheer drop. Will was feeling nervous.

"You've got to go for it," Rick said.

Will took in a breath and gently pressed the accelerator pedal and kept pressing it. It wasn't quite to the floor, but the car was roaring and the tyres scrambling and weaving in an attempt to find grip. The car flew up the hill, but as it got closer to the top the wheels began to struggle more. There seemed to be less and less to stick to and they'd almost reached the summit. But it was no longer just snow. It was mostly ice. The wheels were spinning and there was no forward motion.

"Shit," Will.

There was no question of it. Now they were moving backwards. They were sliding backwards. At first it was just at a creeping pace, but then they started to gain a rearward velocity.

"There's a sheer drop at the end of this," Will said with a quiver in his voice.

There was silence in the car. Now they were all passengers.

"Turn the wheel!" Rick shouted.

Will tugged at the steering wheel, not a hundred percent certain of what he was going to achieve. But the car turned and came to a halt as the rear end buried itself in a deep bank of snow.

"Thank fuck for that," Judah said after a pause.

"What the fuck do we do now?" Will asked.

"You should have put the chains on," Al said, who'd woken up on the impact.

The car was stuck diagonally across the narrow road. Will got out and fell over. He'd skated on ice rinks that weren't this slippery. He got up and got back in.

"Plan of action?" Will asked.

"Did you pack a shovel?" Rick asked.

Will looked at him.

"That's a no, then," Rick said.

Al sat up. He was a little more accustomed to dealing with emergencies.

"Can you get to the chains from inside?" Al asked.

Will had removed the parcel shelf and left it at home, as they had so much luggage.

"You should be able to climb over. They're under the bags on the left hand side," Will said.

Al dived over the seat and pulled out various bags, which he dumped on Judah until eventually he got to the bottom, and pulled out the chains.

"While I've got the luggage here, has anyone got any spikes?" Al asked.

"Yeah, I've got some," Mac said.

Ten minutes later everyone was out of the car except Will. They positioned themselves around the car. Judah had the spikes on his left foot and Mac had them on his right foot.

"Remember, if it slides back we can't stop it. Dive to the left and Will can put it back in the bank," Al said.

He lay the chains down, tucking them under the front wheels.

"Ease it forward, Will," Al said.

They pushed the car and, with a little more to grip on to, the wheels turned onto the chains. Al fixed the chains and everyone pushed until the car had reached the top of the hill. Will stopped and got out. He could tell that something was wrong. Everyone was looking at each other. Will walked to the rear of the car using the roof rails to steady himself. He looked at the rear of the car.

"Shit," Will said.

There was a large dent in the rear wing.

"At least they match now," Mac said, and turned and took a piss down the side of the mountain.

Chapter Thirty-Seven

An hour later they arrived in Val Thorens. Will had driven for twelve hours and it hadn't been a very relaxing twelve hours. Al had slept for eleven and a half hours, Judah for six, Mac for four and Rick for two hours. They were raring for a drink. Will looked through the papers until he'd identified Jim Beresford's apartment and got out the car.

"We're up there," he said.

Jim's apartment was on the top floor of a handsome timber-clad apartment block. Will parked the car next to the front door and they shifted their bags into the lift. They huddled into the remaining space in the lift and pressed the button for the top floor. The lift beeped and refused to move. There were weight issues.

"Mac, you fat bastard," Judah said, having got in the lift first.

Mac stepped out and the beeping stopped.

"That sorts that," Rick said and pressed the button again.

The lift doors closed and a few minutes later they were on the top floor. Will fumbled with the keys and opened the front door.

"Nice," Rick said.

They stepped into a large sitting room with huge leather sofas and fur throws, and a bank of windows which opened onto a balcony overlooking the heart of the resort.

"Very nice," Al said.

They dumped their bags quickly, choosing bedrooms randomly, and got back in the lift.

"Where's Mac?" Rick asked.

"I think I can guess," Will said.

When they arrived at the ground floor, they looked across the road.

"There," Judah said with certainty.

It was the nearest bar and likely to become their local. They walked in and found Mac leaning against the bar. If there was a science, or an art, or an academy, or a university of leaning against bars, this is how it would be done. It was as if the bar was his front room. If a bar could be attached to a man this is how it would look. As if the worn area of bar and floor had been worn by his own shoes. There was an empty glass in front of him. While Mac was often accused of being socially clumsy, this did not appear to be the case when it came to bars or pubs. He had very rapidly acquainted himself with the owner of the bar.

"About time!" Mac shouted and turned to the barman, "Five of your finest lagers, Andre!"

"Who's going to hold the kitty?" Rick asked.

They all knew the answer.

"Let's chuck in fifty euros each and Will can look after it," Mac said.

They moved to the table nearest to the bar and sat down.

"Worth waiting for," Mac said, and passed the other beers out.

"We made it," Judah said.

The bar was a combination of the Alpine style with wooden cubicles and ornaments and ancient skis hanging on the wall, and television screens. Quite a few of them. One was showing skiing events, another football and yet another was showing rugby matches. Although Mac had only been in the bar for a few moments, it was ample time to consume a pint and establish the name of the barman. Andre walked over to them

"My name is Andre," Andre said.

They looked at him. Andre was a big man with a cordial nature. As the owner of the bar he recognised, in a collection of thirsty Englishmen, an immediate rise in profits.

"This is my bar," Andre said simply. "If you need anything, just let me know."

Andre pointed to the not very distant bar and where they could find him, although they wouldn't have to look for him. He had a needy wife to support. They looked at the television screens.

"That's England and France," Mac said.

They looked at the rugby. England were losing. This, they knew, would give Mac some pleasure even though he'd spent most of his life south of the border.

"Done," Mac said putting his glass down.

He looked up for Andre, but Andre was already weaving his way towards them with freshly filled glasses.

"Good man, Andre," Mac said, adding, "it's nice to see England losing to France."

Andre responded as quick as a flash.

"We have England defeats on a constant loop," he said.

His delivery was deadpan, and it took a second for them to realise he was joking.

"Hold on," Rick said, "don't we win this one?"

Andre deployed a time-honoured shrug, as if it had been passed down to him through generations which, in a way, it had. Andre was to shrugs as Mac was to leaning on bars.

"Per-haps," Andre said.

Andre was capable of speaking English with a very minimal accent, as he'd worked in Newcastle for several years, but he liked to adorn his English with a suitably French slur.

"Do you have any of the Scottish losing?" Al asked.

"Ahh," Andre slurred, "the tapes, they are only so big."

Mac had nothing to say to that so concentrated on his third beer. The others were beginning to catch up.

"It's thirsty work, sitting in the car," Rick said.

"That's what all the women say," Will said.

He realised immediately that this, in front of Rick, was a bit of a faux pas. But Rick didn't say anything, and Will launched into his first beer. He needed to park the car properly, but he needed a beer more.

"Sorry," he said quickly to Rick, but Rick waved his hand.

Will looked around. This was plainly a sports bar, and there were collections of newly arrived skiers: some families, a few youngsters, and there were further groups of the middle aged and very nearly elderly skiers. There was also a group of women. He looked back. Judah had already spotted them. Will raised his eyes in light of Judah's recent woman, or perhaps girl, related plight.

"Hey, ho," Judah said.

"Andre, let me introduce our team leader, Will," Mac said.

Andre had returned with more beers, having spent a few moments in the office ordering another barrel. English tourists were like delicate flowers. They need to be nurtured.

"This one is on me," Andre said.

The nurturing process wasn't a complicated one.

"Will you be eating?" Andre asked.

"You can eat here too?" Mac said. "I thought we'd get all our required calorific intake via beer."

"Good idea," Will said to Andre, and Andre returned with menus.

Andre's wife sat in the office. She wasn't, by nature, a friendly woman, and their relationship was frequently a delicate one, although it appeared to be much less so when Andre was making money. She'd flinched at the free round, but she knew, from the countless lectures Andre had delivered on the subject, that it would be a sound investment. But the cook had gone home. Andre popped his head round the door.

"Are you ready for five steak and chips?" Andre said to his wife.

"But they'd haven't ordered yet," his wife protested.

Andre shrugged. There were few things more predictable than a group of Englishmen. The kitchen was next to the office and he nipped in to begin the preparation. The last couple of seasons had been tough and this one had been the worse yet as it either hadn't snowed, or it wouldn't stop snowing. The local taxes had gone mad and the cost of employing people had gone through the roof. They did the evening shift together.

The door was slightly ajar and he was keeping an eye on the beer level, although he knew he'd struggle to keep up with Mac. He wasn't sure if the pump could put it out as quickly as he was consuming it. Andre checked the other tables. The families had left and the others weren't likely to have much more aside from the table of middle aged women. He'd kept his eye on them.

"Andre!"

It was Mac. Andre steered himself out of the kitchen and scanned the other tables as he drew close. The other reason that Andre's wife didn't stray far from him was that he'd been a little inclined to stray himself. But, like the shrug, this was also a time-honoured French custom which had been handed down through the generations. It wasn't his fault, he really couldn't help himself. He took their order and a moment later he popped his head into the office and said to his wife.

"Five steak and chips."

She hated it that he was always right and got up and went into the kitchen and hurled a huge pile of chips into the fryer and began to prepare the steaks. A moment later Andre joined her in the kitchen.

"What are you doing?" she asked.

Andre's wife had honed the accusatory tone to an art form and he responded with a shrug.

"Topping up the Génépi," he said.

"Do they get free Génépi too?" his wife complained.

Andre shrugged. Génépi was cheap, beer was expensive.

"And I've seen you looking at those women," she added.

"Which women?" Andre asked.

He knew that they both knew which women, but he couldn't resist stirring his wife up every now and then. They'd met when he was a young ski instructor twenty years ago and Andre still gave the odd lesson, but his wife, who'd gained a bit of weight and complained about her delicate ankles, hadn't stood on a pair of skis in years. He felt a little freer on the slopes. Twenty minutes later he carried the steaks over.

"Shall we get some wine?" Rick asked.

There was a general nodding and wine appeared a moment later.

"Can you get the news here on one of the English channels?" Al asked Andre.

Andre produced a remote control, as if he as drawing a gun, and fired it at the nearest television. He flipped through the channels until they arrived at a channel which looked suitably English. They were talking politics. As the beers continued their concentration lapsed until a piece that was a little closer to home.

"Isn't that Harry Panter?" Al said.

It was. A second later they saw Judah running from reporters and they let out a cheer – they were on holiday and a few beers in – and Andre looked round. He wasn't sure if he should be impressed or concerned. It didn't matter. He needed to concentrate on keeping the beers and the wine rolling.

Chapter Thirty-Eight

The following morning Will was up early. He always got up early and he was ready for the day. He rummaged through the kitchen cupboards and found a large teapot, and set about making tea for the boys. There had been a lot of snoring through the night and everyone had shuffled to the toilet at least once. There had been fewer visits fifteen years earlier, and the place was acquiring a smell already.

"Morning," Rick said, adding, "I feel like shit."

He sat down at the kitchen table, picked up the remote for the television, which was hung on the wall, and pointed it.

"Tea?" Will said.

"Oh dear god, yes," Rick said.

A minute later Al walked in as if he was still asleep. He bumped into the table and slid down into a chair. Will passed him a cup of tea. Al grunted acknowledgement and sipped the tea. Judah came in.

"Jesus, how much did we drink?" he asked.

Will picked up the plastic zipped envelope, which contained the kitty and far fewer bank notes than had it had at the beginning of the evening. He pulled out a receipt.

"Thirty large beers," Will said.

"Thirty?" Judah said. "That explains why I feel like shit."

"And six bottles of red wine," Will said.

They looked around. Had they drunk red wine? No one could remember.

"With the meal," Will pointed out.

Will had dropped out a little earlier than the others and drank a little less.

"And four scotches," Will said.

"I didn't have a scotch," Rick said.

"Me neither," Judah said.

"Not guilty," Al said putting his hands up.

"That would be me," Mac said making his appearance.

"And how do you feel?" Rick asked.

"Me? Good as gold," Mac said taking a tea and sitting down.

Will got out a skiing map. He'd been studying them all week checking the best lifts up from the apartment. He'd even sent maps to the others.

"Have any of you looked at the maps?" Will asked.

They looked at each other. It was obvious they hadn't.

"Well, anyway, after we've picked the skis up I suggest we ski down here and up this lift," he pointed to the map.

He wasn't sure if they were listening.

"Are we ready?" Will asked impatiently after a further thirty minutes.

Judah and Al looked like they'd been sleep deprived. Rick had more or less recovered and Mac looked bright as a button.

"I'll just visit the khazi," Mac said.

They sat in silence, drinking their tea, with the backdrop of machine gun fire which was Mac taking a crap.

"It's like being in Syria," Rick observed.

When Mac had finished he opened the toilet door, filling the apartment with a new and not particularly pleasant aroma.

"Jesus, let's go," Judah said.

They needed to sort out ski hire and lift passes and nearly an hour later they were fully kitted out and looking down the slope. They were ready to go. The central boulevard was dense with skiers and the lifts were the other side. They'd have to pick their way through, but it wasn't very steep.

"It's been a long time," Judah said.

"It has," Will said.

Will said it with some regret, whereas Judah was feeling a little uncertain. He'd always been the least confident skier, and that was fifteen years ago.

"Where are we going?" Rick asked.

"Down," Mac said, accompanying it with a fart.

"That one down there," Will pointed.

"What, that one?" Al asked.

"No, the one next to it," Will said.

In the intervening years there had been a significant deterioration of their collective eyesight.

"That one," Will said.

"Let's go," Mac said, and set off.

Chapter Thirty-Nine

Rick followed Mac, sliding slowly with his skis making squidgy noises, then he began to gently pick up speed until he drew level with him, and then passed him. He felt his legs and applied weight to one and felt the skis turn, and then shifted his weight to the other leg, and he turned again. It felt good. He'd been one of the better skiers, but it had always been a function of application over natural skill. He liked to think his whole life had been that way. He'd worked hard. Now he was travelling at a reasonable speed, leaving the others behind. He let his mind empty. The wind was rushing against his face and there were a number of skiers of various abilities who were describing a path perpendicular to him. He weaved through them in a way that looked pretty skilful to the others, but he wasn't certain that if events dictated it, he could stop that quickly. It didn't seem to matter.

Rick was through the pack and looking ahead. He vaguely remembered Will saying something about the lift they should stop at, but he didn't feel ready to stop. He'd been a little too stationary for a while and this felt good. He'd once gone skiing with Annie and she'd hated every minute of it. That was the end of that, and the only ski trips he'd taken had been with the boys. He'd always been careful. He didn't see the need now. He'd looked at YouTube skiing tuition videos before he'd left, and he'd read about carving. He tilted his skis into the snow so that two sharp lines appeared behind him and he described a perfect curve. It hadn't occurred to him that he was going too fast to stop at the lift, and he couldn't hear Will shouting at him from a distance, but he could see a clear run beyond the lift. He also didn't notice the sharp drop and the crest that preceded the piste and when he got to it he was airborne.

"Whoops," Rick said to himself.

He liked the sense of freedom that gave him. It was the moment before things went wrong, or they came together. The odd fragility of life and chance. How you meet people was dictated by chance, and Rick had been lucky with chance, and who does, or doesn't, acquire a disease was also random. He'd been unlucky with that. Unless there was a god who deliberately chose to be cruel. He doubted that. It was no more sophisticated than shit happening. He realised that there was nothing random about the collision which was coming his way. He was going too fast. But as he was still airborne there was little he could do. He just had to enjoy the ride and hope for the best landing.

A hundred yards behind him the others had come to a halt. It was a little abrupt and Al fell over.

"Shit," Al said.

"He's not stopping," Mac said.

Rick was in the distance but his orange helmet was easy to make out.

"He's going bloody fast," Judah said.

"Where the fuck is he going?" Mac asked.

"Shit," Al said again.

Will looked down at a map he was holding.

"Les Menuires," he said.

"Where the fuck's that?" Judah asked.

"The next resort," Will said.

"Is that far?" Judah asked.

"Not so far," Will said.

"Shit," Al said for a third time.

They looked round at Al. He was still on the ground. They looked back at Rick.

"Shit," they all said.

They could see Rick rise into the air and then drop out of sight, as if he'd fallen off the mountain.

"Is there a piste the other side?" Mac asked.

"I don't know," Will said.

"Shit," Judah said.

"Shit," Al said.

"We better check he's okay," Will said.

"We can get back up okay?" Mac asked.

Will checked the map.

"Yes, no problem," he said.

They dug their poles in and turned to point in the direction Rick had gone until they noticed that one of their number was down.

"Are you okay, Al?" Will asked.

"No," Al said, "I think I've broken my ankle."

A hundred and fifty yards ahead of them Rick had landed. His orange helmet bobbed as he stumbled and his balance shifted from one side to the other, and the tips of his skis flew up and down and then he stabilised, leaned hard on his left side until he was moving uphill. He slowed to a speed from which he regained control and then threw in an emergency stop to see if he could. He could. He looked back up the hill. It was quite steep, and although it was only a blue run, he'd taken a corner of it which wasn't on the piste at all. With that and his speed he'd travelled a good distance in the air and out of control. It was quite a big mistake for which there were no consequences. He remembered moments when he'd made a minor mistake, a trifling error, he'd taken the current view and he'd gone long. It had taken six months for him to recover his position. Another time he'd bought the wrong stock and it had shot up in value. He looked up until the others appeared in the distance. He waved and waited for them to join them. It took a while until eventually Mac arrived by his side.

"Where are the others?" Rick asked.

"It looks like Al might have buggered his ankle," Mac said.

Chapter Forty

The young doctor carefully handled and examined Al's ankle. But they both knew what was wrong. Fortunately this was a good place for broken bones. They were common on the slopes, although his was a less than heroic injury. He'd just fallen over. The end result was the same and the doctor began to apply the warm plaster cast. It wasn't the first time Al had broken his ankle, although the previous time he'd been young, and it had been broken for him. His father had caught him doing something he hadn't approved of. He'd stamped on his ankle. That characterised his father. Al understood he was still alive, but old and frail, and he had no interest in communicating with him. He hadn't spoken to him for at least fifteen years.

Al had never really talked about it, but a therapist he'd very briefly employed had suggested that it was his relationship with his father which had inhibited his other relationships. In truth he'd not had many. His family, and strongest bond, was with his university mates, although he doubted they knew. That, and his work as a paramedic, which he'd thrown himself into, and which was positive and involved helping people. Although management had suggested he was getting a little too cynical. Al wondered if he'd used work as a crutch for too long.

"Assurance?"

A man in a suit had turned up. He'd shattered the peace that the calm doctor, who'd softly placed his hands on him, had induced. The doctor looked up at him – they locked eyes for a second – and the doctor comically raised his eyes. He guessed that the medics were as fond of the suits in French hospitals as they were in British ones. He reached over for his wallet. He'd taken out insurance a while ago when he'd gone on a trip with Rick. It had invoked climbing and a few of the nutcase things that Rick was currently fond of. Al took out a card and passed it to the man in a suit.

"Merçi," the man in the suit mumbled.

Al had taken out the insurance online and they'd sent him a little plastic card which looked like a credit card. It would have gone with the other credit cards, but he didn't have any. He was cautious with his money and just had one debit card, and that seemed to do. He'd been putting money away for a while. Al had done his time, and the retirement package wasn't too bad. It just seemed like a leap into the old. That was a bit scary, although he wasn't sure if it was about being old, or redundant in the sense of being no longer useful.

"Non," the man in the suit said.

There were moments when Al felt as if he'd let his life pass by. And that was why he wanted to leave the service while he was still young, or he felt young. He wanted to go away and do all the things he'd been too inhibited to do.

"Non?" the doctor said.

The man in the suit showed the card to the doctor. The doctor showed the card to Al. Al read the expiry date.

"Shit," Al said.

He was fairly sure he'd checked it before he left. Or, failing that, he'd ticked a box which would prompt it to automatically renew. He tried to convey this with the man in the suit, but he either didn't speak a word of English, or was choosing not to. The doctor translated.

"He will telephone the insurance tomorrow. You must stay the night," the doctor said.

It was late now and he doubted Will was going to be keen on driving down the mountain, so he shrugged and accepted it. The doctor finished crafting the plaster cast, patted it affectionately and with some pride, and smiled at Al.

"Thank you," Al said.

The doctor nodded graciously and left the room. The nurses were a little less welcoming and ushered him into a room, instructed him to remove his clothes, and gave him a hospital gown. Like the ones in Britain, it closed at the rear, or rather stubbornly refused to close. It mostly exposed his backside. He wasn't very comfortable with this, but they found him a room with a television, and it didn't occur to him that he'd left his clothes behind in a neat pile.

Al resigned himself to the fact that his skiing holiday was a bit of a disaster, but once they'd resolved the insurance, he could at least ensconce himself in the bar, and he wouldn't miss out on the social side, which was the prime reason he was there.

Chapter Forty-One

"Five of my finest lagers," Andre said.

They'd made it to the end of the day and they'd slid effortlessly to the front door of the bar, removed their skis, and entered as if it was home. Andre had the beers ready.

"There's only four of us, but don't worry. We'll find a home for the fifth," Mac said.

Andre cast a rapid eye over the team and noted the missing member.

"Will he be in later?" Andre asked.

"I doubt it," Judah said, "he's in Albertville."

"The hospital?" Andre enquired.

"I'm afraid so," Judah said.

Andre tried not to make his prime concern one of lost revenue, but he also knew that an injured Englishman was one who had nothing else to do but drink.

"Are you going to get him?" Rick asked Will.

"No, I called but they won't release him today," Will said.

"Then you better have another beer," Mac said.

Andre returned to the office. His wife was looking at his laptop checking his internet history.

"Hey, mon cherie," Andre said.

His wife shrugged. Their lunchtime trade was frantic, but their evening trade had been dying on its feet, as the younger crowd had gravitated towards the more fashionable bars. He'd wanted to make changes – play music and employ a young and very beautiful girl – but his wife was resistant to the idea. He'd even lost the group of middle aged women. Andre returned to the more hospitable atmosphere of the bar.

"Okay," Will said, laying out the ski map and making plans, "tomorrow."

But the others were locked in a discussion about whether Andre's wife was his wife, his mother, or a gargoyle he kept in the corner to frighten away evil spirits.

"I bet you can't charm her," Rick said to Judah.

"I wouldn't want to," he said.

"Maybe, but that's not the right question. If I gave you a hundred euros could you charm her?" Rick said.

Judah took a look through the door, which was always slightly open, and the other side of which Andre's wife sat spying on the goings on in the bar.

"Hold on," Judah said.

Judah's concentration had gone. The group of middle aged women had appeared. They cast casual glances their way, and then found a table as far from them as possible.

"A hundred euros," Rick repeated.

Judah brought his eyes back to Andre's wife. A hundred euros didn't seem enough.

"Five hundred," Judah said.

"The challenge is to charm her, not marry her," Rick said.

"Or fuck her," Mac added.

"I'm not sure that's possible," Judah said.

Judah needed the money. He just needed to edge it a little higher.

"Two fifty," he said.

Will had stopped looking at the ski map. They looked through at Andre's wife. And, because Mac was possessed of less discretion than the others, he waved and shouted, "hello." Andre's wife froze and Andre appeared from nowhere. He had no objection to people taunting his wife, he might even encourage it, but there was an empty beer glass on the table and he wasn't having that.

"I'll throw in fifty," Will said.

"Me too," Mac said.

Andre looked at them, unaware of what they were raising money for.

"Tell me, Andre," Mac asked casually, "is the young woman in the office your sister?"

"No," Andre said, "that is my wife."

It was the least cheerful Andre had been so far.

"Ahh, the trouble and strife," Mac said.

"The ball and chain," Will added.

"The bag for life," Judah said, and then wished he hadn't.

They spent thirty seconds in silence, as if they were remembering fallen heroes, and then Andre said, "More beer?"

They were back on track and when Andre left, Rick said to Judah, "Done." It was his way of subsidising Judah's trip without being too obvious about it. Although he had a feeling Judah was going to have to work for his money.

"Where are we going to eat?" Will asked

They looked at their beers and the comfort of their surroundings and Judah correctly figured out that the route to seducing Andre's wife would be to spend more money.

"Here?" Judah said.

It didn't take long to indicate to Andre that more meat was required and Will had a quick look through the kitty. It had sustained sizeable losses already, and twenty minutes later Andre brought in the food, which they tucked into with the relish that only a day's skiing and a handful of beers, could ensure.

"Fifty euros," Will demanded, peering into the plastic wallet.

Judah looked in his wallet. He'd visited the cash machine and it hadn't been very responsive. He feared that the vice chancellor had made an unfavourable decision regarding his employment.

"Tomorrow," he said to Will.

Will doubted there would be money tomorrow, as did the others, but it didn't matter. It was part of the sport. They'd had a few beers already and, despite the weightiness of the previous evening, they were good for a few more.

"Five more of my finest lagers?" Andre asked, forgetting they were one short.

"What else," Mac said.

Judah looked through the crack in the door at Andre's wife. He knew what he had to do. There was no avoiding it. He was going to have to try and charm her. But she had a face like a bruised shovel. It was as if a smile hadn't flashed by in years. Andre came back to the bar.

"Will you be introducing us to your wife?" Judah asked.

Judah had intended to say lovely wife, but he couldn't quite manage it. That might be too obvious or, worse, seem like he was taking the piss.

"My wife?" Andre said, as if someone had asked to inspect the drains.

Andre had been in this business a long time. He'd seen many things. He'd heard many tall tales and strange requests. But no one had ever asked to be introduced to his wife.

"I shall ask," Andre said, less than confidently.

He went to the office. His wife did the accounts and, as he hated the accounts, he had no objection, although he suspected she used it as an opportunity to restrict his pocket money. She was quite controlling and she didn't like to interact with the punters.

"Ma puce," he began.

His wife looked up. This was a term of affection, literally meaning my flea, and the fact that he had deployed it suggested he was after something. A little part of her tensed. He often deployed it when he was in pursuit of sex and it looked like this time was going to be no more successful.

"Oui," she said slowly and with, an outsider might observe, some malice.

"Ça va?" he asked.

Obviously this was tactically a disastrous move, although it reflected his every move with his wife. Everything he did was wrong. He looked down. She was going through the lost property. She was a little more ruthless with it than him. A couple of years ago a group of Englishmen had appeared wearing Superman outfits.

They'd left them behind and he'd wondered what to do with them.

"Poubelle?" she asked.

Andre shrugged and finally got to the point.

"My English friends would like to meet you," he said.

The words hung in the air like the smell of decaying meat, at least that was what her expression suggested, and she looked at him. Andre knew he couldn't get his wife to do something she didn't want to do. It had characterised their sex life.

"You will have to meet them soon," Andre said.

Andre was going to see his mother. She'd phoned him suggesting that she wasn't feeling well. She did this every now and again to get Andre to visit her and, for the most part, Andre's wife had no objection. She had quite a valuable house. And Andre didn't mind either, as it gave him an opportunity to stray.

"Perhaps later with the Génépi," Andre said, and grabbed a full bottle.

He knew this would irritate her. She'd have no way of controlling the flow of the Génépi and he intended to be very generous with it. He left the door open. She looked out at the group of men until one, the one who wore his hair long, looked in. For a second it seemed as if he'd caught her eye. It made her nervous.

"How do we define charm?" Judah asked, leaning in and lowering his voice.

Judah was preparing his campaign. If all it required was a smile, that didn't seem too difficult in return for a week's spending money.

"Good question," Rick said.

Rick was the negotiator, and while he was more than happy to give his money away to Judah, he wanted him to work for it. It was for their entertainment.

"More than just a smile," Rick said.

The others agreed and, were she not married to Andre, who was their principle purveyor of beers, they would have been a little inclined to push for a full seduction. But, looking at Andre's wife, that seemed a little cruel. They were friends, after all.

"We need her to come out of the office with a smile on her face and greet you," Rick said.

The others nodded. This was the terms of engagement. Judah was grateful it didn't require much more and finished his beer. He was going to require a level of fortification. He looked up at Andre, who was walking their way with a bottle, and he made a motion with his hand for another round. Andre stopped, put the bottle on the bar, and poured five more beers. He'd stopped marvelling at the Englishman's capacity for consuming lager, but he remained grateful of it. A bar full of Frenchman watching their national team rarely drank as much as five Englishmen with a thirst on.

"Five of my finest lagers," Andre said forgetting again they were one short.

The bar was emptying and Andre was clearing tables around them. The evening was coming to an end, although if they'd ordered more lagers, he would have brought them. But he could see that they were slowing down.

"Would you like to join me at the bar?" Andre asked.

They got up, cleared the table for Andre, and walked the short walk to the wide, mahogany bar, which had acquired the scars of the vast number of drinks that had crossed it. They sat on the collection of stools.

"Génépi?" Andre asked.

As this was clearly on the house, the answer was a number of thankful nods. Andre sloshed it into the glasses with little attention to the remaining polish on the bar. That would irritate his wife. There were seven glasses on the bar. He turned and said in a loud voice, "Ma puce!" Andre's wife bristled. She had a natural facility for bristling and she made a mental note to deny sex to Andre for a further month as punishment.

"Oui," she said, with all the enthusiasm and charm of a traffic warden.

In another life she might have trained short haul carriers in the dark arts of indifference, but meeting Andre had changed that. But she was aware that this put her in an awkward position. She had to tend the bar soon, so she might as well put them off now, she reasoned. She got up. She tugged down her Decathlon sweat shirt. It was the flamboyant pink one, as the others were in the wash. She entered the bar with the grace of a dog who'd just crapped on the carpet.

"Ma puce," Andre said warmly.

He watched with pleasure as she seethed inside. This, he knew, was not going to help the drought that was his sex life, but he had plans. He wasn't just going to his mother's.

"Mac, Will, Rick and Judah," Andre said.

It had not been difficult remembering their names. This *was* his business. They nodded and mumbled their greetings, except Judah who stood up from his stool and offered his hand. It hung there for a while as Andre's wife looked at, as if he'd just unblocked a toilet with it, until she reluctantly took it and Judah leaned in and kissed her on both cheeks. She hadn't seen that coming and her face managed to redden and darken at the same time. She stiffened. There were more friendly gargoyles hung on the outside of churches. Judah had felt the cold of her skin. He'd encountered stone statues with more warmth. This was not going to be easy money.

"Enchanté," Judah said and stepped back.

He attempted to hold her gaze, but she wasn't having any of it. Her face was slumped, as if gravity had just stepped up a couple of notches, and was pulling it to the ground. Andre realised he'd underestimated her reaction. This was going to cost him and he knew she was hunting for an excuse to leave. Then her eyes fell on the bottle of Génépi between them. Andre grabbed it and poured more into the glasses which had been collectively emptied. One gaze from his wife and anyone could down the hardiest of alcoholic drinks.

"A bientot," Andre's wife muttered, although it didn't sound like she wanted to see them soon.

She grabbed the bottle of Génépi before Andre could give more of it away. But they were all feeling tired and wrapped the evening before it could get too messy.

Chapter Forty-Two

Sir Harry Panter was masturbating in the bath. It had been a terrible day and he was finding a way to ease the pain. There was a large scotch by the side of the bath. It had helped, but it wasn't enough. He'd walked through the House and he'd heard people mocking him. They were making groaning noises and saying 'harder, harder'. He had become a laughing stock.

"Damn and blast," Sir Harry said.

And he'd so very nearly made it. For a moment everything had aligned in his favour, like those spinning staircases in Harry Potter, and the keys to Number 10 were practically his. And then those staircases had rearranged themselves and directed him to the rubbish tip. His career was in the tip.

"Sod it," he muttered.

He'd given up masturbating. He wasn't getting anywhere. It was as limp as his career. He looked at it. Was it getting smaller? He hoped not. He'd spoken briefly to Rumball, although he'd sensed that Rumball no longer had the time for him, and he was sure that he'd said something which implied he'd lost his balls too. It was as if the situation couldn't get any worse. It was so bad he'd almost thought about going to the country and seeing his wife. But she didn't have time for him either. His phone was vibrating. He picked it up.

"Hello," Sir Harry said.

It was Shankly. Shankly wasn't Sir Harry's kind of chap. He was coarse, and had the manners and disposition of a concentration camp commander. He wasn't big on pleasantries.

"The fucker's left the country," Shankly growled.

"Oh," Sir Harry said.

This scandal had reduced Sir Harry from the shit-kicker he could occasionally be to the kind of man who said effete things like 'oh'. He tried to think of something useful to say.

"Do we know where he might be?" Sir Harry enquired.

He was aware that his voice still had that effete tone and he wondered what he should do about it.

"We don't," Shankly said. "But we can find him."

"Good," Sir Harry said uncertainly.

Sir Harry was still entirely rudderless with not the slightest idea how to proceed. He knew that when he'd finished with Shankly he'd run some more hot water. He'd probably have to stay in the bath until he could come out of the political wilderness.

"We could send some boys over," Shankly suggested.

"Boys?" Sir Harry said a little alarmed, "What do you mean?"

Sir Harry had thought he was talking to a lawyer, not a gang land thug, not that he'd met any. But he was desperate. He'd do anything to restore his reputation.

"Intimidation," Shankly said.

Sir Harry took a sharp intake of breath. While he thought this Judah character was clearly a bit of a rotter, he didn't want to get himself into any further trouble. He'd worked bloody hard to be as legitimate as possible. He'd moved his offshore money, declared his dividends, resigned from posts in which he might seem partisan. It was why he was attempting to masturbate in the bath. It stopped him straying into all the temptation that a man with money, power and good looks could be prone to.

"Of the legal kind," Shankly added.

That sounded better. Sir Harry didn't know what it meant, or what it would cost. But it was action and, as the only thing he could think of doing was masturbating, and he was unable to even do that, it sounded like a plan.

"Excellent," Sir Harry said with more confidence.

And the line went dead. Shankly had been given his orders and he hadn't bothered to garnish them with his goodbyes. Sir Harry felt better. There was a Bill that night he was interested in that wouldn't hit the table until at least ten, and probably wouldn't start voting until midnight. He'd go back into the House. More than that, he'd confront the mockers. He wasn't going to take any more shit. Sir Harry lay his hands on the side of the bath to ease himself out and then he looked down. Was it him, or did his penis look rather more substantial? He leant over and ran more hot water into the bath and took himself in hand. He had plenty of time.

Chapter Forty-Three

Andre's wife was having a disturbed sleep. She suspected her husband of having an affair, but she'd thought that ever since they'd met. One part of her thought she shouldn't care. Why should she pander to his whims, or even the whims of society? She was her own person. It wasn't her fault that her face did not fall into a natural default expression which resembled the popular conception of happiness. She was happy in her misery, wasn't she? Andre was snoring. He could sleep through an earthquake.

Her sleep had been a little more fragile and delicate, which were two adjectives which had never been applied to her. She was tossing and turning. Someone had left a woman's magazine in the bar, and it had fallen into lost property, and she'd nearly thrown it away. Nearly, but not quite. She'd read it secretly. It was a little shocking. She was shocked by the things women did to retain their appalling husbands. She couldn't see the point. She looked at Andre. He grunted, farted and turned over. Why, she asked herself, did she need that in her life?

She wafted the duvet and then wished she hadn't. She hated to admit it, but she was pretty sure she could tell what her husband had eaten from the smell of his farts. Who needs to live that closely to someone? She also knew what his mother was going to feed him, and she'd keep a nose out for anything that smelled more exotic. It had happened before and the till had been short a hundred euros. There had been a piece in the magazine about women taking revenge against their cheating husbands. She'd really enjoyed that. She thought about it a bit, and concluded that if there was incontrovertible evidence of Andre meandering, she'd rather keep him at home and torture him than let him leave. She wouldn't want him to leave.

She really wished she hadn't thought that. How the hell was she going to get to sleep with a thought like that buried in her mind? It was Andre's fault. If she didn't have reason to believe that he might philander, then she wouldn't be thinking what she was thinking and, if she wasn't thinking that, she'd be asleep. His snoring was getting louder. She wondered if she should wake him up. But if she did he might get the wrong idea. She wasn't having that. There was another piece in the magazine about keeping your man and it involved doing some quite revolting things. If they really had to have sex she was perfectly happy on her back, and he could kiss her mouth if he wanted to, and he could even insert his tongue. Most other insertions were forbidden. She turned over and tugged the duvet.

There was yet another piece in the magazine that had also disturbed her. It was about the menopause, and she was pretty certain she was going through it. There were hot flushes and occasional irrational thoughts popping into her head. They upset the natural order of things. She'd read about the absurd urges of some shameless women and she pitied them for their lack of dignity. That they should stoop so low. That was the upsetting thing about these strange thoughts, although they were less thoughts, and more urges. There was obviously a biological reason for it, and she had no control over it. It might be her body's last chance to procreate and she was a victim of nature.

"Putain de merde," she muttered.

She was having one of those hot flushes. Worse, she was wondering if she did wake up Andre, and he did get the wrong idea, whether that would be so bad. She found that thought process a little horrifying. She promised herself that she would throw the magazine away the following day. It had put strange ideas in her head. It was either that, or the Englishman who wore his hair slightly long. He'd looked at her in the most piercing way. She didn't know such a thing was possible. She turned over again. She was not going to let herself think about that.

Chapter Forty-Four

Will had got everyone up early, but they were all a little slow and creaky. They were getting on a bit. Will gave them tea and encouraged them to get dressed until eventually he led them out and suggested a 'warm up'. And that was what Rick had intended to do. But his mind had wandered and he'd picked up speed again, and with it the cool wind on his face had blown the cobwebs away. When Rick reached the same drop he'd flown over the pervious day he didn't recognise it and then, when he did, he was going too quickly. He knew this was a little suicidal, but another part of him thought it would be okay. Rick had a fleeting thought about learning from his mistakes – the kind of thing he might say to Judah – but, by the time he applied the brakes, he was airborne. He flew for a while, but he was buoyed up by the feeling that he didn't mind what happened. It was quite liberating. When he landed he was going even faster and he waved goodbye to the others, who had no intention of keeping up with him, and he carried on down the mountain.

When Rick got to Les Menuires he thought about stopping in case the others had followed him, but he realised there was more down to go, after which there was still more down. Eventually he made it to a pretty town which looked more like a functioning village than a ski resort. The only way from here was up. It reminded him briefly of something a grief councillor had said, and then he was reminded about a joke about a grief councillor – his grief councillor died, but he'd done such a good job he got over it immediately. Rick used to be a very focused person, the sort that was currently called goal-driven, but now his mind couldn't focus on anything. Or he kept it that way to make sure it didn't focus on something that hurt him.

He looked around. This was St Martin de Belleville. It was lower down and the fringes of the snow were tinged with green as the grass was pushing through. He'd got to the end of the run and he stopped, took his skis off, and walked into a bar. It was a little less polished than the bar in Val Thorens, with plastic chairs and table cloths, but it had a charm of its own. Despite the money Rick had made he was often just at home in the workers' bar, as he was in the Ritz. He'd met people who'd worshipped the accumulation of money and defined themselves by it, but he was less impressed by it.

"A beer, please," Rick asked the barman.

He wondered if he should have asked in French, but he'd yet to encounter someone who didn't speak English. It was the bane of the Englishman abroad. Rick decided to make more of an effort.

"Une pression s'il vous plait," he said.

The barman raised his eyes and a stream of what he assumed was language spewed from him. Rick was unable to identify a single word.

"Only kidding," the barman said.

His accent didn't sound French. It didn't sound English either.

"Are you Australian?" Rick asked.

"Bloody right, mate," the Australian said.

He handed Rick his beer with a smile.

"The name's Rick," Rick the Australian said.

"Me too," Rick said.

"Cheers to that," Rick the Australian said.

"What brings you here?" Rick asked.

"The skiing and the women," he said.

"In which order?" Rick asked.

"I'm not choosy," Rick the Australian said.

In the next half an hour, and two further beers, Rick learned about the life of Australian Rick, which was entirely free of worry and stress.

"I have a theory," Australian Rick said.

Rick nodded waiting to hear Australian Rick's life philosophy.

"You start with your hierarchy of needs – food, shelter, sex," he began.

It was clear that Australian Rick did not have a long list of needs.

"And you stop there. Like a primitive human might have. Not burdening yourself with all the stuff that gives you stress, anxiety and hassle. Like the cat, Charlie."

Rick looked at Charlie the cat. The cat strolled casually into the sun, as if he was making an effort to be languid and relaxed. He looked like a cat who'd just Bogarted a substantial joint.

"Charlie," Australian Rick said, "Does not concern himself with the notion of a higher being, or existential thoughts, or the possibility of a universe populated with other creatures. He just does what he wants, when he wants."

As Australian Rick said this, Charlie the cat turned revealing quite the largest pair of testicles Rick had ever seen on any animal.

"Like that," Australian Rick said.

They watched as Charlie stopped and sprayed a tree with a never ending stream of his pheromones. It was quite a display.

"Excuse me," Australian Rick said.

As lunch was approaching the bar began to fill and, regardless of Rick the Australian's philosophy, he was forced, by virtue of the renumeration he received for his services, to serve them. Everybody is trapped in one way or another, Rick thought. Except Rick didn't have to be at the beck and call of any employer. In this regard he was entirely free. But he couldn't live like Charlie, the cat with big balls. His balls had been a bit deflated by events.

"Have this on me," Australian Rick said.

Another beer appeared in front of Rick. Even Rick worried that a fourth might be reckless, although these weren't like the large beers that Andre served. But he had to get himself back at some stage. He picked up the beer thinking that Charlie the cat wouldn't have given it a second thought.

"Cheers," Rick said.

Rick took the beer and went outside. Despite the low ambient temperature it was warm in the sun, and the chairs that had been empty on his arrival were now mostly filled, aside from a bench with a girl talking animatedly on her phone. Rick waved to her to see if she was okay with him sitting there, and she motioned for him to take a seat. Rick sat down and watched as people slid down the mountain. There was a small drag lift opposite and he imagined that was where he should go next. He should also get a map, but a little part of Rick wanted to follow the example of Australian Rick, and just go with the flow. He turned to face the sun. He'd spent the last year keeping himself busy and avoiding moments when he could be languid and relaxed like Charlie. It gave him time to think and he didn't like that. His thoughts were interrupted by a sobbing noise. It was the girl at the end of the table. He took a better look at her. She was less of a girl and more of a woman, maybe forty, although he couldn't tell, and, now that she'd removed her hat and sunglasses, he could see she was a very good looking one. Rick leaned over.

"Are you okay?" he asked.

The girl looked up. She really wasn't okay. Things had gone wrong, very wrong, and she lived in a small town in which everyone knew her. And she'd made a big mistake, a catastrophic error, and they'd ostracised her for it. It made her life feel very small. She had nowhere to turn and no one to talk to. Perhaps, she thought, she could unburden herself on a stranger.

Chapter Forty-Five

"Where the fuck is he?" Mac asked.

"No sign of the orange helmet," Judah said.

"Let's stop here," Will said.

They'd arrived at Les Menuires and made their way to the most centrally located bar. There was no sign of Rick. There were rows of table and chairs, which had begun to fill as the sun was out, and lunch was approaching. Mac went in. He looked around and came out with three beers.

"Beer time," Mac said.

Judah and Will didn't complain. They looked for a spare table until Judah spotted one and steered Mac in the direction of a table which was in full sun, but more crucially, located next to a table of young, blonde girls.

"Here," Judah said.

Mac didn't complain and they sat and admired the sun and the girls who, despite the ambient temperature, but as a consequence of the heat of the sun, began to remove clothing.

"Dutch," Judah observed.

"Will you ever change?" Mac asked.

When they'd been at university together Judah had been the quiet one until one day, as if a switch had been flipped, he became the rampant one. His life hadn't changed much since then.

"I don't think so," Judah said.

He'd checked Will's iPad that morning and it seemed as if the press had begun to grow bored of him. His moment of infamy had come and gone. That wouldn't stop the university firing him, or the charges being pursued, or Harry Panter or someone suing him.

"It's kind of put you in the shit," Mac said.

"Once again," Will observed.

"It kind of has," Judah acknowledged.

They drank their beer and Mac and Will looked at the skiers coming down the mountain, and the slightly less elegant architecture in Les Menuires. Judah was looking at the Dutch girls. One of the blonder girls had removed both her jacket and her fleece.

"Jesus Christ," Judah said.

Mac took his eyes off the slightly bizarre church, which was probably built in the seventies, and followed Judah's gaze.

"Jesus Christ indeed," Mac said.

A couple of the other girls had followed her example and they were now sunning themselves, with their eyes closed, wearing tight vest-like tops, and not very much else.

"Does no one wear a bra anymore?" Mac said.

"It seems not," Will said.

"I'm very grateful for it," Judah said.

The combination of the sun and the low ambient temperature was providing a display which Judah found very distracting.

"Hold on," Mac said.

The table next to them had cleared and a collection of middle aged women had filled it.

"You're not tempted by someone a little closer to your own age?" Mac asked.

Judah shrugged.

"There's no substitute for a young one," Judah said and then, giving it more thought, and as if he was presenting an analysis, "almost all women look good when they're young."

They looked at the young Dutch girls and then the middle aged women.

"If you look at the girl at the end, really look at her face, and then imagine it in twenty years time, what do you see?" Judah asked.

They looked at the structure of the young girl's face and attempted to picture it with a couple of decades of living imprinted on it.

"She looks like she might be fairly ordinary," Mac said.

"Exactly, but with youth and a general lithesome quality, she is currently a goddess." Judah said.

"Okay," Mac said turning to the table with the middle aged women, "if you look at that woman in the middle, she must have twenty years on her."

"More," Judah interrupted.

"Maybe more," Mac acknowledged, "but she's a good looking woman. What would she have been like twenty or so years ago?"

Judah looked at her and attempted the calculation. The woman was tall and elegant with good bone structure. If they'd guessed her age correctly she'd aged well.

"That woman would have stopped traffic," Judah said.

As he said it she turned and looked at him for a fraction of a second, and her eyes flickered into the tiniest of smiles, and she held his gaze for a millisecond longer than was necessary. And then she turned away.

"Interesting," Judah said.

Chapter Forty-Six

Rick wouldn't normally talk to single women, on their own and clearly in some distress. It might have been the beers, or Rick the Australian's life philosophy, or it could have been Charlie the cat with big balls. But, without thinking and perhaps reacting to someone who was unhappy, he'd slid over and there had been a pause. It was a pause in which the distressed woman weighed up whether she wanted to accept his help or reject it.

"Are you okay?" Rick asked.

She was someone who, until recently, had waltzed through life with a lightness of touch and an easygoing demeanour. She sniffled a little laugh. She clearly wasn't okay, far from it, but people had been rejecting her rather too often recently.

"Not really," she said.

"Can I help you?" Rick asked.

She couldn't immediately see how he could help her other than listening to her woes. But she wasn't sure she wanted to reveal them. She was, she hated to admit, ashamed.

"Can I get you a drink?" Rick asked.

She was nursing the remaining dregs of a beer and Rick, in an uncharacteristically bold move, picked up the glass and went into the bar. He found Rick the Australian.

"Two small beers, please," Rick asked.

Rick the Australian raised his eyes. St Martin de Belleville was a small town and gossip travelled fast. It moved at lightening speed around the bar.

"Be careful, mate," Rick the Australian said.

Rick could hear the note of caution and rather than ward him off it made him protective of someone he didn't even know. The Englishman rooting for the underdog.

"Why?" Rick asked.

Rick the Australian tapped the bar. He wasn't malicious by nature, and he didn't want to be cruel. But it was good gossip.

"She used to be a ski instructor, but she stole some cash, three or four hundred euros, I think. She got caught on the cameras and they kicked her out," Rick the Australian said.

"Why did she do that?" Rick asked.

Rick the Australian pondered this for a while. He hadn't really thought about her motive.

"Do you know, I've no idea," he said finally.

Rick walked out into the sunshine with the two beers, but the girl was no longer at the table. He sat down and was reminded of those who'd made a monumental mistake for which there are no consequences, and those who'd made a small mistake and lost everything. Although he could see that stealing money in a small community wasn't exactly a tiny mistake. He looked up and saw someone waving at him. It was the girl. She was standing by the drag lift with her skis on. He thought about ignoring her. But it seemed too cruel. He took another mouthful of beer, put his jacket and helmet on, got up and put on his skis. When he got to the drag lift she was already going up and he followed her. At the top she skied for a hundred metres until she arrived at another lift. She waited for him.

"I didn't want to stay there," she said.

As most people were at lunch they didn't have to wait long and, a few moments later, they were sat next to each other as the bench swayed slightly and took them up the mountain.

"I'm Rick," Rick said.

"Sondra," Sondra said.

It left an uneasy silence, as neither was sure who should go first.

"Did the barman tell you about me?" Sondra asked finally.

"He said you used to be an instructor," Rick said.

"And he told you why I'm not anymore?" she said.

Rick felt a bit embarrassed and nodded. There was a further silence interrupted by a fresh wind which brushed their faces. Rick felt it was his turn to speak.

"We have all made mistakes," Rick said.

It didn't seem enough and he searched for something to help appease her.

"Last week I lost my driving licence for speeding. I nearly went to prison and, if I'd had a job which relied on a car, I would have lost that too," he said.

Sondra raised her eyes. Speeding did not have the same criminal sting as theft, they both knew that.

"I used to work in finance. I once made a bad decision and lost the bank two million," Rick said.

They also both knew that a bad decision wasn't the same as committing a fraud, and if he'd done that he probably wouldn't be there. He needed to change the subject.

"Are you out of work?" he asked.

"Skiing is all I know," Sondra admitted.

Rick thought about his morning skiing fraught, as it was, with near collisions and crashes.

"You could teach me," Rick said brightly.

He looked closely at her. She had dark hair and bright eyes with a slight panda shadow where she'd worn sunglasses. It might have been the clear air, or the sunshine, or the white snow below them, but her brown eyes had a shimmering quality he hadn't seen in many women.

"Are you sure?" Sondra asked.

Rick had spent his life making decisions on instinct, although not so much on impulse, and he was sure.

"Of course, it will be fun," Rick said.

"If you're sure," she said.

"I am," Rick said, adding, "I could do with tuition, I nearly had a monumental crash,"

"If you're sure, but I don't know how much to charge," she said.

Rick wondered about the price of crisis. His had been Annie, which seemed like a much bigger turn of events than four hundred euros. That was the price of an airfare or a couple of tyres. He'd bought meals for that. Now that he thought about it, he'd bought bottles of wine that were more expensive.

"How much does the ski school charge?" Rick asked.

And the consequence of her theft was that she'd been ejected from her apartment, and her two children had fallen into the custody of her in-laws. It was as if she'd held up a bank with a shotgun.

"You mean, how much do they pay me?" Sondra asked.

And she'd lost her job. It was the only job for which she was qualified and the ski school was a closed shop. Sondra had become a virtual outcast. She was born in the Alps, practically on skis, and had spent her life in a small community. It wasn't until now that she realised just how small that community was, and how intolerant it could be.

"No, how much would I pay the ski school?" Rick asked.

There were other areas where the same applied. Rick had once known a banker who'd got caught insider trading more than once, and he was more or less banished. The last he heard he was running a children's adventure centre somewhere. But he wasn't a social outcast. London is a big city, people come and go.

"Are you sure?" Sondra asked again.

"Of course," Rick insisted.

"Where are you staying?" she asked.

"Val Thorens," Rick said.

"We shall finish there," she said.

She raised the bar as the lift reached its destination and they skied off. Sondra pointed to the left and he followed her. They hadn't quite agreed on the money and Rick didn't care. She skied in front of him and then she suddenly jumped, flipped and skied backwards. She was going as quickly backwards as Rick was going forwards. She assessed his style, and flipped back and then slowed to a halt.

"Not bad," she said, "but you need to work on your stance."

She dropped into a skiing stance and Rick copied it. She prodded his knees, and patted his back, and eased his shoulders back. Rick couldn't tell whether this was an impersonal, professional prod or something more, but she encouraged him to stand as he should.

"Better," she said, and she turned and skied down.

Rick paused for a second, conscious that he had, as Judah might have said, checked out her backside. He didn't have time to give it a further thought, as he followed her. She turned and shouted, "in my tracks."

Rick followed the clear curves she'd made in the snow and he noticed he had greater control that he'd had that morning. He was going as fast as he had before, but he felt he could stop if he had to. The afternoon passed in a flash until they arrived at a hacked up and lumpy section of piste which Rick recognised as the run that led back to Val Thorens. He'd had a good time.

"Tomorrow?" Rick asked.

"If you're sure," Sondra said.

"Of course," Rick said.

"Okay," Sondra said with a smile, "we'll meet tomorrow at 9.30?"

"Great," Rick said as she skied in one direction and he skied down to Val Thorens and the bar. It didn't take long to find the others. There was a collection of empty glasses in front of them.

"Where've you been?" Will asked.

Chapter Forty-Seven

Despite the outside temperature, which was some way below zero, it had been a torrid night. There was no other way of putting it. The sheets were covered in sweat. It didn't make sense. The dreams had flowed and they were lurid. Lurid had never happened before. They'd never even been mildly explicit. These were in another category and had prompted a cold shower.

"Putain de merde," Andre's wife muttered.

This was the menopause coming her way. It had to be. She was burning bright. But the cool shower brought things down and she went back to bed. Andre was at his mother's and, despite normally sleeping on the left side of the bed, she now seemed to be occupying all of it. Ten minutes later the lurid thoughts had returned and she was sweating again. She couldn't sleep. She got up again.

"Putain de merde," she said.

It might have been nerves. She hated running the bar. She never knew what to say. She couldn't understand why she was required to do more than just deliver the beer and take the money. Why do people require a conversation too? Worse, it was such an inconvenient time for the symptoms of menopause to suddenly appear. And the worse thing was that Englishman who wore his hair long. He kept looking at her. One time they'd accidentally locked eyes. It was certainly accidental as far as she was concerned. But it had never happened before. Or it had, but not for several decades. Maybe longer.

"Putain de merde," Andre's wife said again.

She'd tried to piece it together and that had made things worse. She was still blaming the menopause, but she feared it was something else, something worse than the menopause. The problem was that although she hated running the bar she didn't normally give it much thought. She was very good at being indifferent to the customers. She tried to think about something else. She wondered what she was going to wear the following day.

"Putain de merde," she said.

Andre's wife never gave her clothing a moment's thought. She wore jeans, which were slightly baggy, and a sweatshirt from Decathlon. She'd never thought about wearing anything else, so she had no idea why she should think it now. What was wrong with her?

"Damn the menopause," she said to herself.

She stopped thinking about what she was going to wear, and started wondering whether she should wear some mascara. And then she stopped herself. That just demonstrated the grip of the menopause. She hadn't attempted to apply makeup to her face since her sister's wedding and her sister had been divorced for years. She doubted she had any mascara. She went into the sitting room and turned the television on. They were talking politics. She hated politics and two hours later she woke up as the sun had come up.

"Putain de merde," she said.

She'd fallen asleep on the sofa, but the politics on the television hadn't changed much. Andre's wife took a shower. She wasn't in the habit of taking a daily shower, and she pretended that she'd forgotten that she'd had one the previous evening, as well as the cold one in the middle of the night. She drew on her baggy jeans and looked for a Decathlon sweatshirt. Then she stopped herself.

"Putain de merde," she said.

One part of her mind was reasoning that it wouldn't be a bad thing to experiment with clothing which hadn't been bought at a huge sports store. She was, after all, interfacing with clients. Her choice of alternative clothing wasn't a vast one and she wondered if a summer dress would look strange. It was often hot in the bar and, god knows, she could be very hot indeed. Positively burning up. Returning space capsules had nothing on her. She hoped the menopause wasn't going to last long.

"Putain de merde," she said to herself.

She'd look a fool. But Andre wouldn't be there and the staff hardly noticed her. She put the dress on. It had a more plunging neckline than she'd remembered and she might have put on just the tiniest amount of weight. She found a safety pin. That sorted that. As a matter of curiosity, entirely academic and of no meaning she told herself, she opened the little drawer under the dresser. And there it was. The mascara.

It looked at her with malicious intent. It was like Clint Eastwood saying, 'Go ahead. Make my day'. It was quite alarming. But she knew plenty of women who wouldn't leave the house without it. She looked at it. It was the kind that professed its waterproofness. She decided to give it a go. It wasn't easy, as she had to apply it without her glasses. It was a kind of Catch 22. Ten minutes later she discovered two things. The first was the mascara had very nearly dried up. Very nearly but not quite, which meant there was sufficient for one eye. The other was that when they'd said it was waterproof they weren't kidding.

"Putain de merde," she said.

It was a phrase she was going to utter many times that day, but the eyeliner wouldn't shift. It seemed pretty permanent. That was embarrassing. She checked the time.

"Putain de merde," she said.

She couldn't understand how time had passed so quickly. She had to get down to open the bar. She looked in the mirror. Somehow there had been a battle between the slight weight she may have put on, and the safety pin. It wasn't clear who was winning. She re-fixed it. She looked at herself again. She put her glasses on. They were for reading, and she wasn't that close to the mirror, which meant her view was a little blurry. Blurry was good. She had to go. She cursed the menopause again, as that was clearly the problem, and she left the apartment.

"Putain de merde," she said for no particular reason.

Chapter Forty-Eight

The following day Rick left the others and met Sondra at the piste above Val Thorens, where she'd suggested the previous day. He did so a little hastily.

"What's that about?" Mac asked.

Will shrugged.

"Best to give him some space," he said.

They watched as Rick skied off at great speed either to get there quickly, or dissuade the others from following. For reasons he couldn't explain, or chose not to, he'd mentioned to the boys that he was thinking of taking a lesson, and he'd exaggerated the cost to put them off. The previous evening had involved less beer, although about the same amount of wine. He felt a little battered, but not too bad.

There were a large number of people also waiting for instructors and a huge gaggle of small children who looked like R2D2 units, as they were short, helmeted and wearing goggles. A figure slid by him.

"Good morning," Sondra said.

He would never have recognised her, and it occurred to him that it probably wasn't a good place to meet, as they were surrounded by her former colleagues.

"This way," Sondra pointed, "we'll start with a warm up."

Although her English was good she pronounced 'this' as 'zis' which, for no particular reason, made Rick smile. He followed her as she skied expertly until she came to a halt and turned. She pointed down a piste.

"You ski and I'll follow to see what you've learned," she said with a smile.

Rick felt a little apprehensive. He was being judged and, although it was for his benefit, he wasn't used to that. Or maybe it was something more. Her tone had lost the warmth of the previous day.

"Go," she prompted.

Rick went down the slope gently and in the manner he thought was expected of him, which was a good deal less maniacal than the previous day, but was neat and controlled. When they got to the bottom there was only a small collection of people and no instructors. She removed her helmet and her hair tumbled out like a television commercial. She took off her sunglasses and a scarf that hid the rest of her face. And she smiled.

"Good morning," she said again.

Rick was a little taken back by it and then he realised he should do the same. When he did she leant in to kiss him. It was a formal kiss, and of no more significance than shaking a hand, but it gave him a little jolt.

"Perhaps we can meet here tomorrow," she said.

Rick understood why and nodded and smiled. Sondra put her sunglasses and goggles back on and resumed her disguise and her tone.

"You need to move your legs more and your body less and you need to stand like this," she said.

She assumed a skiing stance and Rick attempted to copy it. She leaned over and prodded him in a few places like a rag doll until he was standing in the same way. It made him giggle although he wasn't sure she'd noticed. The skiing gear was quite insulated, like a space suit. When she'd finished and seemed satisfied, she turned and looked at him.

"Where would you like to go?" she asked.

"Wherever you think," he said.

She considered this. As she'd been skiing in that area all her life she didn't require a map and she knew she'd be more comfortable if she was a little further away from her home town.

"I think you can ski faster," she said.

"I can," Rick said with a smile.

And with that she turned and shot down the hill. It took Rick a second to catch up and then he followed her. It wasn't quite as fast as he'd travelled the previous day, but it was pretty brisk and she turned and pointed to the tracks she'd made in the snow. This was an instruction to follow the same route and Rick obeyed. A moment later they arrived at a point which required speed in order not to grind to a halt on the upward course that followed. They were going in a straight line. Once they got up some speed, Sondra jumped into the air and turned a hundred and eighty degrees. She was now skiing backwards at the same pace as he was struggling to go forwards. She made gestures indicating how he should be standing and then flipped herself back in the right direction and somehow accelerated. Now Rick was really motoring.

When they got to the bottom they took a lift which took them high and then they skied across to another and then a further lift until they were by the glacier. The sky was blue, and Rick had loosened his jacket and then opened the vents in his trousers. Now that they'd moved to a less popular area there were fewer people queuing for the lifts until they found themselves sitting side by side and on their own.

"It's a beautiful day," Rick said.

"It is," she said, adding, "you can see the snow melting in the sun."

The texture of the snow was changing fast and they squinted as the chairlift faced directly into the sun. There was a small distant boom.

"Avalanche canon," she said by way of explanation.

Rick nodded and looked into the distance. She wasn't sure what to say.

"You learned everything about my life and told me nothing about yours," Sondra said eventually.

He couldn't see her eyes, but he could hear the tone no longer had the edge that she'd used when she was instructing him. Rick smiled, but didn't say anything. He'd not volunteered information about his own life to anyone for years. That was one of his problems.

"Do you have a wife?" she asked.

Even though he knew she was going to ask, he always felt like it was a smack in the face, as he could never deny her existence, even if she was no longer alive. Despite that he kept it simple.

"No," he said.

"Children?" she asked.

"Sadly, not," he said.

"Gay?" she asked.

He turned to her, a little affronted, and she smiled.

"I thought not. Do you live with your mother?" she asked.

He knew she was teasing him now, but he couldn't think of a witty reply. He knew he had to take control of the conversation. He knew he had to overcome his resistance to reveal a little of himself. But she was ahead of him.

"What is your work?" she asked.

Rick was still arranging his thoughts, when she decided to take a guess.

"Are you a dentist?" she asked.

Rick would have bared his teeth to demonstrate that this was unlikely, but he felt if he did he'd look like a horse showing its age.

"An architect?" she asked.

He shook his head.

"A plumber?" she said and then added, "No, I've seen your hands. You work in an office."

Rick smiled. This was closer. He'd given up trying to take over and decided to let the enquiry take its own course.

"A bank," she said.

The difference between what he did, or what he used to do, and a banker was considerable, but it was too complicated to explain or, more importantly, not remotely interesting.

"Kind of," he settled on.

Five minutes later they were back on the snow. Despite the altitude it was warm and he took some pleasure in passing slower traffic as she always seemed to pick a route which made it possible.

"Where are we going for lunch?" Rick asked.

"Are you taking me to lunch?" she asked.

"Of course," he said.

"How much do you want to pay?" Sondra asked.

"I don't care," Rick said.

She pointed down the mountain and said, "Courcheval." That, they both knew, was one of the most expensive resorts in the Alps.

"Isn't it full of Russians?" Rick asked.

Sondra shrugged. She hadn't expected him to buy her lunch, but had no objection if he chose to.

Chapter Forty-Nine

Al was used to having his sleep interrupted, as he often worked nights followed by day shifts. But today the movement of the hospital had woken him up. It was that and the need to take a piss. He hated to admit it to himself, but that was an increasing requirement. One of the tragedies of getting old, he'd decided. The nurses were less friendly than the doctor, and they gave him breakfast, which was not brilliant, although it bordered on a gastronomic masterpiece by the standards of the British system. He knew the biggest problem with any hospital stay was the boredom, so he hoped to see the man in the suit and get the hell out of there. By lunchtime he'd not arrived. Eventually he asked a nurse, who didn't speak a single word of English, but conveyed the message that he didn't work on Mondays. How could you expect him to? An hour later he approached another nurse.

"I'd like to leave," he said.

Once again no one seemed to have even the slightest understanding of one of the world's most universal languages. He could see the machinery marked in English, yet no one appeared to speak it. He'd have made a run for it, but it looked like they weren't going to release his clothing until the issue with the insurance was resolved.

"Helicopter," one of the nurses explained rubbing her fingers together in the universal sign of money.

Al knew this, as he'd worked with helicopter rescue crews, and he'd been told that a big machine – much like the one that had picked him up – cost a thousand quid an hour in fuel alone. He always liked the jobs where real help was required. He wasn't so keen on people who were self destructive.

"When will the doctor be in?" he asked.

It took a moment for them to understand that and they pointed to the clock. Later it seemed. That would give him something to look forward to in a dull day. He took his phone out and called the insurance company. It rang for a while and they reassured him that his call was very important to them, and then proceeded to give him about half a dozen options none of which applied to the position he'd found himself in. He went for sales as, in his experience, they tended to answer far faster than claims. He was right.

"I'll have to put you through," a voice said.

It returned him to the same schedule of options and he tried the claims department. Despite the apparent importance of his call, he waited for twenty minutes until finally a bored voice told him.

"That's not covered by the claims department. I'll just put you through," the voice said.

Before he had the opportunity to plead with them, he was back to the main menu, and the many options which didn't apply. Ten minutes later he was through.

"So you say you've paid for another year?" the voice said.

Al said he was certain even though he was becoming less certain. He was sure he'd seen something on his statement and he should have started with that. Then the line went dead. It took a moment to realise it was his phone.

"Damn," he muttered.

He looked at the phone in frustration. It was quite an obscure make, as he'd got fed up with his iPhone, and wasn't prepared to pay for a Samsung Galaxy and consequently he'd entered into a contract for a thing called a Fairphone. He wondered if any of the nurses had a charger. He got up, grabbed the crutch which was leaning against the wall and had been given to a previous patient, readjusted it and staggered into the corridor and towards the nurses station. He showed them his phone. It was the kind of phone which prompted laughter in people. It wasn't *that* basic. He showed them the hole where a charger could be attached.

"Non," they said.

That meant he was going to have to wait for the man in the suit who didn't work Mondays. He hoped he worked Tuesdays. It was time for dinner. It wasn't bad and he put the television on. He didn't understand very much and it wasn't very interesting. He decided, because he could, to take a nap. He woke with a jolt and found the smiling doctor looking in on him.

"Are you well?" the smiling doctor asked.

Al was feeling much better now that the smiling doctor was here, as no one else seemed to understand him.

"I'm fine," Al said, "but they won't let me leave."

The smiling doctor inspected his ankle although, with the cast, Al couldn't see why, or what he'd achieve. But it was reassuring and he handled it carefully.

"A problem with your insurance?" the smiling doctor asked.

"Yes, I tried getting through, but my phone run out of battery and I don't have a charger," Al explained.

"Perhaps, I can find you one," the smiling doctor said.

Al took out his phone and showed it to him. The smiling doctor turned it round as if he was unable to identify it as a mobile phone.

"The nurses don't have one," Al said.

"I'm not surprised," the smiling doctor said.

He gave the phone back to Al and, for the first time, Al wished he'd bought another iPhone. It wasn't the functionality, it seemed to work as well as the phone that had preceded it, it was more that he feared it made him a social pariah. What was wrong with society? Or what was wrong with him?

"And the man in the suit doesn't work on Mondays," Al said.

The smiling doctor laughed. One of the nurses came in and caught his attention and then he disappeared with a wave. Al was back on his own. Al had wanted to explain to the smiling doctor that, he too, worked in the medical business, but he always found that doctors could be very variable in their response to that. Some had worked with, and respected paramedics, and others looked down on them.

Al wondered what he'd say if he retired. He'd been defined by being a paramedic and he couldn't imagine being defined by being retired. It sounded too much like doing nothing, which didn't sound great.

Chapter Fifty

"You will see me," Shankly said.

The vice chancellor hated confrontation. He'd led a quiet life as a respected academic and would have remained one until his wife read a piece about vice chancellors and their salaries in the Slime-Online.

"I'm a little busy," the vice chancellor protested.

"I don't give a fuck," Shankly said.

The vice chancellor was rather taken aback. He would have thrown him out of the office, but he didn't have the courage. It was all his wife's fault. She couldn't believe just how highly paid some vice chancellors were, and she'd grown fed up with their twelve year old Honda and holidays in Cornwall. She'd told him she hated Cornwall.

"I think that's a little inappropriate," the vice chancellor said.

But the vice chancellor couldn't quite meet Shankly's eyes. He found himself walking backwards until he nearly tripped over his desk. His wife had also told him she wanted Caribbean holidays and granite worktops.

"Okay, what can I do for you?" the vice chancellor managed to say.

And his wife had got them. She'd also acquired a membership at the local golf club, personal tuition from a world renowned pro, as well as a wardrobe full of designer labels and a collection of handbags. The vice chancellor had no idea she was so interested in material things.

"Judah Wheeler," Shankly spat.

The vice chancellor looked through his papers, as if he hadn't the slightest idea who Judah Wheeler was, and the problem might go away. This was a big mistake.

"Don't fuck with me," Shankly said.

The vice chancellor was fairly sure he'd said he was a solicitor and he'd never heard a solicitor talk this way before. It was quite shocking.

"Oh yes, of course. A most unfortunate incident. Very regrettable," the vice chancellor said.

Shankly waited. He could have sent someone else, but no one in the office did this sort of thing as well as he did. And he was enjoying himself. He began to tap his fingers on the desk. It would have put anyone on edge, but the vice chancellor was already at the edge, and in danger of tumbling down.

"And?" Shankly demanded.

He'd once confronted an East End crime boss. He'd not sworn then, as that was a language the man could understand. But it was perfect for the vice chancellor. The man was oozing panic.

"I'm sorry," the vice chancellor stuttered, "And what?"

Shankly drew in his breath. He took a very long time doing it, as if he was inflating a large balloon, and he could see the vice chancellor's hands. They were shaking.

"What have you done?" Shankly demanded.

The vice chancellor had done very little. He favoured the path of least resistance. He'd operated the same policy with his wife and she appeared to be much happier, although there were moments when her credit card statements made him pretty angry.

"I've attempted to schedule a meeting with him," the vice chancellor said very reasonably.

"After which?" Shankly asked.

After which, the vice chancellor hoped, the sordid mess would go away and he wouldn't have to deal with it. But he sensed this wasn't the answer that Shankly was looking for.

"We shall review his position here," the vice chancellor finally managed to say.

"And?" Shankly asked.

Shankly was growing bored. He needed to hurry this along to an appropriate conclusion.

"And you will fire him," Shankly said.

"Well, there are legal considerations," the vice chancellor said.

Shankly leaned over. He took out a business card and placed it on the leather-topped desk. He placed his hand over the vice chancellor's and drew his face close.

"You do not need to worry about the legal issues," Shankly said.

The vice chancellor was not the most intuitive of men, but he recognised the path of least resistance in this negotiation.

"He's fired," the vice chancellor said quickly.

"Excellent," Shankly said, adding, " and do you know where I can find him?"

The vice chancellor was now more than happy to tell all. He'd offer his wife if it would get this man out of his office, although his wife was currently in Paris.

"No, but I understand from the television that he has gone on a skiing trip," the vice chancellor said.

Shankly leant back. His work was almost done here. It had been a thoroughly enjoyable hour, which he'd bill as two hours, and which made his job worthwhile.

"His mobile phone number," Shankly said.

It wasn't a question and the vice chancellor produced it as quickly as his shaking hands would allow.

"Here," the vice chancellor said.

It would take most of the day, and very probably the rest of the week, for the vice chancellor to recover from this ordeal. He'd felt Shankly's breath and he wasn't entirely certain that his bladder hadn't loosened its hold on his morning cappuccino.

"Thank you," Shankly said and left the office.

Shankly knew a man who could track mobile phones.

Chapter Fifty-One

It was Rick that chose the restaurant and it was even more lavish on the inside than the outside had promised. It was part of a hotel and they removed their ski boots at the door. They could see a spa through a glass wall and a jacuzzi which lay outside and from which plumes of steam were rising.

"Nice," Rick said.

"Are you sure?" Sondra asked.

Her recent life had not included the lavish, and she feared that she was taking advantage of him. It didn't occur to her that he might want something from her, as he didn't appear to be like that.

"We've got our boots off now," Rick said.

A uniformed woman of sublime elegance led them to a table located next to a vast glass wall. It gave them a view of the mountains and despite the cold outside they were forced to remove further layers, until they were both in tee shirts. Rick tried not to look. But he had something he had to get off his chest.

"I was married, but my wife died," he said.

It was a simple sentence, but it was one he'd not uttered in the last eighteen months, as if he'd hoped it wasn't true.

"I'm sorry," Sondra said.

Rick didn't say anything, and the menu arrived a second later. It was fine dining and, for him, difficult to choose.

"Shall we go for the degustation menu?" he suggested.

This was the one with eight courses and, Sondra noticed, an eye-watering price.

"If you're sure," she said.

He wasn't sure if she was teasing him.

"I'm sure," he said.

The courses came with different wines that had been chosen to complement the various dishes, and with the wine they both relaxed a little. Sondra told him a little more about her life and her two children, and Rick did his best to reciprocate. When the final plate was cleared, an uneasiness returned as if they were both unsure how to proceed. Sondra went first.

"Coffee?" the waitress asked.

They looked at each other.

"As your ski instructor I suggest we get back to it," Sondra said.

"Of course," Rick said and made a gesture for the bill.

The bill arrived and Sondra tried not to look at it. He picked it up quickly and presented a card, but she'd seen it. Four hundred euros. What was life-changing for some was small change to others. They collected their things and stepped outside. The wind had increased and the weather began to look less hospitable. It was snowing hard. Rick could feel his legs aching from the morning's exertion and the time they'd spent in the warm restaurant.

"I know where I can buy you a coffee," Sondra said and skied into the gloom.

Rick followed her shadowy figure until she came to a halt.

"You have to let go here, otherwise you won't make it up the other side," she told him.

And with that she threw herself down the piste. Rick didn't stop to think whether the advice might have been a life lesson, and followed her a second later. He let himself go, as she'd instructed, and picked up speed quickly until the wind was whistling in his ears, and he was going too fast to worry about his aches and pains. He looked ahead. Sondra had leaned right over into a downhill skiing position and she was along way ahead of him. He knew he was going fast enough already, but he dropped his body in the same way, and soon he was hammering down the mountain with his legs and knees bobbing like suspension components in a car. A moment later he'd reached the bottom and the slope started to rise and with it he began to slow down. By the time he reached Sondra he was going little more than walking pace.

"Nice," he said with a smile.

"Over there," she said.

Rick could barely make out a snow-covered building through the haze and it looked like it was above them but, as they slid towards it, he knew it wasn't. A strange optical illusion, he thought. Inside there were low timber beams like an English country pub, and stuffed animals hiding in holes dotted around the room. There was a log fire in the corner and it seemed the natural place to gravitate to, although they had to strip down to teeshirts again.

"I'll get the coffees," Sondra said. "My treat."

Rick watched while Sondra went to the bar. He remembered something his Sensei had said about fighting: it involves concentrating but not thinking. It was something he'd held onto and it had distracted him. He was doing the same looking at Sondra, but it wasn't to distract him. Even in the skiing salopetes he could see she was slim-hipped yet curvy. Judah would have had something to say about that.

"Are you okay?" Sondra said, returning with two coffees.

"I'm fine," Rick said.

He took a sip of the coffee and said, "that tastes good."

"The best in the Alps," Sondra said.

Rick smiled.

"Didn't you say you studied music?" she asked.

Rick couldn't remember whether he had. He must have when he was trying to dredge up something about his life that didn't involve his wife.

"A long time ago," Rick said.

Sondra smiled and pointed at an old upright piano in the corner.

"The owner encourages people to play," she said.

Rick had a grand piano in the sitting room in the large house in Blackheath and he used to play after a stressful day. It was a form of therapy. But he hadn't played in eighteen months. He hadn't wanted to.

"I'm not sure," Rick said.

Sondra pouted. She hadn't pouted for a long time and, if she'd stopped and thought about it, she probably wouldn't have. But she could see Rick relenting. The pout still had power.

"What shall I play?" he asked.

"Whatever you want," she said.

Rick got up. He had no idea what he was going to play, but he often found that. When the keys were in front of him his fingers would know. He sat at the piano and opened it and his fingers, without consulting him, played Van Morrison's 'Brown Eyed Girl'. He sang along a little less confidently and missed out the last verse, which didn't have the optimism of the rest of the song. He didn't know why he'd done that. When Rick finished the room erupted with cheers and applause and it took him a beat to recognise it was for him.

"That was brilliant," Sondra said.

Rick smiled modestly. He'd missed a section, accidentally added a couple of beats and couldn't remember the words correctly, but he hoped he'd captured the spirit of the song. Sondra got up to kiss him in the sort of chaste way that the French are good at – holding no more significance than a greeting he reminded himself – but a little uncertainty arose in both of them, and she patted his arm. He sat down and shrugged modestly and a moment later they were talking about his skiing, and the uncomfortable moment had passed. From there Rick spoke about his friends, their history together, and their quirks until Sondra noticed the time.

"The lifts will close soon. We need to go," she said.

They got up and dressed slightly awkwardly and went outside. The weather appeared to have relented and the sun had reappeared. It was a short ski to a chairlift and they were heading back up the mountain. When they came off Sondra thought for a moment and took him towards a semi-pisted run, which she'd always liked. It was demanding, but she was confident he could do it. She wanted him to get value for his money.

"This way," she said.

Rick looked down a little dubiously. For some reason his reckless spirit had deserted him.

"Are you sure?" he asked.

"I'm sure," she said.

It had been one of the nicest days she'd had in years and that, and the wine at lunch, and the intoxicating atmosphere of the little bar, had influenced her judgement. When the ground shook she knew it was a mistake. When it came rushing towards them she grabbed his hand, and pointed him down the fall line. But the avalanche was travelling faster than them.

Chapter Fifty-Two

Andre's wife had been getting funny looks from the staff all morning. She'd ignored them, as she had most of the customers. She had a few issues with her dress, but nothing a safety pin couldn't handle. She was grateful that the unwelcome symptoms of menopause hadn't reappeared. She couldn't cope with that as well as running the bar. Not that she was running the bar.

Andre's wife sat at the rear of the bar with an expression on her face which did not say 'welcome'. As a young girl there had been many careers suggested to her, but none that included interfacing with the public. But when she'd met Andre things had changed. He'd been her skiing instructor and despite spending her entire life in the Alps, she'd never quite mastered it. Eventually he'd assumed that she was only taking personal lessons from him because she was interested in him, and he'd asked her out. There hadn't been a flurry of other offers and she'd agreed. That had been some time ago. A barman was waving at her. She had no idea why and hoped it wasn't the slightly flowery dress. Then she noticed the weight of people leaning against the bar, and waiting to be served, was becoming too much for the staff to handle. Andre's wife got up and begrudgingly served them. Although it gave her an opportunity to revisit the till, which was the item in the room with whom she had the most rapport.

"Deux bières," someone said to her.

It was more at her than to her, and she was almost inclined to ignore him, but she knew the till wouldn't fill itself. She stood side-on so that her single mascaraed eye wouldn't look strange. She'd tried wearing her glasses, but the beer and the tap produced issues with her focal point, and she'd poured most of it on the floor. Andre's wife did not like wastage. She presented the two beers.

"Merçi," the man said, and slapped a tenner on the bar.

She took it and, for no particular reason, a thought came into her head. A few weeks earlier she'd gone to fetch her aunt from the airport. The plane had been late and she'd watched as people came through the gates and their faces exploded with joy as they saw their loved ones.

"De rien," Andre's wife said reluctantly.

Literally, it was nothing. Andre's wife's face had never exploded with joy. It was unlikely that the muscles which lay under the flesh were capable of it, as if they'd sat in a hospital bed for years, not done a great deal of exercise, and had atrophied. Her face had barely shifted from her default grimace when she'd seen her aunt. Although her aunt was a miserable cow. But buried in the back of her mind was a further thought. She suspected that these unexpected, uninvited and unwelcome thoughts were a further consequence of the menopause and, as she was not terribly cerebral by nature, she did not much care for them. But this one persisted as if it were practising to become a Jehovah's Witness.

"Madame," someone said.

It wasn't said with much charm and she was half inclined, were it not for the hunger of the till, to pretend she hadn't heard and go back into the office. But this was their busy period. People were coming off the slopes and grabbing beers and lunch. She raised her eyes in acknowledgment and the man, who was thirsty and on holiday away from a wife who monitored his drinking, decided to find another bar.

"Putain de merde," Andre's wife muttered under her breath.

The thought had returned. She was going through a really troubling time, what with the hot flushes, but this thought had jammed its foot in the door of her mind. Andre's wife tended to blame everyone else for their rudeness, but this thought had the temerity to suggest that they were only reacting to her. It was nonsense, of course, but there was no harm in experimenting with it. Testing it. She attempted to rearrange her face. It was reluctant, as it had spent the last thirty years looking as if someone with digestive issues had just broken wind.

"Bonjour," she said to someone who had approached the bar.

"Bonjour Madame," he replied.

And then he went on a rambling diatribe about what a beautiful day it was. What made him think she was interested? People were incredible. But he'd noticed her face fall, like she'd just had a stroke, and he ordered his drinks. And the thought began to nag at her again.

"Merçi," she said.

But he'd turned and was on his way to find a table. The experiment had been less than successful. But it wasn't her fault. Why had he chosen to test her smile stamina? She wanted to go back to the office, but people were piling in as if the beer was free. Thankfully it wasn't, far from it, and she consoled herself with that thought when she served someone else with her normal grimace intact. From a business point of view it was much more efficient.

"Bonjour," someone else said.

She could tell immediately he was English. She wasn't fond of the English. Andre loved them, but she was sure he just said that to irritate her. He seemed to do everything to irritate her. Andre's wife didn't like to get eye contact with the English, as it put them off assaulting her with their ghastly language. She barely knew a word. Although she wasn't too bad at numbers.

"Cinq bières," the voice said.

She nodded and began to pour and deliver the beers. That thought came back to her again. The thing was that she would have quite liked to have been greeted at the airport with an explosion of smiles. But that experience had always eluded her and she had no idea why. She was fairly sure, when she looked in her soul, she was a good person. Or a reasonable one. Or something.

"Merçi," a voice said.

But that was why the thought was tugging at her like a small child desperate to pee. Were people reacting to her? If that was the case she needed to attempt another rearrangement of her facial muscles. It was a bit of an effort, but she felt she'd done a pretty workmanlike job. She was never going to win an Oscar. That wasn't her thing. She didn't like to draw attention to herself like some people. But she could knock together a smile as much as anyone. Andre's wife looked up. And there he was.

"Salut," Judah said, with his well-practised charming smile in place.

Andre's wife realised she'd forgotten about serving side-on. She quickly shifted her legs, like a boxer, and then she looked at him. And in an instant the symptoms of menopause returned with a vengeance. And worse, her chest heaved. She had no idea what prompted the heave as it had not heaved before, in fact it had led an entirely heave-free existence. Today was its first heave and with it the safety pin gave up its unequal battle and pinged through the air. They watched until they heard a plopping noise. She looked down. It had landed in Judah's beer.

"Putain de merde," Andre's wife muttered.

There was clearly an elephant in the room and there was some debate afterwards as to what had happened next. There was no question that much of Andre's wife had tumbled out. Another way of putting it was that her décolletage had rearranged itself or, as most of the others put it, her tits fell out. But Judah, ever the seduction professional, had kept his eyes locked on hers. Or one of her eyes. It was hard to tell. He wondered if she had a glass eye. But in his peripheral vision he could see a sea of flesh. Andre's wife didn't know what to do. The eyes were locked in something close to an embrace and she could feel herself flushing. It was rising up uncontrollably. She wanted to say, 'putain de merde', and she didn't want to break the spell. But she did want to put her tits back in.

"Merçi bien," Judah said, and turned away so as not to embarrass her.

He took the beers back to the table and, as it was busy, they were in the far corner. It took a while for him to get there. But they'd seen. When he got there they were putting money in the whip.

"What's up, guys?" Judah asked casually.

"We're paying up," Will said.

"Respect," Mac said and gave Judah a little worship bow.

Judah's kitty had been paid for the week.

"Where's Rick?" Judah asked.

"No idea," Will said. "We've tried calling him."

Chapter Fifty-Three

Rick woke to a whiteness which could have been heaven or a hospital bed. It certainly wasn't hell. It was cold. It was a clear, but muted white light. He took a moment to find his bearings. He still couldn't locate them. Where the hell had his bearings gone? He stepped back a bit. Not physically, as he was trapped. He'd been skiing. His mind flitted through the day, the restaurant, and the bar with the piano, and then the ski back. He'd seen the snow move, but didn't immediately associate it with an avalanche. It was like the first televised tsunami in which people just looked at the receding sea and the fish flipping themselves in the sand, unaware of what was about to happen. Strangely the snow didn't seem to be moving *that* fast. He was wrong about that. Rick was buried in the snow. It was then that he realised that he was lying on top of Sondra. His elbows were dug into the snow either side of her. Their faces were inches apart. He could feel her breath.

"Sondra?" he said.

His focal point had moved away with age, but she seemed to be clear to him. They were in a kind of trapped embrace. An embrace, he realised, which had given them a small pocket of air. He guessed he'd not been out long, his recent high risk exploits had made him no stranger to being knocked out. He also guessed that the pocket of air wouldn't support them for long.

"Merde," Sondra said.

He looked at her. His eyes were adjusting to the light and he couldn't help noticing that Sondra, despite being winded and trapped under a pile of snow, had a kind of serene beauty. She also had brown eyes. He was certain he hadn't noticed that before.

"Are you okay?" he asked.

Sondra's eyelids flitted a little. She managed a smile.

"Oh, wonderful," she said.

She pronounced every syllable in a beautifully French way and Rick realised he was happy to be there. If this was how he was going to go, there could be worse ways. Too many people have a heart attack when they take their final shit. He wanted to kiss her. Rick had not wanted to kiss another woman in a long time. It didn't matter, as his natural English reserve stood in the way and, given that she was unable to move, it would seem a little bit rapey. That said, perhaps he should consider it when they're approaching their final breath.

"Spit on me," she said.

Rick was not, by nature, a fetishistic man and he'd never considered spitting on anyone in his life, and certainly not for pleasure. He wondered if she'd made a linguistic error.

"I beg your pardon?" he asked.

Sondra actually chuckled. He could feel her body against his. It sort of rippled.

"Spit on me," she said again.

For Rick it rather took the sheen away from what might have become a new, and long awaited romance, but there wasn't much air left and this appeared to be her last wish. He spat.

"Interesting," he said.

The saliva slid down the side of his mouth. It took him a beat to understand the significance of this. He wasn't on top of Sondra. She was on top of him. It sort of amused Rick.

"We don't always know which way is up," he said.

It was a philosophical thought and Sondra, as a Frenchwoman, interpreted it that way. They'd both had their lives turned upside down.

"Can you move your hands?" she asked.

He realised his hand was very probably resting on her breast. He couldn't have contrived that if he'd tried. He tried to move it. It was held with the weight of the snow and her own weight. She wiggled underneath him. It loosened. She wiggled a little more. He tugged and his hand sprang free. He pushed it up. As he did so snow fell and began to fill their air pocket.

"Shit," Rick said.

He stopped. If he pushed more he feared he'd lose their small space.

"The pole," Sondra said.

The strap to the pole had slid down his arm. They looked at it.

"I'll try and get a hand free," she said.

"Where's you hand?" Rick asked.

She began to move it.

"You've got to be kidding," he said.

Her hand was resting on his crotch. If this was fate attempting to get him close to a woman, then fate had a sense of humour. She wiggled her hand.

"That's nice," Rick said.

She smiled and Rick wiggled until her hand was released. She tugged the pole and it moved an inch at a time until she could plant one end of it in the snow. But the space wasn't big enough to push it into what they guessed was a vertical position.

"We're going to have to push it upright," he said, knowing that the snow might fall and fill their space.

"Rest a second," Sondra said.

They were breathing more heavily, which they both recognised as a bad sign.

"Go for it," Rick said.

They grabbed the pole and between the two of them they edged the pole into the space between them until it was as vertical as they could get it, although as they hadn't known which way was up, this was likely to be a bit hit and miss. They pushed it upward. The pole moved easily. It continued to move. Snow fell.

"Putain," Sondra said.

She'd heard many stories about people trapped in avalanches and she knew that if the surface was further than the length of the pole, then they were in big trouble. That would be a shame, as she'd been enjoying the day, and she hadn't enjoyed much for a while. The pole suddenly moved very quickly and they were rewarded with a blast of cold air.

"That's better," Rick said.

They weren't going to die, or at least not in the next few minutes. They took in urgent breaths. Rick could feel her body writhe on top of him.

"What next?" he asked.

If there had been a moment when a kiss was a possibility, it seemed to have passed. Survival was on the cards. He watched Sondra frown, as if she were thinking.

"Can you reach my mobile?" she asked.

"Where is it?" he asked.

She nodded in the general direction.

"Inside my jacket," she said.

"Okay, I'll try," Rick said.

He snaked his hand in the direction of her jacket. He paused as he came across an obstacle. It was a zip. He pulled it down until he'd made an opening, which was wide enough for his hand. Then he retracted his hand.

"I think I need to take my glove off," he said.

He snaked his hand back and tried to grip the end of the glove with his teeth. Sondra was close enough to bite another finger. The glove slid off and Rick resumed his journey. He stopped when he met warm flesh. It felt disproportionately warm.

"The other side," Sondra directed him.

Rick reminded himself that they were instigating emergency procedures. He continued to slide his hand. And then he stopped again. He could feel her convulsing slightly. Then he realised she was laughing.

"That's my breast," Sondra said.

"Oh god," Rick said, "I'm really sorry."

"You English," she said.

Rick released her breast and moved his hand until he found a layer of clothing.

"Closer," she said.

He wasn't sure if she was saying so in an ironic manner. He slid his hand a little further until he found another zip. There was even less room to manoeuvre the zip open but, after a bit of fiddling, the tips of his fingers found something solid and phone-like.

"Got it," he said.

He pulled it out and looked at it. There were further issues with his focal point which required him to step back at least a foot. He turned it to Sondra, who was younger.

"Can you see that?" he asked.

"Putain," Sondra said.

The screen was smashed and the phone looked dead.

"Mort," she muttered.

For a second they didn't say anything. They were breathing at the same time. Rick didn't have the excuse of his last breath to kiss her.

"What about your phone?" she asked.

"It's in my pocket," Rick said.

"Which pocket?" she asked.

"By my side," he said.

"It's my turn," she said.

Rick could feel her hand snaking down his abdomen and towards his crotch. He felt a little tense, although he doubted she was going to shove it in his trousers as he had with her.

"Hold on," she said, "is it the latest iPhone?"

"I guess," Rick said.

"Is it thin?" she asked.

"I suppose," he said.

"Then we're in trouble," she said.

They stopped. She looked directly at him.

"Do you know what, Mr Rick?" she said.

"No," Rick said slowly.

"You're a nice man," she said.

Nice men had been in short supply in her life. Her problems had started with Gilbert and his bullying family. They'd taken her children from her. They'd hadn't shown much sympathy or kindness. She kissed him.

"Hey," Rick said, a little taken back, but the kiss was interrupted.

"What's that?" she said.

They could hear noises.

"Move the pole," she said.

Rick shook the pole excitedly. They could hear voices. Russian voices. Very nice Russians. And another voice in English. They could feel the snow moving. There were people above them moving it with their hands. A few minutes later Rick could see the sun. They were digging them out.

"Are you okay?" someone asked.

"I think so," Rick shouted, although he would have preferred to have been saved five minutes later.

Chapter Fifty-Four

Andre's wife was burning hot with the embarrassment, or it might have been the menopause or, she was beginning to fear, something else. She probably shouldn't have read that magazine. The Englishman, who wore his hair slightly long, had stood in front of her and her chest had heaved. What had happened? She'd scurried back to the office and didn't care how many people were waiting to be served. She should never have deviated from the Decathlon sweatshirt. She was safe in that and handily warm, although she was no longer in pursuit of warmth. She picked the magazine up and threw it in the bin. Then she looked at it lying in the bin.

"Putain de merde," she said.

She picked it up again. She had an evening shift to get through and there wasn't enough time to go back and change. She checked the lost property. There was nothing useful, just those strange Superman costumes, and she wasn't putting those on. She looked ridiculous enough already. She reached for the first aid kit and opened it. There were a number of safety pins. That should hold back the tide, Andre's wife thought. She struggled with it for a while. She really needed a third hand to hold her dress together, but she couldn't think of anyone who could perform that task. And then, for no reason she could discern, she blushed, or it might have been a flush. What had she been thinking? She knew what she'd been thinking. She just didn't want to admit it to herself.

"Putain de merde," Andre's wife said, and slumped back in the chair.

She flipped through the magazine. There was an article entitled 'Are You Having Fun?'. Andre's wife had to consider the concept of fun for a minute and then discard it as shallow, immature nonsense, entirely inappropriate for her age. Although she had seen, through her natural grimace, other people having fun. There was a list of boxes to tick to ascertain whether you were having fun. She couldn't tick a single one. She couldn't remember the last time she'd had a drink. Andre's wife didn't like to drink the profits.

"Putain de merde," she said and stood up.

She needed to sort her dress out. In the absence of a third hand she might have to take the dress off, pin it together, and then put it back on again. She locked the door to the office and started to remove her dress. Then she stopped and checked the lock again. It was fine. Then she began to pull the dress over her head and stopped. She checked the door again. It was locked. She removed the dress and lay it down on the desk. She looked up. There was a mirror. She couldn't believe she was practically naked in the office. It made her flush again. She stopped looking at the mirror and got on with it. Five minutes later she had the dress back on. She sat down. She looked at the mirror again.

"Putain de merde," she said.

She could see her uneven mascara. She found a wet wipe in the first aid kit and scrubbed her eye. It stung a bit and made her eyesight even more blurry, but eventually it came off. She looked a little less ridiculous. Andre's wife wondered if she should take a drink to medicate against the menopause. She hoped it would alleviate these strange feelings she was having. She was thinking things she didn't want to think. The same lurid thoughts had haunted her in her sleep. Andre's wife got up. It was time to go back to work and the Englishman who wore his hair long was probably back on the slopes. She tried to open the door. It wouldn't open.

"Putain de merde," she said and gave it a tug.

The handle came off in her hands. This was Andre's fault. She was always telling him to do things and he never listened. Despite that, she wished he was here. She wouldn't be in this mess. She put the handle back on and tried again. The door opened. She peaked through the small opening. The bar had calmed down and the Englishman who wore his hair slightly long wasn't there. She came out. The staff looked at her strangely. Andre's wife stood tall. She was going to be on her own in the evening, but the rest of the afternoon passed rapidly, and without event. She even felt quite relaxed.

But as the early evening drew closer she began to feel tense. She couldn't help herself and she had no idea why. She'd checked the safety pins and they were all good. Her eyesight was still a little blurry, but at least her eyes matched. She'd tidied and organised the bar and had checked the till, removed some cash and placed it in the safe in the office, and tried to occupy herself. And then she turned and there he was.

"Bonjour," Judah said.

There was a pause while Andre's wife searched for the correct response. It should have been automatic, but she felt suddenly flustered.

"Bon soir," she corrected.

She hadn't meant to, but the evening had arrived.

"Je peux achetter une boisson pour vous?" Judah said.

He was asking to buy her a drink. No one had ever done that before. She could feel a flush rising in her and she thought back to the magazine. She could really do with a drink. What harm would a little cognac do?

"Oui, merci," Andre's wife said a little dumbfounded.

She didn't know it, but her dumbfounded expression was a huge improvement on her normal hatchet faced demeanour. She poured herself a cognac and raised it in thanks prompting a further, less grimace like, expression.

"Et cinq biers s'il vous plait," Judah said with a smile.

Judah took a tray and returned to the table with five beers, although there were only three of them. He'd already collected on his charm reward, but he didn't want to humiliate Andre's wife. This was their local, after all.

Chapter Fifty-Five

"Are you okay?" a voice said.

Rick knew he didn't have any life threatening injuries or, if he did, the close proximity with Sondra had put his mind off them.

"I think so," Rick said.

"Are you sure?" Sondra asked.

"No, I'm not. I'll have to wait until I get up. Are you okay?" Rick asked.

A little part of Sondra knew that it had been unwise to take the off-piste route she'd chosen, there had been avalanche warnings on the lifts, but she'd felt a little impetuous.

"I don't know. I think so," she said.

Ten minutes later they had been dug out and Rick reluctantly rolled off Sondra. It didn't feel like anything was broken. It felt more like something had been fixed. Sondra stood up. There were people filming them with their camera phones. She gave them a little wave.

"I'm okay," she said.

Rick struggled to get up, although this was more attributable to his fifty-seven years than being swept away by an avalanche. He stood up.

"Me too," he said.

Their rescuers looked at each other.

"Are you staying in Courcheval?" someone asked.

"No, I'm at Val Thorens," Rick said.

"The lifts have closed and the wind means a helicopter can't get over and the main road has closed. You'll have to stay here," the rescuer said.

Rick wasn't sure what that meant.

"If you go to the medical centre they'll check you're okay and find you somewhere to stay," another voice said.

"Okay, thank you," Rick said.

"If you're okay we need to check for other survivors," another voice said.

"We're fine," Sondra said, "we can ski into town."

Rick wasn't a hundred percent sure about that as his limbs were beginning to ache, but that might also have been to do with his age, a long lunch and an energetic day. The rescuers collected their skis and poles and helped them get ready.

"I think I've lost a pole," Sondra said.

She'd dropped it when she'd grabbed hold of Rick and she suspected it wouldn't reappear until the summer.

"This way," Sondra said.

She skied slowly and precisely, as she might have had she been teaching a junior class, and Rick was grateful for it. When they got to the centre of the town it was snowing again and it looked like a Christmas scene. They followed the signs to the medical centre until they could ski no further. They took off their skis and walked past a hotel. It had a number of stars and the word 'luxury spa' written below. If Courcheval is full of Russians, Rick thought, they like their spas.

"Sondra," Rick said, "I could do with a hot bath."

She stopped and looked at him. He pointed at the hotel and, as he did so, a number of thoughts cascaded through his head. One was a sense of guilt, as if he was proposing an infidelity, the other was that he'd been a little presumptuous. He hadn't meant a shared bath.

"I mean," he explained, "I'll get two rooms," adding, "with two baths."

Sondra didn't know what to say and that prompted Rick to elaborate.

"I mean a bath in each room," he said.

He knew that it was unlikely, despite the spa nature of the hotel, that there would be two baths side by side, and also knew he should stop talking.

"Are you sure?" she asked.

"Of course," Rick said.

She suspected that a room would be more than four hundred euros a night – that figure seemed to haunt her – but she didn't think Rick cared about the money. And she was exhausted.

"I could really do with a hot bath," she admitted.

When they entered the hotel it didn't occur to either of them that the hotel might not have rooms available, but they did, and ten minutes later they were running baths in two rooms located on the top floor, and next to each other. They were fabulous rooms but they weren't, as Sondra had thought, four hundred euros. They were three times that. When they got into their respective baths ten minutes later they were unaware that they were indeed side by side, but separated by a wall. The hot water felt good for both of them and after a furious day skiing it gave them both time to reflect.

Although Rick was trying not to reflect. Reflection, he reckoned, would just be a reason not to act. But he didn't know what that meant. They had shared a kiss, but it had been brief, and it might have been prompted by their threatened mortality. Would they have kissed otherwise? He wouldn't have had the nerve or the courage, or whatever was required. He wondered if everything happen for a reason. Rick felt he wouldn't have got close to Sondra if she hadn't been vulnerable. Had he taken advantage? He hoped not. That wasn't him.

Sondra was also trying not to reflect. She feared she'd taken advantage of him. His generous spirit and something else. She took a while to figure out what that was and concluded it was his vulnerability. It wasn't as if she didn't find him attractive. She'd thought so when she'd looked up and seen him on the bench next to her. She'd been speaking to her ex. It reminded her of where she was. Despite the lavish surroundings she found herself in, she was ostracised in her little village, and only allowed limited access to her children. She didn't want to use Rick because he had money. Or was that what she was doing? She hoped not. That wasn't her.

Rick had not taken a bath in a long time. He'd never had the time and when he'd had the time he hadn't wanted one. Who had time for baths? But, although he felt okay, he also felt that just about every part of him was bruised. It was odd that he could barely recall the moment when the snow had engulfed them. It was like being swallowed by a whale although, as he'd never been swallowed by a whale, this might not have been an appropriate metaphor. It was more gentle, as if he'd been consumed by sleep. But it was a little more violent than that. He remembered a little jolt of adrenaline and worrying that this would be his final moment, which was curious as it hadn't bothered him in all his recent brushes with death. He wondered why his life suddenly mattered to him.

Sondra hadn't taken a bath in years, primarily because her apartment didn't have one. It did have three little bedrooms and a nice view of the mountains. There was a local school nearby and for a time she'd been happy. But her partner had changed. She wasn't sure why, but there always seemed to be less money in the account. The four hundred euros had paid for school uniforms. And then her life had turned into a nightmare after which there were moments when she didn't care what happened to her. But, when the snow had engulfed them, she'd realised that she did care. And she'd held onto Rick.

Despite his aches and pains, Rick couldn't stay any longer in the bath. He got up and grabbed one of the white towels. It was beautiful and thick and well worth stealing. He thought about texting Sondra, but his phone was, as she'd suggested, in a rather sorry way. He thought about phoning her through the hotel system, but that seemed a little odd. That only left knocking on her door.

Chapter Fifty-Six

Judah placed the tray on the table. There were only three of them, but they'd got into the habit of ordering five. Although they were slowing down a little.

"Cheers," Mac said.

Mac had slowed down a little less than the others.

"Have you heard from Rick?" Mac asked.

"No, I've tried calling, but it just goes to voicemail," Will said.

"That seems strange," Judah said.

"What about Al?" Mac asked.

"I called him, but he was engaged," Will said.

"Who's next?" Mac asked.

They looked at him. His face was florid with beer and high blood pressure. There was no question who they'd put their money on.

"You, you fat bastard," Judah said.

"You mustn't underestimate the Scottish gene," Mac said finishing his pint.

The others had barely started theirs.

"I'm going for a piss," Mac said and got up.

They watched him as he marched towards the toilet.

"You'd think he'd be dead by now," Judah said.

"Don't underestimate the Scottish gene," Will said.

Mac returned a few minutes later.

"I've sprayed the Villeroy and Boch," he said.

The toilets contained a single toilet which was adorned with the words 'Villeroy and Boch' but not, they'd all noticed, a toilet seat.

"We need to persuade Andre to get a toilet seat," Judah said.

"Next year," Mac said.

Will raised his eyes. That was interesting. They hadn't even made it through this trip. But he was encouraged by this.

"What's going on?" Mac asked.

The room had become quiet and people were huddled around a television set. They got up and joined them. There was a general muttering.

"An avalanche," Will said.

"Where's that?" Mac asked someone.

"Courcheval," someone said.

"That's not far," Will said.

They watched shaky camera footage evidently from someone's mobile phone as people were being pulled out of the snow. There was another shot of the snow moving down the mountain with a life of its own.

"Shit, that looks nasty," Judah said.

The shot finished with the camera immersed in snow. It cut to another shot. People were being dug out.

"They seem okay," Will said.

There were two people trapped below the snow. They heaved out the first. The slim shape suggested a woman.

"She looks okay," Judah said.

The others looked at him disapprovingly. He hadn't meant 'okay' in the sense of unscathed. A few minute later they pulled out a man. He looked a little shaky, but he also seemed okay.

"He's got an orange helmet like Rick," Judah said.

It took them all a beat to recognise the significance of this.

Chapter Fifty-Seven

Sondra wished she'd had the opportunity to pack, as she'd liked to have changed into something a little smarter than the salopettes, thermal underwear and red sweatshirt she'd arrived in. The hotel room was beautiful and serene. Her experience of hotels rooms, particularly expensive ones, was minimal and this bordered on the surreal. As if she'd died in the avalanche and this was the waiting room before her ultimate destiny was decided. She wasn't sure how judgemental God was, she hoped he was a little more tolerant than those in her village, but as theft was on His list, this moment was as good as it gets. Now that she thought about it, what she'd actually liked to have changed into would be a little more than smart. It would be sexy. She couldn't believe she'd thought that. She had no idea what was going on in Rick's mind.

"Bugger," Rick said.

Rick's mind was in turmoil. He'd stood outside Sondra's door with his hand poised to knock, but it hadn't seemed right. He'd started to get dressed and realised that the clothes he'd arrived in were rather unpleasantly sweaty. He didn't want to put them on, but he had to wear something. He'd established that the hotel had a restaurant, and a rather fine one at that, but they had rules regarding clothing. He'd have had the food delivered to the room, but that seemed presumptuous. Ideally he'd wear a white sailor suit in the style of *An Officer and a Gentleman* even though he wasn't American, and had no interest in being a sailor.

"Bugger," he said again.

He put his knocking fist back in his pocket and walked to the lift. An idea was forming in his mind. It was worth a try. When he arrived at the reception desk he found a young, attractive girl. She had a lapel badge with her name.

"Hello Celeste, I'd like to eat in the restaurant tonight, but I only have these clothes. We got caught in the avalanche," he said.

Celeste raised an eye. She'd noticed them, as very little escaped her notice in the hotel. But the manager wasn't there that evening and they had rules regarding suitable attire. She'd get in trouble if someone said something.

"What I was hoping," Rick continued confidently, "was that there might be some clothes that I could rent, borrow or buy. It doesn't matter which."

Despite the vast cost of the hotel, Celeste was not highly paid, although she lived in the hotel in a basement room which would have been additional parking, had the planning committee not decided against it. The room didn't have a window, but it was a good size. Celeste sized him up. Literally, as she'd once worked in a dress shop.

"For me and my…" Rick struggled to find a suitable name to describe his relationship with Sondra.

"I saw her," Celeste said.

Her manager was around the same size as Rick and he was required, when they held certain events, to wear a dinner suit. And Celeste was a very similar size to Sondra. Rick could see she was struggling to make up her mind. He could have presented many arguments to help encourage her, but instead he opened his wallet. He held out two fifty euro notes. He would have had more, but he'd given Will some cash for the kitty. Celeste looked at the money. She looked around. Celeste could be resourceful, should the right incentive present itself. It had.

"Rent?" she asked.

Rick nodded.

"Give me five minutes," she said adding, "Do you want the black jacket, or the white one?"

Rick chuckled. It wasn't quite an *Officer and a Gentleman*, but it was the next best thing.

"White," he said.

Celeste went down to her room. She opened her wardrobe and ran her hand through the dresses. She liked clothes and had collected a number of labels from the end of season sales. Each dress had a purpose. She did not have to be massively intuitive to guess where this couple's evening might go. She picked out three dresses. The blue silk dress with the oriental pattern was sophisticated and slightly chaste, the black dress was a little less chaste, but was tightly fitting and was quite multifunctional depending on how it was accessorised. It could be sexy and it could be smart. Then there was the red one. She'd not worn it much herself. She'd tried it on many times, but never quite made it out of the room. It was certainly sexy, but she feared it was a hair breadth away from slutty. It certainly was on her, but it might look quite different on a more athletic body. She grabbed all three. He might as well get value for his money. She stopped off at the laundry room where the recent dry cleaning had been stored including her manager's suit, and she returned to the desk, and handed it over to Rick.

"Good luck," Celeste said.

Rick mumbled something, a good deal less confidently, and thanked her. Then he remembered something else.

"Oh, and can I book a table for eight o'clock?" he asked.

"Of course," she said with a smile.

Celeste was looking forward to finding out which dress would be chosen. That might set the course of the evening.

"Thank you," Rick said.

As the lift wobbled to the upper floors, he started to feel nervous. That was strange. When the doors opened he knew he needed to act before he gave it any thought. He knocked on Sondra's door. She opened it slowly.

"Hey," she said.

"I got you some clothes," Rick said and handed them over.

"Great," Sondra said a little dumbfounded.

"I've also booked a table for eight," he said.

Sondra wasn't sure quite how to react.

"About forty minutes?" Rick added.

She nodded. He nodded.

"Okay," he said, and went to his room.

Chapter Fifty-Eight

Julie had gone to the country house. She was lying in a hammock strung between the three hundred year old yew trees which an ancestor had planted. She was thinking about her life. She'd had a slightly rough time, but she was pretty resilient by nature.

"You can't mope around here all day," Julie's mother said.

Julie's mother wasn't anxious. She was horny. She'd been creeping round the house with Jesus – he pronounced his name with an 'H' – her tennis coach and, while the idea of having sex with him while her daughter was in the house didn't inhibit her, it was proving a problem for Jesus. He just couldn't relax. She'd explained he'd have to do rather better than that if he wanted to get her sponsorship for that tournament in Barcelona.

"No, you're right," Julie said.

But Julie wasn't ready to go back to uni either. It would be awkward. She was generally immune from embarrassment, but she'd heard that Judah had been fired. She did feel responsible. She had lured him. Not that he'd required much luring.

"Perhaps a little holiday," Julie's mother suggested.

Julie had been considering it. She was getting a little bored in the country house and didn't fancy going to London.

"How about Barbados?" her mother said.

The family had owned the beach front property for over fifty years, from the time of the British rule, and a vibrant town had grown around it. Julie thought about it, but she didn't have a particular yearning for either the sun or a black man, although she was frequently partial to both. She needed something more energetic.

"Or you could catch the end of the skiing season," Julie's mother said.

She'd been thinking about a trip there herself, but there was a tennis tournament coming up, and she had no intention of coming second. While Julie's mother liked to spend money, she hated throwing it away. Jesus *was* her tennis coach after all.

"That's an idea," Julie said.

She'd also heard that Judah had gone on a skiing trip to the Alps – gossip was flying like a snowstorm – and she owed him an apology. But she didn't want to go on her own. She gave that some thought.

"G and T?" her mother asked.

Julie put a thumb up and her mother went off towards the kitchen. The villa in the Alps had been bought a while ago, when her father had held some money offshore, and a tax-efficient deal had come up. It hadn't been that expensive but, as the Russian community had grown around it, it was now worth a fortune. But the Alps are huge, and she thought it unlikely she'd be able to track Judah down.

"Thanks," she said to her mother, who'd returned with a gin and tonic which, in contrast to Jesus, could fairly be described as stiff.

Julie had upset Terry with her withdrawal of her promise of sex and wondered whether she skied. She doubted it, but it might make up for it. She took her mobile out and tapped out a message. Why not, she thought. She'd been outed as the daughter of Sir Harry Panter and it was no secret that he was wealthy.

'Fancy a skiing trip?' she texted.

She didn't think that a trip to the villa would amount to a reversal of her position regarding sex with Terry, and Terry had been on a number of demonstrations in which she'd asserted the right to insert whatever she chose, or not. She'd understand. A second later the text arrived at Terry's phone and she didn't understand it at all. She'd spent the evening opining the lack of lesbians to a gay man who was only half listening, and who went on to spend the rest of the evening with Alf, Peter, Adam, and would have attempted James, but his body wouldn't have it.

"Shit," Terry muttered.

She'd never skied in her life, although she understood that posh people spent most of their time drinking cocktails, and making patronising comments about those who were less fortunate than them. She could be a bit of social warrior at times. She wouldn't have the right clothes and she'd probably feel out of place and uncomfortable. But if this was an opportunity to get into Julie's knickers she didn't care. She'd kick herself if she didn't go. She texted back.

'That would be great,' she wrote.

It wasn't the language she'd normally use, which suggested she was getting into character already. But Julie didn't notice as she remained resolutely the same person regardless of any social situation.

"Ma," she said with a languid tone that could only be achieved by someone who had consumed a truly stiff gin and tonic drunk in their family's ancestral home.

"Yes, my lovely," Julie's mother said.

Julie's mother had been thinking about her backhand. She'd never quite mastered the double hander and the power that those two hands lend the shot. It was a distinct weakness in her game. She'd get Jesus to work on that this afternoon.

"I think a skiing trip is in order," Julie said.

"Excellent. Will you get onto Cleo?" Julie's mother said.

Cleo was the family's personal secretary and organised a number of things, including flights.

"Right now," Julie said decisively.

Julie's mother smiled to herself and stopped thinking about her backhand and the use of two hands and started thinking about other things that Jesus could do for her.

Chapter Fifty-Nine

Sondra sat on the bed and looked at the clothes. She didn't have a huge collection of her own and was more inclined to wear a tight-fitting pair of jeans with a tight-ish shirt. She'd spent the last twenty years on a pair of skis. She was slim and fit. She looked at the dresses. She'd not actually worn one in a while, and wasn't sure which to start with. She liked the silky feel of the blue, geisha-style dress and started with that. She took off the thick, white towelling dressing gown and stood up. Had she known at the beginning of the day that she'd end up in an expensive hotel with what looked like a date, she would have made different underwear decisions. Not that she had a vast selection, but the sports bra lacked shape and was, she had to admit, rather grey in colour. It probably wouldn't matter. She put the dress on. It was beautiful and she checked herself in the mirror.

"Pas mal," she muttered.

It wasn't bad, but it was slightly wide at the waist. It wasn't a brilliant fit. She took it off and tried the black one. This was a better fit. This, she thought, was the one. She looked at herself in the mirror. It was very smart. Then she remembered the little purse in her skiing jacket. There wasn't much in there. Just twenty euros, a debit card she wasn't certain would work, and some lipstick and mascara. She was surprised she still had it with her. It was an old habit. She applied a little of both and looked at the mirror again.

"Beaucoup mieux," she said.

She did look better. She was ready. Sondra didn't have any shoes, so she'd have to go barefoot, but this was a hotel with deep carpets, probably like the pockets of the residents. She wondered if she should knock on Rick's door, or wait until he knocks on hers. She wasn't sure. She sat down on the bed and waited. She felt oddly nervous and turned on the television. She tried to relax, stretching her arms wide. She put them down. One hand landed on the red dress. That one had not been given much of a chance.

"Pourqoui pas," she said and got up again.

She slid off the black dress and put the red one over her head. It didn't want to go on. She wriggled and tugged until eventually it relented and they were united. She was a little hesitant about looking in the mirror, as she feared this was the dress that bypassed the need for an imagination. She looked at herself.

"Putain de merde," she said.

It looked too much. Way too much. She didn't want to be mistaken for someone who was working in the hotel. And she didn't mean working in a good way. The worse thing was it looked spectacular. The even worse thing was the awkward lines her bra was making in it, and the grey straps which were visible. It was only even worse because she knew it would look better without the bra. She started to take off the dress, but curiosity got the better of her. She had to at least see what it looked like without the bra. It took a while to release the bra, which felt like it was protesting against her with moral issues of its own. Eventually she was free and she pulled the dress into shape. Sondra had never met Celeste, and had barely noticed her, but she was discovering she was more of a slut than she looked. But it did look good. Sondra had never worn anything quite like it. But it was too much. She attempted removal, but found that this was a dress which didn't want to be parted from her. And there was a knock at the door.

"Merde," Sondra said.

What was she going to do? She breathed in and told herself it had been a hell of day. It might as well be a hell of an evening too. She opened the door. Rick looked at her. She couldn't be certain, but it was possible his mouth might have fallen open.

"Do you think this it too much?" she asked.

Rick had argued and parried with the boards of listed companies. He had provided quotes and handy aphorisms for the financial press. He had spoken at huge conferences, without notes, and to hundreds of people and at no point had he been unable to find the words he required.

"It's..." he began.

He seemed to be having breathing difficulties too. Words were tumbling in his head, but they were all a little confused and overwhelmed.

"Shall I change?" Sondra said.

She was having a crisis of confidence, but then so was Rick.

"No," Rick managed to say, "you look spectacular."

Sondra took a look at Rick. He looked pretty good too.

"Shall we?" Rick said and offered his arm.

She took it and they walked to the lift. He was a little hesitant about looking directly at her, but it was all he wanted to do. The lift, like many lifts, was lined with mirrors and by the time they'd arrived at the reception he'd concluded that he was out of both his league and his depth. The lift dinged and the doors opened. Rick looked up to see Celeste. She was smiling broadly. Luck, Celeste decided, wasn't needed.

Chapter Sixty

The following morning Will led the team through the main boulevard. But the team was just him, Judah and Mac. They'd left a little later than the previous day as they were beginning to slow down. But Will had practically forced them into their skis and onto the pistes. He'd planned a route.

"When can we stop for a coffee?" Judah asked.

Will ignored him and they skied a little further.

"I fancy a beer," Mac said.

The others looked at him.

"It's nearly lunch," Mac insisted.

"Too early," Will said with authority.

They spent the morning exploring simple routes which weren't too far from the apartment. But Judah was getting tired.

"You go round again, I'll grab a coffee," Judah said pointing to a small bar.

Will nodded and picked up his things. He hadn't noticed the group of middle aged women who'd just walked in. Judah had them in his sights. He watched as they circled looking for a table. There was an empty table next to him, but he had a sense that they'd seen him, and were looking to sit as far from him as possible. This wasn't good. It was too late, as someone else was about to take the table. For a second he thought about following Will, but there was something interesting about the person that was weaving her way towards the table next to him. She had a slightly exaggerated way of walking, as if she was swaying from one hip to another along a catwalk. But they were at quite a high altitude and it was cold outside. Her face was covered with a scarf and she wore a helmet. Judah decided to stay.

He looked at her. It was impossible to tell her age, or whether she was the kind of beautiful woman who would prompt men to throw themselves in front of a train for just one night together. Although he might be tempted to throw himself in front a train so as not to spend a night with Andre's wife. She removed her gloves. He looked at her hands. They were perfectly and expensively manicured. There were diamond rings. But they weren't the hands of a young woman. He lowered his expectations. She removed the scarf. She wore immaculately applied makeup on a very fine face. He didn't need to lower his expectations. She removed her helmet and her hair tumbled out like an advertisement for shampoo. She slid off her skiing jacket revealing a tight fitting jumper and breasts generous enough to question their authenticity. But she had some style. This was one classy lady.

Judah's lengthy history of women didn't tend to include the sublimely classy, and his numerous one night stands favoured the outrageously slutty. He might have been out of his depth. She suddenly turned and looked directly at him. Judah wasn't aware that she'd removed her clothing with aching slowness entirely aware of his stare. She smiled. He recognised her. He'd sat next to her a couple of days earlier and she'd held his gaze for the tiniest of fractions longer than was necessary. Or he thought she had.

"Hi," Judah said.

"Hi," she said.

She was French. The kind of Parisian French who dined in Art Deco restaurants and shopped in exclusive boutiques laden with brass and mirrors. Even her labels had labels. She knew the designers personally and moved in a circle which spanned politicians to opera singers. The kind of woman who'd been instructed in the fine art of lovemaking. Judah had read a lot into that 'hi'. He was in love. Or it might have been lust.

"Are you on your own?" Judah asked.

She shrugged. Shrugging was normally an art form perfected by French men, but she was well versed in it too, and Judah understood that it meant not exactly.

"My friends ski too slowly for me," she said.

She said it with a twinkle and Judah chose to interpret this as an indication of her general fastness in other areas.

"Me too," Judah lied.

He could barely keep up with Will, but he was going to have to raise his game now. The waiter appeared. He'd been curiously reclusive when Judah had sought him, but this woman had merely raised an eye at him.

"Un café et…" she paused.

If she was toying with him he had no idea, but the pause held everyone's attention. Even the people in the table next to the table next to theirs. She'd grown a little bored of the day and sought entertainment.

"Cognac," she said.

It was pretty early and even Judah, who was a little dissolute by nature, wouldn't have ordered a cognac. But she was showing the way.

"La même chose," Judah said.

She raised an immaculately plucked eyebrow at him by not much more than a millimetre. It might have been less. But this, Judah recognised, was progress in the right direction.

"Do you need a skiing partner?" Judah asked.

She shrugged again. She wasn't going to make it easy for him. She liked her men to work a little.

"Peut…" she paused, "…être."

There was no woman more expert at saying the word 'anticipation'. She could take a short city break between the third and last syllable.

The coffees and cognacs arrived. She stirred the coffee and downed it. Then she turned her attention to the cognac. It didn't stand a chance. A second later she put her jacket back on, then her scarf, and finally her helmet. Judah watched entranced. She got up. That, Judah thought, was that. But she made an infinitesimally small movement with her head. If he'd not been studying her he wouldn't have noticed. And then she turned and left.

It took a moment for Judah to register that was an invitation. He got up and hurriedly dressed, as she'd already reached the door, and was about to leave. He followed her in a stumble. He couldn't help noticing she had a very neat backside. A moment later he was out in the cold. He looked around until he'd located that neat backside and then grabbed his skis. She was already stepping into hers. He marched up to her, he was already a little out of breath, and then she turned, offered the same minuscule tug of the head, and then she was off.

"Fuck," Judah said.

She'd shot straight down the fall line. He wasn't sure he could do this.

"Fuck," he said again.

If he was going to make that observation a possibility he was going to have to follow her down the hill. How desperate was he? Desperate enough as it turned out. He threw himself down the hill.

"Oh fuck," he said.

This, he now recognised, was a mistake. Was this a black run? He hadn't noticed, but it was full of lumps and bumps and his legs were bouncing up and down like a hare being chased across a field. And on each landing he was just a trip away from total wipeout. He'd stopped thinking about the woman with the neat backside. This was about survival. He tried to look ahead, but all his facilities were already operating on overtime. There was a school of children crossing the piste.

"Oh fuck," he said.

But he was unaware he'd said anything. This was wipeout time. He was a moment away from hearing the helicopter. He'd hit a mogul and he was airborne. He flew through a gap in the train of children and landed, stumbling first from one foot to the other. This was it. But the gradient had turned. He was going uphill or, more crucially, he wasn't going down hill. He was slowing down. A few stumbles later he was back in control, and a little after that he attempted to resume some level of style, as he was aware that she'd stopped and turned. Then she entered another small restaurant. He was fairly sure she'd issued another of her discreet tugs to suggest he follow her. He couldn't tell. He was shaking too much. He might have pissed himself, he wasn't sure. It took him a while to get his skis in the slots provided outside the bar. Eventually he managed it, took a few breaths, and entered the bar. He couldn't immediately see her as the contrast in lighting made it seem very dark inside. Then he saw her at a table. She had two coffees and two cognacs in front of her. He needed that cognac.

Chapter Sixty-One

When Claude had been a singer-songwriter he'd sung about his love for Claudette. It was, he'd said, the highest mountain, the deepest ocean, the birds that sing in the trees, the colours of the rainbow, the brushstrokes of a Monet. Claude had been pretty big on his love for Claudette, and then one day she'd relented. He would have sung about that moment too, but there wasn't much conversation, just a hand-job in the back of his car. He'd tried writing about the majesty of that hand-job, but even Claude could see it was a bit tacky, as was the vinyl seat after the deed was done. His romance with Claudette had blossomed followed, as it was, by a brief shuffle in a cleaner's cupboard in which she'd given him another hand-job and he'd inserted two fingers into her.

When he woke the following morning he grappled with how he could elevate this moment to a passion that would rival Anthony and Cleopatra, but she must have accidentally steadied herself and put her hand down onto a surface on which there was something corrosive, and then applied it to his penis. He'd itched like mad for a few days. And then she disappeared. It was a long few days of radio silence in which he penned four more tunes, one of which captured the nation's imagination, and secured his fortune. It was entitled 'My Love For You Is Like a Very Fine Creme Brûlée' and was his first attempt at writing in English. He was unaware that his international success was more of an ironic nature, as he was not a man who liked to laugh at himself. But this song brought him overnight fame.

It might have been that success that heralded Claudette's return, and this time they came very close to full sex. But, as Claude had elevated Claudette to goddess status of the purest kind in his songwriting, he'd come all over her knees. Again this incident brought a halt to his writing. He'd checked a thesaurus for the possible rhymes with knees and found none satisfactory. The following week he'd taken her to Paris's most celebrated restaurant and back to his suite at the Grand Hotel du Palais Royale. He'd taken the precaution of masturbating that afternoon to ensure that there was no repeat of the knees business. He discovered that as soon as he thought of Claudette his penis sprang to life, and he vowed that he would never masturbate to any other image for the rest of his life. It was a vow that he'd kept. But, prior to her arrival at the restaurant, and just for good measure, he'd nipped to the toilets and fired out another. It might have been that, or the three brandies he'd had after the bottle of wine, but when they got back to the room he was entirely incapable of getting it up. This frustration prompted a further song which came close to the success of 'Creme Brûlée' and in which he disguised the central theme of not being able to get it up as a lasting and burning passion. It was a further week before he was able to see Claudette again and this time, when he did, he managed a pretty creditable job and, after he'd shown her his latest royalty cheque, Claudette was his, and with it his creativity dried up.

It was a chance encounter, involving a creme brûlée, which started his career as a chef. He found he had a natural talent for it, and a further talent for presenting his work to camera with an appropriate rolling of his 'r's and a brooding nature, which the female audience interpreted as passion. Claude had become France's most successful celebrity chef, and his love and passion for Claudette had never faded. But it had been tested.

He'd caught her with the sous chef, the gardener, the pool boy, and her tennis coach, who he'd been certain was gay. He had suspicions about the old man who ran the cafe at the end of their street. He had to choose his staff very carefully and, if there had been an agency which specialised in supplying people with facial warts, he would have subscribed to it, because every time he caught Claudette *in flagrante* he was filled with a rage which blinded him to reason. In the old days he would have harnessed this to write songs, quite possibly in the heavy metal genre, but now he had his kitchen and he would spend an hour cutting up onions. Claude had a large collection of the finest and sharpest knives which had been imported from Japan. He never travelled without them and today he was heading for the Savoie region as he'd been invited to knock up a tarteflette, although he was mostly there so that he could check in on Claudette. She'd promised she'd be good and he mostly believed her.

Claudette had insisted he buy the apartment in Meribel, despite his suspicions about her skiing instructor, and he'd relented. She maintained that it would be good for their marriage and had got down on her knees and performed a blowjob which was so expert it almost caused him to wonder, for the very briefest of seconds, as to how she'd acquired such outstanding skills, and then he'd just given into the pleasure. He'd thought about calling her and telling her he was on his way, but then he'd decided against it. He tapped the steering wheel. He should be in the studio in and hour, and at the apartment a few hours after that. He conjured up an image of Claudette and he smiled. It always worked.

Chapter Sixty-Two

Rick had panicked. He'd spent the evening doing a lot of panicking. He hadn't been out with that many women and this one, Sondra, was something else. The restaurant was filled with glamour, but it was a kind of monied glamour. Foreheads were botoxed, lips were filled and smiles were fixed. His eyes had danced over the other diners and he'd noticed that, but not taken a second look. And he'd looked at Sondra. He'd been filled with so many conflicting thoughts he didn't know what to do. A little part of him was thinking, 'yes, she is with me' and another was feeling distant pangs of guilt. It might have prompted him to drink more wine than was wise.

The wine was excellent, but he didn't really remember it. And the food was gastronomic, although he had no idea what he'd eaten. And the conversation flowed, but he couldn't recall what they'd spoken about. He hadn't noticed the restaurant empty. Suddenly he'd looked round and it was just them. He knew that it was time to go to their rooms. He should have been tired, but he felt more alive than he had for years. He suspected that if he did go to bed he wouldn't sleep. He knew that convention dictated that he make a move. But he couldn't bring himself to, which was not to say he didn't want to. It was when they'd arrived at their respective rooms, that he'd panicked. He'd said goodnight. There was a pause. It felt like a pause into which the director's cut of Titanic could have been squeezed in. It was so wide a truck could have been reversed into it. And

Sondra had broken convention, which was why she lay next to him lightly snoring.

It was morning. The good news was that he hadn't drunk too much wine, although he felt that if he'd consumed four bottles he would have been fine. Sometimes desire can overcome anything. He wondered what was going to happen next.

"Salut," Sondra mumbled.

"Hey, did you sleep okay?" Rick said.

"The best in years," Sondra said.

She drew close to him and Rick no longer had to wonder what was going to happen next. Although he did wonder what would happened *after* what happened next.

"What time is it?" Sondra asked twenty minutes later.

Rick looked for his phone and then realised that it had expired in the avalanche. That was yesterday, yet it seemed a long time ago. He checked his watch, although he often found it was difficult to tell the time without his glasses. He showed her the watch.

"Merde," she muttered, "I have to go. I need to see the kids."

It was a prosaic realisation which brought them crashing down. And then she said something. Ten minutes later Rick was alone. He'd panicked again. He hadn't made any arrangements. Was this it? He got dressed slowly, unsure what to do next. But the worse thing, the thing that plagued him, was her parting words. He tried to ignore them. When he got to the reception he gave the clothes back to Celeste.

"A good evening?" Celeste asked.

"Very," Rick said.

Ten minutes later he was on a ski lift. He was asking himself a question. Was this a thing, or was it just a passing fancy, a one night stand? Was this what he needed to move on, and nothing more? He'd certainly needed it and was grateful for it. It just seemed too fleeting for him. He'd kept the hotel room, just the one. He'd come back the following day and check out, which made it a twelve hundred euro commitment. It took him a while to get back without Sondra to guide him, and he made a mistake and had to ski down and back up and catch a different lift. It was nearing lunchtime when he got to Val Thorens. He wondered if the boys were at Andre's. He kept thinking about the last thing Sondra had said to him: "You don't need someone like me in your life."

Chapter Sixty-Three

Al was wondering why the others hadn't come up and seen him, or at least contacted him. But it took a lot longer to get there in a car than it did in a helicopter. These had been the old tour rules. If you fall you have to get up on your own. But they were older now. The nurses had changed to a new crew, and he thought it might be worth showing them his phone. It wasn't clear to them why, and he made hand motions to suggest adding charge. They looked at his phone, as if it was a piece of medieval medical equipment used for dentistry.

"Non," they said.

Al went back to his room and pondered about how isolated he felt without a mobile phone. He led a busy life, and wasn't accustomed to having time on his hands. He'd always taken every shift and he'd run around in the rig with the sirens blaring. Al knew he had a tendency to live through the lives of others. He'd sort of avoided having one of his own. His work gave him purpose and made him a very useful member of society. He needed to stop hiding, or figure out what he was hiding from.

He put the television on. It didn't help distract him. He knew he had to make a few decisions. There was a newsreader who looked about the same age as him. Al imagined him finishing work and going back to his chic apartment with his young and impossibly gorgeous wife, his third, and their two small children. He played with them in the way he hadn't with the older two who were now in their twenties. When he'd been too busy playing with other gorgeous women, and drinking little coffees in chic cafés. The lives of others always seemed preferable to his own. And he preferred to think about them rather than his own life.

Al had noticed from the patients he'd encountered that some people knew how to lead their lives. They were good at extracting pleasure and satisfaction, and others found it difficult. A problem for one person would be a hiccup for another. He tended to avoid thinking about which camp he sat in, although he sort of knew. Al forced himself to think about his own life, but then he saw the weather man. He didn't look as slick as the newsreader, as if he was the same man, but stripped of gloss. The sort of polish Al didn't think he had either. He switched off the television.

The retirement decision was too big to make. Perhaps, if he didn't retire, he'd take fewer shifts. He could download a dating app. He'd been on his own a long time, apart from a slight flirtation a few months ago. He thought he could make it more, but he'd spent a long time alone. He wasn't sure he knew how to. Al didn't feel comfortable talking about it. There was little point in asking Judah, and he didn't want to ask Rick. He decided he needed to talk to Will. He knew he needed to change. He just hadn't decided in which direction.

Breakfast passed and lunch appeared not so long afterwards. He realised he was actually relaxing. And then the man in the suit turned up. He had lots of forms with him, but no greater grasp of the language. It would have been useful if the smiling doctor had been there, but Al understood how they allocated resources in a hospital, and he was not a high priority. An hour later they'd ascertained that Al had not renewed his insurance. He wasn't insured. They had yet to arrive at the total bill, although much of it was in the cost of the helicopter, but it was growing larger every day they kept him there. The man in the suit's plan was to recover the money from the British National Health Service. Al had worked for them for long enough to not be entirely reassured by that.

"Can I leave?" Al said.

The man in the suit looked blank.

Al thought of the French word, or another way to express it so that the man in the suit might understand. He tried hand gestures, but they seemed to offend him.

"Go," Al said.

The man in the suit shook his head. He'd received a memo from management telling him to crack down on this sort of thing. Tourists were costing the hospital a fortune. Al signed a few forms, although he had no idea what he was signing, and the man in the suit left. He could hear him talking to the nurses, although he had no idea he was telling them to put Al's clothing in a locked drawer.

In the afternoon Al dozed in the hope it might pass the time. Then he tried the television. By the evening Al was beginning to feel like he was being held hostage. He got up and took a walk. It was a little inhibiting with a hospital gown and his evidently bared backside. But he needed to move. He'd begun to notice the shift changes and the periods when the hall was unattended. He walked through the wards without being stopped. He'd have liked to have stopped and had a coffee, but he'd put his cash in the kitty, and Will had that. He was enjoying the freedom and wondered if he could get outside. He'd noticed some wooded grounds by the helicopter pad.

"Are you okay?" a voice said.

It was the smiling doctor. Al covered up his bared backside, but suspected it was too late for that, and the doctor was a doctor. He'd seen plenty of backsides.

"They won't let me out," Al said.

"They do that sometimes," the doctor admitted with a smile.

"And I haven't got any money. I can't even buy a cup of coffee," Al said.

"Give me a few minutes and I'll get you one," the doctor said.

Al waited in the hall. It looked like every other hospital he'd ever seen. It was labyrinthine. A few minutes later, as promised, the smiling doctor appeared and directed him through a series of what seemed like shortcuts until they arrived at a coffee shop.

"Take a seat," the smiling doctor said.

Al was grateful of that, as he'd now exposed his rear end to most of the hospital. The smiling doctor returned with two coffees. He hadn't expected that and was grateful for the company.

"I think I may have found something to charge your phone," the smiling doctor said.

He passed him a charger with a lead which had a number of different jacks.

"Thanks," Al said.

"So you're a paramedic," the smiling doctor said.

"How did you know that?" Al asked.

"It's on the forms," the smiling doctor said.

"Of course," Al said. "That's me running around with sirens on and occasionally saving people."

Al didn't need to tell him about the alternative.

"What about you?" Al asked. "Are you permanently here?"

"I am now. I've got family here," the smiling doctor said.

"A wife and kids?" Al asked.

"No, I don't have those. But my family are all involved in skiing. I'm the black sheep," he said.

"The doctor is the black sheep?" Al asked.

"Kind of," the smiling doctor said smiling.

Al's family had not been particularly interested in his education, or what he did with it. He'd mostly used it to get away from them.

"Me too," Al said.

Chapter Sixty-Four

"Wasn't that fun?" the woman with the neat backside said.

Judah wanted to say it was hell and just a breath away from a full body plaster and traction. It was an unending nightmare and please don't ask him to do it again.

"Great," Judah said.

He removed his helmet. His hair was a little longer than it should be. He'd always had a touch of the hippy about him, although now it was more about holding onto a youth which was slipping away faster than he'd come down that hill. His hair was matted with sweat. He attempted to reorganise it, but it was a case of arranging deckchairs on the Titanic. He was going to have to order at least one more cognac to recover. Maybe two.

"Did you feel the adrenaline?" she asked.

She pronounced adrenaline as if it was a girl's name. The wild one at a party. The kind who'd done coke in the toilets. But he was pretty sure she'd seen him stumble. Judah wasn't sure whether to come clean on this one. He wasn't going to do it a second time. Nothing could convince him to do that.

"I certainly did," Judah said, "I nearly shit myself."

Judah wasn't normally inclined to admit weakness, but she was in a different league in almost every way.

"Noo," she said with some exaggeration.

"How long have you skied?" Judah asked.

"All my life. After I walked, I skied," she said.

"That would explain it," Judah said.

He downed the cognac and successfully ordered more. His hands had stopped shaking, although his knees were still trembling.

"And you?" she asked.

"I haven't skied in fifteen years, and I didn't learn until I was nearly forty," Judah admitted.

He would normally be reluctant to mention his age, but he could see that this woman was, as the French might say, of a certain age. She even seemed a little proud of it.

"I can teach you," she said and downed the second cognac.

Judah liked to think of himself as a man who had lived. He'd seen things and done things, but she made him feel like an inadequate teenager.

"You can?" he asked.

This was his attempt at gaining back some power. He thought the inference was sexual and before she answered he followed it with, "perhaps I can teach you something too."

She smiled. She doubted there was anything sexual that she hadn't done. She'd travelled so far in the lexicon of sexual activity that she'd recently gone back to basics. Back to the simplicity of when she'd first discovered sex and the art of touch, suspense and, her personal favourite, anticipation.

"I doubt that," she said.

Judah doubted it too.

"Always worth a try," Judah said.

"Per-haps," she said slowly.

Judah noticed her watch. It sparkled with diamonds and he had no doubt they were the real thing. Then he noticed the time.

"Is that the time?" he asked.

She glanced at her watch with a casual disdain. It would take Judah a while to get back and there was a risk that the lifts would close. She could get back in two minutes, quicker if she felt like it.

"Where are you staying?" she asked.

"Val Thorens," he said.

"I have an apartment in Meribel," she said, pointing down the hill.

They were sitting next to the window and Judah looked out and down. Hold on, he thought, was that an invitation? If it was, she was very definitely in charge in this encounter and he had no objection to that.

"Nice," Judah said.

"But can you keep up?" she asked.

This *was* an invitation. Another man might have thought of recent sexual endeavours in which discretion could usefully have paid a bigger part, but Judah didn't think like that. She was taunting him into being bold.

"Of course," he said.

He didn't say it with any great conviction, but it didn't seem to put her off. She started to put her clothes back on. She did so slowly and seductively, although that was how she did everything, so she wasn't particular aware of it. Judah was, and it was making him quite excited. A few minutes later they were outside. She'd moved away from the pack of skiers and he'd followed. Then he realised why. It looked like a sheer drop. He needed to slow things down. It occurred to him that they'd yet to exchange names. It would be rude not to.

"My name is Judah," Judah said.

He was hoping he could talk her out of this particular piste. He looked again. It wasn't a piste. It was the side of a mountain on which snow had settled.

"Claudette," Claudette said, and then she threw herself down the mountain.

Judah stood rigid with fear, which was not the kind of rigidity he'd hoped for. He looked down at her neat backside receding in the distance. And he knew something for certain. He could go back into the restaurant and order another cognac and relax. But if he did he would wake up in the middle of the night and wonder what sex with Claudette might have been like. He would agonise over the lost opportunity. A gift he'd throw away. Judah couldn't stop himself. He tipped his skis down the mountain while he could still see her. Around fifteen seconds later Judah couldn't stop himself even if he'd tried.

Chapter Sixty-Five

Al had charged his phone and had meant to call Will again, but the smiling doctor had come in and they'd chatted. He'd lost track of time and realised there would be little point in calling him. Will would be too pissed. Al also didn't want to drag him away from the slopes, as he knew how much Will liked to ski. He was the most passionate. Al had always liked the skiing trips, but for him it was more about the friendship and camaraderie, than sliding down the slopes. He should have paid more attention. If he had he wouldn't be lying in a hospital bed. He got his phone out and called his insurance company again. He had nothing to lose. It took a while to get through, but he had time on his hands.

"I'm afraid we didn't receive your renewal premium," Tracey from Newcastle said.

Tracey had been the most helpful and sympathetic, but it kept returning to the same thing. He hadn't paid.

"But I ticked the box to automatically renew," Al said a little whinily.

"I'm afraid," Tracey from Newcastle said, "we have no record of it."

There was no point in rephrasing the same question again.

"Okay. Thanks," Al said at last.

Al knew he was in danger of being saddled with the whole bill and he wasn't keen on that. That helicopter trip had been expensive. He turned on the television. There had been an avalanche. He tried to follow it and it took him a while to gather that it wasn't far from the hospital. They showed pictures of survivors.

"Hold on," Al said.

Was that Rick? He recognised his orange helmet. It would explain why Will hadn't called him. The team had other problems. It was strange watching him on television, but Al suspected he'd always been a spectator, while the others had got on with their lives. He watched a video someone had recorded on their phone of the snow sliding down the mountain like a tsunami. It didn't seem that fast, but it was taking things with it on its way. But Rick was fine. He appeared to be with someone. A girl or a woman. He suspected it was more of a coincidence, as he knew that Rick had had a tough year. But Rick was okay, he wasn't in any immediate danger.

Al, on the other hand, was being held hostage. The man in the suit had secured his belongings and kept him captive. He would be held until the British National Health Service paid the ransom. Al had worked for them for years and knew that if there was immediate and necessary surgery, or treatment, he'd be fine. But getting money out of them would be another thing. He was going to be marooned here for the rest of his life, like a drug runner in a Turkish prison. The strange thing was that he wasn't finding it to be so objectionable. He feared he was beginning to suffer from Stockholm syndrome – that classic moment when the hostages held in a 1972 bank robbery bonded with their captors. He was enjoying his chats with the smiling doctor. He'd felt comfortable enough to ask him what he should do. Should he retire and face the world, or continue hiding from it? Not that he'd put it that way. He'd been conditioned to use his work as his life and there was more, the smiling doctor had told him, to life than that.

The hours on his own had forced him to think about his life. Al wondered if Tracey from Newcastle was happy with hers. She sat at a desk, probably with a headset on, and told people they didn't have insurance. Although it was possible she spent all day helping people and gained a lot of satisfaction from it. But it was most likely she did her job, then went home to her family. Al imagined her husband, Gary, who was a plumbing engineer. He took some pride in his neat installations but, when he got home, he didn't give it another thought. He earned a good living, and they had a nice four bedroom house on a modern private estate. And two children. Al reckoned that Gary and Tracey would be quite aspirational in nature and their two children would be called Tristan and Imogen. Imogen would have a pony. They'd be doing well at the local school and Gary would wear a jacket when he went to the parent teacher gatherings. While he wouldn't deny his working class background, he wouldn't shout about it either. He couldn't stop himself clipping his accent slightly and he had, after all, voted conservative. He'd leased a new van with the name of his company – which wasn't his own – but a larger sounding business, which would be useful when he took on more blokes. He would have done so sooner, but he'd taken a bit of hit on a timeshare in Marbella, and was out of pocket twelve grand. Then he got slammed on a number of installations when a property developer went bust, which really 'fucked him over' and for a second he thought he was going to have to declare himself bust, but his brother, Darren, helped him out. Gary got back on his feet but then, a year later, Darren got arrested and he'd had to fork out a fortune for a lawyer. He had no choice. He couldn't tell Darren he had Tristan and Imogen to think of, as his brother had been there for him. And Tracey had stood by him despite that awkward thing that happened at a Christmas party. In Gary's defence, he was 'well pissed' – his accent could be a bit variable depending on the circumstances – but when he was pissing it up with the lads it tended to revert. Who'd have thought that Sharon had a thing for him? And in Sharon's defence she was on her fifth Campari. He practically choked when she'd shoved her tongue down his throat. He was, as he'd explained to Tracey, more of a victim. This was not an argument that washed well with Tracey, who'd never much liked Sharon, particularly since she'd had her breasts done. They look like two balloons strapped to a life jacket – Sharon could get a little plump – she'd told Gary. Gary could certainly feel the buoyancy aids, but thought it best not to mention it to Tracey. He did prefer them natural and had told Tracey on a number of occasions who, despite her severe criticism of Sharon's breasts, had reservations about her own. It was alright for men. They didn't have to breastfeed. But mostly Tracey and Gary got on great. They had date nights, regular sex, and laughed together.

And Al drifted off to sleep content that he'd been able to really spend time thinking about his own life, while Tracey from Newcastle had stopped off at Harry's, who was a graphic designer and not her husband, on the way home. Harry was a vigorous lover and her own husband, who coincidentally really was called Gary, was a senior policeman fifteen years older than her and needed, as Tracey put it, a 'crank start' to get it going. They'd not had children and retirement was motoring her husband's way, and the thought filled her with terror. They hadn't had a meaningful conversation in years and the best part of her day was spent strapped to a headset – as Al had correctly guessed – speaking to strangers. She'd come across Harry when he'd fallen off some rocks on a climbing holiday. She could have posted the cheque, but then she'd noticed Harry's house was on the way home. And Harry was fifteen years her junior and not remotely serious. This was just fun. She knew she'd be upgraded for a younger model and part of her knew she deserved it, as she'd replaced Gary's first wife. Now, with the benefit of hindsight, she really wished she hadn't. She was a grumpy old cow, his first wife, and coincidentally was called Sharon, and she was exactly what Gary deserved. Tracey knew she had to think about the future and make a big decision but she was afraid to. Gary wouldn't take it well, and she'd have difficulty getting her share of the house, let alone part of his pension. Who knew what lay ahead for a woman like her of a certain age?

Chapter Sixty-Six

Judah was going so fast he daren't attempt to slow down as that would certainly end in a crash. But as he was hammering down the mountain without the slightest facility for reducing his speed, a crash was beginning to seem inevitable. He managed a parting glance at Claudette's incredibly neat backside and then he was no longer on his skis. And his skis were no longer on his feet. They'd shot ahead with no intention of waiting for him and, although he was unaware of it, in Claudette's direction. But, as she'd made a very precise calculation as to where the fall line lay, that might have been inevitable. He was sliding on his backside, the upside of which was that he was now travelling quicker than he had been on his skis. But his backside was beginning to burn like he'd had a heavy evening on the curry. He needn't have worried. He hit a lump under which lay a rock, and he stopped sliding, and began to tumble. The flashes between the white of the snow and the blue of the sky were like a rapid strobe light and would have made him throw up, but he hit another lump and now he was sliding again, but this time on his face. This, he knew, was not going to end well.

As he was now a passenger in this event, his mind had the time to think about other things, not least was why he always got himself into the same kind of trouble. He could have been sitting in the restaurant sipping a further cognac. Instead he was hurtling down a mountain on his face. He didn't anticipate death, but was certain that what lay ahead was the injury that insurance companies refer to as life changing. He'd avoided the vice-chancellor, who was likely to give him the news that he was out of a job. He remembered the line from 'Educating Rita' in which the lecturer, played by Micheal Cane, said the only way he could lose his indentured position was to bugger the Bursar. He hadn't needed to go that far. But he'd certainly buggered himself up. It was all to do with the regret of missed opportunities. He just couldn't walk away from an offer of sex. It wasn't his fault. He was a victim of his own lusts.

Judah reckoned that some men were made for gentle lives. Will was one, as was Rick, but he was littered with more lusts and desires than the pair of them put together, and that was just how he was. He'd once attended a sex addiction help group. He'd got off with one of the women, a housewife with three children and a vibrator collection which – she'd told the group – could furnish a museum. After that he attended regularly for a while. There was no more certain way of getting laid than joining a collection of sex fanatics. There was as many women as men. He would have sighed at the thought, but Judah had stopped sliding. And the reason for this wasn't a good one. He was airborne. He'd fallen off the side of the piste, which wasn't a piste, and now he was testing maximum velocity to an inevitable death.

"Bugger," Judah thought.

But he'd always known that it would happen this way. His life was not the kind that ended sat in an armchair surrounded by his grandchildren, or in bed with his wife of fifty years. His would be finished in pursuit of Claudette and her neat backside. And if hadn't been her it would have been someone else. Then Judah landed.

The previous night the piste bashers had come down the mountain in their monster machines creating a corduroy-like tapestry for the skiers to enjoy. They'd dumped quite a bit of snow in a huge pile and, on the north side, it had frozen into a concrete-hard surface. Fortunately Judah landed on the south side, which had had the sun on it all day, and which provided an airbag softness, in which he made a man-shaped hole six feet deep. And then he came to a halt. He was on his back.

"Fuck," Judah muttered.

But he knew that being able to mutter anything was a good thing. He was winded. He was bruised. He was scratched. He was bleeding. He hurt everywhere. He couldn't move or didn't want to. He lay there looking at the sky. It was blue and more beautiful than he normally found it. That was either the recognition that he was still alive, or the possibility that his organs were about to shut down, and were just torturing him with a last glance.

"Bugger," he said again.

What the hell had he been thinking? Of course, as usual, he hadn't been thinking. When one sense is fully engaged, it tends to disengage the others. His penis had done the thinking. Again.

"Are you okay?" a voice said.

He recognised the voice. It was Claudette.

"I hurt," Judah said.

He could see her face peering down at him. He didn't really want to get up. He wanted to sleep for around eighteen hours. He wanted to close his eyes and keep them closed.

"Shall I kiss it better?" Claudette volunteered.

Judah's hierarchy of needs had been reshuffled and none of it included sex. That was completely disengaged.

Chapter Sixty-Seven

Al was going stir crazy. He was thinking of escape and he'd almost made a run for it when the nurses had changed their shift, but he'd been too late. He'd only had about five minutes and he'd bungled it. He sat back in the bed and picked up his phone. He called Will. He didn't answer.

"Bugger," Al said.

Will was chasing his way down a red run with increasing speed. It was all coming back to him and he missed it. It cleared his mind in the way that other forms of exercise hadn't. He'd felt stressed at work. His work load fluctuated with the property market and the economy, although most of his work was corporate and not domestic, but he'd built up relationships with developers and he was in demand. He didn't think his partners recognised how dependent the workload and the income was on him, while at the same time fearing his own obsolescence. Hard work stopped him feeling that way. And the junior partners were biting at his heels. They wanted a share of the pie. That left the last issue. The question he'd been asking himself.

Will was skiing on his own again. The others couldn't keep up and most of the time he was happy to go at their pace. But today he'd let rip and he'd arrived at a crossroads. The metaphor wasn't lost on him. He'd been wondering whether he actually enjoyed the work. Did he find it challenging and satisfying? He'd lied to himself that he did, but he was finding it increasingly repetitive. The same disputes and complaints with roughly the same solutions. It was dull. Will had a choice. There was the blue run ahead of him, a red to the left and a black run to the right. He looked down the black run. It was steep, more like a sheer drop than a slope. But it didn't look bumpy. He'd spent his life taking the blue run in front of him. Will took a right and headed to the black run.

"Oh my god," Will said.

A hundred yards later he realised a few things. The first was that there was no going back. It would take him all day to climb back up the hundred yards and he doubted it was even possible. The only way was down. The other thing was that now he was closer he could see it was bumpy, very bumpy. It looked like a minefield where the mines had exploded.

"Shit," Will said.

He could feel his phone vibrating, but he daren't reach for it. It was too steep. If he slipped he'd slide down on his arse and that would hurt. His pulse was racing. He looked back up again. He nearly fell over with vertigo. He had to calm his nerves and pick off a few turns at a time. He let himself slide across the mountain, as far from the fall line that would prompt movement and not plummeting. It was a wide piste and there were few opportunities for falling off, he reassured himself. But he had to make a turn soon. He remembered he had to put his weight on the downhill ski which, when you're trying not to tumble down a mountain, is pretty counterintuitive. He turned, but he hadn't committed his balance as he should have and suddenly, as if a switch had been thrown, he was travelling very fast.

"Shit," Will said and crashed.

He managed to hug the slope enough to stop him falling and, as crashes go, it wasn't too bad. He hadn't lost his skis. Such was the slope it was easier to get up than he thought it would be. He'd learned a lesson. Firstly, fully commit and, if it goes wrong, it won't hurt that much. And at least he was pointing in the right direction, even if a crash had got him there. He let himself slide. It took him across the piste and he was able to avoid the larger humps and he slid until he had no choice and turned again. And crashed.

"Shit," Will said.

He wasn't even pointing the right way, but he'd landed on the softer snow on the top of one of the bumps. He'd been trying to turn on the smooth, icy lanes between the bumps, perhaps that was a mistake too. He put himself in the widest and most basic snowploughs and heaved all his weight on the downhill ski. He turned, came off the bump, and now he was facing the right way. That hadn't been too bad. Another lesson learned. If it gets difficult remember the basics and slow down. He wasn't sure what he could do other than work as a lawyer, although in the back of his mind he had a distant idea. When he got to his next turn he dropped his weight, applied it all to the downhill ski, opened his skis a little, which was not quite a snowplough, mounted a bump and turned.

"Beautiful," he said.

This time he went a little quicker across the slope, bending his knees to absorb the impact, and mostly steering round the bumps until finally turning on one. Now he was motoring. He could feel the cool air whistling past his ears. There was nothing to fear from learning new skills. His legs were beginning to burn with the exertion, but they were burning in a good way. He saw a slighter flatter part of the piste ahead and came to a halt for a rest. He was breathing heavily. He looked up.

"Fucking hell," he muttered.

The point he'd started at seemed a long way away and it looked even steeper looking up. He'd nearly cracked it. Once he'd caught his breath he set off again. It was less steep than it had been, and the bumps seemed more ironed out, and he lifted his foot from the brake or applied the accelerator, he wasn't sure which, and now he was flying. He stabbed his skis in for a tight turn and then realised he'd approached the turn at too high a speed. He grappled to find his footing, but it wasn't there. This time he lost both his skis and tumbled down the mountain. But he was nearly at the end of the piste and a few seconds later he stopped falling. Someone ahead of him had grabbed his skis and held them, and he considered his last lesson. While he shouldn't fear change, he shouldn't be over confident with it either.

Chapter Sixty-Eight

Claudette had sought entertainment and not a nursing job for which she clearly had no vocation. But she felt a little responsible. She knew Judah wouldn't be able to cope, but she also didn't think he'd be stupid enough to try. Men were extraordinarily stupid.

"Shall I get help, or do you want to try and get up?" she asked.

It was another reminder that Florence Nightingale she was not. It was unlikely that Florence Nightingale had a wardrobe full of the most exotic and sensual lingerie and had blowjob skills which could render a man useless for days. But history doesn't always record such events. Claudette sighed. She was going to have to get into the hole.

"I need a brandy," he said.

"Cognac," she corrected him.

"Perfect," Judah said.

"I'm coming down," she said.

It was quite steep, and quite deep, and she hadn't intended to land on his thigh.

"Fuck," Judah said with the pain.

"Later," Claudette said.

Judah's body was doing its own assessment of the severity of his wounds and he noticed an unintentional twitch at what sounded like a pretty solid promise of sex. It was his penis. His penis had got him into this mess and it was holding a meeting with his other organs and attempting to get him out of it. Out of it and into her, preferably. But Judah knew this was a good sign.

"Can you lean up?" Claudette asked.

Judah tried. Not much happened. Claudette kneeled down and lay one hand on his inner thigh and the other behind his back. It wasn't clear which hand was the trigger, but he eased himself into a sitting position.

"Move your hands and your legs," Claudette ordered.

She was very close to the end of her patience.

"I'll try," Judah said in a slightly pathetic whine.

He tried and everything seemed to move as it should.

"I'll help you up," she said.

She squatted over him, leaned forward and put her arms round him. He could feel her breath on his neck. His major organs were making complaints to his penis. They needed the blood more. It seemed to work as he was suddenly on his feet. He felt a little fragile but nothing, as far as he could tell, was broken.

"Do you need a doctor now?" she asked.

Judah didn't think he did. He watched as Claudette scrambled out of the hole. She really did have an extraordinarily neat backside. When she got to the top she stabbed one pole in the ground and held the other down for him. It took a while, but eventually he made it to the top. He lay on his back and took in some air. She wondered if he was going to be of any use to her.

"That," she said, "is the door to my apartment block."

She pointed. It wasn't far away and this time she helped him. By the time they got there he was moving better. He found his skis, which were skewered in a bank of snow next to the door. He decided to leave them there. They entered a locker room.

"Take off your boots," she said.

He obeyed. His boots felt like they were welded to his feet, but eventually his feet found freedom and some of the pain disappeared. He was feeling stronger. He walked to the lift with barely a limp and she pressed the button for the top floor. There were mirrors and he caught a glance at himself. There was a bruise across his face and his hair looked like straw. She, on the other hand, looked like she'd just got out of an air conditioned Bentley. Not a hair out of place. The lift dinged. She led him to the apartment, fumbled with the keys for a moment, and they went in. It looked like the kind of accommodation that would be featured in a magazine. It was huge and opulent. If Judah was out of his depth he wasn't unhappy about it.

"Take a shower," she ordered and pointed to a bathroom.

Judah didn't question it. He needed a shower and the opportunity to do some repair work. He took his clothes off. They were soaking with sweat and the snow. It was a bathroom with a number of mirrors and he looked at his naked self. He looked like an old steak which had been beaten to make it tender. There were marks all over him. He pulled his stomach in. For someone who took so little exercise he was in remarkably good shape. He got in the shower and thought about Claudette. He looked down. There was no question of it. He was recovering. He wondered what that neat backside looked like naked and he felt even better. He washed the sweat out of his hair and a few minutes later he was ready.

"Showtime," Judah muttered.

Then a slight hint of anxiety set in. He looked in his wallet. There was a small zipped pocket – almost impossible to find – in which he hid what he thought of as his emergency viagra. There were three pills. He knew from his very brief acquaintance with Claudette that she was going to be a demanding woman. She was going to set a pace – a little like she had as they'd skied down the mountain – and he wanted to give his best. Or rather more than his best, via the delights of the pharmaceutical industry. He swallowed a pill. There was no immediate response. He wondered if he should take a second. A second pill seemed excessive, but he doubted he'd have another opportunity like this, and he'd had quite a rough time. His body was bound to require more help than usual. He popped another pill. He looked at the remaining pill. That would certainly be excessive. It would be completely over the top. He looked at himself in the mirror again. He didn't look well. He wasn't well. He'd just fallen down a mountain.

"Fuck it," Judah said and took the final pill.

He felt better already.

"Excellent," Judah muttered.

He took one last look in the mirror and realised that he hadn't required the pills at all. He was ready to go. There seemed little point in putting his clothes on, as he had every intention of taking them off. He imagined that Claudette was reclining on the sofa dressed in the lingerie of the highest class. He looked down again. Those chemicals must have found their home, as he wasn't just ready. He was iron-bar ready. Even Judah knew that there was something a little tacky about this approach and for a second he faltered. Then he picked up his clothes and held them in front of him. That was better. And then he stepped out of the bathroom and into the hall.

"Hey," he said to Claudette.

And Claudette smiled. He dropped his clothes. She raised her eyebrows. There *was* more to him than met the eye. Then the front door clicked.

Chapter Sixty-Nine

Claude had finished in the studio and he was pretty pissed off. They'd compared him to an English chef who swore a lot, and he was pretty fucking outraged by the comparison. He expressed his outrage by deploying every known French vulgarity. He went on to explain that English food is shit, and annoyingly it just seemed to reinforce their view. He explained that there weren't any English chefs. Everyone knows that their cuisine is fetid, suppurating merde. That the sewers of Paris flowed with more palatable food than an English kitchen. The suggestion that anyone from that fated land could be used in the same sentence as him was like crapping on the French flag. Like squatting over the tricolour and covering it with merde.

Claude had flambéed something in cognac, and he'd taken a few sips of cognac himself just for good measure. He'd actually consumed quite a bit, as he'd then suggested a suitable wine, and he'd drunk most of that too. He shouldn't really be driving, but he felt that if a gendarme did stop him, he'd recognise him and thank him for his contribution to French culture. He really was quite iconic. His thoughts returned to the English chef and his mind blackened. The notion that an Englishman could cook was wounding enough, but to be compared to him... that filled him with horror.

Claude floored the throttle. He loved the Bentley. The wood and the leather and the jewel-like clock, which sat on the dashboard reminding him that he needed to get a move on. His was a frustration that only his cherie could whisk away with her magic lips. He patted the steering wheel. He was happy to let an Englishman select and polish the wood for his dashboard, or choose the finest hide for the upholstery, but he was certain they'd make a mess of the most basic omelette. They probably wouldn't know that it required an egg. They would struggle, if there was such a thing as a food line out, to recognise an egg. They'd have to google it and check. The English had no feeling for seasoning. These things weren't acquired. They were handed down through the generations by word of mouth and genetics. If your grandfather's grandfather hadn't been lauded for his creme brûlée, then you wouldn't know where to start. It wouldn't be in your soul.

"Mon dieu," Claude said.

He'd been told to curb his language and fucking hell he'd tried. But the English. Please. Claude had once been invited to a catering school in a place called Slough. It was before his fame had really taken off and the money had seemed good at the time. Now he wouldn't fry an egg for the same money. But then he'd needed it and he'd not known just what a revolting place Slough was. The thought, the memory of it, made him feel a little queasy. He pressed the accelerator a little further down and the car roared in return. He understood that his particular Bentley had been engineered by the Germans, and he was thankful for it. He didn't like the Germans either. Of course, their food was shit, and their idea of sophisticated cooking was to wrap some mince meat in a skin, and call it a sausage. What kind of cooking is that? He decided to call his cherie. He brought her number up and stabbed the appropriate button. Nothing happened. He tried again.

"Putain de merde," Claude said.

He could never get his phone to connect with his car. He was certain that some Englishman was responsible for that particular design anomaly. If they'd left it to the Germans he'd be talking to her now. He checked the time. The little clock was a Breitling. They'd asked a Swiss person to do the clock and he was fine with that. That was their thing. Of course their food was shit. Don't ask them to cook or they'll hurl everything into a gooey mass of ordinary cheese, and call it a national dish. As tasty as a bird poop on a pizza. That brought him to the Italians. Of course, their food was shit. They had not the slightest idea when it came to assembling ingredients into something exceptional. It was lazy cooking. Pizza and pasta. Give them a car and they're fine – Claude's other car was a Ferrari, but he didn't use it much as it scared him – but most of them couldn't tell a frying pan from a ladle. He sighed.

He'd been so insulted he'd nearly cut himself. Not that it was difficult to cut himself with a Master Raf knife. Master Raf was the sixth generation of knife makers with skills passed down through teaching, skill and, once again, genetics. There had been a formal ceremony when he'd picked them up – he liked the Japanese, they were so respectful – they had recognised his contributions to the art of cooking. It was an art and not a lot of shouting as Claude had maintained, although if his sous chef failed to follow his instructions to the letter, he might easily unleash a stream of well selected insults. The Japanese understand the importance of order. Of course, their cooking is shit.

The idea of mixing cold vinegared rice and raw fish was an insult to a finely honed palate.

"Pas loin," Claude muttered.

He wasn't far, not that he was feeling any more relaxed. He saw a sign which reminded him of a shoot he did in America. He wouldn't have gone, but the money was so good he couldn't stop himself, and when he was there they had treated him like the royalty he often felt he was. He'd shown them how to make a steak special. He'd refused at first, as it was like asking Monet to paint a toilet block – it was hardly an expression of his talents – but it reflected American tastes. Claude was convinced that they were equipped with about a quarter of the taste receptors of a Frenchman and, of course, their cooking was shit.

Claude was off the motorway and hammering up the mountain. He didn't tend to recognise the possibility that other road users might have the same right to the road as him and he overtook and weaved. He was getting a little excited. His cherie always did that, although his thoughts had helped put the world in perspective. It didn't take long to get to his building. He reached for the remote control which opened the gates and manoeuvred the Bentley into his parking space. He turned off the ignition and patted the steering wheel. Claude always dressed in black and he had a spare set of clothes in the apartment. He took out two small cases from the boot of the car. One contained a toothbrush, underpants and socks. He liked to wear a fresh pair of socks every day. He didn't like them once they'd been washed. The other wooden box was beautifully inlaid and told the story in Japanese of the knife makers and their contribution to the samurai culture. This box housed his knives and they were like a Stradivarius. They were more valuable than the Bentley and he never travelled without them. He pressed the button for the lift.

He looked in the mirror and rearranged his hair, which could go a little manic particularly with the heat of the kitchen. He checked his profile. Claude was equipped with a large nose, some might say it echoed de Gaulle, but it was just another instrument to taste and assess. The lift binged and he got out, fumbled with his keys and entered the apartment.

"Claudette," Claude said.

"Claude," Claudette said.

"Shit," Judah said.

Chapter Seventy

When Bruno got the call he was sitting on the toilet. He had the shits. It was embarrassing, as he'd spent the afternoon with his mistress, and he'd spent most of it scurrying to the toilet.

"Who?" he asked.

He'd spent ten years in Paris and had dealt with all kinds of criminals and gangs. It had become a little tiring. He'd viewed the Alps as half way to retirement. Tourists getting pissed and nothing more.

"Claude Cretet," his sergeant said.

Bruno had heard the name, but he couldn't place him.

"Who?" he asked.

"The chef," his sergeant replied.

"Putain," Bruno said.

He did know who he was, and it prompted an inkling of an idea. There could be a payday in this one. Bruno would have got off the toilet, but he couldn't be certain that his bowels had finished their unplanned evacuation. He needed to go to a doctor. He lit a cigarette and phoned Jean-Paul. Jean-Paul was his big-shot brother-in-law, who he didn't much care for, but he ran a newspaper and it was the kind that would be grateful for this kind of information. A gratitude that would be expressed in euros, which was the kind that Bruno liked. The phone rang and remained unanswered.

"Putain," Bruno said.

Jean-Paul lived in a seven window wide apartment that overlooked the Seine. It was worth millions. He viewed Bruno as a carrot-eating, straw-chewing bumpkin and Bruno hated him for it. He sent him a text.

He wasn't going to give away too much information, but he used the word 'siege', as that sounded long lasting and newsworthy. And if it wasn't a siege he'd make sure it was.

His phone rang. It was Jean-Paul.

"Who?" Jean-Paul demanded.

"A very well known chef," Bruno replied.

"Yes, but who?" Jean-Paul asked.

"How much?" Bruno replied.

He did not trust Jean-Paul a millimetre, which was coincidentally the measure by which Claude intended to remove his hostage's penis. It was a nice touch and he'd mentioned it in the text.

"Millimetre by millimetre," Bruno said.

Jean-Paul had a dog called Johnny. He'd been tempted to name him Bruno, but his wife had objected. He credited Johnny with having significantly more intelligence than Bruno, but Bruno was holding out. He tried a different tack.

"How famous?" Jean-Paul asked.

"Very," Bruno said.

"Is it JF?" Jean-Paul asked.

"No," Bruno said.

"Is it Malin?" Jean-Paul asked.

"No," Bruno said.

"Claude Cretet?" Jean-Paul asked.

And Bruno paused. He really hated his brother in law.

"Millimetre by millimetre, you say?" Jean-Paul said.

Jean-Paul was beginning to enjoy this exchange. Still, it didn't matter. What did matter was that he loathed Claude Cretet. He'd tried on three occasions to get into Claude Cretet's restaurant and had been rejected every time. Jean-Paul moved pretty skilfully through Parisian society and he resented this very deeply. If Cretet had given him the finest table, at the shortest notice, he would have brought a halt to proceedings right now. But he hadn't, and now he was going to pay for it.

"A kilometre," Bruno said.

"Eh?" Jean-Paul said.

"That is the closest the press will get," Bruno said.

Now they were negotiating and five minutes later Bruno felt certain his run of diarrhoea had come to an end and Jean-Paul was straight back on the phone.

"We're going to need a helicopter," he said.

He had a plan which would double circulation and overload the internet. A news and televisual treat. He rubbed his hands together and phoned around until he found a crew nearby. Doris was a cross-dressing helicopter pilot who'd seen action, as Derek, in Afghanistan and Syria. He could land the thing on a spike, in a storm with a hale of gunfire. Actually, he could probably do that and still apply mascara. Today he was in full bloke gear, apart from his fingernails, which he'd left on after a slightly wild night.

"Alright, Doris?"

Boris was the cameraman. Boris and Doris often worked together and they'd arrived at an understanding. They both took the piss.

"I am, my sweetness, I am," Doris said.

He weaved the helicopter around, as he knew it irritated Boris, and would induce sickness. Boris was built like a tank, although a rather flabby one, and he was sensitive to criticism.

"Enough," he shouted, and Doris righted the helicopter.

They both had no idea how this drama would unfurl. What they did know was that the helicopter was very expensive and it would be in their interests to make it as dramatic as possible.

Chapter Seventy-One

"Claudette," Claude said.

"Claude," Claudette said.

"Shit," Judah said.

The scene was such an outrage to Claude it took him a few seconds to assimilate. It was as if, for a second, he couldn't believe his eyes. His eyes were lying to him. Then he realised it wasn't his eyes that were doing the lying. It was his wife. Claude wasn't angry. Anger did not express his feelings at that moment. Claude was incandescent with rage. There were situations which could be misinterpreted, in which someone could legitimately say, 'it's not what it seems.' But a naked man with an erection was not one of them.

"I'm going to blanch, boil, bake, fricassee and caramelise your balls," Claude screamed.

He dropped his small briefcase and opened the knife box. He would normally give it some thought as to whether he required the paring, filleting, boning, peeling or carving knife. But he knew what he wanted. He wanted the biggest knife. It looked like a meat cleaver,

But, in Claude's view, a meat cleaver was as blunt as an Englishman's palate. This was much sharper. Claude raised it above his head and brought it down as hard as he could on the part of Judah which was demonstrating that this situation was exactly as it seemed.

"Fuck!" Judah yelled.

He put his hand up. Judah was not a man who would ordinarily be lauded for the speed of his reactions. He was feeling a little battered too, but a primal sense of survival stepped in. There was no question which of his organs was his favourite, and he was prepared to sacrifice a finger if it was necessary. The cleaver sliced through the air and Judah leaped into the bathroom, almost tripping over his clothes. He turned and locked the door.

"Fuck," Judah said.

There was blood on the floor. *His* blood. He checked his penis, from which a flag could easily be suspended and, given the horror of the previous few seconds, was a tribute to Pfizer and their contribution to keeping men stiff. There was blood all over it. It took a moment to realise that it had come from his finger, the top of which had been sliced clean off. From the other side of the door it wasn't possible to tell whether they were looking at part of a finger, or part of a penis.

"Claude," Claudette said.

She was attempting to find a way to placate him, but she'd never seen him quite so furious before. Angry English chefs had nothing on Claude. The whites of his eyes were bright, as if he was having a rabies fit.

"I'm going to cut it off centimetre by centimetre," Claude yelled.

He'd shouted so loudly that the people in the floor below could hear, as could those in the neighbouring block. Then Claude hesitated. That was an insult to Master Raf. That didn't do his finally honed product any justice.

"Millimetre by millimetre," Claude corrected himself.

Claudette and Judah had no doubt he wasn't kidding. Judah looked around for his clothes, but they were in a pile the other side of the door. He looked around for a towel. He'd dumped that with his clothes as well. There was nothing to cover himself. A second later it seemed less important as Claude had brought the knife down so hard on the solid wood door that it sliced straight through.

"Fuck," Judah said.

He looked out the bathroom window. This wouldn't be the first time he'd made his escape through a bathroom window. He was eight floors up. He looked down. It was a bloody long way.

"Stop, Claude," Claudette pleaded.

Claude turned his head. His eyes were crazed. Claudette feared he'd turn on her. She'd only just met Judah and, although he seemed nice enough, she wasn't prepared to sacrifice herself for him. Her family hadn't got rich doing that.

"Mais…" Claudette said.

Claude turned his face to the door. He wasn't stupid. He'd heard words like 'shit' and 'fuck' and guessed that this wasn't a man with a sophisticated vocabulary. And he was English. For a second he remembered the comparison that had been made between himself and some Englishman who claimed to be a chef. The word should be protected, like Brie or Roquefort. Only a Frenchman could be called a chef. The rest were just taking up space in a kitchen.

"Connard," Claude screamed, and pulled the cleaver out of the wood, and brought it down a second time.

It had been constructed by a carpenter down in the valley who had painstakingly matched the grains, and each door weighed fifty kilos, and was designed not just to last a lifetime, but to be passed through the generations. He was the sixth generation cabinet maker, although his son had chosen to throw this heritage away and become a DJ in Ibiza and take a lot of drugs. But this was a Master Raf knife.

"Shit," Judah said.

This was a real level of panic. He did not wish to have his penis sliced like a saucisson, or any other part of him, but he wasn't keen on tumbling to his death either. He opened the window and screamed, 'Help!'. But Claudette had already called the gendarmes. She'd reasoned that if she didn't her husband would commit murder, and that wouldn't be good for either of them. Judah was considering his self preservation options.

"I didn't touch her," he shouted through the door.

Claude had just removed the cleaver, it was a remarkably effective device, and he considered the words. There was an outside possibility, marginal in the extreme, that nothing had happened. But, if he'd listened to his idiot producer and stayed a further fifteen minutes to retake something, that erection would have been planted in his wife. And he wasn't having that. He brought the cleaver down. The door splintered a little more, but it had a number of sturdy crosspieces which were holding it together and preventing Claude from entering.

"Nothing happened," Judah pleaded.

Chapter Seventy-Two

"Five of my finest lagers," Andre said proudly.

"There's only two of us," Mac said, "but don't worry, I'll find a home for the others."

Andre eyed Mac curiously. His Englishmen were becoming less reliable and his wife had gone mad. There was something up and he couldn't figure out what. If it was another woman, someone who absolutely wasn't his wife, he might suspect she was having an affair.

"What happened?" Andre asked.

"Al is still at the hospital, and Rick got caught in an avalanche, and I'm not sure where Judah's gone," Mac said.

"Oh," Andre said and added, "nice kilt."

They'd gone back to the apartment and changed and Mac had put on his kilt, which he'd dumped in the bath to remove the vomit, and which was now dry.

"Scotland are playing," Mac explained.

"Of course," Andre said.

Will and Mac sat down. They looked around for Judah.

"He's not here," Will said.

"Where did you leave Judah?" Mac asked.

"He was in the restaurant at the top," Will said.

"The other side of Meribel?" Mac asked.

"That's the one," Will said.

"I doubt he'd have gone down to Meribel," Mac said.

"He doesn't like to ski far," Will said.

"Not keen on heights, either," Mac said through gulps of lager.

"I'll try him again," Will said.

"Anything?" Mac asked.

"It's not even ringing now," Will said.

Andre had drifted back into the bar even though they had a more than adequate supply of lager in front of them.

"Putain," Andre muttered.

"What's up, patron?" Mac asked cheerfully.

Andre pointed to the television. He pulled out a remote control from his apron and raised the volume. It was a newsflash which had interrupted the program.

"Putain," Andre said.

"Doesn't the match start soon?" Mac asked.

"Putain," Andre said again.

They looked up. There was a helicopter flying round a tall building. The rotors were shifting the loose snow on the roofs of the neighbouring building creating a bit of a snow storm. There was a camera on the ground which occasionally shifted to the viewpoint from the helicopter. They could see a man waving from a window. There was a constant stream of commentary.

"Putain," Andre repeated.

"Where's that?" Mac asked.

"That is Meribel," Andre said.

"Just up the road?" Will said.

"Yes," Andre confirmed.

They watched a little more but, as they had no idea what was going on, they lost interest. Andre explained.

"Do you know who Claude Cretet is?" Andre asked.

"No," Will said.

"He is a famous chef. A very angry chef. He swears a lot," Andre said.

They nodded and carried on drinking their lagers.

"Does that mean they won't be showing the match?" Mac asked.

Andre shrugged.

"He has found a man with his wife," Andre said, adding wistfully, "a very beautiful woman."

Although Andre had a habit of prefacing the phrase 'a very beautiful woman' when describing any female member of the species, he was in this case correct. He always said it with some bitterness, as his wife had been described as many things in her life, and only once was it beautiful. But the myopic war veteran had collected very little money that day. Mac nodded and turned to Will.

"I wanted to see the match," Mac said.

Will shrugged, but he wasn't as good at it as Andre.

"I quite fancy eating at the duck restaurant this evening," Will said.

They'd found a restaurant which seemed to only serve duck, and they'd agreed that they'd go there at some stage during the week. Today seemed as good a day as any.

"He is holding the man hostage," Andre said.

They looked up at the television. That seemed a little more interesting, if not actually as riveting as Andre appeared to find it. Andre laughed.

"What's up?" Mac asked.

"Cretet is threatening to slice off the man's penis millimetre by millimetre," Andre said.

"Not nice," Will observed.

They went back to their planning and would have continued, but there were two words that interrupted their train of thought.

"What did he say?" Mac asked.

"An Englishman," Andre said and then, as he said it, the centime dropped.

"Do you think that might explain where Judah is?" Mac said.

"It sounds like him," Will said.

Now they were all riveted to the television. The commentary flowed at great speed. There were news anchors adding their views and a few excerpts of Claude at work, mostly, it appeared, swearing. The bleeps they understood. When the narrative shifted back they could see gunmen taking position on neighbouring buildings. The camera turned to the hostage. They zoomed in.

"Putain," Andre said.

"Shit," Will said.

"It bloody is," Mac said.

Then the zoom continued beyond Judah to the door behind him. It was sliced apart and they could just about make out a manic looking face and a hatchet.

"That's Cretet," Andre said.

"Here's Johnny," Mac said, less than tastefully.

A ladder fell out of the helicopter. It dangled outside the window, bouncing about like a bungee rope. The camera pulled back

"That's a long way up," Mac said.

"It is a long way down," Andre said.

"He's not going to..." Will said.

"He is," Mac said.

They could see Judah leaning out for the ladder. But it was swaying about, with the downdraft from the helicopter, and the snow was flying everywhere.

"Shit," Will said.

"It's that or getting his penis cut off," Andre said.

Will and Mac looked at each other.

"He's going to get on that ladder," Will said.

"No question," Mac confirmed.

They watched as Judah leaned out further and finally caught the ladder. He looped his arm through.

"He's naked," Will said.

"No, he's got a towel on," Mac said.

A second later Judah was out of the window and on the ladder.

"He's naked now," Will said.

The towel whipped up, as if he was Marilyn Monroe over a subway vent, and then it flew away. Will and Mac stood up and moved closer to the television.

"So that's what all the fuss is about," Will said.

"Looks pretty small to me," Mac said.

"It is very cold," Andre pointed out.

Andre's wife had often made derogatory remarks about his tackle and he was very sensitive about it. It *was* very cold.

"Shit," Will said.

They watched transfixed as Judah was hoisted up into the helicopter and, as this was French television, they saw no need to pixilate his nakedness. The whole world was given a view of the Judah Crown Jewels. Claude Crete's head had appeared at the window.

"That was close," Will said.

They sat down again. Despite appearances, the boys had cared for each other for over thirty years. If one was down the others would be there to support him. It was understood. What was also understood was that it was never openly expressed. Andre was a little taken back by their apparent indifference.

"What about the match?" Mac asked.

The news flash finished and the match appeared. It was the final few minutes and Scotland were losing.

"Shit," Mac said.

"I'm hungry," Will said.

"Do you think we'll need to book the restaurant?" Mac asked.

"Probably not with just the two of us," Will said.

"Duck it is, then," Mac said.

Chapter Seventy-Three

Judah looked out the window. It was a bloody long way even if he didn't have an issue with heights. His legs were shaking. He was going to die or have his penis cut off. He looked at his penis. Despite the pharmaceutical industry's best efforts, the fear, the cold draught from the open window, and the prospect of its imminent removal had practically reduced it to Braille. But it was still attached to him and he wanted to keep it that way.

"Fuck," Judah said.

There was no question of it. He'd rather die than have his dick cut off, particularly a millimetre at a time. The fall would be less painful. Then, suddenly, a ladder appeared. It was a rope ladder, and it had sprung from nowhere. He looked up. It wasn't nowhere. It was a helicopter. And this was a lifeline. He looked around for something to cover himself up with. His clothes were the other side of the door. He grabbed a towel. It wasn't a very big one, but it was better than nothing.

"I didn't touch her," Judah shouted.

It was worth a try. He had nothing to lose. Then he could hear a phone ringing. It sounded like his. The chopping stopped. There was a pause in proceedings. Perhaps he'd been saved.

"Merde," Claude shouted.

Judah heard a scrunching noise. That used to be his phone. Then the onslaught on the door continued. He hadn't been saved.

"Putain de merde," Claude screamed.

The door, solid as it was, was not going to hold up forever. It was a splinter away from collapse. Of course,

Judah could face him and fight him like a man, even if the man was manic and in possession of a very sharp knife.

"Fuck that," Judah said, and leaned out and grabbed the ladder.

It was bobbing about in the wind and the helicopter was struggling to keep it still. He looked up.

"Fuck," he said.

It was a bloody long way up, but it was also a bloody long way down. Then he heard the door make a noise. It was the kind of noise that suggested it was nearly over. He stepped onto the window ledge and put his foot on the ladder. He curled his arm round it as he'd seen people do in films. And then he was free. He dangled for a second and then the ladder began to move. It was then that he noticed two things. The first was that the towel had flown away. He couldn't reach out and grab it for fear of falling. The other thing was it was bloody cold. Properly freezing. He held on. He daren't look up or down. A few minutes later he was inside the helicopter.

"Evening, love," Doris said.

There was a lens in Judah's face followed by a barrage of questions from Boris. But Judah couldn't answer them. He was shaking too much. He was shaking with the trauma and the cold and he was seconds away from his body shutting down.

"You wanna get a blanket round him," Doris said.

Boris looked around. He couldn't see any blankets. Or anything.

"Where are they?" Boris shouted to Doris.

Doris shrugged. He'd been scrambled at short notice and this wasn't his unit.

"I think he's going to freeze to death if we don't get something on him," Boris said.

"He probably won't," Doris said rationally.

Judah was still shaking and didn't take much comfort in this exchange.

"He'll just get frostbite at his extremities," Doris added.

Judah knew what that meant and he clung to his extremity to keep it warm. Oscar Wilde would have had something to say about nearly losing it to a maniac with a knife and then losing it through frostbite.

"Fuck," Judah managed to say.

His vocabulary was breaking down. Everything was breaking down.

"Okay," Doris said.

Doris turned the helicopter and headed down the hill to Albertville, the nearest hospital. He had a sports bag next to him. It was his overnight case and he had some clothes inside it. He threw it back to Boris.

"He looks about the same size as me. There are some clothes in there," Doris shouted.

Doris looked round at Judah who was lying prone on the floor and shaking as if he was having a fit. Doris cast a not inexperienced eye over Judah's shrivelled genitals and added, "maybe not the same size, but the same height and build."

"Okay," Boris said.

Boris unzipped the bag and pulled out the clothes. There seemed to be an excessive amount of lingerie. Then he found some thick denim. It looked quite warm. He held it up.

"It's a fucking dress," Judah managed to say, despite being two steps away from hyperthermia.

"That's a Milly Elisa," Doris said proudly.

Judah looked at it. He didn't have a choice. Boris helped him get in it and then found a florescent pink cardigan. They both looked at it.

"Fuck it," Judah said, and put it on.

The ride to the hospital was a short one in a helicopter, but Judah was unaware that Bill Tuft had been in his office in Fleet Street. There was a chatter to the news room as articles and items drifted past his desk. He nearly missed it, but then the name rang a bell. A bell which would give him an opportunity to regurgitate the sadomasochistic story about the MP's daughter and the lecturer. It didn't take him long to get someone on the ground. He had contacts and when Judah alighted from the helicopter in a denim dress with a pink cardigan, that too was recorded by the world's press.

"Fuck it," Judah said.

Chapter Seventy-Four

When Al woke up he wondered whether he should call Tracey and check on Tristan and Imogen. Then he realised he'd made them up. Not Tracey, she was real, but the children. He toyed with the idea of calling her, but he feared he'd get Mary. Mary was from the west coast of Ireland and from a family of nine. They were catholics. She'd fled when their local priest had made an advance, although it made a change from him touching her brothers, which at least explained why they called him Father Bi-Barry. She thought it was because he had a stutter. He was certainly stuttering when he'd placed his hands on her. He was breathing heavily too. She'd found England to be a strange land. No one knew anyone. Where she was from everyone knew everyone and all their business. Not that it had stopped Father Bi-Barry, who looked set to extend the alliteration and become Bishop Bi-Barry. She couldn't make out for what services he was being rewarded. And the clothing had been a shock to her, although this was the north east of England, where a night out involved flaunting it all. And a bit more. She'd worn less revealing underwear. Despite that she met Tom on a trip to the pub and he seemed a nice boy with a good career. Al shook his head. He realised he was dreaming about the lives of others again. He turned the television on. There was some sort of siege.

"Bloody hell," Al said.

He couldn't believe it. He'd seen Judah on the television. How was that possible? It all seemed a little surreal. His time in hospital had been a little surreal.

He'd had a patient once who was dying and she talked about destiny. She felt that it was all part of God's design, and there was nothing anyone could do. Al didn't believe that. He'd been taught about the mechanics of the body. The airway, the breathing and the circulation. She'd said there was more to life than that. Al didn't know what she meant, although he guessed it was an allusion to the soul. He didn't believe in that either. Maybe when management had said he was getting a little cynical there was some truth in it. He'd seen too many people die. But that didn't explain destiny. And surely he was the master of his own? He stopped this irritating reflection and concentrated on the television. He didn't understand a word. Fortunately the smiling doctor appeared.

"That is my friend, Judah," Al said.

The smiling doctor watched.

"But I don't understand what he's done," Al said.

"According to this," the smiling doctor said slowly, "he was caught with another man's wife."

"That sounds like Judah," Al said.

"But the other man is a famous chef, Claude Cretet. He is very aggressive," the smiling doctor.

The smiling doctor pronounced aggressive in the French way, as if it ended with an 'f'". It had a charm about it which made Al smile.

"And Claude is threatening to cut off his penis millimetre by millimetre," the smiling doctor said.

"Judah wouldn't like that," Al observed.

"Who would?" the smiling doctor said with a smile.

They watched as Judah was hoisted naked through the cold air and into the helicopter.

"That looks cold," the smiling doctor said.

"It bloody does," Al said.

After that there was a piece about hair loss, which they both watched, although neither were particularly interested in it. Conversation had flowed from the smiling doctor, but today he appeared a little hesitant.

"I have to say goodbye," the smiling doctor said.

"Goodbye? Are you doing your rounds?" Al asked.

"No, I've done them, but I'm off for the next three weeks," the smiling doctor said.

Al felt a little irritated he hadn't mentioned it earlier, but then he knew he wasn't going to stay there forever. This wasn't his destiny, if there was such a thing. Although, it would be useful to figure out what his destiny was. That said, he shouldn't have to, destiny was just what was going to happen to him. He couldn't stop it.

"It was nice to meet you," the smiling doctor said and got up.

And that, Al thought, was that. They shook hands formally and the smiling doctor smiled.

"Where are you going?" Al asked.

"A bit of travelling. Rome, Venice, Paris, Berlin and Amsterdam," the smiling doctor said.

"Not London?" Al said.

"Too expensive," the smiling doctor said.

"You can stay with me," Al said.

He couldn't believe he'd said it. He was immediately embarrassed, as if he'd overstepped a line. But friendship wasn't so easily come by these days. The smiling doctor nodded with a smile and disappeared into the labyrinthine corridors of the hospital. Al was left on his own. He tried watching the television, but it bored him. He thought about Tracey, but this time he couldn't conjure any images of her life. He couldn't even think of a name for Imogen's pony. He fiddled with his phone. He tried phoning Will.

"Come on," he said as the phone rang.

He really was ready to go and now he was feeling a little let down by the team. They'd completely deserted him. He tried Will again. Nothing. He tried Rick. It didn't even ring. Then he tried Judah. There was no reply, although that might have been because he had problems of his own. It was as if they'd sent him to Coventry. Al patted the bed. He wasn't sure what he was going to do. Then he knew exactly what he had to do. He had to escape. His Stockholm syndrome had come to an end. There was nothing keeping him there. This bank robbery had come to an end. And if he had to escape with his arse hanging out of his gown, then so be it.

Chapter Seventy-Five

Terry was finding her first skiing trip to be bordering on the surreal. She understood that Julie's family were wealthy, but she'd no idea how the truly wealthy live. Cleo, the family secretary, had got them onto a private jet which was apparently owned by someone called Oleg. Who had friends called Oleg?

"Fucking hell, it's cold," Terry said.

It wasn't as if she hadn't seen snow before – she came from a village near Oldham – but she couldn't believe how much there was of it. It was everywhere.

"Don't worry, there's some skiing gear in the villa," Julie said.

Terry had never flown in a private jet before, and it seemed to have gin and tonic on tap. And, as the weather conditions were too bad to land in the short runway in Courcheval, they'd hopped into a helicopter for the last part of the journey. That was a first time too.

"Hi Doris," Julie said to the pilot.

"Doris?" Terry said, a little confused.

Julie shrugged. She'd had a few drinks with Doris in the past and knew where he could he found should she need him.

"Nearly there," Julie said.

She'd dozed through most of the journey, while Terry had taken the opportunity to avail herself of the evidently endless and free booze on the plane. Her eyes were no longer flitting over Julie's lithesome body. They were mounting an invasion. The helicopter landed gently on the snow.

"Duck," Julie said, as they got out.

Terry's denim dungarees and her nylon coat were no match for the downdraught of the blades, the wind, and an ambient temperature of around minus six.

"I'm fucking freezing," Terry said.

Her teeth were chattering. She couldn't believe that rich people put themselves through this torture.

Twenty minutes later they were in the villa. It felt sauna-warm by contrast to the outside, and it was vast. The sitting room was larger than her parents' house. The whole villa seemed to be about the size of the village she'd been brought up in.

"If you're cold you might want to grab a bath," Julie said.

Despite the cold and the awe of the place, Terry interpreted this as a very good sign, although she'd been given her own bedroom with its own bathroom. But there was no one else there.

"Sure," Terry said.

She ran the bath and practically lost her hands when she pressed them into the white towelling dressing gown. She'd never felt luxury like it.

"Fancy a g & t?" Julie shouted from the sitting room.

Terry didn't really, but she reckoned it was likely that Julie would bring it to her and, as she'd be naked in the bath if she got a move on, that would be good.

"Please," Terry shouted back.

Terry turned the taps on full, as she knew she'd look a little silly sitting in a half empty bath. It filled quickly and she threw off the dressing gown and stood naked for a moment. She looked around the bathroom. There was more marble than there was in Oldham town hall. And mirrors. The rich, she'd noticed, like their mirrors. She forced herself to look at her reflection. She was a little pink and plump but she didn't look *that* bad. She pulled her stomach in and stuck her breasts out.

"Not so bad," she said to herself.

There was no question she would. But she wasn't very objective about the matter. She was desperate to have sex. Terry made the mistake of fantasising about how it might go. The bath was double ended and could easily accommodate the two of them. That would be nice. Although, before that, she'd like a good old fashioned snog. Was that too much to ask?

"No problem," Julie shouted back.

Julie had no idea that Terry had consumed so many gins on the plane, as she hadn't really paid much attention. She grabbed a couple of cut glass tumblers. The remote control for the television was lying on the sideboard next to a collection of spirits. She fired it over her shoulder and continued with the process of assembling a gin and tonic. Cleo had made sure there was both ice and lemon in the small fridge which had no other purpose, and Julie didn't give it a second thought. When she finished she turned and looked at the enormous screen.

"Bloody hell," she said.

Given where her thoughts had been, it was a little surreal. Was that? She couldn't be sure. She moved closer to the screen. It was. She couldn't believe it. It was Judah.

"Oh dear god," she said.

His towel had whipped off and he was naked. He was a lot smaller than she remembered. She watched as he was hauled into a helicopter. She studied the helicopter. She recognised it.

"Doris," she muttered.

It must have been his next call after dropping them off.

"Hey," she shouted to Terry. "You'll never guess who I've just seen on the telly?"

Julie walked into the bathroom and dropped the g & t by the side of the bath. Terry lay there naked. Her arms were pinched in, pressing her breasts up. Her pink nipples were little islands in the water. There was symmetry and, when she moved them, ripples evenly intersected each other. It could have been an art installation. But she couldn't guess, even if she'd tried.

"Judah bloody Wheeler," Julie said.

A little part of Terry withered. Had that bloody man come back to haunt her again? He was the Antichrist of her sex life. Terry watched as Julie left the bathroom. She hadn't once cast her eyes over Terry's naked form. It hadn't even occurred to her.

Chapter Seventy-Six

The duck was magnificent. It had been served and cooked in five different ways, mostly dripping in fat, and it had been followed by more Génépi than either they, or the patron, could count. The starter had also been a duck variation in which even more fat featured, and the selection of puddings appeared to have been chosen for their likelihood to induce a heart attack.

"I'll just nip out for a fag," Mac said.

There was a side door from which people were encouraged to smoke and Mac found the patron, Louis – or Louis the duck as he was often called – lighting a cigarette from the remnants of his previous cigarette.

"Bonsoir," Louis muttered through an enormous moustache.

Mac had swept his yard with less luxuriant brooms. He was holding a cognac in his other hand. He looked at Mac.

"English?" he asked.

"No, no, no," Mac insisted. "Scottish."

Louis raised his glass, but then realised there was an issue.

"Attendez," Louis said.

Mac lit a cigarette and looked at the slopes. In the distance he could see the piste bashers performing their nightly task, and he could hear the music from a bar filled with the young. They were spilling out onto the street. It was all part of the mating process and a little part of Mac envied them, but the larger part was grateful he was with Anita and didn't have to go through all that. Louis reappeared and handed Mac a glass of cognac.

"Salut!" Louis said.

"Salut!" Mac replied.

Louis had worked in the tourist industry all his life, he'd even lived in England for a couple of years, and he came across English-speaking people every day. Louis didn't speak a word of English and had no interest in trying. He operated the same policy with his menu. He liked duck. Mac realised it was up to him to communicate and unearth whatever French he possessed. He started with the duck. His mind went blank and then he remembered 'Only Fools and Horses' in which Rodney had explained to Del Boy how to say duck.

"Bon canard," Mac said.

When Del Boy had heard the word he'd interpreted it as 'fucking hard', but Louis had got the point, and explained in rapid French precisely how he selected and cooked the duck. He spoke with great passion and for no obvious reason Mac appeared to understand.

"Et vous?" Louis said.

Mac understood this to be a question regarding his occupation and he'd heard the French express it before.

"Ar-she-tect," he said.

Louis raised his eyes in appreciation and they clinked glasses. And Louis chuckled.

"Avocat," he said, "pas bon."

Louis did not like lawyers. He didn't like them during his first divorce nor the subsequent three.

"Je n'aime pas les avocats," Louis said.

Mac wondered at what point he'd tell him that Will was a lawyer. It was too good not to mention.

"Et les banquers," Louis said.

He put his thumb down at them. He was not fond of bankers. Mac wondered if he should mention that Rick had been a banker, but he wasn't there so that would have to wait for their next trip.

"C'est vrai," Mac said, raising his glass.

They clinked glasses again and Mac lit another cigarette and offered one to Louis. Louis looked at it. It had a filter tip and was low in tar. Girl cigarettes, in Louis's view. He took one anyway, as he wouldn't want to offend, and he raised a glass in thanks.

"Attendez," Louis said.

He took the two glasses and went inside. A moment later he reappeared with fresh cognacs. He handed one to Mac.

"Salut!" Mac said, adding by way of a conversational opening, "Ta femme?"

This set Louis off on a diatribe which involved quite a few Latin words, which made it easier for Mac to follow, and which featured quite a bit of divorce.

"Et toi?" Louis asked.

They'd shared enough cigarettes and cognacs to move from the 'vous' form to the 'tu' form. Mac explained, as best as he was able, that he'd been married to the same woman for some time.

"Combien des anneés?" Louis asked.

Mac went through the numbers in his head.

"Plus de trente ans," he said.

Louis's mouth fell open. This was not possible. There must have been an error in translation. He hold up three fingers. Mac held up ten fingers, then dropped them and followed with a further ten fingers, and then dropped them and raised another pair of hands.

"Putain," Louis said.

Louis clinked glasses and began to cough. A few years after his heart bypass he'd had stents put in and now, as far as he was aware, his stents probably had stents. He'd been told to alter his lifestyle and he had. He smoked more, exercised less, ate fattier foods, and drank more. When he stopped coughing, he realised he was getting cold.

"De dans," Louis said.

Mac held up his cigarette. Louis peered into his restaurant. There was only Will there, as everyone had paid and left.

"C'est bon," Louis said, and they went in.

"Where've you been?" Will asked.

"We've been putting the world to rights," Mac said.

He sat down and coughed. He really ought to think about giving up smoking, Mac thought. He then coughed a little more. It appeared to chime with Louis who coughed ferociously, as if they were competing.

"Oh god," someone said, but it was hard to say, with all the coughing, who had said it.

"I don't feel very well," someone said.

"Are you okay?" Mac asked.

Will had turned an ashen colour. The blood had drained from his face.

"No," Will managed to say. "My chest."

Chapter Seventy-Seven

"What do you think, Blossom?" Beth asked.

Beth had not had a good week. The humiliation of the vomiting escapade hadn't quite left her. She'd been unable to return to her own party. And the carpet had been a mess. She'd had it replaced the following day, although she could have had it cleaned, but it only cost twelve thousand dollars.

"What was that?" she asked Blossom.

Blossom had farted. Beth had barely eaten anything all week and she'd given much of her fairly rich food to the dogs. They were having difficulty adapting to it. Or their stomachs were.

"Well, what do you think?" Beth demanded, as if she expected an actual response.

She'd also not touched a drink. While the weight hadn't actually fallen off her, some of it had made an apathetic exit, and she was back in the dress. The dress was remarkably unscathed as most of the vomit had flown over it. Which, given the size of her breasts, was a surprise.

"Not bad, eh?" she said to Blossom.

She was finding Blossom's responses a little unsatisfactory and was thinking about going into the next room and asking Peachy. But she wasn't ready for movement. Wearing the bloody thing was enough.

"Sigmund," said I had to wear it.

Sigmund was her therapist. It wasn't his birth name and nor was the German-Jewish accent he affected, but this was California, and both were good for business. He told her she needed to confront the dress. That meant putting it on, and not tearing it to shreds, as she'd originally intended. That wasn't the only confronting she needed to do.

"Do you think a Scotsman would like it?" she asked.

She'd forced herself not to watch any further television that featured the Scottish. It hadn't helped much. Although her recollection of events was less than forensic, she did remember him saying something about ravishing her. It had helped that most of what he had said had been entirely incomprehensible to her, but that word had stuck out. She studied the plans he'd drawn up that morning. They were, she seemed to remember him saying, preliminary. Although a word like preliminary in a Scottish accent could be anything. But she liked what he'd done. He'd understood her vision.

"Shall I call him?" she asked Peachy, who'd just walked into the room.

She knew she had to call him. But what was she going to say? Her stomach was growling again. She had to take the dress off. She couldn't remember how she'd achieved it the last time. For a second she tried to pull it over her head, and then realised that there was no possibility that the fabric designed to wrap round her waist was going to accommodate her breasts. The only way was down. It took a bit of pushing and then it flew off like a cork exiting a champagne bottle. She tottered naked for a second and then she stepped back and collapsed onto the bed. She pushed her face into the duvet. She wished she could undo the whole event. She'd mentioned it to her therapist and his eyes had lit up.

"Maybe I can," she said to Polly, who'd also just strolled in.

Beth had agonised over it all week and now she'd made a decision. She was going to talk to Mac about something, perhaps a new extension as the house was only ten thousand square feet, and pretend nothing had happened. She wasn't going to refer to it and she was sure, because he was a gentleman, that he wouldn't either. For a second she panicked that he wouldn't want to work with her. She had no idea how much he required the money. She grabbed her mobile from the bedside table. She retrieved his name and was about to press send when she realised she was naked.

"Not a good idea," she muttered to herself.

She put on some track pants which had never visited a track and a stretchy top. She went outside onto the small balcony that overlooked the hills and she sat down. But it still didn't feel right. She was thinking about a cocktail. No, she decided, she had to be disciplined. She dialled the number. But there was no response. Was he ignoring her? She hoped not.

Chapter Seventy-Eight

Mac wasn't slightly tipsy, or a tad over the limit, or even mildly jolly. He was comprehensively pissed. He wasn't aware that his phone was rumbling in his pocket. He had other priorities.

"Where are the lights on this thing?" Mac asked.

They were sat in Will's Volvo. Will removed his arm from his left side and pointed. Mac put the lights on. He didn't do a huge amount of driving in London and when he did it was in a small town car. The Volvo seemed vast. He reversed it into a lamppost.

"Sorry about that," Mac said.

There hadn't been a helicopter available and the medical centre was closed, and Louis the Duck had pointed out that he didn't have much of a choice. It was either drive, or have another cognac, and let your friend die. It started to snow.

"Wipers?" Mac asked.

Will pointed. He couldn't believe it. He didn't smoke. He drank, but much less than the others. He went for runs. It didn't make sense. But it felt like someone fat, like Mac, had sat on his chest. There was another problem.

"Left," he said.

Mac was a terrible driver. He was making an effort to get there quickly, as he understood that time was critical in these matters, but he was giving Will the impression that they were both going to die before they got to the hospital.

"Slow," Will said.

There was a hairpin bend approaching – one of a number as they began to snake their way down the mountain – and Mac was heading towards it at some speed.

"I see what you mean," Mac said.

He'd managed to bury the front of the car in a snow drift. It would have been a soft landing, but there was a steel barrier behind it, which had taken out one of the headlights.

"Sorry about that," Mac said, attempting to engage reverse.

The five large beers at Andre's, the handful of Génépis and the enormous cognacs with Louis the Duck had added a further level of inebriation, which was having a detrimental effect on Mac's motor functions. His eyesight was a little blurred too. And now he was going down the mountain with fifty percent less lighting than he'd started with. He was driving a fraction quicker than walking pace. Will was wondering whether he should take over. He wasn't sure he could.

"A little faster, perhaps," Will suggested.

He hated making the suggestion, but he was beginning to think he was going to die on the journey. Mac speeded up to the point when a corner arrived quicker than he'd anticipated and when he exited the corner he was on the wrong side of the road. A car was hurtling towards him. Mac tugged at the wheel and the car seemed to disappear.

"Shit, that was close," Mac said.

It was so close the wing mirror had been ripped off.

"Sorry about that," Mac said.

"Kill me now," Will said.

It wasn't clear if he was joking. Mac thought he should reassure him.

"It doesn't matter," Mac said, "I wasn't using it anyway."

Will was not reassured by this. He gripped the seat, although the pain in his chest seemed to be subsiding. He assumed that it was doing so just prior to his remaining organs shutting down. The removal of the pain was just a temporary kindness.

"Sorry about that," Mac said.

He'd hit a kerb. It was odd as the road contained very few kerbs, yet he'd managed to find one, and hit it. It took out a little chunk of the alloy wheel which Will had kept scrupulously clean. It was followed by a long section of kerb on which Mac had mounted two wheels. He wasn't sure if Will had noticed and didn't want to draw attention to it. The approaching hairpin gave him no choice. They bounced off.

"Sorry about that," Mac said.

As the car fell the tall kerb clipped the front valance. It was quite a heavy car and it dislodged it. It would have been saveable, but Mac carried on going and drove over it. It made a scrunching noise and he wondered whether he should turn the radio on to mask the noise. It involved taking his hand off the steering wheel, but there seemed little harm in that. He also needed to look down.

"Roundabout," Will said.

Curiously Will was feeling a good deal better and he still hadn't decided whether this was to do with his impending demise, or if he wasn't quite as ill as he'd thought. They'd almost made it down the mountain. The car jumped as they travelled directly over the roundabout. There were small metal plates marked with arrows to indicate the direction of travel, which Mac had failed to follow. One had embedded itself in the wing.

"Sorry about that," Mac said.

Then there was an explosion which very nearly induced a heart attack in both of them. It was the radio which had burst into life and, with Mac's fumbling, was on full volume.

"Jesus Christ," Will said, stabbing it off.

They'd finished the descent and, now that they were on the edge of the town, there was street lighting. They were out of the woods.

"Left here," Will said.

The hospital signs were clearly marked and the road was wide and clear. Despite that, Mac managed to clip another kerb.

"There it is," Will pointed.

They were a hundred yards away and Will was beginning to relax. Whatever had been sitting on his chest wasn't there anymore, but he wanted a doctor to look at him.

"We're nearly there," Mac said, adding, "I think that went pretty well."

Will looked at him. They were not going to arrive at a consensus as to what constituted pretty well.

"What's that noise?" Mac asked.

"Oh shit," Will said.

A second later the noise was accompanied by flashing lights. Mac carried on going.

"I think you'd better stop," Will said.

Mac stopped and got out of the car. Two gendarmes appeared. They both played for the local rugby team.

"Bonjour," Mac said.

He hoped to continue the linguistic success he'd established with Louis the Duck, although they appeared to be a less responsive audience.

"Mon ami," Mac began pointing to Will.

He then made movements with his hands against his heart, which were intended to suggest a heart attack, but which they interpreted as love of the kind they weren't keen on.

"Hospital," Mac pointed.

The gendarmes looked at each other. When the gay pride march came to town they were the only two in the force not to do overtime. One of them walked back to the car and returned a minute later.

"Gonfle le ballon," he said.

"I beg your pardon?" Mac said.

It had been much easier with Louis the Duck and he wondered if there was any cognac in the car to ease translation. Will got out of the car.

"He wants you to blow in the breathalyser," Will said.

"The what?" Mac said.

"Breathalyser," Will confirmed.

Mac watched as Will walked away.

"Where are you going?" Mac asked.

"The hospital," Will said.

Chapter Seventy-Nine

Shankly floored the throttle. It prompted a cacophony of visceral sounds and the car shot through the road toll barriers. He knew that if a job needed doing aggressively and unpleasantly there was only one man for the job. He was on his way to the Alps. As a child he'd assembled his Action Men and fired his father's shot gun at them. That had taught them something about the realities of battle. He'd taken the space capsule and hurled it out of a fourth floor window. That was re-entry. At school his rule had been merciless. He'd trodden on toes, delivered Chinese burns and, when he was sent to boarding school, he'd upended beds. There were few people who'd encountered Shankly who hadn't, at some point, used the word 'bastard' to describe him.

When Shankly failed his 'A' levels he had an epiphany. He recognised the brutality of his own talents, but there wasn't a war on. He wasn't the kind of man to travel and fight other people's wars. There was only one solution. He was going to go into organised crime. The profit margins on drugs, arms and short term loans were astronomical. Violence and aggression were positive assets. He'd even told his father, who'd just gone through a bruising experience where he wasn't sure who had fleeced him most, and he introduced him to the even more astronomical returns a lawyer can make. Shankly was astonished that anyone could be paid so much for an hour's work. Not least because there was no way of knowing whether an hour had been worked. He'd buckled down and passed his exams.

He flashed his lights and then, as the car in front of him had responded in a less than instant way, he left the main beam on. When road testers had reviewed his AMG modified Mercedes they had described its power delivery as brutal and unmanageable. The engine was over six litres in size and, if that wasn't enough, the engineers had bolted on two turbochargers. This thing flew, and Shankly was enjoying his easy progress through France. It was getting him in the mood for serious intimidation. Not that he was ever out of the mood as his ex wives would, and did, testify. Now he consoled himself with the occasional prostitute and, as they were on the payroll, he could he as abusive as he liked.

Shankly was going to perform a citizen's arrest and take Judah Wheeler back if he had to handcuff him himself. Legally he was on dodgy ground, but this was the ground he favoured most. He'd get it sorted with some bullying and bluster and then throw him in the car. And, as well as the obvious pleasure this would give him, it would also prompt an avalanche of billable hours.

"Bring it on," Shankly said to himself.

He'd reached the part of the journey where the snow-capped mountains were in sight and half an hour later he began his ascent up the mountain. The conditions weren't perfect, but the traffic was light and he could, with a blip of the throttle, pass slower traffic between the hairpins. All traffic was slower.

"Out of my way," he growled.

The only irritation was that Judah Wheeler's phone signal had cut out. It had blipped and faded last in a building in Meribel which Shankly had identified, and would be his first port of call. Although, like the good sex he'd never had, he didn't want the experience to be over too quickly. He wanted to savour it, while at the same time charging Sir Harry Panter a small fortune. It wasn't a problem, as he'd checked on Sir Harry. He was a man with a large fortune.

"Hold on," Shankly said.

The roads were getting more slippery and, for the first time, he'd felt the car weave. But he had a lot of confidence in his ability to control the car. He kept his foot down and the rear of the car slid round and then shot up the hill. This was fun. He was travelling so quickly he hadn't had the time to look down at the dashboard and at the outside temperature. It was a long way below freezing. He wondered if he should grab a room when he got there and perform the eviction the following day, as a return journey without sleep would be tough. It was as he was wondering this that a car appeared in front of him. He didn't have time to notice what kind of car, it might have been a Volvo, but he could see that it was on the wrong side of the road. On *his* side of the road. He yanked the steering and the cars clashed removing wing mirrors, as if they were knights jousting on horses.

"Bugger," Shankly said.

He'd arrived at the next corner rather quicker than he'd expected. He wondered if he could perform the same trick and power out and into the straight. The rear of the car kicked out, and then it kicked out some more. And then he was travelling backwards. Shankly yanked the wheel, as if he was dressing down a subordinate, until he was no longer going backwards. He was travelling sideways. He was confident that the big fat tyres would find some tarmac and grip and they might have, but there was no more road. The car was sliding down the mountain. It would have remained sideways, but it hit a tree, and that spun him into the right direction until he met the road below. He might have regained control, but a truck was making its way up and, as the brakes in the Mercedes were proving useless on the snow and ice, he watched as it came into view.

"Fuck," Shankly managed to say.

Collision seemed inevitable, but the truck had seen him and had chains fitted. The truck braked. But it wasn't in time, and it caught a corner of Shankly's Mercedes and spun it round again. But there was no road left and Shankly plummeted down the snow covered mountain. He was unaware that the mayor's house was below him. The mayor's family was away and Jean-Jacques, the mayor, was in the process of buggering Brian. This would have been devastating news for the community and his family, but he simply couldn't help himself. It wasn't made any better by the fact that Brian was a local priest and on loan from the church. Although it would have surprised the church less. The car ploughed through the roof with tiles flying like surf and it almost came to a halt. Almost, but not quite. It fell from the roof. As Shankly was travelling backwards he didn't see the tree which skewered the car through the rear windscreen, which was just as well, as it took his head off.

"Fu…" Shankly almost said.

It would take a while for Shankly's body to be recovered, as the noise made when the car had careered along the roof had sounded like the wrath of God to Brian and had jolted Jacques to the point where Brian sustained a serious injury. They couldn't see the car, as it had dropped a further hundred metres into the darkness below, which reinforced the wrath of God theory.

It wasn't until the sun came out in the summer and the snow melted that anyone noticed the Mercedes and, as the tree was blossoming and growing through it, it would have stayed that way. But someone dropped their watch and it was valuable enough to attempt to retrieve it. Three months after that, at Shankly's funeral, there were a few attendees, but no mourners. Shankly's son would have made it but Arsenal were playing and, his son reasoned, it was what he would have wanted. It was a big game and Arsenal lost, which prompted serious questions in his son's mind about the future of Arsène Wenger.

Chapter Eighty

"You need to lawyer up," Claude's agent told him.

That didn't sound good. Claude realised he'd got himself in some trouble. He'd just lost his head a bit and the world's press had recorded it. He'd met the prosecutor. Or the prosecutor had met him. He was lucky to get out on bail, but the consensus was that his fame would make it too difficult to flee. And the charges were serious. The prosecutor wasn't going to accept a charge of assault, or even attempted assault. He wanted attempted murder. The evidence spoke for itself.

"Merde," Claude muttered.

He really should lawyer up – as his agent put it – for a divorce. But when Claudette had been so contrite she'd dropped to her knees, and he knew he couldn't divorce her. She was a wonderfully skilled woman.

"He's talking about a custodial sentence," his agent added.

Claude's agent had many qualities, but few of them were human. When he'd heard the news of Claude's violent and dangerous exploits, his client's wellbeing was not his principal concern. He wondered how he could profit from it.

"Putain," Claude muttered.

If he went to prison he'd never be able to control Claudette. That would be it. She'd be in the arms of another man quicker than he could say pass the soap.

"Attempted murder," his agent said.

His agent had to balance a few things. It was possible that Claude would lose the television show, but he reckoned he could get him a better deal elsewhere that would play on his murderous intent.

"Putain de merde," Claude said.

But, his agent thought, that would only be any good if Claude had a short sentence – a few months ideally and, if he could arrange it, somewhere brutal. But if he got a long sentence – ten years or so – he'd have to take him off the books. That would be bad. Claude had become one of his best clients, although ratings were falling.

"We need to broker a deal," his agent said.

By 'we' he meant 'I' and by 'broker' he meant with commission. To him. He liked the word broker as, for him, it was always a win-win situation.

"With the prosecutor?" Claude asked.

He wasn't sure he could survive in prison. It wasn't the violence or the buggery that concerned him, it was the food. He couldn't manage if he was forced to eat institutionalised food.

"No," his agent said slowly.

Claude's agent was always astonished at just how stupid some of clients were – dumb as dingbats – but he was there to make their lives easier. Or perhaps he wasn't. That didn't matter. What did matter was how he could monetise the situation. Reality shows had been on the phone already, although another plan was emerging in his head. It would be a challenge to get it past Claude.

"With the Englishman," the agent said.

It reminded Claude of the sight of the naked and plainly excited Englishman who had every intention of inserting that excitement into his wife. It made Claude shudder with anger.

"No," Claude said.

That morning Claude's agent had called Master Raf. He'd suggested a television advertisement for his knives. He'd been working at an appropriate strap line, but Master Raf had not responded well to 'There's only one way to slice a penis'.

"But yes," his agent insisted.

Claude couldn't grasp the indignity of it. The idea of actually paying the man who had every intention of fucking his wife was a step too far. He'd rather go to prison. And then he thought about the food.

"How much?" Claude asked.

Claude's agent smiled to himself. Now they were negotiating and he liked to negotiate. Of course, how much they paid depended on the Englishman, but he'd made preliminary enquiries and it suggested that – as the English might say – he did not have a pot in which to piss.

"Good question," Claude's agent said.

Often, in a case like this, he'd opt for what they might call an 'undisclosed' amount and then leak it anyway. But the bigger the sum the better the publicity and Claude could afford it.

"Million," Claude's agent said.

Claude spluttered as if he was about to have a heart attack. Was the man crazy? That wasn't going to happen. A million euros for the man who tried to fuck his wife? What did he take him for?

"No," Claude managed to say.

Claude's agent knew he'd say that, as he knew precisely how the conversation would now go, and the sum they were likely to arrive at. He would have the same conversation with the Englishman, or his agent, and eventually they'd get to a figure which would make the world's press and, in terms of advertising his client, it would be a bargain.

"More?" Claude's agent asked to amuse himself.

Claude stopped looking like he was having a heart attack and started to look like he was having a hernia. He needed to get this negotiation in line immediately and said, as his agent knew he would, "cinq cent mille euro." And that was where he wanted Claude to be before suggesting his alternative plan.

"There is another alternative," Claude's agent said.

Chapter Eighty-One

"How the fuck did you get here?" Al asked, although he knew the answer.

Judah didn't know where to start. He'd never felt so cold. He thought he was going to die or lose some extremities at the very least. He knew that his life would be a good deal simpler if he lost one extremity. It had got him in trouble all his life.

"It's a long story," Judah said.

"And why are you wearing a dress?" Al asked.

"Do you know, I have no fucking idea," Judah said.

"Nice jumper," Al said.

"Thanks," Judah said.

"But you came up in a helicopter," Al said.

"I did," Judah said.

"My insurance company is refusing to pay and they've taken my things until they do. They're holding me hostage," Al said.

They'd wondered why Al hadn't reappeared but, as things had been a little hectic, they hadn't got round to picking him up.

"Is that why you're in that gown with your arse hanging out?" Judah asked.

"Yes," Al admitted.

"And you didn't think that a bit odd for a broken ankle?" Judah asked.

Al shrugged. He'd been duped, but was reluctant to admit it. He'd stopped attempting to close the gown. He'd grown used to it, like a naturist on a beach. He wasn't sure if it was it was preferable to a dress.

"You'll probably have the same problem with your insurance," Al said.

"I doubt it," Judah said.

Al looked at him. Thirty years ago he'd envied Judah. He had an ease with women and living crazily, which he admired, but now realised wasn't for him. He needed to know that everything was in order, the house, the mortgage payments, while Judah didn't seem to care. He'd never cared.

"Why not?" Al asked.

"I'm not insured," Judah said and got up.

"Jesus, do you know how much a helicopter trip down the mountain costs?" Al said.

"No idea, but mine was free," Judah said.

That didn't make any sense to Al, but then Al had missed quite a bit.

"Why?" Al finally asked.

"It was a news helicopter," he said.

"Of course," Al said.

That was typical of Judah. He never picked up the tab. The door swung open and they looked round.

"Hi guys," Will said breezily.

"About time," Al said, "they've kept me hostage here."

Judah took a second look at Will.

"Why have you got a gown on?" Judah asked.

"Ah, that," Will said.

He was a little embarrassed. He told them about Louis the Duck, the journey down the mountain, and Mac's subsequent arrest.

"So you haven't had a heart attack?" Al said.

"No, apparently not," Will said. "More a very bad case of indigestion."

"Tosser," Judah observed.

"And where's Mac?" Al asked.

"I think they took him down to the police station," Will said.

Will felt a little resentful of the damage done to his car and thought that a night spent in a prison cell was well earned.

"So where's the car?" Al asked.

"I'm not sure," Will admitted. "I guess it must be where we got stopped by the police."

Al nodded. A plan was forming in his mind.

"Have you got the keys?" Al asked.

It was a good question and one that hadn't occurred to Will, although at the time he thought he was having a heart attack. He had other things on his mind.

"I guess Mac must have them," Will said.

"Or it's been stolen," Judah said.

"We're going to need them soon," Al said.

"Why?" Will asked.

"I've studied the routine of the nurses. In two hours their shift changes and there is a five minute period when there is no one guarding the place," Al said.

"Are you talking about nurses or prison guards?" Judah asked.

"Same thing," Al said, "then we need to get in the car and get the hell out of here."

"The keys aren't a problem," Will said.

"Why not?" Al asked.

"I've gaffer taped a spare underneath," he said.

"You still do that?" Judah asked.

Will had acquired a car from his grandparents when they were at the polytechnic, and he'd been warned by his father not to use it as a 'virility symbol'. It was an ageing estate car bereft of style, but they'd once crammed ten people in it. It had been fun. He'd also lost the key on three occasions and took to gaffer taping a spare to the chassis.

"Old habits," Will said.

"We're going to need our clothes," Al said.

"My clothes are lying on the floor of a penthouse apartment in Meribel," Judah said.

"Whoops," Al said.

"Where are your clothes?" Judah asked.

"I think they're locked in the cabinet behind the guards," Al said.

"The nurses," Judah corrected.

"The guards," Al insisted.

"What time do they change?" Judah asked.

"Seven," Al whispered.

"I'm going to take a doze," Judah said, "Do you want to wake us when you're ready to go."

"Will do," Al said.

Chapter Eighty-Two

Rick stopped at the apartment. It was empty. He had no idea where everyone had gone. He made himself a tea and sat down. But he felt restless. He knew Sondra had problems with her ex. It sounded like she was being bullied and he didn't like bullies. But this was a one-off thing, wasn't it? It felt like more to Rick. He left his tea and went to the next most likely place he'd find his colleagues. Andre's. He crossed the road and entered and looked around before he approached the bar.

"Bière?" Andre asked.

Rick nodded and sat down. He did feel very slightly guilty that he'd deserted his ski team, but not enough to trouble him. He knew they'd understand. Andre appeared with the beer.

"Where is everyone?" Rick asked.

Andre sighed and looked around. The bar wasn't busy.

"Attendez," he said, and came back a moment later with a beer, and sat down opposite him.

"Where to start," Andre said.

He'd sat down for a further reason. He wanted to talk to Rick about Sondra. He wanted to warn him.

"Judah," Andre began, "with the long hair."

"That's Judah," Rick said.

"Do you know Claude Cretet?" Andre asked.

"No," Rick said.

"He wrote the very famous Creme Brûlée song and now he is a famous chef," Andre said.

"Okay," Rick said unsure where this was going to go.

"He is a very angry man," Andre said.

"Oh dear," Rick said, getting more confused.

"He caught Judah with his wife," Andre said.

"That sounds like Judah," Rick said.

Andre explained the helicopter ride and the dress. He'd seen it all on television, and what he hadn't seen on television he'd heard through the grapevine. And Andre seemed to be the conduit for all information. He knew someone at the hospital, and a secretary at the gendarmerie. He'd had his eye on her for years.

"And Will had a heart attack," Andre continued.

"No," Rick said, shocked.

"But it wasn't a heart attack," Andre explained.

"And he's okay?" Rick asked.

"I believe so," Andre said, adding, "but Mac drove him to the hospital."

"I don't suppose he enjoyed that," Rick said.

"No. Mac got arrested for drinking and driving. He's in the gendarmerie," Andre said.

"Shit," Rick muttered.

"Indeed," Andre said.

"Where's Al?" Rick asked.

"He's still at the hospital. There is an insurance issue. They won't let him out," Andre said.

That brought Rick up to date with his colleagues.

"And you?" Andre asked casually, "What have you been up to?"

Rick took a mouthful of beer. What he had done in the last few days was just live. He hadn't reflected or analysed. He'd just done. And that was refreshing.

"I've been learning to ski better," Rick lied.

It wasn't a complete lie – he did ski much better – but that hadn't been the principal feature of the last few days.

"Who is your instructor?" Andre asked casually.

He could tell that Rick was reluctant to open up and he knew the solution.

"Attendez," Andre said, and went to get two more beers.

The one thing he'd learned about the English was that they were more than a little partial to a beer or two. And a free one even more so.

"It is Sondra," Andre said when he'd put the beers on the table.

"How do you know?" Rick said.

Andre shrugged. He liked his contacts to appear mysterious. But everyone knew. They'd seen it on television.

"Yes," Rick said and looked into his beer.

By not reflecting and analysing he'd also not faced up to what his relationship with Sondra might be. Was she the crutch to get him back on his feet?

"It's been nice," Rick said.

Andre gulped a little of his own beer, as if he was pretending to be an Englishman.

"She is complicated," Andre said.

Rick recognised the warning tone immediately. And he wanted to rail against it. He was, by nature, a loyal person and he felt that while Sondra may have aired, she had more than paid the price.

"I know," Rick said.

But it made him wonder. Was this more than a holiday romance? Leaving her had been like leaving a part of himself behind. Not that he'd left her. He wasn't sure what he'd done.

"I like her," Rick said after a pause.

Andre sighed and shrugged and wondered how to proceed.

"She's paid a high price for what she did," Rick added.

Andre got it. He looked closely at Rick and realised that Rick had got it too. He'd got it big time.

"Actually, l like her a lot," Rick said after a further pause.

Andre got up to serve some people, which gave Rick a moment to do the reflecting he'd been avoiding. And he did feel a little guilty. He was fairly sure that Sondra had asked for his help – not directly – but she'd asked. It involved her two children and her partner's family. They had pretty much kidnapped her children. But intervening in that was getting him in very deep indeed. Except, he was already in very deep. He'd been hit by an avalanche.

"Bière?" Andre said, reappearing.

"No," Rick said with determination, "Do you know where Sondra lives?"

Andre, as a purveyor of gossip in addition to beer, did know where Sondra lived, although he wasn't sure it was a good idea telling Rick.

"I do," Andre said slowly.

"Well?" Rick said with a rather harder tone than Andre had heard before.

Andre shrugged and explained where Sondra lived.

"I've got to go and help Sondra," Rick said with determination.

Andre could sense something bad going down.

"Help? How?" Andre asked.

Rick had drawn himself up to his full height. He'd made up his mind. This was more than a holiday. This was something he couldn't walk away from.

"She's having problems with her partner's family," Rick said.

"You don't want to go near them," Andre said. "That's a very bad idea."

But Rick was out of the door and putting his skis on.

"Merde," Andre muttered.

He really shouldn't have told him where Sondra lived.

Chapter Eighty-Three

"Breakout minus fifteen," Al whispered.

Al had been up all night. He threw furtive glances from one side to the other. He'd crept through the corridors avoiding the nurses. He nudged Judah again.

"Breakout minus fourteen," Al whispered.

Judah was asleep. He wasn't just dozing, he was buried in a very deep slumber in which a maniac was hacking his way through a sturdy door with the intention of slicing up a saucisson which they were going to share with a glass of cognac. This had yet to happen in his dream, but he knew that it would and, after a brief and agreeable conversation, they would then go on to share his very beautiful wife. It would have irritated the hell out of Al if he'd known this. He shook Judah.

"Breakout in thirteen," he hissed.

Al was worried he might be overheard. He would have dressed himself in black, but that was one of the problems. Phase one of the plan was to recover their clothes.

"Breakout in twelve," he whispered a little louder.

But Judah had opened the door, shook the man's hand, and they were discussing which cognac they should sample first. Hennessy was a favourite, but then that was not to ignore Courvoisier, Martel and Rémy Martin. They settled on a Baron Otard.

"Superbe," the man said.

He was a man who knew and appreciated his cognacs. Whatever had happened in Judah's life it had never prompted bad dreams and this one was shaping up very nicely. There were moments when it seemed a shame to wake up and face the world. Judah was frequently late for things.

"For fuck's sake," Al said, shaking him.

The shaking was useful as they'd moved past the cognac and onto the moment when the man had removed his wife's clothing for Judah's delectation and pleasure. And it was giving him some pleasure. The wife had a body constructed with fabulously undulating curves. She was perfection. Slim but curvy. It seemed like an impossible combination – almost a contradiction in terms – and yet there it was, in Judah's dream. For a second his mind wondered what Claudette might have looked like naked, and then it moved on.

"Breakout in eleven," Al practically yelled.

He was beginning to feel a little foolish saying 'breakout' but he was starting to panic. He didn't want to walk out on his own as it was pretty cold outside, but he didn't want to spend another day there either. He'd completely failed to charm the nurses. It wasn't that he was incapable of charm, he just wasn't very good at it. Judah would have had them eating out of his hand, or something worse and more lurid that Al daren't contemplate.

"Get up," Al shouted.

But in the dream Judah was having no difficulty getting it up and the wife had thrown him on his back and was about to mount him. There were moments when Judah could be a tiny bit lazy and it might have been for this reason that he currently favoured this kind of coital arrangement.

"Is he ready?" Will asked.

Will had appeared. He was ready and rested. His blood pressure was back to normal and the ECG had confirmed that he hadn't had even a hint of a heart attack, and that his pump was in good working order. He wanted to get back. They had another day skiing.

"I can't wake the fucker," Al said.

Will shook Judah.

"He's in a pretty deep sleep," Will said.

Al leaned over and placed his mouth next to Judah's ear.

"Breakout minus ten," Al said.

"Breakout?" Will said.

Al hadn't meant to say it, but it had just come out.

"Yes," Al said indignantly.

"Okay," Will said and returned to Judah, adding, "Jesus, is that what I think it is?"

Judah was lying on his back. A small tent was forming on his crotch.

"For fuck's sake, that's bloody typical of the man," Al said, more than a little irritated.

"It looked pretty small on the television," Will said.

It didn't look so small now, but then in Judah's dreams he was being mounted by a goddess with a sublime body, and with the encouragement of her husband.

"Someone's coming," Al hissed. "Under the bed."

They crawled under the bed revealing, should someone look, two naked backsides. The nurses peered in. Judah was a bit of a celebrity. They chatted together for a second and then left.

"It's shift time," Al said from under the bed. "We only have five minutes."

They scrambled out and Al decided to take charge.

"Wake him up," he ordered Will, and went to the nurses station.

Will continued to shake Judah, but that just seemed to encourage him. It wasn't working. He couldn't understand how anyone could sleep so soundly. It didn't seem possible. He wondered if it was the medication. There was a plastic clipboard at the end of the bed. It was quite flexible. He didn't bother to read it, as he was unlikely to understand it. Instead he picked up the board and smacked it on the lump in the middle of the bed.

"What the fuck?" Judah said.

"We've got to go," Will said.

"Okay," Judah said.

A little part of him was still in the dream, but it was retreating fast, and reality was dawning. He got up. They went into the corridor.

"Have you got the clothes?" Will asked.

"Bugger," Al said.

There was a locker below the desk where he'd seen the nurses place his clothes. He'd grabbed the handle. It wouldn't turn. He looked around for a key. There were lockers and cubby holes. But he couldn't find the key.

"I can't find the bloody key," Al said.

"How much time have we got?" Will asked.

Al checked his watch. He'd set the stopwatch after the nurses had left. He was in breakout mode.

"Seventy-two seconds or we'll have to abandon breakout," Al said.

"Breakout?" Judah asked.

Will shrugged. They weren't infused with the same tension as Al.

"Fuck it," Al said. "We'll have to go like this."

Chapter Eighty-Four

"Go! Go! Go!" Al hissed.

There were issues. Someone had taken the crutches, which just left a Zimmer frame. He had no choice. But they made a run for it with Al hopping and using the frame. The sun was on the edge of the horizon and about to make an appearance and the whiteness of Will and Al's buttocks, as the gowns fell open and closed, were like beacons in the night light.

"Fucking hell it's cold," Will said.

The denim dress which Judah wore had a lining and was considerably warmer. When they got to the car they stopped and looked at it.

"Jesus, what happened to the car?" Al asked.

Will's face darkened when he looked at the newly acquired dents on his formerly pristine car.

"Fucking Mac," he said.

"Oops," Judah said.

Will slid under the rear bumper and searched for the spare key. He patted around in search of it.

"I need some light. I can't find it," Will said.

"I'll have a look," Judah said, and leant under the car.

They patted about furiously, but neither could find it.

"All we need is some light," Will said.

"Maybe there's a torch inside," Al said and opened a door.

Judah stopped and looked at Will.

"It wasn't locked," Al said.

"He didn't bloody lock it," Will muttered.

"There's something else," Al said slowly.

"He didn't leave the bloody keys in it, did he?" Will said.

"He did," Al said.

"That's bloody typical," Will said.

Will scrambled into the car, adjusted the seat, and started it. He turned the lights on or, more accurately, the remaining functioning light. He was trying not to feel irritated.

"Let's get the fuck out of here," Al said, throwing the Zimmer frame into the back of the car.

Will drove the car round the corner, and out of sight of the hospital, and stopped.

"What now?" Judah asked.

Will paused. Firstly, he needed to warm the car up. It was bloody freezing. Next, they had to see if they could pick up Mac, although part of him wanted to leave him there.

"I guess we need to find the gendarmerie," Will said.

"How are we going to do that?" Al asked.

"Anyone got a phone?" Will asked.

"No, mine got stamped on by that chef," Judah said.

"Mine is with my stuff," Al said.

There was a silence.

"What about the Sat Nav on the car?" Al asked.

Will tapped some buttons and a few seconds later a destination appeared.

"Six minutes away," Will said.

"Great, let's go," Al said.

But Will hadn't moved.

"What's up?" Al asked.

"Who's going in there?" Will asked.

"Well, you. You're the lawyer," Al said.

Will sighed. He knew there was no point in saying that this wasn't his kind of law, but there was another issue.

"I'm not going in there dressed like this," Will said.

"Nor am I," Al said.

"And you speak better French," Will said to Judah.

They turned and looked at Judah who had got into the back of the car.

"You've got to be fucking kidding," Judah said.

"You have every right to self identify with which ever gender you choose," Al pointed out helpfully.

"And we can't go in there with our arses hanging out," Will said.

Will put the car in drive and began to follow the instructions on the screen. As far as he was concerned it was settled. Six minutes later he came to a halt outside the gendarmerie. He didn't move. He tapped the steering wheel.

"Fuck it," Judah said and got out.

Despite the brief time since their escape, the sun was coming up fast, and it was almost daylight. He walked into the gendarmerie. There was a counter, after which he could see a waiting room more like a dentist's surgery than a police station. There was no one at the counter.

"Hello?" Judah said.

He looked into the waiting room. There were posters scattered on the walls warning people about security, speed limits and alcohol consumption. He saw Mac. He was on slumped on a bench in a small cell with open bars, asleep and snoring loudly. Judah leaned in and shook him.

"Fuck," Mac said.

He looked up bleary eyed. But Mac was accustomed to the bleary.

"What the fuck are you wearing?" Mac asked.

"I believe it's Milly Elisa," Judah said.

Despite the gender issue with his clothing, he had to admit it was actually quite comfortable, and the best argument he'd come across for cross-dressing. Mac started laughing.

"Do you want to be rescued or not?" Judah asked.

Chapter Eighty-Five

Yves had been in his own apartment for nearly a month and things were changing. He'd spent the last half hour following a YouTube video, and he was quite happy with the result. Flower arranging was harder than he thought. Leaving the family home had left him free to express his artistic nature and his little space was coming together nicely. He'd borrowed his mother's sewing machine and he'd launched into the curtains. He liked the ruched look and favoured lighter petal-like colours. His brothers might call it pink, but he had no intention of letting them in. This was his private space and he didn't wish to have it invaded.

Yves' father was a gendarme and his grandfather had been a gendarme, as were all three of his brothers. His cousins were in the military and he had further cousins who were firemen. They all played rugby. At school Yves had demonstrated great talent as an artist and had shown a greater facility for French poetry and the classics than his siblings, but his destiny was always set. He was going to be a cop. Not that he minded the job, but there were times when he wished his upbringing had been a little freer. He'd once been tempted to run off and study accountancy, but his father had talked him out of it. Instead he'd taken a discreet post in the Alps, away from the family, but still in the force.

Of course the force was changing, and he'd recently attended a course about women's rights, and those of the new community of sexually depraved people. At least that was how his father had described them. There hadn't been much debate at the kitchen table, aside from the qualities of certain rugby players, so Yves had found it quite eye opening. He'd also learned that people had a right to self identify their gender. That seemed a little strange to him, as he'd always thought that God defined your gender, and there wasn't much you could do about it. But he'd learned it was a political minefield and he was ambitious. He wanted to get on and, although he'd never told his brothers or his father, he thought that this was the way forward. This was the modern world and they needed to adapt to it. It was why he'd sought a transfer away from the family home in the Massif Central.

Albertville was big enough to have a good size gendarmerie, although he'd really hoped that there would be a small garden which he could quietly tend. He hated seeing roses which weren't properly deadheaded. There was a bush outside his apartment block and he'd gone out late at night, when no one was looking, and given it some basic maintenance. Of course, he differed from his brothers in other ways and right at the moment he was in a state of shock. His brother had visited him the previous night – he was still asleep on the sofa – and there had been revelations. Revelations he was still reeling from.

Frank, his big brother, had been the prop forward. He'd almost become a professional, but his father had told him his destiny. He could hear Frank gently snoring on the sofa. And Frank wanted to leave the force. More shocking, he'd started a relationship with someone called Rock. It seemed an unusual name for a woman and Yves had assumed it was a nickname. If people had the right to decide on their gender, then they could call themselves whatever they liked.

Frank had to spell it out. Despite this, it had taken a few minutes for Yves to grasp the message. He would have liked to have phoned Peggy, but Peggy was on the nightshift, and he couldn't disturb her. Peggy stayed three times a week and she encouraged him to embrace his artistic side. They both knew they'd get married eventually, but the time wasn't quite right. When Frank had dropped the bombshell there was no one to share it with and make sense of it. Yves had kept asking him if he was sure.

And Frank was as sure as he'd ever been. Yves had always been the black sheep in his family, although no one had ever said it, and now it turns out that his big brother was a raving queer. As Yves had encountered no one, as far as he was aware, who embraced an alternative lifestyle, he'd yet to acquire an appropriate vocabulary to describe it.

He had to think about the course he'd taken. He wasn't sure what to say. But curiosity, after the fifth beer, got the better of him. Did they really take it... he'd begun to ask, and then wished he hadn't. His brother told him about the number of pleasure receptors which are located in the anal canal, and Yves didn't know what to do with himself. Eventually he had to excuse himself, and go to the bathroom, where he washed his hands several times. When he got back to the table, and saw the sea of beer bottles, he panicked. He couldn't tell which was his. He opened a new one to be sure, but he knew it was going to take some while to rid himself of the image his brother had provided for him. He was grateful when dawn came and he could go to work.

But Yves was still reeling from the revelations when he took the short walk to the gendarmerie. Who would have thought it? Frank. Although now Yves thought about it, he remembered Frank's fondness for body building magazines, but he'd assumed that was just an interest in bulking up his upper body. Or that was what Frank had said at the time. He had wondered why the pages were often stuck together.

It had just brought his mind back to the equality course he'd attended and the alternative lifestyles people chose. It wasn't that he was *that* ignorant. He knew that there were men who lived with men, women who lived with women, and men who liked to dress as women and even – what was the phrase? – self identify as women, but it was just alien to his upbringing. He didn't quite understand much of it, as he'd always been clear about his own sexuality. He just liked pink flowers. When he got to the station it was empty except for two people. His colleague wasn't there. The smoking ban was proving a problem for him and he was probably round the back.

"Bonjour," Yves said.

There was a couple waiting. It took Yves a second to recognise that the person in the cell was wearing a skirt, but it looked like a man. It was one of those Scottish skirts. Yves nearly addressed him as Madame. But the other one with the long hair and the denim dress was obviously his wife.

"Madame," Yves said politely.

She was probably collecting him after a drunken spree. It wasn't uncommon. The woman turned and looked at him. He'd read that there were signs such as large hands and Adam's apples that gave away such things, but this bloke, despite his long hair, just looked like a bloke. Yves wondered if he should have made more of an effort. He'd ask Peggy next time he saw her, but he thought a little bit of basic eyeliner and lipstick would have helped enormously.

"Bonjour," the man dressed as a women said.

It shocked Yves that he, or perhaps it would be more politically correct to say she, made no effort to raise the tone of her voice. He knew at that moment that he had to be careful. This was the minefield they'd talked about on the course. He had to treat them with the utmost respect. He wondered if he should wait for his colleague. But he didn't want to be seen to be dragging his heels on that one.

"J'ai venu pour mon ami," the man dressed as a woman said.

English, Yves thought. He'd heard, or rather his father had told him, that they were all that way in England. It was what had prompted the fall of their empire. He remembered making the mistake of asking how, and his father had said sodomy. That brought his thoughts back to his brother and the pleasure receptors. He felt a little queasy. He wanted to go to the bathroom and wash his hands, but he knew it would look a bit odd. But who would have thought there were pleasure receptors in the place where you shit? Yves really wished he could un-think that thought. He certainly couldn't keep the man incarcerated due to his proclivities. He grabbed the keys from the desk and opened the cell door.

"Okay, pas de probleme," Yves said.

The Scotsman looked a bit surprised by this and stood up, but Yves knew it would be wrong to detain them for longer than was necessary just because they were this way. He felt a little sorry that they couldn't share what he had with Peggy. He watched them walk out. They didn't embrace or appear to be together, but that was probably just a function of the length of their relationship, Yves thought.

"That was easy," one of them said to the other, but Yves's English wasn't very good.

Chapter Eighty-Six

Will drove carefully up the mountain. Not that it mattered, as the car had received a dent in every panel. When they arrived at Val Thorens he realised they had a further problem.

"Who's got a key?" he asked.

"Not me. It's with my clothes in Meribel," Judah said.

"Mine is in the hospital," Al said.

"Shit," Will said.

This was embarrassing. His was also in the hospital.

"We need to find Rick," Judah said.

"You want to go up and see if he's in?" Will said to Mac.

Mac grunted and got out of the car. Ten minutes later he came down.

"No. We might as well try Andre's," he said.

Will parked the car as close to the door to Andre's as he was able.

"Do you want to ask him if he has any spare clothes?" Will asked.

"Okay," Mac said and went in.

He came back ten minutes later clutching a collection of clothing. It was the clothing that a previous group of Englishmen had left behind and Andre had been unsure what to do with it. He was pleased to get rid of it.

"Andre seems pretty agitated," Mac said throwing the clothing into the car.

Al picked up a piece of clothing and tried to figure out which end was which.

"What the fuck," Al said.

"Why's that?" Will asked.

"Something about Rick," Mac said.

"What the fuck," Al said.

"What about Rick?" Will asked.

"Andre reckons he's got himself in trouble," Mac said.

"What the fuck," Al said.

"What's the problem?" Will asked Al.

Mac and Will turned round.

"What the fuck," Mac said.

Al had put on the clothing Andre had found for him. It was a onesy.

"Superman," Will observed.

"Hey, why not?" Mac said.

Five minutes later they entered Andre's bar. They were all dressed in Superman outfits, including Mac.

"What's up, Andre?" Mac asked.

Andre paused.

"Is everything okay?" Will asked.

"No," Andre said.

Andre looked as she if he was composing his thoughts.

"What's the problem?" Will asked.

"It's Rick," Andre said.

They looked at each other.

"He's gone to help Sondra, but her family, are difficult. Violent," Andre said.

He pronounced 'violent' as a Frenchman – vee-oh-lon – and it seemed to carry more weight.

"He needs help," Andre said.

"Okay," Will said slowly. "Where does she live?"

Andre scribbled down her address.

"Vite! Vite! Vite!" Andre said.

Andre felt a little responsible.

"We better go," Mac said.

They headed to the car.

"Shall I drive?" Al suggested.

"That sounds like a good idea," Mac said.

"With a broken ankle?" Will said.

"Its an automatic, I won't need that foot," Al said.

Will sighed and got in the passenger seat. He checked the Sat Nav, and headed towards St Martin de Belleville, which was a lower resort, and back down the mountain. Al pressed his foot to the floor as if he was in the rig, with the lights flashing, and on the way to an emergency.

"Jesus," Will said.

Al was storming down the mountain and they were gaining time.

"Hairpin," Will shouted.

This was going to be the end of the car and him. He doubted there were any panels left that weren't dented, but this was going to sort that out. The rear of the car slid wide, Al applied some opposite lock and caught it and they shot out the corner.

"Hey, this is fun," Mac said.

Will closed his eyes and decided that if they ever do this again, they were going to fly. He opened his eyes. There was another hairpin and he could see a car ahead.

"Shit," Will said.

Al had shot round the corner, floored the throttle, and overtaken the car before arriving at the next corner. Will was feeling a little car sick. He was wondering if he should suggest he take over the driving. He didn't think that was going to happen.

"Not far," Al said.

There was a longer straight. It was downhill and covered in snow and ice at the end of which was a sheer drop. Will held on.

"You're bloody good at this," Mac said.

They'd somehow managed to turn a corner and pull off the road and down towards St Martin de Belleville.

"It's behind the church," Mac said.

The church spiral was easy to find and Al headed for it. A minute later they turned the corner.

"There he is," Mac said.

Al stopped the car and they got out.

Chapter Eighty-Seven

Rick was on his way to Sondra's. He tried to keep his mind empty, as if he was concentrating, but not thinking. But in the back of his mind was the notion that he was about to make a significant, and romantic, gesture. The kind that in the movies would be 'you had me at hello'. The house was not difficult to find and without deliberating he walked up to the front door and knocked. He could hear a commotion behind it, which stopped as he knocked. The door opened slowly. It was Sondra.

"Merde," she said.

As the door opened wider Rick saw three men looking at him. They were not welcoming faces. They were faces marked with aggression and violence.

"Bugger," Rick said.

He knew that as an opening line, and a romantic gesture, 'bugger' was not what he originally had in mind. One of the men pushed past Sondra and, with the flat of his hand, punched Rick in the chest. Rick staggered back and would have fallen were it not for the boots, and the gravel on the drive. There was only a fine covering of snow at this altitude.

"This isn't a good idea," Sondra said to him.

Rick's introduction to Sondra's partner's family was not proving to be a very pleasant one. He had three brothers. Two were slightly bigger than him. The third was a monster.

"They have no right to hold your children," Rick said.

Outside the sparring he'd recently been practising, his experience of street fighting was limited. Limited to nothing. And this looked like it was going to be unpleasant.

"You are the children's mother," Rick insisted.

She told them, but Rick knew they weren't responding well. A further man appeared at the door. He was the partner, the father of her children. He was shouting.

"You have to go," Sondra said.

One of the reasons Rick had taken up mixed martial arts was because he'd been bullied when he was younger. He bore the emotional scars of defeat, and it had always hurt to think about it. But he was outnumbered, and they were younger than him. He'd be a fool to take them on. He held his ground for a second longer until he realised that one of the brothers was moving towards him. What had he been taught? He moved his right foot back and raised his fists to a ready stance in a fraction of a second. He was side on and left foot forward. This was the fighting stance and in the class it was always accompanied by a "Yah!" Rick wasn't aware that he'd done that instinctively, but it didn't matter as things were happening quickly. He'd practised blocking a wild punch – the kind he'd been told that a drunk or someone with no skills might throw – and he thought about the instructions Sensei Joe had given him.

"Stop," Sondra shouted.

Rick reminded himself of the things he'd learned. Don't stiffen up, relax, move, side step. Despite that, the punch came a little quicker than he'd expected, and he only just managed to get his arm up in time to block it. It landed on his forearm and, in an automatic movement, he dropped his right shoulder, twisted his shoulders and punched through. The punch landed on the top of the jaw just under his nose. This was part of a combination of moves, and the next move was a roundhouse kick. He'd also learned not to look down before throwing the kick. It gives it away. Rick swivelled his hip and kicked hard. He'd aimed for his opponent's side – he needed to warm up to get much higher – but the brother was falling and Rick hit him squarely on the side of the head. He'd once heard someone use the expression 'falling like a sack of shit'. He'd wondered how anyone would experience such a fall, as most people were reluctant to bag their faeces. But the brother went down like a sack of shit.

Rick landed on his right foot, one step ahead. He now had his back to the second brother. He was out of stance – his right foot was now forward – but he'd been trained to fight from both stances. He'd always had trouble with the spinning kicks, which were required for him to achieve his next belt, but he was half way round already, and the second brother was moving towards him. Rick continued turning and raised his leg to kick the second brother in the stomach, any lower or higher was not allowed in the sparring classes he attended, but Rick missed. He caught him square on the knees and there was a cracking noise. The second brother collapsed as if his legs had been pulled away from under him. Instinctively, and because it was part of a combination, he followed with a side kick, which was high and landed flat on the second brother's face. He flew back.

Rick stood on the balls of his feet, with his left foot forward, and his fists raised in the fighting stance. The big brother looked at him. Then he looked at his car. Then he looked at Rick and he raised his hands in defeat and walked to his car. A little part of Rick was grateful that he'd taken up kickboxing, although he was unaware that there were four Englishmen dressed as Superman standing behind him, although one was leaning on a Zimmer frame. Rick looked at Sondra's partner.

"I do not want to fight you," Rick said.

He'd meant to say it in a rather peaceful way, but his short and very successful bout had got him in character. It wasn't quite as menacing as Clint Eastwood, but it held the implied threat that should they fight, Rick would win. It was a bit of a bluff, as Rick hadn't been taking martial arts lessons for *that* long. He wouldn't have put money on himself and now that his adrenaline level was coming down, and two men lay on the ground in front of him, he was wondering whether he might have overdone it.

"You need to find a solution to this," Rick said quietly.

Rick turned and noticed his polytechnic friends standing behind him.

"Hey," Rick said,

"Awesome," Mac said.

"Are you okay?" Will asked.

"I think so," Rick said and then, after a pause, "What the fuck are you wearing?"

Chapter Eighty-Eight

Rick skied back to the apartment. He needed to pack, but he'd given his key to Will, and there was no one there. It wasn't a problem. He knew where to find them.

"Hey," he said entering Andre's.

But Andre wasn't there. Andre's wife was manning the bar.

"How did it go?" Mac asked.

Rick thought about it. It had been complicated. They'd sat down and talked. As the adrenaline had declined, his hands had started to shake. He realised he'd been a little mad to take on the brothers. It was the first time he'd feared for his own life for a while. Sondra had introduced him to her children. Annie had never managed to get pregnant and there had been moments when she'd been anxious and upset, but eventually it had passed, and they became their own family. It was a strange time in life to take on parental duties.

"It went well," Rick said.

"Beer?" Mac asked.

As the Catholicism of the pope wasn't in question, they sat down.

"How's the leg?" Rick asked Al.

Al tapped the cast.

"It doesn't hurt," he said.

"And the ticker?" Rick asked Will.

"What a pussy," Mac observed.

"And you've still got your dick," Rick said to Judah.

Rick raised his glass, "Cheers!"

"Cheers!" the others said.

This was the final evening. There was no question: it was going to get messy, and it was unlikely they were going to eat anywhere else. They were rooted for the night. But it was clear the week had stirred something in them. A beer or so later Will asked the question.

"What about retirement?" Will asked.

"What are you talking about?" Judah said, "we're too young."

"Rick's retired," Will pointed out.

Rick hadn't exactly made a decision to retire, but he'd lost interest in trading, and was sufficiently solvent not to require it. He'd only meant to take some time off. At first it was just a long weekend, but then it turned into a very long weekend.

"I'm not retired," Rick said, "I'm just taking a sabbatical."

"For the rest of your life?" Will asked.

"I don't think so," Rick said uncertainly.

Rick hadn't told them about his most immediate plans. He was still coming to terms with them himself. He felt a little nervous, but not in the sense of anxious. He was excited.

"I'm not going back with you guys," Rick said. "Not for a while, or maybe not at all. We'll see how it goes."

There was a little pause as they all took this in.

"Cheers to that!" Will said, and they all raised their glasses.

Now that Rick had covered that he wanted to steer the conversation back to where it had come from.

"What about your NHS pension?" Rick asked Al.

"I can take that in three years," Al said.

"Will you?" Will asked.

"Probably," Al admitted.

"And then what?" Judah asked.

"I'm not sure," Al admitted, "and you?" he asked Will.

"No one's mentioned it, but I can hear the junior partners making moves, so maybe another three years too," Will said.

"Jesus," Mac muttered, "how did we become such a bunch of old cunts?"

"I take it you have no retirement plans?" Judah asked Mac.

"Not in the slightest, no plans, no money, nothing," Mac said.

"More beer?" Judah asked.

"Excellent idea," Mac said.

Judah went back to the bar. He wasn't sure whether this was the fourth or the fifth, but each time he'd made the walk to the bar.

"Cinq plus, ma cherie," he said to Andre's wife.

And each time he'd bought Andre's wife a drink. She had now downed four cognacs, or it might have been five, she wasn't sure. It was the most she'd consumed in around thirty years and it was doing a very good job of relaxing her. It prompted a whole change in the arrangement of her facial muscles. She had no idea what Andre was up to and, at the moment she didn't care. He said he'd gone down to Albertville to pick up some parts for the coffee machine which had been playing up. She wondered if he'd sabotaged the machine and it was just an excuse. He'd said that since he had to go there he might as well eat with his mother. Either way she was going to lie in the following day. He could get up and deal with the bar. Although, with the amount of cognacs she'd consumed, she'd probably *have* to lie in.

"Et un cognac pour toi," Judah said.

There was no question that it was appropriate addressing her in the 'tu' form, and from there he'd moved on to 'ma cherie'. They both knew it was a harmless flirtation, but Andre's wife was grateful for it. No one had flirted with her in thirty years. He returned to the table with the five beers.

"Okay," Will said, "last retirement question. You must have a pension, Judah, from the college."

"I'm not sure I have a job," Judah said.

"You want to find that out," Mac said.

Judah shrugged. He ought to, but he didn't like to face bad news.

"Okay, enough about retirement," Will said, "here's to the ski team."

They raised their glasses again and drank appreciatively and then turned. Someone was calling.

"Judah!"

It was Andre's wife. She was waving. Judah got up and went to the bar. He didn't notice a man standing there.

"Judah Wheeler?" the man asked.

Judah nodded cautiously.

"I'm here on behalf of Claude Crete," Claude's agent said.

"Oh," Judah said.

His last experience with the chef had been a rather unpleasant one. It prompted an automatic, protective, Pavlovian cupping of his genitals.

"He sends his apologies and asks that you don't press charges," Claude's agent said.

"I don't think so," Judah said.

"I understand," Claude's agent said with a well practised sigh, "but he would be willing to compensate you."

Judah's concept of compensation was closer to a free meal than a sizeable bundle of cash and he shook his head. It had been a very unpleasant ordeal and the chef had been maniacal.

"Generously," Claude's agent added.

Judah broke his lifelong habit of making bad decisions and paused.

"One moment," he said and returned to the table and explained the situation.

"Rick," Judah said, "could you negotiate for me?"

"My pleasure," Rick said and got up.

Judah followed him, but Rick stopped him.

"Stay there," Rick said.

They watched as Rick negotiated with Claude's agent. It was hard to make out what was happening. There were hand signals and nods and sighs. And then Rick shook his head.

"That's not acceptable," Mac said, and took a drink.

Claude's agent was talking. Rick was nodding and then he was shaking his head again.

"Nor that," Will said, and took a drink.

Rick was talking. He was using his hands, although they had no idea what he was attempting to illustrate, or whether it mattered. Then Claude's agent shook his head.

"That too," Al said, and took a drink.

Then Rick was shaking hands with Claude's agent. The deal had been done. Rick came back to the table. He'd written something down on a small piece of paper. He took a deep breath.

"Well?" Mac asked.

"There's just one thing," Rick said slowly.

"There is?" Judah asked.

"I'm assuming you've lost your job at the university," Rick said.

"I don't know for certain, but it seems so," Judah said.

"I've got you another job," Rick said.

As Judah had decided that there was very little for which he was qualified, he had no idea what that might be.

"A television job," Rick said.

They looked at him expectantly.

"A cooking show with..." Rick paused. "Claude Cretet."

It took a while for the others to stop laughing.

"You've got to be kidding," Judah said. "There's no way I'm doing that."

"I can think of a few reasons," Rick said.

"How many?" Mac asked.

"About seven hundred and fifty," Rick said.

This didn't mean anything to Judah who was recounting his experience and not finding it to be a pleasing one.

"What do you mean seven hundred and fifty?" Judah asked.

"For your new television career," Rick said.

"That won't cover the cost of this trip," Judah said derisively.

The others looked at each other.

"Not seven hundred and fifty," Rick said.

As large sums of money had never tumbled into Judah's account before he was struggling to comprehend the experience.

"No, it can't be," Judah said.

"Seven hundred and fifty *thousand* euros," Rick confirmed.

"Fuck," Judah said.

"You'll have to sign something confirming that you won't take action," Rick said.

"Fuck," Judah said.

"But I'll run it through my foreign exchange account first, so you can get the best rate," Rick said.

"Fuck," Judah said.

"We're going to need some more beer," Mac said.

"Fuck," Judah said.

"Are you okay?" Al asked.

"Fuck," Judah said.

"You need to go and see Andre's wife," Will said.

"Fuck," Judah said.

"Cheers to that!" Will said and they all raised their glasses.

Judah got up a little unsteadily. Who'd have thought he'd have been rewarded for trying to fuck someone else's wife? If this had happened throughout his life he'd be a rich man. He approached the bar and grabbed Andre's wife with both hands and kissed both cheeks. He guessed the word 'compensation' was the same in French and he said it with a French flourish.

"Compensation," Judah said.

"J'ai entendu," Andre's wife said.

She'd heard and, as she'd drunk at least five cognacs, she was feeling unusually merry and relaxed.

"Celebration," Andre's wife said and went to fetch the more exclusive cognac and a bottle of champagne.

She wasn't sure if she was giving it away, or selling it, as Andre's wife had arrived at a point where it didn't seem to matter. Judah waved the others over and Andre's wife passed the champagne over for Judah to open. He was about to open it when Rick pointed at another bottle.

"Magnum," he said.

Judah was more acquainted with the ice creams than the double bottle of champagne. It had sat there for a while, and had been originally bought for a wedding that had been called off.

"Biensur," Andre's wife said, and picked up the bottle.

She laughed with everyone else and Judah opened the bottle, spraying a little of it, but not too much, on his friends. He poured everyone a glass including Andre's wife, who was beginning to wonder whether she should slow down. But then she wasn't offered champagne every day of the week.

"Santé," Andre's wife said.

And they cheered. They'd got through the week. It hadn't been without incident but they remained in good spirits. They were in such good spirits Al felt relaxed enough to say something that had been troubling him.

"There's something I'd like to say," Al said.

They looked round expectantly. Perhaps he should've kept quiet, but then if he can't tell his polytechnic mates who could he tell? He could feel a piece of paper in his pocket. It had been left on his bed in the hospital. It was the smiling doctor's telephone number.

"I'm gay," Al said.

"Jesus," Mac roared.

Al recoiled. This was the reaction he feared. His father's reaction had been brutal and he'd kept it to himself ever since.

"I thought that closet door would never open!" Mac shouted.

"You knew?" Al asked.

"We've always known," Will said.

"Cheers to that!" everyone shouted and raised their glasses.

A couple of hours later, and more than half a barrel of lager, they were flagging. Will had to drive the following day and he couldn't be certain he'd be under the limit in the morning.

"Pour la route," Andre's wife said and got out the Génépi.

The bar was empty and they all turned, as the door opened, and a young, very attractive girl appeared.

"Julie," Judah said.

The others looked at him.

"Why are you here?" Judah asked.

"I heard you lost your job," she said.

"That confirms it," Rick said.

"And I wanted to apologise," Julie said.

It prompted a number of raised middle-aged eyes.

"No problem," Judah said, "have a drink."

They cheered and for a moment no one noticed Andre enter the bar. To Andre it was one of the most perplexing scenes of his life.

"Andre!" Andre's wife called.

Chapter Eighty-Nine

Andre had had a terrible time. Covert affairs were incredibly difficult to conduct and he didn't have the stomach for it. Literally. He'd eaten with his mother – there had been quite a lot of food – and then his uncle had turned up with a selection of cheeses, after which he'd been in a bit of a panic. He'd agreed to meet Marie and Marie had insisted that they eat. He couldn't object, as he understood the currency of sex was an expensive meal. He'd never really noticed before what a chunky lass she was and, now that he'd eaten with her, he knew why. She ate practically everything on the menu and insisted he try it too. He couldn't fit any more in.

And then the farts began. It might have been the beans. It could have been the asparagus, or the broccoli. It could even have been the cabbage. He'd always been prone to wind and, now that he thought about it, it was a wind inducing menu, but this wasn't his wife. He couldn't break wind in front of Marie, and certainly not in a restaurant, which was likely to cost more than the hundred euros he'd taken out of the till. Suppressing farts only added to the pressure building in his stomach. It had become taut like a drum. He could probably play tunes on it.

He'd had to excuse himself a number of times, but the toilet wasn't far from their table. He'd stood there for a few seconds and wondered how he could most effectively muffle the noise. Should he open his buttock cheeks, or force some toilet paper against the offending orifice? He'd experimented with both and he was fairly convinced the whole restaurant had heard. But when he'd returned to the table Marie did not appear to notice. She was too busy eating. She'd ordered more food in his brief absence. It was going to be a very expensive fart.

He realised he'd left the door to the toilet open. He didn't want to wander over and close it, as it would imply he was closing it for a reason, which he was. It didn't take long for the smell to drift their way. He really wished he hadn't eaten the sprouts. It was quite appalling and he could hear other people complaining. He wasn't sure if they'd noticed him going to the toilet, he hoped they were all preoccupied with their own lives, but he was certain someone was pointing at his back. A waiter came over and closed the door and threw an accusing look at him. But Marie didn't seem to notice. Then his stomach started gurgling like a blocked drain. It was quite noisy and the background music had come to an end. His stomach stopped gurgling and started making farting noises even though no air was leaving his body. It was very embarrassing and his fellow diners now knew for certain he was the culprit.

The rest of the evening had not gone well. Paying the bill had been a challenge. The hundred euros wasn't sufficient. It wasn't even close. The first card hadn't gone through, they didn't take the second one, and after that he'd gone to the cash point across the road. He wasn't sure Marie had even noticed. She was still eating.

He'd checked his watch. It wasn't going to plan. He only had a limited amount of time, after which his wife would suspect him, and then she'd ring his mother and check what time he'd left. He couldn't be certain she wouldn't gather further evidence from his uncle. Time was of the essence and Marie had wanted to have a further aperitif at the restaurant. He'd drawn the line at that. She'd not responded well to that, nor his suggestion that they could have aperitifs at her place. How the hell else were they going to get there and have sex? She'd told him he was being tight fisted and he pointed out that he'd paid for the digestifs, three starters, one main and two puddings and she shouldn't eat so much. He might as well have pulled the pin and thrown a grenade at her. She certainly reacted as if he had. People at neighbouring tables had to take cover. For a big girl – he'd really not noticed how large she was before – she could really shift. She slapped him across the head. His ears wouldn't stop ringing. They were still ringing when he got in the car.

He'd set off with the windows open despite the cold, as he suspected his wife would identify the beans, and his mother never gave him beans. He'd never wondered why. Once Andre had abandoned the idea that sex was on the cards, and bailed on Marie, and driven the car a good kilometre, he'd let rip. Mozart had composed symphonies with fewer notes than he'd achieved and the simple pleasure of unleashing the trapped wind was likely to he the only pleasure he'd have for some time. When he got to the bar he was a little dazed by the experience and feared he may blow his cover. His ears were still ringing. He entered the bar.

He saw a woman at the bar in a dress. She was laughing. For a second Andre thought he'd completely lost it. He was hallucinating and had entered an alternative universe. The English crowd were at the bar. There was a forest of glasses around them including small Génépi, cognac and champagne glasses. Champagne glasses? And it was a magnum. They were laughing. He looked back at the woman. It was Marie. That wasn't possible. It was his wife. He'd never once noticed how much Marie looked like his wife. They could be sisters. It was as if he'd spent the whole evening trying to get into the knickers of his own wife. Of course, he'd done that plenty of times with the same result.

"Andre!"

It *was* his wife. She was calling him over. As he approached the bar she picked up the bottle of Génépi and poured it into a collection of glasses, as if it was given away free. She pushed one in his direction. His wife had just poured him a drink. This was surreal. But it didn't end there. When the Englishmen had finally run out of energy and left, and they'd locked the doors, she'd dragged him into the office. He assumed it was for the purpose of pointing out anomalies in the accounting – quite possibly an unaccounted for, and very much absent hundred euros, but instead she pulled his trousers down and threw herself to her knees. As he'd been married for some while there were many things he might have anticipated happening, prime among them being the possibility that she was going to attach electrodes to his testicles and flip a switch. Next was that she was going to pick up two bricks, or at the very least wield a meat cleaver. He had no way of knowing what she was going to do and it put the fear of god into him. And then he felt something warm and wet on his retreating genitals. Was that the wet sponge that was used before electrocutions? A moment later he discovered it wasn't.

"Mon dieu," Andre gasped.

Chapter Ninety

"Are you okay?" Mac asked.

"Just," Will said.

Will was exhausted. It had been a tiring trip. He'd thought about sharing the drive with Al, but Al was asleep and he wasn't keen on Mac driving. Not that it mattered. But, although it was far, the roads had been clear and he'd set the car on cruise control, and managed not to fall asleep.

"Here we are," Will said.

They were home. It felt like they'd been away longer than a week. Amanda appeared by the window.

"Hey," Will said, getting out of the car.

"You guys look wrecked," Amanda helpfully observed.

Al hobbled out of the car.

"A Zimmer frame?" Amanda asked, looking into the back of the car.

Al shrugged. He'd almost forgotten about his broken ankle.

"Small skiing injury," he admitted.

"And where's Rick?" she asked.

They shrugged. It was a long story.

"He stayed on," Will said, saving the details until later.

This was complicated. There were tour rules that shouldn't be broken.

"And where's Judah?" Amanda asked.

"That's a long story too," Will said.

"I told you you were too old," Amanda said.

"You think?" Mac said, coughing.

"But you've got it out of your system?" Amanda asked a little pointedly.

"Of course," Will said.

"Until next year," Mac managed to say through a further fit of coughing.

"Definitely," Al said.

Amanda raised a cynical eye. She was going to have to work on Will, as there was clearly more to be told. She stepped back.

"Jesus Christ," Amanda said, "What the hell happened to the car?"

Will looked at the car. It was covered in dirt, but that wasn't enough to disguise the bodywork which was peppered with dents, nor the missing headlight and front and rear bumpers. There wasn't much point in cleaning it. It looked better dirty.

"It's only a bloody car," Will said.

Nearly the end...

Epilogue

"Today, ladies and gentlemen, we are going to revisit one of my classics. The creme Brûlée," Claude said.

The camera panned back from Claude's face to the studio, which was designed to look like the kind of kitchen Claude had at home. But it didn't complete its journey and turned to the left, resting on Claudette's glowing face. She smiled.

"Are you ready, ma cherie?" Claude asked.

Claudette nodded enthusiastically and seductively. The camera moved back showing a variety of ingredients which were arranged in front of her. She was ready to go. Ready to follow the Master.

"And you?" Claude spat.

He said it contemptuously as if he was standing over an open and very blocked drain oozing effluent. But, for Claude, it was worse than that. The camera panned back until a second student appeared. He wasn't immediately recognisable as Judah. He'd had a bit of a makeover. His hair was shorter, his teeth whiter and the creases in his face had been botoxed into a distant memory. But the consensus among the production staff was that he looked pretty hot. One had even said he was hot to the point of smoking. Judah smiled and soon his face filled the screen.

"Ready and raring to go," Judah said and Claude's face darkened a little.

Claude turned to check the oven had been pre-heated to the correct level and, for just a fleeting second Claudette moved her hand and rested it on Judah's, and social media went a little crazy. When Claude turned back his face was florid with anger. The doors of the oven were quite reflective.

The End
Many thanks, as ever, to Steve Caplin without whom I wouldn't have got this far…
www.gilescurtis.com or email me, if you like, at gilescurtis@mail.com

If you enjoyed this book you can find more Giles Curtis comedies on Amazon –

'Love, Lust and Hoovering'

Magda cleans up – and it's more than just housework. She knows all about the call centre worker's fake dating profiles, and what the prospective MP gets up to when he slips into something more comfortable. She even knows about Claire's secret inheritance, which is more than Claire does – and she knows how to tease out Claire's husband's infatuation. But can Magda turn a profit from all this knowledge? A hilarious romp through the private lives that only a cleaner really sees.

'The Hundred Grand Banana'

Andy has been kidnapped. He's in Africa, and the only telephone number he can remember is his parents'. But Andy's mum and dad have issues of their own. Andy's dad has been forced into retirement and doesn't know what to do with his time, and is horrified to discover that a friend has been telling Andy's mum that she has a constitutional right to an orgasm. Andy's girlfriend, Ali, is in New York on a work trip. She thinks it's time for them to get married, and has dropped monster hints which Andy has been resisting. But now Ali has come under the spell of the mesmerising Jemima. How will Andy get back?
And it all started with a banana. A hundred grand banana.

'Hell, Hull and Epiphanies'

Gerry doesn't get out much, but when he does he encounters Mandy – free, a little wild, and half his age. But by day Gerry is Gerrard, who is not only married, he's a vicar. A vicar with doubts. Although Lucinda, his wife, has very few doubts when a trip to Birmingham goes startlingly right. And ageing gigolo Nelson never sees himself as a messiah until Albert convinces him he can walk on water – or is that just revenge for Nelson having put his head down the toilet at school?

Does Gerrard really witness the Second Coming? Will Lucinda's American prove himself in Hong Kong? And will the Late Contessa ever retrieve her Bentley?

Find out in Giles Curtis's twelfth rip-roaring, hilarious romp through the intricacies of fidelity, faith and epiphanies.

'Five Minute Warning, Harry'

Harry feels downtrodden. Downtrodden by senior management, who have decided to retire him, and by his meddling, sex-obsessed father in law. But mostly by his wife, Hilda. And she tells him they must retire to Cornwall.

There is talk of reconnection, but neither can remember being connected in the first place. Harry takes up a creative writing course, through which he can live out his fantasies – fantasies of murdering his wife. But Hilda reads his story and, lost on Bodmin Moor, is confronted with devil worshippers, a convicted call centre worker with a habit of cutting off fingers, and a birdwatching hitman. In her absence, and befuddled by his writing tutor's hallucinogenic muffins, Harry looks very guilty. indeed.

'Faecal Money: A Very Lucrative Crap'

Sam's trousers were round his ankles. The microwaved chicken – long past its sell-by date – had made a hasty exit. He was down a ditch in the middle of nowhere, and there weren't any tissues. Suzy had dumped him. Things weren't going well. He was only one wipe away from his life changing forever when he found a blue IKEA bag packed with banknotes. Gary wants to kill him. So does Vlad. Ashton wants to paint him naked and then there's the Contessa. Suzy isn't certain they've broken up. One thing's for sure: Sam's life has been turned upside down.

'Newton's Balls'

Martin is dying and he has one wish. He asks his daughter, Megan, to find a man. But not a normal man, he is the product of Martin's quest, and obsession, for higher intelligence. A man made from the finest genetic material, a cocktail of stolen DNA, including the forefathers of science. A super human who will solve the world's problems. At least that's what Martin hopes. But Kevin is a man with a rampant hedonistic thirst, a talent for deception, and the centre of the ensuing chaos that brings a city to a standstill. He is a man who knows how to throw a hell of a party.

'The Hedonist's Apprentice'

Travis's life is perfection. He has the looks, the car, the apartment and the women. Lots of women. Debbie says the sex is revelatory, which doesn't help Sheryl. And then there's Colin.
Colin's life is bleak and without hope, and his sex life is so inconsequential that it is hard to assign it a proclivity in any direction. All Colin's dreams come true when, thinking he's working for MI6, he shadows Travis's life

and goes on a journey of orgiastic debauchery. But things aren't quite as they seem as the noose tightens on Travis's perfect world.

'The Calamitous Kidnap of Oodle the Poodle'

Bryan Brizzard, a notorious bastard, and owner of short haul airline company Bryanair, hates everyone. He hates his suppliers, his employees, his passengers and his wife and children. But, Dom Hazel discovers, he really loves his poodle, Oodle. And Hazel is an animal assassin. But this time it's a kidnap and Brizzard's mansion is set in the Essex Woods where Hazel, who's trying to be faithful to Julie, finds temptation and confusion. And dogging. The plan threatens to fall apart as Hazel leaves behind more of his DNA than he intends.

'The Badger and Blondie's Beaver'

Madeleine misses her old life in Paris. Her work as a forensic scientist is going great, but now she's marooned in the country and her social life, or more accurately her sex life, is a disaster. When she's called upon to extract a severed head from a weir, she meets Sam. Sam is her perfect man, but murder, mannequins, cocaine, the drug squad, Customs and Excise, multiple arrests and the Mafia get in the way.
Sam, Oliver and William are three young graduates desperate to make a fast buck. The plan seems so simple, it just involves the not entirely legal business of transporting silver which, by way of a cunning disguise, has been fashioned into dildos. But the journey refuses to go to plan.

'A Very UnChristian Retreat'

Hugo has only himself to blame. The bookings in their holiday complex in France are few and Jan, his wife, is forced to organise a yoga week. She remains in Godalming, which leaves Hugo alone with the irresistible Suzanna, who gives off signals he has difficulty interpreting. Jan is talked into hiring a private detective to lure Hugo, but his problems have only just begun. Hugo meets Lenny and Doris who claim to run art parties, which turn out to be more of the swinging sort. Hugo's friend, Gary, books in his gay friends, who have a penchant for the feral. But wild is how Lenny and Doris like it. Hugo doesn't tell Jan, and an unpaid telephone bill means she can't tell him about the Christian Retreat group who are on their way.

And then the chaos really begins.

'It's All About Danny'

"How does he manage to go away for a few weeks and come back a Nobel fucking Prize winner?"

Kathy can't believe it. Nor can Danny, who has tripped through life gliding past responsibility, commitment and anything that involved hard work. But when he is rejected by all the women in his life: his girlfriend, landlord and his boss at 'Bedding Bimonthly,' he has no choice. His better looking high-achieving brother, whose earnest phase has taken him away from the big money in the city, invites him to build a school in Africa with him.

Danny discovers that all the flatpack battles he has fought have given him a talent for it, and it lends his life new purpose. But his life changes when, during a fierce storm, he saves the only child of an African chief, who claims to have mystical powers. The chief invites him to make a wish. Danny can't decide whether he should wish for world peace, a cure for cancer or to be irresistible to women. Shallowness prevails.....

Does the Chief have strange powers or has Danny changed? He misses Kathy his girlfriend, who realises she's made a mistake. And then the wish turns into a nightmare...

'Looking Bloody Good Old Boy'

Arthur Cholmondely-Godstone is in the business of pensions. He offers a unique pension, from a nonreturnable sum, and he introduces his clients to a new way of living. He encourages them to explore radical views, try extreme sports and to eat, drink and smoke as much as they can. Or put another way, Arthur does his best to kill them.

Born from an old family and gifted with the family gene, which ensures him an unbreakable constitution, he is also the last in line and the family need an heir. But the family gene is cursed with a minimal sperm count, and his dissolute ways don't help. He is certain there is a child in his past, all he has to do is search his back catalogue of women, while keeping his clients in bad habits.

Brayman is proving to be irritatingly indestructible and Eddie B, the rock star who used to be a rock god, is trying to kill himself, which would be great, but he needs to finish his gigs before Arthur can collect all the money.

And someone is trying to kill Arthur.

'The Wildest Week of Daisy Wyler'

Daisy had lived her life as if on a merry-go-round, and she'd never stepped on a roller-coaster. There had been a husband, children and even grandchildren, but things had changed. A change dictated by her fickle ex-husband, and which prompts a new life in London.

But Daisy wants more. A bigger life, a wilder life. An exciting life. She finds an unlikely friend in Sophie, her neighbour, and there is an imminent party planned for Sophie's 'sort of' boyfriend, the dissolute Lord Crispin. Crispin's parties are legendary and favour the excessive. And so begins the wildest week of Daisy Wyler.

Find out more on gilescurtis.com or email me on gilescurtis@mail.com

Printed in Great Britain
by Amazon